ALSO BY STEVEN W. HORN

The Pumpkin Eater:
A Sam Dawson Mystery

Another Man's Life

WHEN GOOD MEN DIE

WHEN
GOOD
MEN DIE

A Sam Dawson Mystery

STEVEN W. HORN

GPP GRANITE
PEAK PRESS Cheyenne

Cheyenne, Wyoming
www.granitepeakpress.com

GRANITE PEAK PRESS™
Granite Peak Press
www.granitepeakpress.com

Although the author and publisher have made every effort to ensure the accuracy and completeness of information contained in this book, we assume no responsibility for errors, inaccuracies, omissions, or any inconsistency herein. Any slights of people, places, or organizations are unintentional.

This book is a work of fiction. All references to real people, actual events or places must be read as fiction. The characters in this book are creations of the author's imagination. The dialogue is invented.

First printing 2015

ISBN: 978-0-9835894-5-7
LCCN: 2015944683

ATTENTION CORPORATIONS, UNIVERSITIES, COLLEGES AND PROFESSIONAL ORGANIZATIONS: Quantity discounts are available on bulk purchases of this book for educational purposes. Special books or book excerpts can also be created to fit specific needs. For information, please contact Granite Peak Press, P.O. Box 2597, Cheyenne, WY 82003, or email: info@granitepeakpress.com.

FOR TRAPPER

Deep Lake, Minnesota—1933

The noise grew louder, a low rumbling punctuated with an occasional shout. There were no children's or women's voices. It was a man-crowd. The volume intensified.

"Sounds like a logging truck on a foggy morning," Rubber Man said, pursing his lips over his toothless gums.

"More like a lynch mob to me. The kind that took my pappy when I was a young'n' in Mississippi," William said matter-of-factly. He rose from his kneeling position near the turnbuckles that kept the ring ropes taut.

The first figure dashed into the intersection at the far end of Main Street, then another, and suddenly an entire swarm of writhing humankind, jumping and shouting, loose around the edges and tight in the middle. Arms were held high in the midst of the throng of dark clothes and fedoras as everyone pushed their way toward the center. Clamorous but coordinated, the mass turned left and flowed slowly down Main Street toward the midway of O'Brien's Wonders of the World Travelling Show.

"Jesus jumped-up Judas Priest," Doc O'Brien whispered slowly when he spotted the mob heading toward them. He pulled the ever-present cigar butt from his lips; his mouth remained open. "What the hell is that?"

At first it appeared that the crowd was carrying something large high above them. But as the mass moved closer, the details snapped into focus.

"What is it, Doc?" Curly Martin, the carnival's advance man, said, squinting into the sun low on the horizon. "Some guy on stilts?"

"A giant," Doc said. "It's an honest-to-God giant."

"What's he carrying?"

"Trapper—somebody find Trapper!" Doc shouted without taking his eyes from the approaching spectacle.

"What's he carrying?" Curly repeated.

"Railroad ties. He's carrying railroad ties, new ones, one on each shoulder. Trapper!" Doc shouted. "Where's Trapper? William, fetch me the megaphone."

"Just 'cause I'm a Negro and work for ya, don't mean I'm your boy. What do you say, boss?"

Doc stared at him for a moment, unbelieving. "*Please*, damn it, fetch me the megaphone."

"That's better," William said as he turned and trotted toward Doc's trailer.

"What's he carrying railroad ties for?" Curly said, pushing his hat back on his head and scratching above his ear as the crowd slowly advanced.

"How the hell should I know?" Doc shot back. "Because he can, that's why. Trapper!" he shouted again.

The giant approached from the west. The crowd's noise contrasted with the ear-ringing silence that had settled over the mildewed tents of the carnival midway. Incoherent whispers of disorder drifted among the amusements. They were carried on the mist of dust particles that rose and bent with the waves of heat escaping the bruised canvas. Raw-boned carnival workers stood silently, their gaunt bodies wet from last-minute preparations; their heads cocked, they listened. Operators, talkers, shills, and roughies faced west. Cigarettes hung limply from parched lips; eyes amid weathered faces squinted into the late afternoon sun setting behind the worn-out Minnesota town. There was anticipation.

"Jesus jumped-up Judas Priest," Doc whispered again, the cigar butt clenched in the side of his mouth. He stepped toward Curly. "I thought you told me this town was wide-open."

"I took care of it, boss—the town marshal, the mayor. I even bought off the ole hen that rules the local temperance roost."

"What about the thumpers?"

"I didn't miss a trick, boss. All we got is mackerel snappers and Lutherans. The priest was an easy mark. But I had to tell the Kraut there was no kootch show and contribute to their building fund. The rest of the townies were chumps. The place is greased, I tell ya."

"Trapper!" Doc yelled, his voice desperate.

Hans Rudolf Gottlieb—"Trapper"—moved easily through the maze of motionless workers and tangled moorings that established both the ring and the tent protecting it. His calfskin wrestling shoes, with the laces tied together, were draped over his shoulder. He was a handsome man, almost baby-faced with a full head of light brown hair slicked back in a pompadour. At a distance he did not stand out; he melded into crowds. But up close, it was easy to see why he was one of the toughest carnival wrestlers in the country.

"Strike the sidewalls of the ring tent!" Doc yelled. "Now!" he screamed. "Get all the canvas away from the ring. That mob will tear this center joint to hell and back." Turning back toward the cheering crowd he found Hans standing at his side, also looking toward the oncoming mob. Doc stared at Hans's cauliflower ears, chiseled features, and nineteen-inch neck. "What do you think, Trap?"

"He's over eight feet, maybe four hundred pounds or better," Hans said without looking at Doc. "Those ties weigh more than three hundred pounds apiece and those leather tie saddles strapped to his shoulders add another hundred pounds." He paused, then added matter-of-factly, "He's strong."

"Jesus jumped-up Judas Priest. I hate these godforsaken logging towns with all their blonde-headed Norman, Norse, Scandinavian fish eaters. The whole town reeks of lutefisk."

William suddenly appeared, slightly out of breath, and handed the megaphone to Doc, who took it without taking his eyes from the crowd. "What do you say?" said William.

Doc looked at him with astonishment. "Oh, where are my manners? *Thank you*, William."

"You're welcome."

The noise had reached a fevered pitch as fists full of dollars were thrust toward the odds makers who flanked the giant, pencils furiously recording on notepads. The glint of brown beer bottles and quart jars of moonshine flashed in a kaleidoscope of moving bodies.

"They're going to tear this place apart and the cops are going to let them." Doc stared again at Hans, measuring him. "You're paid to win. I'll sell you like chattel to another show if you ever lose, but I'm thinking this one time, it might be best if you take a fall."

Hans looked at him from beneath eyebrows of scar tissue and smiled. "They're going to tear this place apart regardless of who wins."

Doc said nothing for a moment and then a smile slowly appeared at the corner of his mouth. "Then kick his ass," he said as he brought the megaphone to his lips. "All carnies, listen up!" he shouted, turning toward the workers. "Save what you can and retreat to camp. Protect yourselves and nothing else. They'll most likely stay in the midway. If they follow, scatter into the woods and regroup here at dawn. Don't give the authorities anything to charge us with. I want out of this town. I need the ring crew to stay behind with Trapper. All right, people, let's move."

"How do you want to play this, Doc?" Hans said, unbuttoning his shirt.

"I'm figuring the longer you keep him in the ring, the more worked-up the crowd will get. Put him down early and you might take some of the wind out of their sails. Two out of three falls will just drag it out and get them more agitated." He looked squarely into Hans's intense green eyes and smiled. "You'll be Jack the Giant Killer for the rest of the season. We'll pack the house in every stinkhole from here to Hannibal."

"And if I lose?"

"You'll be standing in line at a soup kitchen in Des Moines. You can come visit me at the poor farm on weekends. Get your shoes on. I'll try to pitch 'em and do the outside talking, but I doubt we'll get anybody to buy a ticket. If we get separated, we're scheduled to play Fargo next Friday. Good luck, Hans."

Hans offered a half-smile. Doc O'Brien only called him by his given name when he was drunk or dead serious.

The crowd numbered close to three hundred, an impressive figure for Deep Lake. Saturday-night lumberjacks and farmers blowing steam from a week's worth of dragging logs and picking rocks. They sounded mean.

"Yawza, yawza, yawza!" Doc yelled into the megaphone as the tip of the throng started up the midway. "Ladies and gentlemen!" He dragged out each syllable and then realized there was neither in the crowd. "Step up. Don't crowd." He looked around to see if anyone was paying attention. "Don't crowd? What the hell am I saying?" he said softly to himself. He glanced toward his trailer and saw Madame Marguerite watching from the doorway. He tipped his hat, and she turned and disappeared inside, shutting the door behind her.

Hans twisted from side to side as he stretched his torso in the far corner of the ring. He had shed his shirt and dungarees and stood bare-chested in his high-waist wrestling tights. He wore his trademark, snug-fitting, black leather hood and mask; his eyes appeared large, catlike. Broad, square shoulders and huge, bulging biceps helped shape the massive V that defined his chest.

Hans's attention was drawn to a distant figure standing in front of a storefront whose sign read "Thor's Trim, Cut, and Shave Barber Shop." The barber's white smock was illuminated against the dark mass that flowed down the sidewalk and street. Hans stared at him, captivated by the contrast—a white pebble on a black beach.

Them are good eats," the waitress said, nodding toward Sam's plate. She was thin and anemic-looking with recessed, dark eyes.

Sam struggled to not correct her grammar. "Those are," he said, gently pushing the remainder of his breakfast away from him. "Could you please scrape what's left into a doggie bag for my traveling companion?" Sam motioned with his thumb toward the antique vehicle parked in the gravel lot just outside the window. An aging billboard with a giant northern pike leaping from a reed bed, a red-and-white daredevil spoon hooked in its lower jaw, loomed over the restored 1953 Willys Station Wagon and 1958 Airstream Bubble. Sam's dog, L2, sat rigidly in the passenger seat of the Willys, staring at him. A glistening strand of saliva stretched from her mouth to her shoulder.

The vintage rigs had been expensive distractions purchased with the proceeds from the sale of his perfectly good Winnebago motor home. He had spent several years and much of his savings restoring them. He found the Willys near Encampment, Wyoming, in the Sierra Madres, a "For Sale" sign on the windshield. The old prospector who sold it to him claimed it came from an abandoned mine near timberline. The vehicle identification number had been removed and there was no registration or title, but Sam paid the fees and filed the applications and was now the proud owner of America's first SUV. He found the Airstream in Laramie. The elderly woman he bought it from was the original owner of the two-hundred-fifty-eighth Airstream Bubble to come off the assembly line. Sam had meticulously restored the fifteen-foot trailer to its original specifications even though the absence of air-conditioning, refrigeration, and a shower were an inconvenience. He liked seeing America from the back roads at speeds below sixty.

The waitress looked at him with total indifference, obviously not impressed by either the rig or the dog. The right side of her nose was inflamed from the tiny diamond stud that had been rudely punched through her nostril. "What kind of dog is that?"

"The hungry kind."

"No, what kind is it, really?"

"Bloodhound."

She turned and disappeared into the kitchen, apparently satisfied with her feigned interest and obligatory customer relations. She knew the tip would be between one and two dollars.

Sam sipped the dregs of his coffee and looked above the rim of his cup at L2. It was hard to believe she would be seven years old in a few weeks. It seemed like yesterday that Annie had surprised him with a puppy, a replacement for Elle, who had been struck down in her prime. L2 was still with him, but Annie was gone. He missed her. Neither spoke of Colorado and the trauma they had experienced there, nor of the love they had shared in Iowa. They still talked on the phone, but it was becoming more infrequent. She usually started the conversation with "Jeez O'Pete, Sam, do you know what time it is?" The last time he called, Mark answered. Sam heard a muffled "It's that old guy, your cousin" as Mark called Annie to the phone. The age difference had been a minor issue, he believed, but the genetic relatedness was like a bucket of cold water thrown on copulating dogs. "It's just too creepy" was her final proclamation. Coitus interruptus was the story of his life, both romantically and professionally. At forty-four he was still alone, had no close friends, had spent most of his savings, and would rather sleep than work.

Minnesota had not been his idea. Sam's vision of taking pictures of dead trees—snags, in remote high-altitude settings had not panned out. The boxes of unsold books in the publisher's warehouse were a painful reminder of the public's fickle taste. He resented the fact that his customers did not share his appreciation for the beauty of nature. His loyal alpine imagery fans had bought a few books and he had sold a few calendars in the usual venues, but not enough to pay the bills. He believed the real issue was the public's fascination with electronic readers and the increasing obsolescence of books, especially expensive coffee table books. Pat, his publisher, had insisted the market was still ripe for Sam's pictorials of obscure cemeteries, especially in the Midwest.

He had done the fall shots in southeastern Minnesota along the Mississippi drainage. The hardwood colors had been spectacular from Red Wing to Winona. The winter had been dry in the southern part of the state. He had captured the starkness of small-town cemeteries from Moorhead to Mankato, grain elevators hovering over abandoned rail spurs in the background. Small towns on the verge of an uncertain death clung to their agrarian roots, hunkered down against the scouring wind and unpredictable economy. He knew how to find cemeteries around farm towns, but as Sam worked his way north in search of snow for the winter shots, he felt the anxiety of uncertainty descend on him. At the same time, he worried about pulling the Airstream on slick roads. His weight distribution hitch made the Willys squirrelly unless it was in four-wheel drive. Duluth's cold wind off of Superior turned him westward. The thought of International Falls' boreal chill blunted his northward advance, and he decided to finish the seasonal shots that Pat demanded somewhere between Grand Rapids and Bemidji. Looking past the parking lot with the giant jumping pike, the small green highway sign read "Deep Lake 1 Mile." It had started to snow.

Deep Lake, Minnesota—2007
Day 1, 8:01 a.m.

The external world was silent. Hans preferred to be deaf. It allowed him to hear the past better, to see it better too. He could visit years gone by without sleeping and he liked it. The past was familiar; he took refuge there.

Leafless trees reached into a gray sky that rested heavily on the tiny greenbelt just south of Whispering Pines Care Center. Paper birches, their black-and-white trunks in Morse code patterns, silently telegraphed unknown messages to each other. Black spruce provided contrast—dark pyramids that braced for the snow beginning to fall.

Hans's aged eyes appeared glassy and small, the morning cold biting at their corners. His dry lips trembled as they parted in an expression of recognition. He heard them first, a distant murmur, unintelligible vocalizations of an ancient species. Lifting his eyes, he saw them coming. The agitated mob flowed toward the ring tent, a restless serpentine mass that was both beautiful and foreboding. At its center the giant appeared unaffected by the weight of the railroad ties he carried above the heads of the agitated mass. It had been seventy-four years, but Hans could see him clearly. The world was no longer silent. He was young again. He focused intently through the gray clouds of cataracts and time. The odor of hot canvas from so long ago reassured him.

They could not see Hans. He peered out of the eyeholes of his mask, hidden behind a curtain of leather; the executioner's identity was secure. The filling and flushing of his lungs was rhythmic, keeping cadence with the dull resonance of his heart buried deep in his chest. He felt the warm tingle of blood rushing to his extremities as he stared at the giant. All else faded around him. The transformation was complete. He had become Trapper. Without rising from the park bench, he turned his time-worn body stiffly to the west and gazed into the past.

Deep Lake, Minnesota—2007
Day 1, 8:05 a.m.

Has anyone seen Hans this morning?" Aimee Pond, the nursing supervisor, asked as she approached the nursing station from the south hall of Whispering Pines Care Center. The chest-high counter that separated the station from the three long hallways and common visitor's area was covered with flowers. Pots wrapped with colorful foil and vases with bright ribbons were lined up atop the counter. Aimee thought it interesting that the nurses and staff so easily disposed of human remains but could not discard the flowers that arrived with the news of death. Their combined fragrance caused her stomach to roll in the mornings and did little to mask the stench of death and dying. The large flat screen TV, sound muted, flashed above the homey-looking common area. The crawl across the bottom of the screen declared President Bush's troop surge in Iraq a success while California wildfires still burned out of control.

"He's not in his room?" Taneesha Jeter asked in a falsetto voice. The rotund nurse's aide did not look up from the tray of tiny white paper cups in which she was placing the morning allocation of meds that sustained the Whispering Pines residents.

"Gone again," Aimee said matter-of-factly.

"Where does that old man go?" Taneesha said, shaking her head. "You want that I should call security?"

"Security won't go after him anymore. Administration threatened to fire them if they turned in any more workers' comp claims. Let's wait until I'm done with my rounds, then we'll find him." She looked out the window at the light snow fluttering in the air. "He's probably at the greenbelt again, staring across the bike path. He acts as if he's waiting for someone."

"Did I tell you he spoke to me yesterday?" Taneesha said.

"Really? That's rare," Aimee said, looking up from her chart. "What'd he say?"

"When I walked into his room carrying some towels, he lifted his head and said, 'William?'"

"That's it? That's all he said? Who's William?"

"Got me. Do I look like a William to you?" She paused. "You best be careful in how you answer that."

Aimee was used to the incoherent ramblings of patients with dementia. They were sincere, often enthusiastic in their pronouncements and wanted her to share their excitement. But there never seemed to be any context, just random statements without relevance. More frequently, she believed her life was equally without history or direction. Sometimes she imagined herself slumped forward in a wheelchair pointing a bony finger at an imaginary participant, profane words spilling from her mouth like a toilet overflowing—all the things repressed from a lifetime of disappointment rolling out of her mouth for the world to hear.

Aimee attempted a smile but knew it came out as a sigh. Strong coffee and estrogen replacement, she told herself, made it possible for her to show up every day. She looked at the calendar, another picture of a loon looking beady-eyed below the bold numerals "2007." She was beginning to hate loons, wolves too. One thousand seven hundred and thirty-six days until retirement. She mentally put a dark X through Monday and then glanced at the clock above the counter. Another loon graced the clock's face. The administrator and, it seemed, most of Minnesota had a thing for the goofy-looking fish eaters. Aimee wished the administrator would take as many loons as she could stuff into her Louis Vuitton briefcase back to Los Angeles, along with her MBA degree.

"Oh, Taneesha, remember to check on Mrs. Dawkins. If she hasn't had a bowel movement by noon, we'll need to give her an enema."

Taneesha raised her eyebrows, exposing the whites of her eyes that contrasted with her ebony skin. "She'll have a BM all right, even if I have to borrow one from somebody else."

Aimee smiled and looked at the clock again. It was 8:15 a.m. as the clock chimed its mournful quarter-hour loon call. *One thousand seven hundred thirty-five days, seven hours and fifteen minutes*, she thought.

Deep Lake, Minnesota—1933

Yawza, yawza, yawza!" Doc O'Brien yelled again through the megaphone. "One hundred dollars paid to the man who can beat the mighty Trapper! Step right up, no need to crowd. No need to crowd," he repeated softly to himself in wonderment. The air under the tent seemed to grow stale as the angry crowd sucked the oxygen from it. Doc wiped the back of his neck with his soiled handkerchief as he nervously considered his escape options.

Noisy men with mouths open and excitement in their eyes flowed and swirled from the midway into the area surrounding the ring. Desperate men emboldened with liquor, mindful of their wagers and what was at stake for their children. Caught up in the primordial excitement of the hunt, driven by maleness, they had no choice.

"Trapper, the greatest wrestler in the world, descended from Greek gods. Invincible, unconquerable, inviolable, he is un-de-feat-able. Come one, come all, step right up, no crowding," he smiled. "Ten cents, one thin dime, one tenth of a dollar is all it takes to see the greatest wrestling spectacle of the modern world." He knew no one would pay. The rules were suspended by their rage. He looked toward the roughies standing helplessly near the far corner of the ring; they each held a roll of tickets and a red coffee can for collecting the entrance fees. Doc shook his head at them. Hans stood in the same corner, calmly holding the top rope on each side of the corner post, his eyes as emotionless as the mask he wore.

The giant stopped just outside the ring tent. Half a dozen men on each side of him hoisted the railroad ties from his shoulder saddles while others unbuckled the leather cinch from around his bare chest and arms. His steer-sized head was topped with a mass of curly brown hair that looked like a crown of thorns. Sad eyes, one slightly lower than the other, peered out from below the broad shelf of his forehead. A massive, long, square jaw, dark with stubble, appeared rock solid, belying his cartoonish gap-toothed grin. Without the railroad ties he stood stoop-shouldered, almost arthritic. With arms as big as an ape's and the legs of a giraffe, he stepped over the ring ropes and stood awkwardly in the corner opposite Hans.

"How much you weigh, Clem?" Doc yelled up at him.

"Four hundred sixty-five pounds," the giant said in a voice as big as the rest of him.

"What's your name, Clem?"

"Milo Knuteson."

The crowd quieted as they attempted to hear Doc, who had assumed the role of referee. They pushed closer, surrounding the ring in a uniform mass of heads looking upward.

"Yawza, yawza, your attention please! Welcome to O'Brien's Wonders of the World Athletic Show! The Lancashire rules of catch-as-catch-can wrestling apply. One hundred dollars to the challenger who can win by pin or submission; one hundred dollars to the man strong enough, big enough, and smart enough to beat Trapper," he barked as he gestured with a broad sweep of his arm toward Hans, who suddenly looked very small. Doc looked at the giant and smiled. "You're certainly big enough and strong enough, but are you smart enough, Clem?"

"My name is Milo," the giant said menacingly.

"In this corner, weighing four hundred and sixty-five pounds, from Deep Lake, Minnesota, the challenger—Milo the Silo!" Doc yelled through the megaphone.

The crowd roared and twisted in an agitated, writhing mass of dark clothing and pale skin. The smell of liquor and tobacco rose upward toward the ring on the moist heat from their sweaty bodies.

"In this corner, weighing two hundred and twenty pounds, from Clinton, Iowa, the undisputed carnival wrestling champion of the world—Trapper the Giant Killer."

Hans turned his masked face toward Doc in surprise at the new moniker he had given him while the crowd booed angrily. Someone threw a beer bottle, narrowly missing Hans.

Doc stepped to the center of the ring and motioned for both men to join him. The crowd again quieted in an attempt to hear the rules. The giant, bent low at the waist, hovered over Doc. "Milo, you're the biggest son of a bitch I've ever seen. When this is over, come see me. I have a job for you. Trapper, p-eeyuhz-ut h-eeyuhz-im d-eeyuhz-own f-eeyuhz-ast."

Hans nodded that he understood Doc wanted him to put him down fast and responded in the same carny language, "F-eeyuhz-argo n-eeyuhz-ext w-eeyuhz-eek."

"I'll see you there," Doc said. "Gentlemen, to your corners, please." He nodded to William, who was crouched behind the turnbuckle at Trapper's corner. William paused and stared back at Doc. Doc rolled his eyes and then mouthed the word "please." William raised the hammer and then brought it down sharply on the ring bell.

Deep Lake, Minnesota—2007
Day 1, 8:19 a.m.

Sam stood in the cold cemetery, digging through several layers of clothes to reach the ringing cell phone. He hated the intrusive little device and rarely used it to place calls. His daughter, Sidney, had insisted he carry it so she could reach him with messages and had sworn to never give the number to anyone else.

"Hello?...Hi, baby. What's going on? Is everything okay?...Another one? That's the second blizzard this month. Are the roads closed?...It's probably trucks piled up on the side of the mountain outside of Laramie. Did you have classes this afternoon?"

Sam had moved to Wyoming for two reasons: to get away from Colorado and the aftermath of his discoveries there, and to establish residency so Sidney could pay in-state tuition rates at the University of Wyoming. He had told her she could go to college anywhere, but she had chosen Wyoming for strategic reasons, he believed. She would be far enough from her intrusive helicopter mother, Marcie, but close enough to visit when necessary. Most of all she wanted a horse, and in Wyoming horses outnumbered people.

Sam had found a remote and beautiful quarter section of property in the Laramie Range between Cheyenne and Laramie. It had taken him nearly two years, and most of the profits from the sale of his Colorado home, to renovate a long-abandoned cow camp at the end of a winding, wet meadow deep in the forest—an inholding of private land surrounded by the Medicine Bow National Forest. It was still a work in progress, but he now considered it home. The hard, physical, outdoor work had toned and seasoned him. The creases that flamed from his eyes were highlighted by flashes of gray at the temples.

Sidney had moved in with him after her junior year at UW. She had justified the move as a cost-saving measure in light of his poor book sales, but Sam was not convinced. While she hid her hearing aids beneath her hair, she could not hide her increasing apprehensiveness of growing deaf and eventually blind. Her academic advisor had recommended she attend law school elsewhere, but she insisted on staying at UW. A small monthly paycheck from Sam, for managing his affairs and tending house, kept her in gas and hay. Sam complained that the cost to support a horse was more than the cost to support a daughter.

"Best to stay put until they get the roads cleared. Think you can get to the county road without plowing?…Make sure the chains are tight and you might check the oil in the pickup.…Deep Lake. It's in the north central part of the state.…Pat? What did he want?…He knows full well where I am. He sent me here.…He's my publisher, not my mother, for crying out loud.…He's agitated? You think he found out about my proposal to Churchill?…He has no right to be upset. I offered it to him first and he wasn't interested.… No, he's the one who needs to read the contract.…I'm not jeopardizing the contract, and you don't have to tell me we need the advance from this book. Save your oral arguments for class....I'm not killing the messenger, Sid. I guess I'm a little frustrated. Bored and frustrated. Don't worry, I'll handle it....She's fine. She's bored too....I know bloodhounds always look bored. But she's sleeping more than usual. I took her to an old folks' home a couple hundred miles south of here to cheer her up, kind of like a therapy dog....I know you told me to stay away from old people....Pat can't pull the plug if he doesn't know about it. Look, Sid, I'm just trying to maximize my options. It's a good proposal. I think the book will sell, especially to aging boomers....Yes, dear. Look, if I wanted someone to nag me, I would've stayed married to your mother....I'll call him. I promise. Got to go, sweetie. It's snowing here too. I want to finish these shots by noon.... Yes, I'll stay away from old people....Love you too, sweetie. Stay warm."

Sam looked out over the rows of uneven headstones. He had lost most of the available light. A uniform grayness descended on the cemetery as storm clouds continued to roll in from the north. He had been in so many cemeteries in the last ten years that he had difficulty differentiating between them. In a snowstorm they all looked alike. Their colors flowed together into a dark mass of geometric redundancy. He sighed. His fingers were numb as he fumbled with the door handle of the vintage station wagon.

"L2, wipe the slobber off your face and put a smile on," Sam said. "We're going to see some old people. It'll be our little secret." He winked and slid into the driver's seat.

H ans, what are you doing out here?" Aimee Pond
said as she stepped in front of the park bench at
the greenbelt. She was not a tall woman, but her
presence was imposing. Her hands were thrust deeply into
the pockets of her long wool coat. She wore a red stocking
cap pulled over her ears. Snow was starting to collect on her
head and shoulders.

"Fargo next week," he said, looking up at her, his eyes
darting back and forth across hers.

"What's in Fargo next week?" A foggy vapor rose from
her lips.

He looked down and stared at the concrete between his
feet.

"Hans, do you know where you are?"

He raised his head and looked into the distance. Snowflakes landed gently on his eyelashes.

"You're not supposed to leave the care center without
supervision. You know that, don't you, Hans?"

He looked at her through cloudy eyes, the intense green
washed out by thick, gray cataracts. The ridges of scar tissue
above each eye were lost within pale folds of skin that had
succumbed to gravity. The misshapen lumps that had once
been ears still told the story to the astute observer.

"Hans, can you hear me?" she said loudly. "We worry about you. What if you get lost? What if you fall and hurt yourself? Aren't you cold?"

Her lips moved, but he did not hear. He stared past her. The snowy haze of the present lifted slowly; he could see the other side. There was no noise. From the sides of his eyes he could see the crowd boiling angrily as the giant charged across the ring toward him.

Deep Lake, Minnesota—1933

There was no contest, none of the ritual displays of aggression. It was over so fast that many in the crowd did not see it. A wristlock, a modified fireman's carry, a slam without drama, and a rear naked choke. The crowd went silent as the giant struggled briefly, his arms and legs spread across the ring floor, twitching in spasms. The giant did not have a chance to tap out; there was no time for concession as his brain starved for oxygen. He was unconscious before anyone could react. Hans maintained the choke hold.

Doc dropped to all fours beside the giant. Holding his hand above the mat, he whispered, "Don't kill the bastard." He slapped the canvas loudly and William beat the bell furiously. Trapper released his hold and lowered the man's huge head gently to the floor. As he stood over the sleeping giant, Doc lifted Trapper's hand into the air. "How long will he be out?" he whispered from the side of his mouth.

"Another thirty seconds," Hans said.

The crowd was still silent but began to move restlessly. It seemed to compress inward on the ring as people attempted to see the motionless giant. "Cheater!" someone yelled. Another screamed, "Murderer!"

Doc grabbed the megaphone. "He's fine, folks. Your boy is fine. Let's give the lad a good round of applause for his efforts."

No one clapped. A man scrambled into the ring. With catlike quickness Hans picked him up over his head and threw him into the crowd. William climbed into the ring and stood, hammer in hand, beside Hans. Suddenly, spontaneously from all sides, the crowd exploded. They swarmed into the ring; bypassing their fallen hero, they rushed toward Hans and William. Men yelled, bones snapped, a shot was fired. Then cymbals crashed, drums rolled, and a clarinet hit a teeth-grinding note. The crowd turned their attention toward the midway just outside the ring area.

O'Brien's Wonders of the World Burlesque Show had begun. Colorful feather fans and bright, sheer gauze were all that separated the three women's nakedness from the crowd. They twisted and twirled provocatively to the snake charmer's tune as they slowly followed the ragtag three-piece band down the midway toward the sideshow tent. Madame Marguerite walked slowly along the edge of the concession fronts, motioning discreetly to the dancers, who looked frightened.

"Yawza, yawza, yawza!" Doc yelled into the megaphone as he struggled to his feet, grabbed his hat, and placed it on his head. "The most beautiful women in the world, hand-picked from the far corners of the globe—twelve gorgeous beauties in all. Count them, an even dozen, each with a secret tantalizing display of cultural diversity. Come see the other nine. Naked, one hundred percent nude, disrobed, ungarmented, without a stitch, gentlemen. See them. Free admission this afternoon only."

The mob's tone changed as it flowed from the athletic show into the midway. Whistles and catcalls replaced the angry threats as they followed the scent of the dancers toward the sideshow tent.

"Free admission, gentlemen," Doc repeated into the megaphone. He tipped his hat to Madame Marguerite, who nodded and faded into the shadow of the ring toss concession.

"Dirty rotten pups," Doc said as he stepped over injured, writhing men, abandoned by their cohorts for the lure of sex. He made his way to Trapper's corner and then stood motionless, staring at the pool of blood. Red polka dots trailed from the ring canvas through the ropes and disappeared into the trampled earth.

Does your leg hurt, Hans?" Aimee Pond asked, leaning over the old man in front of her. She could see her breath. A light breeze caused the snow to swirl on the park bench next to Hans.

With both hands, he rhythmically massaged his right thigh just above the knee. In the distance he heard the clarinet's soothing melody. The crowd had become silent.

"Hans, can you hear me?" Aimee said, placing her hand on his shoulder.

With lightning speed his right hand shot upward, caught the underside of Aimee's forearm, and pushed it violently aside, sending snow flying from her shoulder. With the same speed his facial expression changed from dull neutrality to menacing aggression, and then more slowly to wounded submission in apparent realization of what he had just done.

"I'm sorry, Hans. I shouldn't have touched you." Startled, her voice was a little too high and her hand began to shake as she groped for the fanny pack on her hip. She had seen this behavior before. She likened it to a dog snapping at its owner's hand in defense of a bone. She tried not to show her fear. She stood her ground and lowered her voice. "Hans, I've got just the thing for that sore leg."

Deep Lake, Minnesota—2007
Day 1, 8:38 a.m.

Sam thought he might be homesick. Sometimes after talking with Sidney he felt very much alone, even depressed. There was a heaviness that seemed to descend over his shoulders. Taking a complete breath was an effort. A burning deep in his sinuses forced him to think of happy distractions. He reached across the seat and massaged L2's large, soft ear. It did not help.

He was still in second gear after exiting the cemetery when he saw the sign for Whispering Pines Care Center. "How about that, girl? Old people right next to the cemetery, just like I promised. That ought to cheer both of us up." He slowed and leaned forward to study the cookie-cutter architecture of the sprawling, single-story structure behind the row of uniform spruce trees. Red brick below tan, steel siding with large, wood-framed windows and fake shutters gave it the desired homey look. Assisted living, community care center, health and rehab facility, retirement community, and other assorted terms that implied tranquility, serenity, and pastoral settings were all listed under the heading "Nursing Homes" in the phone book. "Not me, girl," he whispered as he turned into the tree-lined driveway and parking lot.

In search of rural cemeteries in several states, he found that nursing homes and prisons were growth industries. Communities actively pursued them and competed for them. Out-of-state, specialized construction companies swooped in and swooped out, leaving straight lines of bricks and mortar behind along with a handful of low-paying jobs. Sam wondered at their similarities and how he might explain them to a visitor from another planet. "Dog pounds for people, girl." Some were incarcerated, others given perfunctory care. All were displaced and confined. "Wag that tail, L2. It's showtime."

Deep Lake, Minnesota—1933

Her dress was purple. When she was a girl, her father called her Morning Glory. Outside her bedroom window her mother had planted purple morning glories that climbed magically up the trellis and delicately scented her room in the summer. Purple was her color. It represented innocence. She believed it masked the harsher tones of her youthful indiscretions.

The late summer evenings had become almost chilly, and she struggled to put on her coat as she closed the door to the clinic behind her.

"Miss, miss!" William shouted from the walkway leading to the ordinary-looking, white clapboard house. "Is this the doctor's office?"

Gloria Halvorson looked up and brushed her long, brown hair from her face. A large black man was half-carrying, half-dragging an even larger shirtless man wearing tights, up the sidewalk.

"Yes, yes, this is the clinic," she said hesitantly, staring only at William. She turned and glanced at the sign next to the door. The bold, black letters spelled out "Deep Lake Medical Clinic."

"This man's been shot in the leg and he's lost a lot of blood," William said.

"Bring him in." She pushed the door open and stood aside. "First door on your right; put him on the table," she said, pulling off her coat.

"Down you go, Trap. You're gonna be fine now," William said as he placed Hans on the examination table in the center of the small room.

Gloria Halvorson had put on a white linen coat. She quickly started cutting away Hans's tights above his right knee.

"Miss," William said, "shouldn't you fetch the doctor? This man's been shot and he's lost a lot of blood," he repeated.

Blood was dried and caked around the wound. She felt the hotness of his skin. "When did this happen?"

"Yesterday about this time," William said.

She peeled back Hans's eyelid, then poked her fingers into his right armpit. "The wound is infected and he's burning up. Why did you wait so long before bringing him here?"

"We was hidin' in the woods north of town waiting for things to simmer down a bit."

"Are you with the carnival that was here?" she said as she prepared instruments in a metal pan.

"Yes, ma'am. This here's Trapper, the undisputed wrestling champion of the world—descended from Greek gods," he added proudly.

"So this is the man responsible for so many broken bones last night. Some of those men looked like they had been beaten with a hammer."

"Oh, that was me, ma'am," William said, smiling. "Trapper calls that hammer my equalizer. He says what I lack in ability I make up for with sixteen ounces of hardened steel. What about the doctor, ma'am? Is he here?"

"I'm the doctor," she said softly without looking up. "What's his name?"

William said nothing, but stared intently at her. "I've never seen a woman doctor before."

"I've never seen a Negro in Deep Lake before," she said, staring back at him. "What's his name?"

"Trapper, I mean Hans. His name is Hans."

"Hans, I'm going to give you an injection that's going to make you drowsy and then some ether to put you to sleep for a while. The bullet passed all the way through your upper leg, but I need to make sure there are no bullet or bone fragments in the wound. You'll be fine. I've seen a lot worse. You're lucky it was a small caliber; I'd say a thirty-two. A forty-five would have taken part of your femur. Do you understand, Hans?"

Hans stared up at her; his lips parted, but the words did not come. The room appeared foggy, a white mist encircling the angel who stared down at him. She was the most beautiful woman he had ever seen.

"Trapper!" William said loudly. "Do you understand the lady?"

He turned his head toward William and scowled. "I was shot in the leg, not in the head," he whispered. "And why are you yelling?"

"Mr....," Gloria said, looking at William.

"Just call me William, ma'am."

"I would like you to wait in the parlor." She nodded toward the door. "I'll come and get you when I'm finished."

William stood staring at her, waiting.

"Please," Hans said weakly.

"Yes, ma'am," William said and started for the door. He stopped and turned, and said, "Trap, I'll be right out here if you need me." He closed the door gently behind him.

"He's very devoted to you," she said.

Hans did not respond. He watched her prepare the syringe and needle. Her hair flowed and curled gently down her linen coat, surrounding her long, graceful neck. Her delicate hands and slender fingers worked adeptly, filling the syringe. Her blue eyes crossed slightly as she held the needle in front of her face and forced the air bubbles from the syringe. He felt only the warmth of her hand as she gently held his arm to administer the shot.

Aimee took her time holding the cotton ball against the injection site on his upper arm. Snowflakes tickled her eyelashes. Hans seemed not to feel the 22-gauge needle slip into the heavy muscle between his elbow and shoulder. She then meticulously repacked the disposable syringe into her fanny pack, pulled out her cell phone, and dialed the center. She watched his pupils dilate and his eyelids begin to droop. It was only half a dose of haloperidol, but would give her the upper hand.

"Hans, we're having meatloaf for lunch today," she said, buttoning his collar. "You like meatloaf, don't you?" She disliked sedating patients, but when it came to protecting herself, she had no choice. "Stay with me, Hans. You're too darn big for me to lift." She remembered from his chart that he was born in 1908. She had never seen a stronger ninety-nine-year-old with as much retained muscle mass. "I'll bet you were a force to be reckoned with seventy or eighty years ago, huh, Hans?"

Drool formed at the corner of his mouth as his chin slowly descended toward his chest. They sat in silence, waiting.

Soon Taneesha arrived with the wheelchair and parked it a few feet behind the bench. Aimee turned and nodded toward her. A sudden breeze rained the last remaining birch

leaves to the ground around them as fall reluctantly gave way
to winter.

••••

Aimee turned a puzzled look toward Sam's Willys and
trailer as she and Taneesha rolled Hans through the parking
lot of Whispering Pines.

"He's a photographer," Taneesha said. "He showed up
here just a few minutes after you left. He's got a real ugly dog.
The inmates are flocking to that dog like bees to honey."

Aimee shot her a scowl. "Residents. Our patients are
residents, not inmates. And he's taking up an entire row of
parking spaces."

"You should meet him," Taneesha said, ignoring Aimee's reprimand. "I didn't see no ring on his finger, and for
a white dude he does look mighty fine."

"Get Hans back in bed. Ask one of the aides to help
you. I'll take care of the white dude. As far as I'm concerned,
he's trespassing."

"Uh-huh." Taneesha rolled her eyes. "Woe be to the
eligible, unwrinkled man who dares to set foot in our care
center."

"He could be a thief. Someone stole Mrs. Ostler's
watch."

"Uh-huh," Taneesha repeated. "That's why he came
here. He needed to steal a cheap watch to pay off all that
fancy camera equipment he was lugging around."

Aimee ignored her and punched the automatic door
opener at the end of the wheelchair ramp. "Nothing to eat

for Hans until the haloperidol wears off. Let's hold off on his other meds until after dinner."

CLINTON, IOWA—1921

The roundness of the rabbit's eyes fascinated him. Hans studied the leaf-like veins in the translucent ears and felt the softness of its fur. He hugged the pregnant doe to his cheek before placing her back in the nest box. The buck in the next cage thumped his rear foot on the hutch floor in protest. Rabbits were innocent. He wondered if they had thoughts, if they were like him and had thoughts about thoughts. He knew they had fears, the same fears he had. They both screamed when his father came for them, a razor strop for him and a hickory bat for the rabbits. His mother always pleaded for mercy for her only child. "Hans," she would say afterward, "your father is a good man who only wants for you to be strong."

His mother's frailty enraged his father, but he never raised his hand or his voice to her. Instead, he beat his equally frail son while screaming insults at him. "You should have died when you had the chance, you namby-pamby daisy!" he would shout in reference to Hans's near-death experience with Saint Vitus' dance. His mother would retreat to her room for days after such outbursts, her muffled sobs drifting down the long, dark hallway. She had wanted more children, other children. His premature birth was the only one that resulted in life. Pale and sickly, his classmates tortured him with ridicule and threats. When his father's coworkers at the railroad yards told of the thrashing a twelve-year-old girl,

Hattie Carlson, had given Hans, his father had stropped him until he bled.

On his thirteenth birthday, March 10, 1921, his mother gave him a book of Wordsworth poems and a membership to the Young Men's Christian Association. He cried. His fate at the YMCA would be no different from that of Longfellow School or Lincoln Middle School. There would be no mercy.

They took the streetcar from Chancy to downtown Clinton. He knew that his mother's escort would result in a beating. He solemnly ascended the granite steps to the cold, gray, mausoleum-looking building; his teeth chattered in fear.

Red Carter, athletic director at the YMCA and former Olympic wrestler, did not intervene when the other boys would form a circle around Hans, pushing, slapping, and taunting. Instead, he discreetly watched him from afar as Hans passively endured his hazing. The boys laughed hysterically at his first swimming lesson when they discovered Hans had no pubic hair and possessed the penis of a child. Bathing suits were not allowed at the Y. Neither was compassion.

Deep Lake, Minnesota—1933

Wiliam dozed in the straight-back chair next to Hans's bed. His chin rested on his chest.

"What time is it?" Hans whispered. He pursed and smacked his dry lips.

William raised his head and looked at Hans in disbelief.

"Please," Hans added in a raspy voice.

"It's time to wake up," William said, smiling.

"What day is it?"

"It's Tuesday, Trap. You slept right through Monday."

"I've got to pee. Real bad."

"The donnicker is in the hall," William nodded toward the doorway of the small bedroom in which Hans lay. "Can you walk?"

"Can you swim?"

William grinned. "Let me help you up," he said, ducking his head and draping Hans's arm around his shoulders.

Dr. Halvorson was waiting for them when they made it back through the doorway. Her arms were folded across her chest. "That's why they make bedpans, Hans."

"He had to pee like a racehorse," William said. "This here's the Trapper. He don't pee in bed."

Gloria tried not to show her confusion with William's logic. She turned from him slowly and looked at Hans. "How's your leg feel?"

Hans stole a quick glimpse of her as William positioned him on the side of the bed. Her blue eyes were slightly almond shaped, turning upward at the outside corners. Her hair shone with the soft luster of a well-groomed thoroughbred. "Fine," he said softly without looking at her. "It's a little stiff; feels like a charley horse."

"You need to stay off of it for a few days. I'll get you a pair of crutches. Do you need something for the pain?"

William snickered and shook his head. "This here's the Trapper. Pain don't mean nothin' to the greatest carnival wrestler in the world."

They both looked at William for a long moment.

"No. But thank you." Hans was still unable to make eye contact with her. "It doesn't hurt near as much as the embarrassment of this dress," he said, referring to the white nightshirt he was wearing.

Gloria Halvorson smiled broadly and her eyes sparkled. "I'll see about getting you some clothes."

Hans's eyes met hers. He could not breathe. His entire body felt as if he were about to shiver. The room seemed to shrink and swell with each resonant beat of his heart. He looked away from her.

"All right, Trap, lay yourself back down and get some rest," William said as he helped him swing his injured leg onto the bed. "Can I get you anything? Are you hungry or thirsty?"

Hans suddenly felt very tired. "I could use a beer and a bag of popcorn," he said, smiling weakly up at William.

A beer and popcorn! We don't serve beer and pop-corn here," Taneesha laughed. This here's Monday, Hans," she said, lowering his head to the pillow. "You know what that means? It's tasteless meatloaf, watery mashed potatoes, and rubbery green beans. Cherry Jell-O for dessert." She put her hands on her hips. "What you mean beer and popcorn?"

"Please," he added weakly. His eyes darted back and forth, searching.

"We'll see what we can do. But Nurse Pond said no lunch for you since she had to sedate you. A beer and pop-corn—you got me thinking about it now. You get some rest first. You've had a busy morning, old man. You're going to need all the rest you can get if you keep messin' with Nurse Ratched. She's as mean as a snake, Hans. You watch your step around her, else she'll put you out for the wolves to gnaw on." Taneesha fluffed the pillow on either side of Hans's head. She stared at the large age spots along his thin hairline. A spiderweb of blue veins radiated across his fore-head and down his temples. His paper-thin skin appeared waxy and yellow. "If I find beer and popcorn around here, you'll have to fight me for it, Hans."

"Thank you, William," he said, closing his eyelids.

Taneesha rolled her eyes. "You old fool," she said under her breath as she left the room.

The late afternoon sun cut through the room in perfect slices of yellow and gold. The office was too neat. It was for show. Professionalism, warmth, and cleanliness were the three take-home messages the Whispering Pines administrator wished to communicate. She had left at dawn for a two-week conference and vacation in Orlando to meet with others of her kind. Aimee was reluctant to sit in the large leather chair behind the walnut desk. Instead, she stood half in the sunlight, half in the shadow near the window. She gazed out at the row of four-foot-high black spruce trees that lined the curved entryway: the whispering pines. Aimee had turned fifty-seven last June. She believed this office should have been hers.

"Do you have relatives at Whispering Pines?" she asked.

"No," Sam said, his hands thrust deeply into the front pockets of his corduroys. L2 lay in a puddle of flesh at his feet.

"Did any of our residents or staff invite you to Whispering Pines?"

"Nope." He studied Nurse Pond. The contrasting light and shadow intrigued him. She was attractive. No, she was pretty, cute-pretty he decided. Sam wondered if that term could be used to describe a woman her age. Sam believed she was older than him, but was reluctant to guess. Handsome might be a more appropriate description. She had wide-set, dark eyes, eyes with heavy lids under upswept brows. She had a habit of tilting her chin downward and fixing you with an upward gaze, like Lauren Bacall. He liked that she did nothing to hide her graying hair, which she wore in a pony-tail, giving her a more youthful appearance. Her hands were delicate with long fingers and well-manicured nails. Sam noted the absence of any jewelry, including a wedding ring. Even in her blue scrubs, he could see her slender, athletic body. He wanted to ask her if he could do a few portrait shots of her. She was more than handsome.

"Mr. Dawson?"

She had obviously asked another question and was now staring curiously at him.

"Excuse me?" he said.

"I was saying this is a private facility and, unless you have an invitation or permission from a higher authority than me, you are trespassing. Please don't make me call security, Mr. Dawson," she added impatiently.

"I was hoping you would give me that permission, Nurse Pond."

"Permission? Permission to impose on our residents, disrupt our staff, to spread God knows what from that, that hound," she waved dismissively at L2. "What is it precisely that you want?"

"I would like to take pictures of some of your resi-dents, with their permission, of course." Sam saw her glance quickly at L2. "The dog serves as a social bridge and as a fa-cilitator," he added. "Older people tend to like dogs. They'll invariably share a story or two about dogs they've owned. The dog makes them happy and they'll bond with her much more quickly than with me. She helps me establish trust with someone who, moments earlier, was a total stranger."

"Is that when you ask them where they keep their money and jewels?"

"What?" Sam felt the hot flush of anger sweep over him. "You think this is some sort of con to swindle old people? Christ, lady, I wish you'd give me some warning before you attack."

"I have my reasons for being suspicious. Nothing personal, Mr. Dawson."

"Nothing personal," Sam gritted his teeth. "You just called me a thief. I take that personally."

"Take it any way you want to. You are not welcome here. Do I make myself clear?"

"Perfectly clear," Sam said, turning and patting his leg for L2 to follow. "I'm sorry I troubled you."

"Me too," Aimee said quickly with no hint of apology.

••••

His ears burned as he and L2 walked briskly across the parking lot. Flakes of snow contrasted sharply against the dark asphalt before promptly melting on the wet pavement. He had not heard the kind farewells from the staff and residents of Whispering Pines as he made his way through the lobby toward the automatic doors. L2 glanced repeatedly at

Sam, her tail tucked and head lowered, a submissive posture meant to mitigate the aggression she sensed from her leader.

"Bitch," he whispered, his jaw still clenched. "Not you, girl," he added in an attempt to reduce L2's fear. "Not a good day, girl. I should have listened to Sidney. Do you wanna know what really gets me?"

L2 rolled her eyes upward and then quickly averted her gaze. She knew a question when she heard one, but this one did not seem to involve food or going somewhere.

Sam looked at L2 and could not help smiling. "Forget it, girl. It's a long list and it's guaranteed to bore you." He opened the door to the trailer, which he had left unlocked. L2, who normally leaped in, hesitated. She sniffed the air, first left, then right. Her tail rose up and attempted a half curl above her back. Her legs stiffened and the hair just above the base of her tail bristled. "Easy, girl," Sam whispered as he slowly eased his head through the open door and looked to the right. Hans Gottlieb sat in the dinette. He was eating popcorn and drinking a beer.

Sam recognized the old man he had seen Nurse Pond and her assistant wheel into the lobby that morning. He eased into the opposite side of the dinette and said, "I know who you are."

CLINTON, IOWA—1921

I know who you are," Red Carter said, staring down at Hans, who sat alone on the locker room bench. The smell of dirty sweat socks and chlorine-drenched towels hung in the humid air.

Hans sat shivering, staring at the coarse concrete floor. Mixed with sand and cement, it was speckled with small agates that shone reddish brown, polished from years of gym shoe traffic. Hans kept canning jars filled with agates and water in his basement. His mother said he was a rock hound. He liked that.

He had disappeared into the equipment room while the other boys showered, dressed, and snapped each other with twirled-up towels. "Where's that little queer, Gottlieb?" he had heard someone yell. He had crouched naked under a leather pommel horse until the locker room grew silent.

"You're a fake; that's what you are," Carter said. He placed his wooden foot on the bench next to Hans. The scuffed shoe was rigid and lacked the creases from normal bending. "You're not fooling me, Hans. I can see through your disguise."

Hans did not look up. He continued to search the floor for agates.

"I know that you see things differently from the other boys. I can see it in your eyes. I see how you read people, how you can tell what they're going to do before they do it.

How you can slow down their actions, analyze their options, and determine their next move. You know what I'm saying, Hans?"

Hans did not look at him, but shrugged his shoulders in an attempt to dismiss Coach Carter's insight.

"Today, when I threw the medicine ball at you, you stepped aside with the quickness of a mongoose and let the ball flatten that big jerk, Thompson, who had been shoving you around. When Napaletano tried to put you in a head-lock, you were behind him so fast he couldn't find you. I've never seen reactions that quick in another person. I think you're faster and smarter than any boy I've ever worked with. But you always hold back. You don't want to draw attention to yourself. You're a fake, Gottlieb."

The radiator clanked loudly and Hans's body jerked in-voluntarily.

"There's another person trapped inside that scrawny little body of yours. Someone you won't let out. It's some-one you're afraid of. You know what I'm talking about? You know who he is. You only let him out at night when no one else can see him. That's when he does battle for you. He settles the score with all the punks that pushed you around during the day. It's you, but they don't recognize you behind the mask. They don't recognize the guy who's faster, smarter, stronger, and meaner than you. You never let him out dur-ing the day, never in public. But he wants out, doesn't he? He wants to show the world who he is. But you're afraid of what he might do. So you keep him trapped inside. You're the Trapper, Hans."

Hans did not respond. Instead, he slid his foot forward and prodded a marble-sized agate with his bare toe.

"I saw your Jew-whore mother the other day. She smelled like a pig," Red Carter said without emotion.

Hans straightened and looked up; his green eyes narrowed and he stared at the coach intently. Carter still wore his red hair cropped short on the sides, military style. His blue eyes were pale, almost gray, framed by red lids. Hans studied his pocked face as if searching for agates. "It doesn't work that way, Coach. Remember," Hans said, "I control him completely. We're one and the same. I keep him trapped inside. I'm the Trapper. And she's not Jewish," he added as though it were an afterthought.

"Let me give you the tools you need, Hans. Let me teach you to wrestle, to box, to defend yourself. You come here every day for a year. You follow my instructions. You eat what I tell you to eat. You lift what I tell you to lift, run when I tell you to run. You do that, Hans, and your life will change. I guarantee it. In four years, colleges will be knocking on your door."

Hans had never considered college. His parents never got beyond grade school. No one on either side of the family had ever graduated high school. He had heard the stories about Red Carter who wrestled for Oklahoma and went on to win a medal in the 1912 Olympics. He won another kind of medal in wartime France, but that one cost him the lower half of his left leg and a year in the loony bin.

"Think about it, Hans. If you want me to talk to your mother, I will. I'd just as soon not talk with that Kraut father of yours. As far as I'm concerned he kissed Kaiser Bill's ass when he stayed here instead of—"

Hans straightened again and flashed a piercing look at Carter. Being a coward was not one of his father's faults. Being a first-generation German-American who did not speak English—until he was forced to in school—gave rise to speculation about his national allegiance. His father chose to provide for his wife and son rather than prove himself to his skeptics. That decision was made easy for him when Hans's mother contracted influenza in 1918 and survived due to the round-the-clock care provided by his father.

"Well, never mind that," Red said. "We start tomorrow after school if you're up for it. Hit the showers." He placed his hand on Hans's shoulder and squeezed gently before he turned and limped off behind the lockers.

"Come in!" Sam yelled in response to the weak knock on the trailer door. He took a swig of beer from the bottle and glanced across the table at Hans.

Aimee Pond leaned in the doorway; snowflakes clung to her hair and scrubs. She attempted a smile as she climbed in and shut the door behind her. "First it was trespassing, now it's kidnapping. You are persistent, Mr. Dawson."

"He was in here eating popcorn and drinking beer when I came back from our little chat this afternoon."

"How many of those has he had?" she asked, nodding toward the amber beer bottles on the table.

"Just one. I didn't know what meds he might be on, so I cut him off. Could I offer you one, or a cup of tea perhaps?"

Aimee inhaled deeply. Her sense of relief was apparent. "A cup of tea would be nice, thank you."

Sam slid from the booth and put the teakettle on the stove. "I figured, another couple of beers and he would tell me where he kept his valuables."

Aimee ignored him and eased into the small alcove across from Hans. She picked up a paper napkin and began wiping at the orange stain around Hans's mouth.

"Cheddar popcorn," Sam said. "He has it all over his fingers too. Is Earl Grey okay?"

"Fine, thank you. Hans, what are you doing out here? We get worried sick when we can't find you."

Hans stared back at her. His watery eyes darted back and forth across her face. He made no attempt to speak.

"He's pretty deaf, you know. Cream or sugar?" Sam said without turning from the stove.

"No, thank you. I had assumed some hearing loss given his age. But deaf—are you sure?"

"Pretty sure. He shows no response to auditory stimuli that would cause an orienting response in an unimpaired person."

Aimee looked up at Sam curiously.

"Trust me, I know about deafness," he said.

"Has he said anything to you?"

"Not *to* me," Sam said. "But he's not mute. Every once in a while he'll say something totally out of context. It's like he's dreaming. Have you heard him speak in tongues? It's some made-up language like pig latin with lots of eeyuhz-sounding words. I've never heard anything like it."

Sam placed a mug of tea in front of Aimee.

"Thank you, Mr. Dawson."

"Please, call me Sam." He paused. "And, may I call you—"

"Nurse Pond," she said without smiling.

"Fair enough. Would you care for anything to eat, Nurse Pond?"

"No, but thank you. May I ask what your plans are, Mr. Dawson, regarding Hans that is?"

"After he tells me where his money and jewels are, I was going to sell him a furnace. Then as soon as he gives me his checking account number, I will transfer the million dollars he won from Publishers Clearing House, minus a small management fee, of course."

Aimee sipped her tea and then smiled.

Hans watched each of them attentively.

"Scoot over, Nurse Pond." Sam slid into the dinette next to her. His hip pressed against hers. He felt her warmth through the thin cotton scrubs she wore and caught the delicate scent of her fragrance.

"Enough sarcasm, Mr. Dawson. I apologize for my earlier remarks."

"Apology accepted."

Hans held out a piece of artificially orange popcorn to L2.

Sam touched Hans on the arm and then shook his head. "Popcorn gives her gas and I have to sleep in this tin can with her," he said to no one in particular. He turned to look at Aimee. "I want to photograph him, with your permission, of course," he added. "I'd like to shoot his portrait and those of others at Whispering Pines, and similar care centers here and in other states."

Aimee's eyes narrowed and her nose wrinkled as if she had smelled something offensive.

"Let me explain before you say no," he said quickly in an attempt to head her off. "I'm a photographer. I make my living selling coffee table books and calendars, mostly landscapes and cemeteries." Sam reached above the dinette and pulled one of his books from the rack, *Forgotten Cemeteries of Colorado.* He placed it in front of Aimee. "I've done four of those. Minnesota will be my fifth. I used to like the medium: black-and-white still life. But I'm tired of taking pictures of the dead, bored I guess." Sam took a sip from his beer. "My publisher won't let me experiment with a new theme. Like the rest of the publishing business, all he wants is more of whatever has sold in the past. It's all about money. Forget artistic expression or literary value. Have you heard of the American painter Edward Hopper?"

"No."

"He was pretty well known in his day. He was a realist who depicted American life in the early part of the twentieth century, mostly oil, but some watercolors and printmaking from his etchings. Anyway, he said something to the effect that all he ever wanted to do was to paint sunlight on the side of a house. I've spent a good portion of my adult life trying to take a picture of sunlight on the side of a house." Sam paused. "Sorry, I digress, but I've submitted a book proposal to another publisher, Churchill, to do a pictorial essay on the fastest growing segment of our population—the elderly. To me they are the sunlight on the side of a house."

Aimee looked up from the book she was examining. "That's interesting, Mr. Dawson. These photographs are amazing."

"Sam. Please call me Sam."

"Sam," she said slowly as if reading it from a Dr. Seuss book.

"The point is, Nurse Pond—"

"Aimee," she interrupted with a smile.

"The point is, Aimee, I want to take a step backward and attempt to capture the essence of a person before they die. I keep trying to tell their story from a few words carved into a chunk of granite, names and dates that don't begin to tell the real story of who that person was. I know that's the appeal of looking at monuments to the dead. It makes you wonder about them as living, breathing people with lives lived. The ancient Egyptians said that to say the name of the dead is to make them live again. I think I've done that. Now I want the reader to stop speculating about the person under the stone and actually see who that person was when they were alive. Am I making any sense here?"

"Yes." Aimee looked at Sam seriously. "But how do you get a true sense of who the person was or is in a single photograph? You would need to do an entire book, a photo essay on each person that explored the complexity of their existence, a sort of photographic biography."

"Holy crap, Hans," Sam said excitedly. "She gets it."

Hans straightened a little and stared back at Sam.

Sam turned to Aimee and smiled broadly. "The answer is: You don't get a true sense of who the person was or wanted to be with one photo. It's impossible. It can't be done in a single, visual expression. If I weren't afraid of getting slapped, I'd hug you."

"Don't even think about it, Mr. Dawson."

Sam pinched his lower lip between his thumb and forefinger. "But what if I told you that I could only use one photo to represent you, not your life necessarily, just any existing or future photo that captured who you think you are or who you want to be? A single photo that was your essence, the real you, the true you." He paused, an even broader smile on his face, his eyes flashing.

"I would have to think about that," Aimee said slowly.

"That's what most people our age would say. It's code for 'Let me make up something good. Stroke my vanity. Show posterity what a great person I was.' People as old as Hans here are much more intellectually honest with themselves. They're more comfortable in their skin than anyone else on the planet. They know precisely who they are. They don't have the luxury of time to reinvent themselves. They don't care if they're remembered as a wonderful, nurturing mother and doting grandmother, a faithful and supportive wife, or a world humanitarian. It's not about contributions or altruism or the number of Sundays without missing church. They're done with doubt. The insecurities of youth and middle age are way behind them. They're finished with regret. The guilt and loss and missed opportunities are long gone. In their final hour they only want to see the truth and be able to take comfort in knowing that they no longer have to fool themselves. They are at peace with themselves."

Sam sat silently for a moment. He shook his head. "We don't expect anything from them and they know it. They can do absolutely nothing and everyone around them is okay with that. Do you have any idea what a luxury that is? Their priorities have changed, and time means little to them at this stage of their lives. They sleep when they're tired. They enjoy the sunlight streaming through a window and take pleasure from a comfortable bed." He paused again and then looked directly into Aimee's eyes. "It's honesty, pure and simple. It's who they really are. That's what I want to photograph." Sam leaned back and pushed Hans's beer bottle to the middle of the table. He waited.

"First," Aimee said, holding up a finger. "Thanks for lumping me into your age category. A woman needs a compliment like that once in a while. Second...," another finger went up, "I think I understand what you want to capture on film, but it's intangible. You can't see what it is that you're trying to take a picture of. Unless you draw little balloons over their heads with images inside, like a cartoon character who is thinking. Sam, you're trying to take photos of ghosts."

"Interesting, but the concept has sort of been tried. I've seen this guy's work where he photographs very old people looking into a mirror. The mirror's reflection shows a much younger person dressed to show who they once were: a soldier, a ballerina, a nurse—you get the idea. It's all very much staged and uses models for the younger reflections. That's not what I want to do. I haven't worked out all the details yet, so bear with me for a moment. Look at Hans here. I mean really look at him." Sam slid quickly out of the booth and opened the blinds above the sink, casting light on one side of Hans's face. "Good strong sidelight, high contrast for facial details. It's black-and-white. I'm using a medium telephoto lens, wide aperture." He brought his hands to his face as if he were holding a camera. "I don't want to smooth out his wrinkles or hide his blemishes." He was silent for several seconds as he studied Hans's face. "Aimee, can you see the wisdom in those wrinkles of time? You don't get those babies without seeing a thing or two." He paused again. "Can you feel his energy? He's like an icebreaker going up the Hudson in January." Again, Sam was silent for several seconds as he studied Hans. "Can you sense the intrigue behind those eyes? There's a story there, several volumes of stories, a whole freaking library behind those peepers. Do you see it? Stare at it long enough and you'll see the whole megillah." He paused again, lowered his head, and looked sideways at her. "There's your ghost. There's the intangible image. Don't you see, Aimee? It's not the image in front of you. It's the image in here," he said, poking his finger sharply against the side of his head. "Everyone will see it a little differently. My job is simply to turn on the projector and focus the viewer's attention on the screen. They'll see it. They can't help but see it. Imagination—it's what makes us human."

Hans, slumped in his seat, his eyelids half-closed, suddenly brought his hands to his ears. He sobbed.

Deep Lake, Minnesota—1933

There was no room in the budget to hire support staff, not since the president had closed the banks. Gloria Halvorson owned some prime, out-of-state property, but there was no one with money to buy it. It had lost its value. The decade of materialism had turned into a new decade of maternalism. Gloria still lived with her mother and worked for barter. The chickens, pickled fish, crocheted rugs, and rusted farm implements would not buy medical supplies or pay for a nurse to provide round-the-clock care whenever a patient required hospitalization. On those occasions, she kept a private room at the end of the hallway and shared her only bathroom. Her mother brought meals from home and left them on the front porch. Mrs. Halvorson was proud that she had never set foot in a hospital in her life and she was not about to spoil her record.

Gloria had spent a year at Saint Vincent Hospital in Manhattan after medical school in Chicago. Secretly she too had vowed never again to set foot in a hospital. She had been to Paree but was quite content to stay at home on the farm. At thirty-one, her mother considered her a spinster daughter, the embarrassment of the family, and the subject of public ridicule. Her father had affectionately referred to her as his "barren doe" and was convinced there was no one within three hundred miles worthy of her attention. She had purposefully rejected the amorous attentions of classmates, fellow residents, and colleagues for a decade. A particularly persistent suitor in Chicago had lavished her with expensive gifts, but she had rejected his attentions. Instead, she had focused on her career, thinking there would be plenty of time for romance, a husband, and a family after she established her practice. She had not expected the narrow time frame that society had established for a woman to marry.

Hans had just finished shaving when he heard the spigots above the bathtub open in the tiny room next door. The cast-iron tub was separated from the stool and sink by an adjoining door. A second door allowed him to exit into the hallway. Preparing to leave, he pulled the string that hung from the single light bulb above the sink. The room turned dark—dark except for the small shaft of light pouring through the keyhole from the tub room. The light flickered and the floorboards creaked with the movements of Gloria Halvorson, disrobing inches away from him. He stared at the yellow keyhole, unable to move, unable to breathe. *Just one quick peek, just for a second, no harm in that,* he rationalized.

The tub room was filled with steam, a wispy gauze that floated sensuously around the room. Pale flesh tones went in and out of focus from behind the vaporous curtain. His breath came in spasms and his knees began to shake. When he swallowed, the lump in his throat was coarse and dry. He knew it was wrong, that he should turn away and leave with his head held high, satisfied he had acted honorably. But he could not. An electrical sensation pulsed from his temples, down the sides of his neck, crisscrossed to each shoulder, and traveled along the backs of his arms to his fingers. *Walk away; you're better than this,* he told himself. He held his breath when the steam suddenly drifted upward and the room burst into a fleshy yellowish pink. His heart beat wildly, his eardrums pulsed, and he thought he might faint. Was this how Red Carter had felt watching him and other young boys through the peephole that connected his office to the shower room? He slid slowly to the floor, his hands placed tightly over his ears as he remembered his own stifled sobs amid the spray of water splashing on concrete, auburn agates glistening, unconcerned. Darkness enveloped him.

S am sat at his dinette and made the call. The first ring sounded like someone gargling mouthwash. He looked at the flip phone. The little flashlight battery icon said it was more than half-charged. The tiny satellite dish had only one bar next to it. He turned in his seat to face the long window. A second bar appeared and the ring was more distinct.

"Pat, it's Sam....Sam Dawson....No. What time is it?"

Ever since leaving the governor's office, Sam never wore a watch and never remembered that the phone Sidney made him carry had a built-in digital clock. This was one of his quirks that she found irritating. It was 10:45 p.m. in Deep Lake, 9:45 p.m. in Denver as he peered into the darkness beyond the Bubble's window.

"Sorry, I didn't realize it was so late. Sidney said you've called a couple of times. What's up?...Fine, fine, everything's fine. I'm just about finished with the early winter shots.... Yes, I know there's a deadline. Have I ever let you down?... Well, other than those few times?...Look, Pat, I can't control the weather here. When the light's right, I'll get the shots I need and then I'll head for home....Send that stuff to Sidney. She keeps my schedule....I can't do both, Pat. When I'm touring and signing books, I'm not taking photos or editing....Who?...I didn't know there was a National Associa-

tion of State Archaeologists. What do they want me to talk
about?...Witching? Sounds like a setup to me. They'll have
a panel of geophysicists, archaeologists, soil scientists, and
any other skeptics they can round up to discredit me. No
thanks....All right, I'll think about it. Send the letter to Sidney."

He knew he wouldn't think about it. He had no intention of speaking to anyone about grave dowsing, divining, or
witching for unmarked cemetery burials. He too had been a
skeptic. The papers he had read all concluded that dowsing
was no better at finding graves than random luck. The dows-
ers cited the "Tinkerbell Principle"—if you don't believe in
it, it won't work—as the reason for the skeptics' failure to
validate the methodology. But it worked for him. He refused
to believe in any sort of mysticism or inherent abilities, yet
his batting average rivaled that of the Great Bambino. An
unauthorized press release from Warren Air Force Base in
Wyoming had implicated him in finding a lost cavalry burial
ground at Fort Russell, the frontier fort that had transcend-
ed into Warren AFB. It mentioned dowsing, and the fallout
had been predictable.

"Look, Pat, you're my publisher, not my agent—...Well,
if I had an agent, they'd—...I know sales are down, but I
need to maintain credibility. I'm not going to jump at every
chance to show people my talking frog....I don't want to be
on TV....I don't want to be on NPR....Pat, are you listening
to me?...All right, all right, send it to Sidney and I'll consider it," he lied. The eggheads couldn't stand the fact that
he had found numerous burial sites, even entire cemeteries,

without an advanced degree in archaeology. "My battery is almost dead, Pat. I'll give you a shout when I get back to Wyoming....I will. You too."

Sam pushed the end button. He tossed the phone on the seat cushion and stared at it for several seconds as he debated placing it under the rear tire of the Willys and rolling a couple tons over it. But he had promised Sidney that no harm would come to it. Sensing his frustration, L2 raised her head and looked at him from above her inflamed lower lids. A strand of saliva stretched from her mouth to the floor.

"Sow," Sam said with a smile.

Deep Lake, Minnesota—2007
Day 2, 3:33 a.m.

Darkness was all around him, strange and cold. Hans lay motionless, aware of his own breathing. The room was again unfamiliar, different from during the day. Something had awakened him. He could feel the sudden pounding within his chest—his heart responding to something he had not yet detected. Yellow light slipped beneath the door from the hallway like it always did. He could not hear the whispering pines outside his window as the wind bent them in a reluctant dance with winter. Without his glasses, objects appeared to blur into the surrounding darkness. Taste and smell were all but gone, yet there was a feeling of presence, inexplicable and intangible. It engulfed him. He was too old to run, too unsure to cry out. Someone or something was in his room.

He remembered the lion that had lived under his bed as a child, and the hideous monster that had frequented his wardrobe. It had been nearly a century, but the fear was still there. He felt the hairs stiffen on his arms as something nudged the side of the bed. He felt the monster's claws against his wrist as it slowly pulled the Speidel Twist-O-Flex band and gold Bulova over his hand. Even in darkness with his eyelids closed he could see the vulnerable parts, exposed and unsuspecting. He knew the pressure points. He knew the sequence. It was showtime. Yawza, yawza, yawza.

Yawza, yawza, yawza! She walks, she talks, she crawls on her belly like a reptile—Reba...," Hans growled into the megaphone, "the Snake Girl. Five cents, one buffalo nickel. Step up; you won't believe your eyes."

The ten-in-one was always on the back end, designed that way in order to bring the lot lice through the length of the midway. The number of sideshows varied throughout the season depending on the sobriety of the performers. Freaks were the most stable. "Where else are they going to go?" Doc had once confided.

The chumps were always the same: big-eyed, round-faced townies in overalls or dungarees with four-inch cuffs, their Saturday-night white shirts with the sleeves rolled up on their forearms. They clutched a bag of popcorn to their chest and radiated hopeful anticipation at the prospect of seeing something they shouldn't, something they would always remember. The fat lady, blade glommer, contortionist, mummified devil's baby, rubber man, a shelf of pickled punks with their deformed faces pressed against glass jars filled with formaldehyde, and Zeus the Fire Eater were the usual attractions. Reba the Snake Girl, Harriet the Hermaphrodite, and the burlesque show were the real crowd-pleasers.

Reba was young, beautiful, and unpredictable—especially when drinking, which was often. She was fond of showing teenage boys more than a few harmless snakes. She worked the evening hootchy-kootchy where the same boys lied about their age in order to see her dance naked. When the carnival closed at midnight, Reba often disappeared. She always had money and was the most generous carny in the show. Agents, talkers, showmen, roughies, anybody down on their luck could get a couple of bucks from Reba. No questions asked.

"Five copper Lincolns, five cents will get you in to see Reba the Snake Girl. Get in line, folks. You won't believe your eyes." Hans hated giving the ballyhoo. He would have preferred to run a ride like the new Tilt-O-Whirl where he did not have to feign interest or interact with the chumps.

He had missed the carnival in Fargo, but caught up with them in Watertown, South Dakota. Eighteen trucks and twenty-eight railcars, mostly flatbeds, had moved the odd community with precision along the planned route.

Dr. Halvorson had arranged a ride for William with a medical supply salesman on his way to Bismarck, while Hans convalesced for another week at the clinic. Then she drove Hans to the train station and purchased his ticket to Watertown. He had forgotten to say thank you.

Doc O'Brien made Hans outside talker at the ten-in-one and gave him two weeks to heal up, or else.

A dozen young men, a couple with dates, had gathered in front of Hans, paid their nickel, and were getting restless. Using a cane for support, Hans hobbled over to the large wooden crate just inside the tent. The open-topped box containing Reba and her snakes had jungle scenes depicted on the sides. A large snake with red eyes, mouth open and fangs bared, was painted on the long side above "Reba the Snake Girl."

"You ready?" Hans said, looking into the box.

"What we got?" Reba asked. She was sitting on the floor of the box, leaning against a corner where several black-snakes, bull snakes, a couple of hognose snakes with rattle-snake rattles glued to their tails, a boa constrictor, and a corn snake with yellow bands painted between the red and black segments slithered on and around her. She wore her usual animal skin, which covered little, and her wild woman wig complete with dirt and twigs.

"About a dozen—two girls," Hans said, trying not to stare at her perky breast prominently displayed through the enlarged armhole of her jungle dress.

She stared up at Hans and smiled. "See anything you like?"

"I'm saving my money," he said, smiling back at her.

"That's what you said last month. I'm beginning to think you like wrestling boys better than girls."

Hans flushed red.

"Easy, big fella. I was only foolin' with ya. But you might think about startin' with Harriet in order to make the changeover."

"Are you ready?" he sighed.

"Let the show begin," she said with a toothy grin as she shook the small cloth bag filled with rattlesnake rattles.

"Remember, Reba, you can't throw hot snakes at the townies. You can only throw the bouncers," he said, refer-ring to the rubber snakes she kept hidden behind her. "That young lady last night soiled herself when you tossed Blackie on her."

Reba smiled; she was obviously proud of herself. "She's a thumper," she said, referring to the young missionary who repeatedly attempted to give Reba a book of the New Testament.

Hans turned back to the crowd outside the tent. "All right, people, approach with caution. You won't believe your eyes," he said, motioning for the eager patrons to enter.

Hans took a deep breath as the last townie disappeared inside. A full moon, glowing orange, rose from the prairie east of town. A light breeze, heavy with the scent of caramel corn and hot dogs, drifted down the midway. Gaudy lights and a confusion of sounds filled the carnival grounds with a sense of excitement. If he slit his eyes, the colorful lights would run together, red and white flashing at the ends of the bright streaks.

Torrents of red and white light lurched around the room from the flashing strobes atop the ambulance and two sheriff's cars in the parking lot. Loud voices, demanding voices that he could not understand, bit hard on the inside of his ears, lifting him roughly from the cotton-soft haze of sleep.

"Get back in your rooms, people! There's nothing to see out here!" Nurse Pond again yelled from the hallway. Garbled voices filled with static, unintelligible words punctuated with numbers, hissed from the radios on the EMTs' belts. Sophie Mickelson's body, elongate and prone, was undefined inside the dark bag on the gurney they wheeled past his open doorway. She was done with life.

"Stay in your room, Hans. Ain't nothin' to see out here," Taneesha said as she gently took him by the elbow to guide him back toward his bed. "Why are your knuckles bleeding? You've got blood on your pajamas, you old fool. And why are you barefooted? You've got slippers right next to your bed. You're as cold as ice, old man. Did you see the caramel corn I left in your room yesterday?" She stole a nervous look at the half-empty bag on the dresser across the room, knowing that she had eaten most of it. "We'll have breakfast in just a little while."

Sophie Mickelson was about his age. She would often talk to him after lunch, but he could not hear her. There was something familiar, kind, and reassuring in her facial expressions. Sometimes she stood next to his table and stared at him without speaking. He remembered her eyes. They were unchanged from when she had stared at him from behind the counter at Fuller's Grocery Store nearly three-quarters of a century ago. He suspected that she remembered him too. Sophie Mickelson's eyes told him she knew why he was there now. Soon there would be no one who remembered the dark-haired doctor with sparkling blue eyes who always wore purple.

The gurney bounced noisily through the front doors as the EMTs discussed the Vikings game from the night before. Like Sophie, Hans was done with life too, but somehow he kept waking up. He liked it better when he was asleep and young again.

••••

Aimee Pond's hands shook as she fumbled with the charts from the night nurse's rounds. She knew the administrator would be upset. She would insinuate that Aimee had brought negative attention to the center. Corporate would surely want someone's head on a pike. But she had no choice. She had called the sheriff. Sophie Mickelson was dead and it had been a horrific death. Aimee had spent years in emergency rooms in Los Angeles and Minneapolis. She knew about trauma. The bruising and cyanosis around Sophie's mouth indicated she had been smothered. The night nurse who had called Aimee sobbed uncontrollably from the dark corner of the administrator's office. She had fallen asleep in the nurse's lounge and had heard nothing. "Jesus, Kate, pull yourself together," Aimee snapped. "I want every resident accounted for, every room checked, every bathroom, nook, and cranny searched. Take a deputy with you. Look for anything out of place or missing. And, whatever you do, don't get the residents upset. Tell them you're looking for a lost dog or doing a routine fire drill or something. They're not to know what's happened here."

Aimee stepped to the window and parted the blinds. The gaudy lights on top of the sheriff's cruisers revolved and flashed around the parking lot. The county animal control van partially blocked her view.

With a long noose pole the animal control officer led L2 to the waiting van. The bloodhound struggled to look at Sam. Sam too struggled to see her as he was being pushed down into the backseat of a cruiser, his hands cuffed behind his back.

Aimee swallowed the sharp lump in her throat. The bond between the man and his dog was almost touching. Sam had asked her if he could park his vintage rig in the parking lot overnight. She had eagerly said yes.

L ook, I watch TV. I have a right to have an attorney
present." Sam sipped coffee from the white Styrofoam cup the sheriff had placed in front of him.
"And I also know that you have to charge me with something if you're going to hold me here, not to mention you
need some sort of warrant to arrest me or search my vehicle."

"Is that how they do it in Wyoming?" The sheriff smiled
and turned his own Styrofoam cup in a circle as if trying to
screw it into the table that separated them. "We do it a little
differently here in Timberlane County."

Sam stared across the table at him. The sheriff had been
a large man in his prime. He now appeared sickly, bent across
the shoulders, his face gaunt and prematurely wrinkled. He
had the voice of a smoker, coarse and on the verge of a
cough. He repeatedly reached with a large right hand for his
empty left breast pocket. Sam wondered how long ago he
had quit smoking.

"First, I don't need no stinking warrant," he said as he
reached for his imaginary cigarettes, his voice like gravel
spilled on a glass table. "Second, I've got probable cause.
I've got a call in to the county prosecutor. He'll approve my
request for the county judge to make a determination. Third,
I've got forty-eight hours to cause this to happen. Your ass

is mine for up to two days. Before that, I don't have to do jack squat."

"What probable cause are you talking about?"

The sheriff held up a plastic bag with a magnetic key-card inside. "We found this on your kitchen table. Whispering Pines is a secure facility with an alarm system. You can't get in after hours without one of these babies." He shook the bag.

"That belongs to Nurse Pond. She was in my trailer yesterday. I found it between the dinette cushions last night. She must have lost it when she slid into or out of the booth. It was after hours when I found it. I was planning to take it to her this morning."

"Have you been sliding into or out of Nurse Pond?"

"No," Sam said a little too loudly. "I only met her for the first time yesterday, for crying out loud."

"She's a looker. Am I right?"

"What are you insinuating?"

"Oh, I don't know. Maybe she got you all horned up and you snuck back into the care center looking for a little action."

"What are you talking about?"

"You know what I'm talking about, you sick bastard." He brushed his left breast pocket again.

"Why would I be sleeping in a camper trailer less than fifty yards from where I supposedly murdered someone?"

"Criminals are stupid."

"I'd like to talk with an attorney now."

"What for? I haven't charged you with anything."

Sam pushed his chair back and stood up. "Then I'm leaving. Will someone please take me and my dog back to Deep Lake?"

"Relax, Dawson. I'll arrange your transportation as soon as you voluntarily give me a DNA sample. A tech from Bemidji is on his way to collect it."

"With all due respect, Sheriff, I happen to know a little about DNA and the right to privacy under the Fourth Amendment. You'll need that warrant based on probable cause. I won't voluntarily submit my DNA for inclusion in the national database. I might as well change my name to Hester Prynne and wear a scarlet letter around my neck."

"What the hell are you talking about?" the sheriff coughed. "Who's Hester Prynne?"

"I have the right to be left alone. You either arrest me or take me back to Deep Lake." Sam was gambling. He knew the backlog at most DNA testing facilities was measured in months. "You'll be voted out of office before you get the results back."

"Screw you, Dawson. You wanna play hardball with me—"

Sam cut him off. "You'll need harder evidence than a keycard to convince a judge to issue a warrant. You're barking up the wrong tree, Sheriff. Time's a-wastin'. You've got a killer out there who's getting away while you're dinking around with a law-abiding citizen." Sam grabbed his Styrofoam cup, poured the remaining coffee into the sheriff's cup, and stuffed his own cup into his jacket pocket. "And by the way, Nurse Pond probably needs her keycard back."

"Not your concern, Dawson. I happen to know she's got a spare."

Someone knocked on the interrogation room door, then opened it slightly. The sheriff, breathing heavily, stepped halfway out. Sam heard muffled voices, then curses from the sheriff, who swung the door open and stared at Sam for a long moment. "Your ride's here," he said with a crooked smile as he again reached for his pocket.

Aimee Pond sat on a bench at the end of the long cement-block corridor.

H ere are your meds, Hans," Taneesha said as she entered the room carrying a small paper cup with a half-dozen pills in it. "Down the hatch." She held the cup in front of him. "I've got no time for any funny business today. Everybody's behind schedule 'cause of what happened here last night. Lordy, can you believe it? Right here in River City." Despite Aimee's orders, word of Sophie Mickelson's murder had spread among the residents. "Everybody's got a bad case of the willies. I can tell you right now I ain't workin' no more night shifts. Breakfast is late. Lunch is gonna be even later. The inmates are as grumpy as old bears. Don't ever get between food and an old person." She rattled the pills in front of him.

Hans reached for the cup with a shaking hand, his fingers crooked with arthritis.

"Hans, I been meanin' to ask you about that tattoo on your arm." She tapped the inside of his left forearm. "Is that a morning glory?"

He turned his palm upward and stared at the faded purple and green tattoo, barely discernible amid the wrinkles of his skin and the discoloration of age spots....She had been angry with him.

Deep Lake, Minnesota—1933

"What would possess you to mutilate your body with a cartoon flower representing someone you barely know?" Gloria Halvorson was upset, but she never raised her voice. "And what are you doing here in Deep Lake? Is your leg all right? Hans, it's seven o'clock in the morning, Sunday morning. What—"

"Who is it, Gloria? Is everything okay?" her mother yelled from somewhere inside the two-story farmhouse.

"Everything is fine, Mother! It's a patient!" Gloria yelled over her shoulder. She was dressed up: a purple-striped gingham dress with a doily-like collar, wool sweater, and a single strand of pearls. Her black shoes were polished.

"I've come to settle my account," he said softly, unable to make eye contact with her. He tried to hide his left arm behind him.

"Your account?"

"When I left in September I was unable to pay you. I didn't have any money with me." He stole a quick glimpse of her face. Her almond eyes were narrowed as if trying to comprehend something without an answer.

"You could have posted it in a letter to me. Can you write, Hans?"

"Yes." He looked at her fully. "I'm not uneducated. Just because I work in a carnival—"

"What? You graduated eighth grade?"

He glared at her, his anger rising.

"High school? I'm impressed, Hans. And then you joined the Navy. Is that where you developed your passion for tattoos? And then you joined the circus?"

He pulled his wallet from his hip pocket and removed several bills from it. "I'll be on my way. What do I owe you?"

Gloria Halvorson looked down and said nothing for a long moment. "Hans, I'm sorry. I didn't mean to insinuate—"

"Yes you did. How much? And don't forget the train fare."

"It's just that I don't get shot-up carnival wrestlers in my clinic every day. I guess I just assumed—"

"That I was carny trash? Times are tough, lady. We do what we have to in order to survive. Not all of us are fortunate enough to live our dream. But I make a living and enough to pay my medical bills. How much?"

"Are you sure everything is all right, Gloria?" her mother shouted from upstairs.

"Fine, Mother!" she yelled and then turned back to Hans. "You needn't lecture me on what one needs to do to survive. You are not the only one who has struggled. Have you had breakfast?"

"I didn't come here to eat. I came to pay my bill."

"And to show me your tattoo. It is even more incredible, given that you are an educated person who purposefully mutilated your body and traveled hundreds of miles out of your way to turn up on my doorstep on a cold Sunday morning to show me your pronouncement of—of whatever. Did you ever stop to consider that by doing so you violated me by stealing something that—that represents me? Did you stop for a minute to consider your presumptiveness? Now answer my question. Have you had breakfast?"

"No," he said, looking down. "You saved my life and I never want to forget that. I wanted to remind myself every day that I owe my life to you."

"Hans, you can't go through life putting tattoos on yourself to remind you of everyone you feel indebted to." She shook her head. "I should have never told you my nickname. I only told you because you insisted, since I knew yours. Trapdoor, or something equally silly."

"Would it make more sense to you if I told you I was drunk at the time?"

"No. Now roll down your sleeve and come in. It's freezing out here." The misty vapors of her breath rose from her perfect mouth in cloudy puffs.

Hans looked over his shoulder, contemplating his response. Stands of leafless paper birch surrounded the farmstead, their cobweb of branches dark against a gray sky. A single black pine, straight and massive, stood in the yard, looking lonely. The tops of its kind rose jaggedly beyond the birch.

Gloria slipped a long apron over her head and opened the firebox door on the cookstove. She placed several pieces of kindling on the glowing coals, adjusted three of the dampers, and opened the shunt at the base of the flue. She did not speak. He sat and watched her, fascinated by the strength of her slender wrists as she hoisted a large cast-iron skillet to the stovetop, and her square shoulders as she levered the handle of the pitcher pump when filling the coffeepot. A flour sifter, white from morning biscuits, sat unwashed on the countertop. He watched as she shifted her weight from one leg to the other while she worked at the sink. He followed the dark vein of her cotton hose from the top of her shoes to where it disappeared under her hemline.

"Gloria," her mother said from the kitchen doorway, startling Hans, who jumped to his feet, his newsboy cap crushed in his hand. "I'm off to church, unless you want me to wait. Please sit down, Mr...."

"Gottlieb," Hans said sheepishly.

"Mom, this is Hans," Gloria said, blushing somewhat nervously.

"Mrs. Halvorson," Hans nodded.

"Gottlieb," the older woman said, looking directly at him. "That's a nice German name."

"Yes, ma'am, it got me beaten up regularly growing up," he said, avoiding eye contact.

The older woman studied him for a moment. "Well, I doubt that happens much to you now. Mr. Gottlieb, would you like to attend Sunday services with us? Gloria sings in the choir."

"Mom, you go ahead. I'm fixing Hans breakfast and will see him off. I'll catch up with you for lunch at the Stephensons'."

"Oh, I hope I didn't offend you by asking you to church," Mrs. Halvorson said. "I assumed you were Lutheran. But of course, you might be Catholic."

"Mom, we don't care what he is. He's our guest and we don't pry or convert." Gloria placed her hand sternly on her hip.

"Oh my, yes. Where are my manners?" the old woman said. She looked at Hans and hesitated, waiting for a response that did not come. "It was a pleasure meeting you, Mr. Gottlieb. Enjoy your breakfast." She turned toward Gloria on her way out, saying, "See you at the Stephensons', dear."

Gloria stared at the door for several seconds, a spatula in her hand. "Please sit down, Hans." She gestured toward the straight-back kitchen chairs surrounding the oak table. "I'm sorry about that. Mom believes there are two kinds of people in this world. You're either Lutheran or, God help you, Catholic. She almost died when I accepted a residency at Saint Vincent's in New York. She needs to know which one you are, so she can adjust her behavior to either patronizing or condescending—I mean acting superior," she apologized as a quick afterthought.

"I know what condescending means, Doctor Halvorson. Four years of college provided me with a good vocabulary."

Her eyes narrowed and her head tilted slightly as she stared at him.

"Of course, two years with the carnival has expanded my vocabulary considerably more."

"How do you like your eggs?" she said softly.

"Scrambled, if it's not too much trouble."

She opened the oak icebox and pulled out a large ham shank. "Ham?"

"I've nothing against the flesh from a cloven-hoofed animal. And no, I'm not Jewish."

"Just who are you, Hans?" She placed her hand on her hip again and faced him.

He stared up at her for a long moment, his eyes darting back and forth across hers. "I'm Trapper, the world's greatest carnival wrestler," he said, his voice barely above a whisper.

E xcuse me," Taneesha said in a falsetto voice, her brow furrowed. "You're who?"

Lying in bed, Hans looked at her, and then at the tray of food she had placed over him.

"What kind of a dream world do you live in, old man?" She was used to the incoherent ramblings of the home's residents. Snippets of conversations, taken at random from lives that still offered hope, would suddenly spill from their emaciated bodies. She believed they were reading their autobiographies when they were asleep. And that is what they did best, sleep. They reminded her of old dogs that slept eighteen-to-twenty hours a day. She tried not to imagine herself in their place.

"Scrambled eggs and ham, your favorite. Yum, yum," she said, leaning him forward and placing a pillow behind his back. "You need to eat up, Hans. You have a visitor waiting for you. He's come a long way, so try to stay awake. Nurse Pond wants to talk with him before he sees you. She'll be back from Walker after breakfast. Probably wants to tell him how naughty you've been and that, unless you straighten up, we're going to put you outside and let the wolves eat you." She pointed toward the window.

He turned his head to look outside. A gray Minnesota winter's haze had settled over the whispering pines.

"Ain't no wolves out there. I was only foolin' ya, Hans. Now eat your food. You're lucky I brought it to you. As much as you like running around, you could easily come down to the dining room. Open your hangar now. Don't make me be the airplane," she said, lifting a fork full of eggs above his head.

Hans stared down at the unnaturally yellow eggs, scrambled from powder, and the bright pink ham that was already cut into bite-size chunks. He closed his eyes and smelled the wood smoke that escaped the firebox as she stoked the stove. He heard the sizzle of the gray, brine-cured ham when she placed it in the pan. He watched her hips as she shifted her weight from one leg to the other while she cracked open the brown eggs on the edge of the mixing bowl. He looked out the window again, his eyes glassy with tears. He heard the high-pitched whistle of a distant teakettle.

CLINTON, IOWA—1925

The whistle's shrill warble ricocheted from the concrete walls and hardwood floor of the underground gymnasium.

"All right, Hans, hit the showers and then twenty-five laps in the pool," Coach Carter barked as Hans slowed his pace around the raised walkway above the basketball court. The other boys had been dismissed more than an hour earlier. It frightened him to be alone in the gym.

"Where are your balls, Hans?"

"What?" Hans's eyes grew large as the sweat dripped from his nose.

"Your rubber balls, for Christ's sake."

"Right here, Coach," Hans said, patting the pockets of his gym shorts.

"They're no good to you in your pockets. I want to see them in your hands when you run. I want to see them in your hands when you walk. I don't ever want to see you without them."

The firm rubber balls that he squeezed during most waking hours had already turned his hands into living vises that could grip and paralyze his opponents. Coach Carter had shown him every pressure point on the human body and drummed into him the fact that wrestling was more than technique. It was a state of mind and the ability to inflict pain with every move. Hans liked seeing fear in the eyes of his opponents. They knew they were about to be hurt, but did not know where or how bad. He thought of them as the rabbits, just before the crushing blow of his father's hickory bat. The coach had taught him holds and moves that had been banned from high school and college wrestling, some of which were still used in the Greco-Roman Olympic contests and the catch-as-catch-can brawls of the carnival. Most of the young men at the YMCA refused to spar with him. Carter had taken him to other Ys as far away as Waukegan to find local toughs willing to spend ten minutes on the mat with him. Hans was surprised to find that at other Ys the boys were allowed to wear bathing suits in the pool.

At seventeen, Hans had lost the gangly look of his youth, replaced by the bulk of muscle. He had gained nearly eighty pounds in the past four years. "You're eating us out of house and home," his father said most every night at the supper table. In the summers, Hans worked for a brick mason as a hod carrier. Troughs of bricks and mortar, hiked up ladders and across scaffolding all day, toned the muscles he developed in the Y's weight room at night. Every Friday he handed over his pay to his mother so she could keep him fed and clothed.

••••

At the end of Hans's last lap, Coach Carter appeared at the pool ladder. He was holding the towel that Hans had hung on a hook above the long gray bench, where naked boys usually sat shivering while the coach delivered one of his sermons about mind, body, and spirit. He stared down at Hans; his rat-like eyes shone red from the pink around them. Hans shivered involuntarily.

"You tell Coach Grooms you're going to wrestle one eighty this season," Carter said, staring down the ladder that Hans clutched.

"I only weigh one sixty-five," Hans said softly as he pushed the hair and water back from his face.

"I don't give a shit if you weigh ninety-five. You tell him one eighty. I'll have you ready. That's only fifteen pounds and we've got three and a half months before your first meet."

"We've got three and a half months of football taking the weight off of me too."

"I wish to hell you'd sit this season out. You're going to get yourself hurt. Football won't get you into college." He considered his last statement for a moment. He knew that scouts from both Iowa universities had already looked at Hans. Clinton had won the state high school football championship the previous season—thanks in large part to their star right end, Hans Gottlieb, who had set the state record for the hundred-yard dash the previous spring. "Well, it won't put you into the Olympics. You'll get hurt and... and another thing: I saw you walking down Eighth Avenue the other day with some sweet little blonde thing. Do you want to know what will steal your future faster than a stroke? Knocking up some young harlot, that's what."

"I like football," Hans said softly, looking down. "We're the state champs."

"You're the hundred-fifty-seven-pound state wrestling champ too. And the year before, the hundred-forty-five-pound champion. And the hundred-thirty-seven-pound champ your freshman year," Carter shot back. "If it weren't for me—" He caught himself. His eyes narrowed. "This is your senior year coming up. It's your one last chance to do something big. To make a name for yourself, to do something no one has ever done before." Red Carter looked to the far end of the pool for a long moment and then turned back to Hans. "Your lard-ass heavyweight won't be coming back this year. His drunk bastard of an old man is moving the whole family to Missouri where they belong. Skinny owes me," he said, referring to Coach Grooms. "I'm pretty sure I can talk him into letting you wrestle one eighty and heavyweight back-to-back."

Hans pulled himself up the ladder and took the towel from Carter. He stepped away and held the towel to his face for several seconds before wrapping it around his waist and tucking it securely. "Coach, I'll have trouble making weight for the one-eighty class. Some of those heavyweight farm boys are coming in at better than three hundred pounds."

"You're faster and smarter than they are. You can't muscle them. You've got to use your head."

"You're talking four five-minute periods back-to-back. That's potentially twenty minutes of mat time."

"I didn't say it was going to be a goddamn cakewalk." Carter's face glowed red. "You'll have to be in better shape than you've ever been before. If I didn't think you could do it, I wouldn't have suggested it. This is it, Hans. This is your one last chance to do something big. Believe me, if you don't do it now, it won't ever get done. You'll spend the rest of your life kicking yourself in the ass and asking what if. The last thing a man wants is regrets."

Hans shot a glance at Carter and set his jaw. He already had regrets and there was nothing anyone could do to take them away.

"Take it from me, kid, when the moon comes calling thirty years from now, you'll be able to go back to sleep knowing that you made the right choices." He paused, then pointed his red-freckled finger at Hans. "You do what I tell you." Coach Carter turned and walked to the pool room door, stopped, and turned around. "Stay away from that little blonde whore too."

"Bernice is no whore."

Carter took a step toward him. "You listen to me and you listen good. They're trouble. They're all trouble. They got one mission in life. Why the hell do you think they're so sweet and firm when they're young? You stay away from that nasty stuff." Carter narrowed his eyes and again shook his finger at Hans. "Do you want to go blind? Do you want to go crazy? That's how you'll end up in a few years. You want your mother changing your diaper, dabbing the pus from the sores on your face, and spooning sweet potatoes into your drooling mouth for the rest of her life? There's plenty of time for females when you're older. Until then, every time you have thoughts about one of them, drop to the floor and count off twenty-five pushups. That'll do you a lot more good." He turned back to the door. "And you won't go blind," he added just before it closed behind him.

That's a lot of pushups," he said, looking up into her translucent blue eyes, her blonde hair dangling in his face. He could smell the shampoo she had used when showering before work.

"What do you mean, Hans?" Her breath hinted of spearmint when she spoke. Her voice was soft and she always smiled when she talked, a tight dimple on each side of her mouth. Her flawless cheek grazed his as she gently pulled him forward into a sitting position. He did not respond.

Robyn Threlkeld, the seventeen-year-old part-time nursing assistant, liked Hans. "Can you believe what happened here last night, Hans? There are police everywhere. They have yellow tape across Sophie's door and nobody can go in there. Taneesha called me in special because she needed the extra help. But that's okay, I hate geometry. It's so boring. It's not a good day to have a visitor, but Taneesha said you have someone coming to see you and that I need to give you a good sponge bath." She held his head gently to her shoulder as she untied his gown behind his neck. Her loose-fitting scrubs, decorated with cartoon characters, hung open at the neck. Robyn seldom wore a bra. The need for support was something she only wished for. "You wouldn't be peeking down my blouse now, would you, Hans?" She pulled away from him and looked into his eyes. "Of course not," she answered herself with a smile. "Surely, a man your age isn't curious about such things."

Ulysses, Kansas—1933

E ven a man my age has curiosities. The one-eyed snake is even more curious, but less discerning," Doc said from the step of his trailer.

Hans said nothing as he watched Yolanda, the contortionist, disappear among the tents of the midway. She was a homely girl, less than half Doc's age. Hans had been the outside talker for her show a couple of times. He called her "Boney Macaroni." She would smile demurely, her biscuit-face turning red. Skinny and flat-chested, with oversized joints, Yolanda could stuff herself into a breadbox.

"When you're as ugly as she is, you have to be flexible." Doc lit the half-cigar in his mouth and tossed the match to the ground with a flick of his wrist. "If Harriet was half as flexible," he said, referring to the show's hefty hermaphrodite, "she could screw herself." Doc smiled from the half of his mouth opposite the cigar and squinted into the smoke. "That'd bring the chumps in," he added in an almost serious tone.

Hans said nothing. He knew better. Doc was Doc and that was all there was to it. Hans thought it strange that Madame Marguerite put up with his wandering eye. The agents and operators all feared Doc, but they feared Madame Marguerite more. Their fearfulness was not based on anything she had done. Rather, they feared her because Doc feared her. The woman was as mysterious as a cobra in a basket.

Rumors, bits and pieces of fact and fiction woven together, had Madame Marguerite as the carnival owner. Close to twenty years older than Doc, the woman had to be pushing eighty. The story told was that she was born to circus parents, ran away early, worked as a prostitute in Cripple Creek, and fell in love with an English-born con man who started the carnival before he died of tuberculosis. Where and when Doc came into the story, nobody seemed to know.

"What the hell do you want?" Doc growled when he returned from his daydream about Harriet.

"I was wondering when we might be going to winter camp?" said Hans.

Doc eyed him suspiciously. "Oh, you were, were you? If you weren't so damn big, I'd tell you it was none of your damn business."

"I'll crush your head like a grape," Hans smiled. He had long ago discovered the best way to deal with Doc was with a mixture of humor and aggression.

"We've got dates in Guymon, Pampa, Plainview, and Odessa before we break for Mission. We'll pull out of Ulysses this weekend. Is that enough for you? Or do I need to wipe your ass too?"

"Just wondering."

"Don't lie to me, you oversized charley horse. Is it a woman?"

Hans looked down, unable to meet Doc's stare. "I need see the doc who fixed me up back in Minnesota, make sure I've healed okay."

"Jesus jumped-up Judas Priest. They must have a doctor in Ulysses. Why the hell would you go back to that tree-infested, lutefisk-reeking land of giants?"

"I've got a meeting in Chicago too; thought I would kill two birds."

"Don't tell me." Doc pulled the cigar butt from his mouth; his dark eyes searched Hans's face. "That horse's ass, Lucky 'Big Ears' Lucello, wants you to go pro."

"Just during the off-season. I could use the money, Doc."

"Lucello is bad news, kid. He's a grafter with a nasty temper. He'll chew you up and spit you out. He's got some kind of numbers game going. Sure, he'll promote you, but he's only interested in one thing and that's scoring the con. I wouldn't trust that dago bastard as far as I could throw him." Doc thrust the cigar back into his mouth and turned to leave. "You watch your step, Hans." He stopped and turned back toward him. "And by the way, your gate has been dropping since we hit Kansas. It wouldn't hurt to lose once in a while."

"Then I wouldn't be the greatest carnival wrestler of all time, would I?" Hans smiled.

"Everybody loses, Hans. The question is when. The secret to success is knowing when to quit. Damn few ever get it right. The ones that die trying might get their statue in the park. Something for pigeons to crap on," he added. He pulled the cigar from his mouth and inspected the soggy, brown end. "None of the chumps will take you on. You have to give them hope. Besides, I'm tired of you beating up my strongman night after night in exhibition."

Myron Jakabowsky was the carnival strongman. Billed as "The Mighty Atlas," the aging immigrant appeared on stage in a leopard skin sarong while the outside talker gave the ballyhoo. The clems would be taunted to step up and, for two bits, attempt to lift the thousand-pound barbell from the stage floor. The fake barbell weighed only about eighty pounds but was held securely to the floor by a large electromagnet under the stage. An operator peeking out from the side curtains would open the switch, turning off the current when the Mighty Atlas bent over the barbell and, with much theatrics, lifted it above his head.

When there were no challengers from the audience, Hans was forced to wrestle Myron in exhibition while Madame Marguerite's girls sold popcorn and soda to the crowd. Usually a good sport, Myron would sometimes lose his temper with a taunting townie, leap from the ring, and pummel the hapless patron.

"I know all about hope, Doc." Hans forced a smile. "There isn't a day goes by that I don't hope to get the hell out of this sideshow and make something of myself."

Doc looked at him for a long moment. He seemed to be debating whether to spoon out more philosophical advice. "I'm sending the advance man into the local saloons this afternoon. We'll offer two hundred bucks to any two men who, together, can whip your ass. No holds barred," he said, raising an eyebrow. "That'll cheer you up," he called over his shoulder as he walked away.

A cloudless blue sky hung over the dusty midway as Hans watched Doc disappear into the chaos of carnival workers preparing for another day.

••••

William rubbed a generous amount of alum powder into the cut above Hans's eye and pinched it shut. "This is round three, Trap. No more foolin' around. You're making Doc nervous. If he has to shell out two hundred bucks, you're gonna be in big trouble."

The large man-crowd bucked and heaved just below the roar. Trapper had given them hope. The two oversized farm boys smiled at each other, shirtless brothers with a vision of California and a fresh start. They would not win. They could not win. They had not paid their dues as he had. They would need to sell a hog or two in order to cover the hospital and doctor bills for setting the bones he was about to break and for immobilizing the joints that he planned to dislocate. California would remain their dream. He would be their nightmare.

Timberlane County, Minnesota—2007
Day 2, 9:45 a.m.

Pine forests rose from the edge of the borrow pits on both sides of the road. Neither of them spoke as Aimee Pond drove her Subaru wagon north on 371, Paul Bunyan State Forest on the left and Chippewa National Forest on the right. Sam noticed the fresh mud caked on the floor mats below her feet. He inhaled deeply and swallowed in preparation to say something, then stifled the urge. His eyes darted nervously toward Aimee. She stared straight ahead, her knuckles white on the steering wheel. She looked tired.

"Does she always smell this bad?" Aimee said without turning. "She smells like a pack of beagles."

L2 sat in the backseat, drool hanging from the corners of her mouth.

"It's worse when she's nervous."

"How can you tell when she's nervous?"

"She stinks and drools."

Silence again descended between them, a cold curtain almost tangible. A cluster of Forest Service signs with arrows and distances pointed the way to several lakes hidden behind dark walls of trees.

"Boy, that sheriff is a piece of work," he said a little too loudly. "He insinuated that there was something going on between you and me."

Aimee continued to look straight ahead.

"Did you vote for that guy?"

Still there was no response.

"I don't think he's long for this world. There's something wrong with him, cancer maybe. You don't think I had anything to do with this, do you?"

"Are you hungry?" She looked at him as if the fate of the world rested with his answer.

"I could eat."

••••

At the diner on the outskirts of Deep Lake, the giant northern pike still leapt above the billboard at the edge of the parking lot. The same emaciated waitress had taken their order and offered Aimee consolation for the terrible thing that had happened at the home.

Sipping his coffee, Sam said, "Word travels fast in these parts."

"Everyone from Grand Rapids to Bemidji will have heard about it by dinnertime." She stared out the window; her eyes became glassy.

Sam noted her nearly flawless skin and that she wore little, if any, makeup. The flesh of her upper lip turned slightly upward, framed by pronounced dimples on either side of her mouth.

"I can't help feeling that I'm somehow responsible for this mess," she said. The tears threatened to spill over her lower eyelids.

"Aimee, neither of us is responsible for what happened to that woman."

"Sophie Mickelson. She had a name." A single tear streaked down her face.

"Yes. I'm sorry. Does she have any family?"

"There's nobody. She outlived them all. She never married. She lived in Deep Lake as long as I can remember. She believed it was the safest place in the world. She used to baby-sit me." A second tear streaked her opposite cheek. "She was a good woman, a kind and gentle woman who trusted me to care for her. I can't help but think I let her down."

The waitress brought their breakfast. Slices of toast spilled onto the table as she set their plates down. "I heard they caught the guy. Some out-of-stater," she added, as if there was comfort in knowing that a local could never do such a thing. She waited for a response.

They both stared up at her. No one spoke for a long, uncomfortable moment. "No." Aimee swallowed the lump in her throat. "They haven't arrested anyone and they don't have any suspects yet. Could you bring some more ketchup, Rhonda?"

They both picked at their food without talking. Sam finally pushed his plate forward an inch, a gesture that he was done eating. "I've never been arrested before. I've had a warrant issued, but never actually been arrested."

Aimee raised her eyebrows.

"It's a long story. It was several years ago in Colorado."

Aimee continued to look at him.

"I hit a guy, a very bad guy who deserved much more than a beating. I was exonerated," he added in an attempt to mitigate the look on her face. "One of the things I took home from that experience was the fact that there are some really bad people out there who are capable of horrific crimes. Not just crimes of passion or anger or motivated by money, but well-calculated crimes committed with absolutely no remorse. One of the cemeteries I discovered—you won't find it in any of my books—contained the bodies of a hundred and three young women, all victims of one man." He had her attention. "And I think there were seven other cemeteries with equal numbers of victims." That was the clincher.

"My God, Sam, what—"

"The point is, Aimee, you can't assume responsibility for the bad things that happen in this world. You'll never sleep again; you'll never be at peace with yourself. Trust me, I know."

"But—"

"No buts. No should've, could've, or would've thoughts. Get back on the horse, do your job, and do your best to make sure it doesn't happen again."

"You think it could happen again?" There was fear in her eyes.

"I'd like to think it was a onetime, isolated event. But that would be naïve. You have to plan for the worst. Let the sheriff do his job and hope the idiot brings in some outside help. Did you vote for him?"

Aimee leaned forward and stared directly into his eyes. "Yes, I voted for him. It's lung cancer complicated by emphysema. No, I don't think you had anything to do with it. And lastly, you tell me: Is there anything going on between us?"

Sam straightened. "Wow, where'd all that come from?"

"Just because I don't answer all your questions doesn't mean I've forgotten them. Excuse my bluntness, but I'm older than you and I don't have the patience for game playing that I once did."

"What if I said I hoped there was?"

"The mere fact that your response is phrased as a question tells me you're more interested in playing *Jeopardy!*, a game I don't have time for, especially in light of everything going on." Aimee turned toward the cook and said something in American Sign Language before calling out to the waitress, "Rhonda, can I get the check and a doggie bag, please?" She leaned back from the table.

"That's it? Do I have the right of appeal?" Sam said.

"Sam, forget I asked the question. I've got way too much on my plate right now to be playing silly courtship games. Go flirt with someone your own age. Let's you and I be friends instead. Okay?"

Sam smiled and shook his head. "If you only knew how many times I've heard that. It's the story of my life." He inhaled deeply and extended his hand across the table. "Friends."

Deep Lake, Minnesota—2007
Day 2, 11:35 a.m.

Aimee stifled a yawn as she glanced at the loon clock on the wall. It seemed as if an entire day had passed, and it was only 11:35 in the morning. She had laughed when the administrator asked if she should cut short her meeting in Duluth to return to Deep Lake. Aimee believed the best place for her was as far away from Whispering Pines as possible. But it would have been nice to have someone else deal with horses' asses, like the one standing in front of her.

"He has good days and bad days. He mostly sleeps," Aimee said. "He rarely speaks and when he does, it's not to us. He called one of the staff William the other day. I assume he thought he was talking to you, Doctor Gottlieb."

"He always called me Will, never William." Dr. William Gottlieb appeared nervous, standing painfully straight in front of the large desk in the small office. He was tall and slender with a full head of gray hair. His Harris tweed jacket with elbow patches atop a V-necked sweater and open shirt were the standard garb for a university professor.

"Are you a geriatrician, Doctor Gottlieb?"

"No, I'm a veterinary pathologist."

Aimee Pond cocked her head slightly and looked at him without responding.

"I'm professor of veterinary medicine at the Veterinary Teaching Hospital at Colorado State University," he offered quickly. "My DVM is from Kansas, my PhD from UC Davis, and my postdoc was at Cornell. I understand the pathology of aging, if that is what you're asking." At sixty-two, he was tired of justifying his competence to the medical community.

"I'll keep that in mind should my cat drop dead. As far as your father is concerned, he's unaffected by the typical geriatric issues of immobility, instability, and incontinence. However, there does appear to be intellectual impairment. He's suffering from some form of dementia, but that's the norm for someone his age." Aimee paused. "I appreciate your coming, Doctor Gottlieb. You're the first family member to visit since he checked in here eight weeks ago." She did not take her eyes from his. There was an accusatory note in her voice and she did little to hide it.

"Until I received a call from your business office, I had no idea he was here," said Dr. Gottlieb. "Apparently my contact information was listed with Medicare. He checked himself out of the assisted living center in Clinton, Iowa, two months ago and disappeared. He has been exhibiting signs of progressive dementia for the past several years. I was considering moving him over to the nursing home side of the facility when Dad walked away one afternoon. He closed his bank accounts and vanished. Magnificent Oaks didn't even notify me. My brother used to take care of all that for Dad."

"You have a brother?" she said, raising her eyebrows.

"He died last year. He was older," he said, his voice becoming tight. "He was in poor health. He lived in Illinois where we grew up. Look, Nurse Pond—"

"Are there any other immediate family still living?" she said, cutting him off.

"No, my mother died over twenty-five years ago. That's when Dad moved back to Iowa, where my brother and I were born. We had moved to Illinois when we were still in grade school and Dad commuted to Clinton, just across the river in Iowa." He looked around the room. Framed artwork in shades of green, brown, and blue surrounded the small office. Loons, wolves, moose, and lakes were the typical Minnesota themes. "Why here?" He returned his eyes to her.

"We were hoping you could tell us." Aimee again made eye contact. "This place is not cheap, Doctor Gottlieb. How does your father pay for this?"

"He has a good pension. He worked for the railroad. He was an engineer, a locomotive engineer. Medicare and his railroad plan pick up a portion. And he lived very modestly. How do you get paid?" he asked suddenly.

"We were sent a check by a law firm in Boone, Iowa, with a quarterly payment. They manage his trust. They must receive his pension."

"Boone? I don't understand. Dad was a railroad engineer. Boone was a division point. He spent most of his career hauling trains between Clinton and Boone. It was where he lived when he wasn't home. But he did all his business in Clinton. We didn't know he had a trust. His home has been sitting vacant for several years, since we put him in the assisted care facility. When he came up missing I didn't know what to do. I couldn't find him."

No one spoke for a long, uncomfortable moment.

Dr. Gottlieb broke the silence. "I contacted the authorities and they told me there was nothing they could do unless I could prove that he was mentally incapacitated. Short of hiring a private investigator—" Finally he asked, "Is he all right? What's going on around here? Why is there yellow tape everywhere? Why are the police here?"

Aimee ignored his questions. "He claims to be the world's greatest carnival wrestler." She smiled. "Which leads me to a rather serious problem we're having with your father; he's hurt both of our security guards, who now refuse to go near him."

Dr. Gottlieb furrowed his brow and shot her a piercing look. "My father is one of the gentlest human beings on the planet. He would never intentionally hurt anyone. I've never known him to even raise his voice in anger."

"Oh, he doesn't get angry," she shot back. "He just puts them on the ground writhing in pain. For a man approaching a hundred years old, he moves like a cat. I've never seen anything like it. We have to sedate him to get him back into his room."

"I find this astonishing," he said, running his fingers through his hair. "Is that why the police are here? Has my father hurt someone?" He shook his head and then looked directly at Aimee. "He was never a wrestler, let alone a carnival wrestler, whatever that is."

Aimee's eyes narrowed. "What about his ears? How do you explain those cauliflower ears and the massive amounts of scar tissue under his eyebrows?"

"Football. He played high school football in the leather helmet days. There were no face masks and very little padding. Hematomas happened."

Aimee looked down at the shiny walnut surface of the desk; her fingertips resting lightly on the polished wood left wet smudges. "Don't misunderstand me, Doctor Gottlieb. Your father, for the most part, is a gentle man. As long as nobody tries to physically impose their will on him, he's fine. But for the safety of our staff, we cannot tolerate aggressive behavior. He has two strikes against him. If it happens again, we will ask that you make other arrangements. Am I clear on that, Doctor?"

Professor William Gottlieb did not like being threatened or placed in a subordinate role by someone he did not view as his intellectual equal. "Crystal clear, Nurse Pond. But understand that I did not make these arrangements. Perhaps we might continue this conversation after I visit with my father. May I please see him now?"

CLINTON, IOWA—1955

The Clinton yards, sixteen sets of tracks across, were wet beneath the gray clouds of October. Ash and coal dust covered everything within sight from the yard office, giving the world a uniform bleakness. Gray men with ice hooks stood atop the wooden refrigerator cars, guiding the huge blocks of ice that slid down the wooden flume from the icehouse on the hill. The cars would be loaded with hanging sides of beef from the slaughterhouse on Beaver Slough. The air smelled of coal, steel, and rotting flesh. Hans disengaged the conveyer from the coal tender to the firebox and checked the pressure gauges one more time.

Will waved from outside the dispatcher's office, his red Schwinn adding the only color to the cinder-covered surroundings. Two longs and a short from the engine's whistle had brought the boy the half mile from home to greet the train. It was a Saturday morning routine he and his father had shared for some time.

The huge drivers slowly brought the wheels to a stop and the engineer set the brakes. The rippling sound of giant steel knuckles compressing was heard fading into the western distance as the slack came out of the train. Hans was bucking the engineer's extra list and had passed the book of rules more than a year earlier, but was still a fireman at age forty-seven. Seniority was the indisputable rule that governed the road. The Depression had lingered throughout the 1940s and good-paying jobs remained hard to come by. When the boys came home from Europe and the Pacific, the job market soon flooded. He did not begrudge the favor shown to veterans by society. Too young for the war to end all wars and too old for conscription into the second war, he had volunteered, only to be turned away citing an occupational deferment. It seemed they needed someone to shovel coal into the bottomless gullet of the steam engines that moved the goods of war across the continent.

Truman had picked a fight with Korea earlier in the decade, and the economy was only now starting to respond. Maybe next year Hans could take the boys north to do some fishing.

The engine crew that would take the train to Chicago was already gingerly stepping across the many sets of tracks between Hans and the yard office. Will waved again and smiled broadly as his father made his way across the tracks, his leather grip in hand. The boy was slight like his mother, like Hans had been at that age. The kid was smart and unfortunately knew it. His mouth sometimes got him into trouble both in school and at home. He always had an answer and it was always right. He could incite his brother or a teacher with a stinging barb that would render them speechless while the insult sank in. But the smile and the sparkling eyes would usually disarm his opponents. On Saturdays, when the weather was good, Will would race to the yard office at the sound of his father's whistle. After the paperwork was signed and the crews had traded good-natured, though oftentimes vulgar, denouncements, they would ride his bicycle home. Will would balance his father's grip in his lap while sitting atop the handlebars as his father peddled. A playing card, pinned to his rear fender strut with a clothespin, clattered against the spokes. His father smelled of sweat and coal. It would be several years before Will would be ashamed of his blue-collar heritage, telling his fraternity brothers that his father was an engineer, conveniently leaving out the word locomotive.

The Saturday morning greeting was always the same. The barrel-chested man with no neck wearing bibbed overalls, engineer boots, and a striped engineer's cap would say, "Why aren't you in school?" Will would beam and respond with "It's Saturday, Pop. There's no school." The greeting was expected. It was their ritual.

DEEP LAKE, MINNESOTA—2007
DAY 2, 11:50 A.M.

W hy aren't you in school?"

"It's Saturday, Pop. There's no school."

They stared at each other for a long moment.

Hans smiled at the ten-year-old boy with sparkling eyes and a broad grin.

Will smiled back at the time-ravaged old man who lay in the hospital bed. A painful lump formed in Will's throat. He studied the ashen face of his father framed by the whiteness of his surroundings. Cataracts had stolen the color from his eyes and white-beard stubble helped camouflage him amid sheets and pillowcases.

Will saw himself in his father's face and it frightened him. He was staring into the fortune-teller's crystal ball, its weight pressing deeply into the pillow. Light-bending distortions blurred the image, but it was him—thirty-seven years into the future. Will had always been too busy and too young to think about mortality, but now it looked him in the eyes and it was smiling. He did not know what to say to the man he suddenly realized was a stranger. He had fathered him, raised him, paid for his education, and now lay dying, morphed into an ancient hulk of a human being, almost unrecognizable. Will heard himself swallow.

S am could feel the eyes of the Whispering Pines residents watching his every move as he pulled up stakes
and readied the tiny Airstream for departure. But for
where? He had no idea. There were plenty of campgrounds
in the National Forest that surrounded Deep Lake. Straightening suddenly from securing the not-so-easy-to-fold-up
step below the doorway, he faced the care center, his arms
extended slightly with palms up, he said, "Take a good look,
folks. I came in peace and this is what I get. Angry? You're
damn right I'm angry. Look what they did to my dog." Sam
pointed at L2 who sat obediently behind the Willys. Her eyes
were even more bloodshot than usual from being choked by
the noose pole that Timberlane County Animal Control had
used to subdue the unruly beast. He was especially sensitive
to any mistreatment of his dog, given the brutal way Elle
had been killed.

He turned his back to Whispering Pines and closed the
valve on the propane tank. "I'm getting just like them," he
said, looking at the forlorn bloodhound. "Inward, cantan-
kerous, self-righteous, and generally pissed off at the world."
He adjusted the anti-sway bar. "I think we've been on the
road too long, girl. I've become disengaged and intolerant
of anyone who disagrees with me. Like that freaking sheriff," he almost yelled. L2 shrank and looked away from Sam,

unsure of why she was being punished. "Not you, girl," he apologized. He did not like to think about it, but he was as isolated as the old people who fascinated him. His daughter, Sidney, and a bloodhound were the extent of his social world. Friends and lovers in Colorado had betrayed him, and his response was to isolate himself further by moving to the middle of nowhere in Wyoming, the least populated state in the nation. He had only Sidney to turn to, but he was uncomfortable seeking solace from his daughter. She, too, seemed reluctant to console him. Give her a problem to solve, however, and she was unstoppable. He would call her.

It was starting to snow again when the sheriff's deputy slowly pulled into the Whispering Pines parking lot. He parked on the far side of the lot, but left the SUV running. The deputy watched Sam. "Really?" Sam muttered as he loaded L2 into the Willys. He snapped the snow from the wiper blades, then cupped his hands over his mouth and blew warm air on his numb fingers. Turning, he saw the residents and staff of the care center lined up behind the dining room windows. They, too, watched him. "How do you people live here?" he asked with an animated gesture. Increasingly intolerant of both cold and hot weather, Sam was as frustrated by his age-related narrow-mindedness as he was by the weather itself. "Being accused of murder brings out the best in me," he said, smiling at L2 as he slid into the driver's seat. He flicked a toggle switch below the dash and heard the electrical whir of the in-line fuel pump. He pulled out the choke and visualized the butterfly closing on the big Holley four-barrel carburetor. He turned the key and pressed the starter button. The Chevy small block roared to life. *If it were only that easy to bring people back to life*, he thought. Sophie Mickelson was not coming back to set the record straight. "It's up to us, girl. Fasten your seat belt. I've got a feeling it's going to be a bumpy ride."

Hans studied the many colors of rounded stones beneath the clear water at the lake's edge. Most were brown, some nearly white, others almost black. He could see his breath. The dark, boreal forest surrounded the small lake, looming over its shores. The southern exposure appeared red from the dead stubble of wild rice poking above the surface of the shallows. It had been a short walk on a well-worn trail that angled north from the backyard of the farmhouse. "Is this Deep Lake?"

Gloria smiled. "Yes, this is it. My great-grandfather built a cabin where the house stands today. The Indians had another name for it, which meant 'too deep for rice.'"

"What about the town? Was it here then?"

"No. The Halvorsons built a combination trading post and mercantile that served both the Indians and Scandinavian immigrants. The town grew up around that."

Hans picked up a small, flattened stone. He flung it with a sidearm pitch that caused it to skip several times across the lake's smooth surface.

"Before breakfast, you mentioned college. Where did you go to school?" she said, smiling nervously.

"Iowa State College. I had a full scholarship—wrestling."

"What did you study?"

"Biology." He smiled, looking down. "I wanted to be a teacher and a coach," he said with a note of finality, hoping that would put an end to the probing.

"And?" Gloria said, her eyes dancing with anticipation as she pulled a strand of windblown hair from her mouth.

"And, I should have graduated in '30, but being a student athlete and all, I was sort of on the five-year plan. Training for the '28 Olympics set me back academically." He stuffed his hands into the pockets of his coat and looked out across the lake. "The crash in '29 changed everything. It was a sucker punch that left us all a bit woozy. Lots of dreams got shattered. My dad lost his job just before Christmas. I quit school in order to support my folks. There you have it, short and sweet."

"Is that when you started with the carnival?" she asked, almond eyes narrowing.

"No. I bounced for some of the bigger gin joints from Omaha to Chicago. I met some nasty people in those days. I guess you might say I was on the supply side of your profession."

Gloria looked into his eyes for a long moment. Lowering her eyes, she said, "I worked for a few of those people myself." She lifted her gaze and smiled. "How did you take up with a traveling show?"

"Doc O'Brien's show came to town one day offering a hundred bucks to anyone who could beat the world's greatest carnival wrestler, Mad Dog Gomelski. I beat him every night for the better part of a week. Doc O'Brien fired Mad

Dog and hired me in order to save money. That was almost three years ago."

"What happened to Mad Dog?"

"He turned pro. He's making a bundle working for a promoter out of Milwaukee. The last time I saw him, he told me I was the best thing that ever happened to him. He's happy as a pig in shi—, as a clam," he corrected himself, looking down and kicking at a tree root exposed between the rocks on the shoreline.

Neither of them spoke. Gloria positioned herself in front of him.

"Hans, why are you here?" she suddenly asked, a note of seriousness in her voice. She brushed the windblown hair from her face again and stared up at him.

"I guess I wanted to see you again," he said softly.

"You guess? You're not sure?"

"No, I'm sure. Look, can't a fella just come calling? Does there have to be a reason?"

"You just don't come calling to the north woods of Minnesota, especially this time of year. And then there's the tattoo," she said, shaking her head. "Why are you here, Hans?"

"You're not going to let it go, are you?" He looked into her eyes. "What do you want from me—a signed confession? I came here because I wanted to see you again, because I have thought about you every day for the past two months. Because when I close my eyes at night I see your face, and when I wake in the morning I smell your hair and hear your voice asking me to take a deep breath. Because I feel the warmth of your hand on my shoulder while you listen to my lungs filling with the same air that you breathe." He paused and looked down again. "I came here because I couldn't stop myself. I need to know if there is any possibility that you could someday share these feelings and, if not, tell me straight up so I can leave here and get on with my life."

"And what life is that, Hans? Beating people up for a living? And if I say yes, does that change your plans? It seems we have two very different goals in life. Mine is to end suffering and yours is to create it. How's this going to work, the doctor and the wrestler?"

The black spruce jutted upward in a jigsaw pattern against the gray sky. Pockets of paper birch intermittently hugged the rocky shoreline, their leafless branches a spiderweb of dark tentacles reaching for the light beyond the shroud of gray. He watched a skein of geese flow gently just over the horizon, hurriedly heading south. "Why are *you* here?" he said softly, turning to look directly into her eyes.

"I live here, Hans. This is my home." She looked down at the same tree root Hans had been nudging with his foot, then out across the lake. There was a long pause, as if she wanted to say more but could not find the words. "After my father died…" She paused again. "Being an only child, it was my place to come back to care for—"

"No, why are *you* here?" he interrupted. "With me?" He swung his right arm, palm up, in an arc to include the lake.

"Oh, well—I'm just being cordial."

"You could have turned me away at the door. Instead you fed me breakfast and took me on a walk to the family lake. Does everyone who knocks on your door get food and a walk in the woods?"

"I'm curious is all," she said. The wind blew her hair across her face again. "I was only trying to figure out why *you* were here."

He took a step toward her and slowly pulled the strands of hair away from her mouth, his hand brushing gently across her cheek. "Answer my question," he said softly.

Gloria stared at him, her eyes darting across his and then narrowing. A slight smile formed at the corners of her mouth. "Why are *you* here?"

Answer me, Dad. Why are you here?" Will Gottlieb said, leaning over the bed, staring directly into his father's face.

Hans stared back at him, his eyes darting back and forth, confusion spreading from the corners of his eyes and across his forehead.

"I have been worried sick about you. Whatever possessed you to sneak off and come to Deep Lake, Minnesota?" It had been more than a year since he had seen his father, and the changes were evident. Hans would be one hundred years old in March. He had always looked at least ten or twenty years younger than his age, but now he looked like a centenarian. His eyes had recessed into blue-gray sockets; his translucent skin was a sickly shade of yellow that barely covered the veins in his face. "Dad, is there something significant about this place that made you want to come here?"

Hans's mouth hung slightly open. His lips came together, then parted as if he were about to speak, but nothing came out.

Will studied his father's face. His questions did not seem to register. Dementia had robbed his father of his ability to comprehend or to formulate a response. Perhaps rephrasing the question would trigger an answer. "Let me ask you this…," he said.

Lemme ask you this: How's that mick bastard O'Brien doin'?" Lucky "Big Ears" Lucello said from across the table at Chicago's Ristorante La Roma. Tiny specks of red sauce were flecked across his ponderous belly; his swollen fingers below dimpled knuckles tapped at the table's edge. The remnants of his meatball sandwich lay strewn on his plate as if something had been killed there.

"He's well. Grumpy as usual," Hans said.

"And Margaret? Is she still alive?"

"Margaret?" Hans asked. "I don't know a Margaret. Do you mean Madame Marguerite?"

Lucky grinned. His gold front tooth shone brightly as he shook his head. "Hell no, I mean Margaret, his whore mother that he lives with."

"Marguerite is Doc's mother?"

"Lemme ask you this: Have you ever heard that mute bitch utter a word?"

Hans thought for a moment. "I can't say that I have."

"That's 'cause her drunken mick husband cut out her tongue when she told him she was leaving him." Lucky smiled again, his tooth gleaming, and his stomach bounced in an attempt to stifle a deeper laugh.

Hans could smell Lucky's bay rum aftershave over the strong odor of Italian food.

"She was just a whore, but didn't deserve how she was treated by that bastard. Word has it that she poisoned his sorry ass with arsenic. Did it real slow so as to drag it out."

"Doc's her son?" Hans asked in amazement.

"Lemme ask you this: Are you stupid? Didn't I just tell you that he's her boy?"

"Yeah, but—"

"She was quite a looker in her day. Hell, she was only seventeen when Doc was born. Somethin' ain't right about a man livin' with his mother in a wagon his whole life. It ain't natural." Lucky paused and looked past Hans. His dark eyes were surrounded by puffy brown lids. "They're Irish! What can I say?"

A small, dark man, nattily dressed, with a light gray fedora entered the restaurant and approached their table. His hat had a deep gutter dent. He wore it at a rakish angle with the brim snapped down and the back snapped up.

"Lemme introduce you to my little Romanian Gypsy-Jew friend, Isadore Blumenfeld."

Lucky waved the man to the chair on his left with the back of his hand, gold and diamonds flashing. When he reached inside his coat to retrieve a silver cigar case, Hans saw the butt of a pistol protruding from a dark leather shoulder holster. Hans rose and offered his hand. "Mr. Blumenfeld."

"You can call him Kid," Lucky said, pulling his cigar case apart and offering one to Hans.

"No, thank you. Mr. Lucello, you contacted me. What's on your mind?" Hans said, wiping the corners of his mouth with his napkin.

"That's what I like about you Krauts. No dancin' around, right to the goddamn point." He glanced at Kid, who had yet to utter a word. "Lemme ask you this: You wanna make some big dough?"

Hans sat back in his chair and placed both hands palms-down on the linen tablecloth in front of him. "These are tough times; big dough is a relative term. I have a job and I'm thankful for it. But I'm listening."

"My sources tell me you're pretty good at beatin' up hayseeds and chumps. Lemme ask you this: You got what it takes to go pro? You got what it takes to go up against someone the likes of Stocky Joe Snow? Or maybe Greasy Grimes?"

"I'm still listening."

"Lemme ask you this: You interested in the world title? That chunk of meat from Scotland...what's his name?"

"The Mighty Angus MacGregor."

"Yeah, that's the guy. They say he's mean, killed a guy in the ring."

"Angus is a swell fella. I beat him on a decision in the '28 Olympics. He's strong, but he's not technical, doesn't use his head. As for killing someone, I heard the guy died of a heart attack a day after the match."

"Whatever," Lucky said, fanning a cloud of smoke away from his round face. "If his promoter is smart, he'll work the rumor to build a bigger gate. And that, Mr. Gottlieb, is what this game is all about. It's all about promotion. It's about juicing the schmucks so they show up at the match. I've got the connections to take this game out of the carnival lots of Hicksville and small-town exhibition halls all the way to Madison Square Garden." He winked at Kid, who still sat silently, legs crossed, staring at Hans. "To do that, I need to sign a stable of talent, people worthy of promotion. That's where you come in."

Hans smiled and shook his head. "You're talking contracts. What's in it for me?"

"A steady paycheck, like clockwork, every Friday; you get paid—win, lose, or draw. Plus, if you're the guy I'm keeping on top, you get a percentage of the gate."

"So the matches are rigged," Hans said, straightening in his chair.

Lucky placed the fingers of both hands on the table's edge, stubby appendages dark against the white tablecloth. "No. I prefer to use the term 'worked,'" He smiled at Kid. "Nobody takes a dive in this game. The key is in the match-up. When two men climb into the ring, the best one climbs out again. The match has to be legit or the fans won't think it's on the level. In this game, the fans come first. They'll get behind an all-American champ."

"Every regional promoter claims they have the one and only champ," Hans said. "How will you get them to cooperate?"

"In less than a year, I'll have hired all their talent away from them. Lemme ask you this: You gonna go where the pay is steady and you're treated right, or where you don't know when you're going to get screwed and when your next meal might be? A guy is as loyal as his last paycheck. I'm puttin' a wad of dough up front to get the talent I need and leave those East Coast promoters out in the cold. I'll take Boston, Philly, Baltimore, and New York so fast they won't know what hit 'em. I'll choose the one and only title-holder, somebody the fans can get heated up about. Only the best will wear the crown. They gotta earn it. It's gotta be somebody fresh, somebody we can build a program around, somebody the fans can get behind and believe in, the old rags-to-riches crapola. That's where you come in."

Hans raised his eyebrows and said, "I'm listening."

"My people tell me that with the right push, you could be the draw I'm lookin' for. Outside the Midwest carny circuit, not many people have heard of you. By workin' the build-up matches and with good promotion, you could be the all-American champ, a real matinee idol. Lemme ask you this: You interested?"

Hans looked beyond the dark, round figure before him and his silent associate, the moving bodies of the restaurant blurring into horizontal flashes of black and white. Through the window he saw a tall, dark-haired woman walk slowly by. She delicately pushed back strands of hair from her face. She turned slightly toward him and paused, but he could not see her face. The buildings behind her appeared as dark and jagged as a Minnesota forest; the pavement, wet with melted snow, reflected light like the surface of Deep Lake.

"Lemme ask you this—perhaps you didn't hear my question. Allow me to repeat it. Are you interested?"

Hans met Lucky's impatient gaze. "I'm here," he said.

Yes, Dad, I know you're here, but why? Why are you here?" Will Gottlieb said, leaning over his father. "Why are you in Minnesota?"

Hans's cloudy eyes darted back and forth across Will's face. A smile formed at the corner of his mouth, but he did not attempt to speak. Instead, he reached out and took his son's hand in his and squeezed it gently. Arthritis had disfigured his hands, but they were as huge and strong as when Will was a boy. The Monel ring he had always worn was still on his right hand. A friend, Will's namesake, had made it for him a very long time ago. Hans had never worn a wedding band. He claimed rings were dangerous when working around machinery and only wore the Monel ring because he couldn't get it off. The nickel alloy was as shiny as Will remembered. He used to sit in his father's lap, rubbing his finger over the smooth metal surface, always wishing he was big enough to wear it. Or, tracing the outline of the tattoo on his father's forearm, he would dream of the day when he would be able to get one too. Cigar bands for rings and bubble gum tattoos made him feel closer to his father, even though he physically resembled his mother. Hans squeezed Will's hand again and smiled. The corners of his mouth were crusty with dried saliva, and white-beard stubble rose in patches from his uneven face.

Will was unsure whether the gesture was one of acknowledgment of his presence or of his question. It was becoming increasingly clear that his father's mental state was deteriorating rapidly. He slipped between wakefulness and sleep as though it were a controlled response to some cue. Sometimes there appeared to be recognition, sometimes even cognition. It was like talking to a dog or a small child, he thought. He found himself speaking slowly in short sentences, as if reasoning with a toddler. It was the same way his father had spoken to him sixty years ago. Will shook his head and smiled with the realization of how he had come full circle in his relationship with his father. "Christ and a bear," his dad would have said as an expression of both surprise and acknowledgment.

Spirit Lake, Iowa—1934

Christ and a bear," Doc muttered to himself as he pushed through the tip gathered in front of the stage of the kootch show. The rubes smelled of sweat and tobacco. Junior Stucken, the outside talker, was presenting the bally. He had just let out a "Hey Rube" for someone to come snatch Penelope the Pinhead from the stage. But Junior was making his final pitch as if nothing had happened, the superlatives bursting from his mouth in florid excess.

"Gentlemen, I want you to come right up close and get a sample, a little peek, a little whiff, a little taste of what you're going to see on the inside. You've heard your buddies talk about it; you've read about how they've tried to shut it down; you've heard the whispers. Now see it for yourself. The most daring display of feminine flesh ever presented, female anatomy at its finest. Take a good look, fellas. These girls are young, they're supple, they're lithe, and they're nubile. They're hotter than a firecracker and too young to know what's decent. They'll bend and stretch; they'll shake and quiver. They've got all the right parts in all the right places. You'll see Bendin' Brenda, Pristine Christine, Holly Oh Golly, Slippery Sadie, and eight other warm, wild, wonderful, willowy women. Two bits, gentlemen, twenty-five cents, one quarter of what it would cost anywhere else. Get your tickets, come inside, feel the heat, hear the slap of flesh, smell the aroma of passion, see what you've dreamed of. You know the dreams I'm talking about. Get your ticket because it's showtime at O'Brien's Wonders of the World Burlesque Show."

Penelope the Pinhead danced at the end of the stage, last in line of the all-girl revue. Penelope, a twenty-seven-year-old microcephalic, wore his trademark white chiffon, sleeveless dress. Heavy cotton hose disappeared into his scuffed and dirty work boots. A pink bow was clipped to the long topknot of hair above his shaven, conical head. His nose and lips appeared huge in comparison to his undeveloped cranium. An imbecile with the personality of a happy coonhound, Penelope could become stubborn when things did not go his way.

"Jesus jumped-up Judas Priest," Doc said as he and William pushed their way through the laughing throng of men and teenage boys gathered in front of the stage. "He'll listen to you, William. Talk him down; promise him anything. Just get him off the damn stage."

William stopped and looked at Doc.

"*Please,* for Christ's sake. But whatever you do, don't let him start pissing on the yokels like a goddamn monkey. Get him back to the freak show, lock him up, tie him down; just get the pinhead back to the end of the lot. Goddamn freaks," Doc added through clenched teeth.

"He'll be okay, boss. He just followed Reba from the freak show. He likes her."

Doc rolled his eyes and looked down the line of girls to Reba, who was grinning from ear to ear.

"Just get him off the stage," Doc growled. "*Please.*"

William pushed up to the edge of the stage and cupped his hands in front of him, one over the other as if hiding a surprise. Penelope stopped dancing; his mouth hung open as he approached William. William made his way to the stairs at the end of the stage and disappeared into the tent behind. Penelope followed, a strand of saliva hanging from his mouth.

Junior Stucken continued his bally, working the situation. "That guy was as normal as you and me before he saw what you're about to see. He paid his two bits and has been happy ever since. Step right up. Get your ticket. I guarantee that in less than five minutes your mouth will be hanging open and you'll be drooling too."

"Everything okay, Doc?" Hans said, sidling up next to him in the crowd. "I heard the 'Hey Rube' call at the other end."

"Well, if it ain't Lumpy. Why aren't you down with your kind at the freak show?"

"Watch it or I'll yell queer and let this hormone-enraged crowd tear you apart."

Doc smiled. "Hormone-enraged? Big words for a guy who wears a mask and sniffs armpits for a living; I forgot you were a college boy." He magically produced half a cigar that he stuffed into his mouth, and he and Hans pushed their way to the rear of the crowd.

"Doc, there's someone I want you to meet," Hans said as they broke free of the tip.

Doc did not respond. It was too late. He had stopped and slowly pulled the cigar butt from his mouth. He stared intently at the tall, slender brunette who stood at the end of the midway. A shy smile appeared on her face. "Jesus jumped-up Judas Priest," he said slowly under his breath as Hans led him across the dusty lot.

"Doc, this is Gloria Halvorson—Doctor Gloria Halvorson," Hans said proudly. "Gloria, this is Doc O'Brien."

Gloria took a small step forward and offered her hand, a bold gesture that made Hans somewhat uncomfortable. She was a professional woman, he reasoned. Or perhaps it was a gesture of emancipation that she had picked up in the twenties.

"Mr. O'Brien, I've heard so much about you. It's a pleasure to finally meet you," she said, smiling.

"Doctor Halvorson, the pleasure is all mine," Doc said, removing his sweat-stained fedora. "I must say, however, that I have heard little about you, which is not surprising, given that Hans is an inarticulate charley horse totally lacking in the social graces."

"Oh, that's contradictory. He told me today that you were, and I quote, an irascible lout with the demeanor of a demented wolverine."

Doc grinned and his eyes sparkled. "I don't know why you didn't euthanize him when you had him in your clinic last year. The very least you could have done was to remove that portion of his brain responsible for aggression. He would have been perpetually happy and much easier to get along with."

"Those options are still on the table." Her smile turned into a toothy grin. "Tell me, Doctor O'Brien, do you have a medical background?"

Doc laughed and shook his head. "It's funny, all these people that call me Doc every day have never asked me how I came by that moniker. The short answer is no. But I earned the nickname honestly. My mother sent me off to college kicking and screaming. I started off studying medicine but soon gravitated toward philosophy. I had a professor at Notre Dame who believed me to be the most irreverent, cynical agnostic he had ever encountered. He encouraged me to pursue theology. I hold a doctorate in religious studies from Harvard."

The three of them stood silent for what seemed a long time.

"Hans, your mouth is open," Gloria said finally.

Hans could not take his eyes from Doc. "All this time you've poked fun at my being a college boy; you've shown nothing but contempt—" He shook his head. "And your vocabulary! You can actually carry on a conversation that doesn't cause my ears to blister and sailors to blush."

Doc stuffed the cigar butt back in his mouth and squinted at Hans. "Tell anyone and I'll kick your sorry ass from here to hell and back." He turned to Gloria, removed his cigar, and said, "I was under the impression you practiced in Minnesota. What, pray tell, brings you to this corn-infested backwater known as Iowa?"

"Hans wrote and asked me to come, so here I am," she beamed.

"It was as close to Minnesota as we were going to get this season," Hans added.

Doc inspected them both, his eyes searching one, then the other. "This sounds serious!" He narrowed his eyes at Hans. "You bring her to the kootch show?"

"We were about to ride the Ferris wheel when the operator yelled 'Hey Rube' at the kootch. I thought there was trouble, so I came on the double."

"You're a real poet," Doc said. "I suppose you'll invite her to the wrestling match tomorrow night?"

The last of the crowd was passing through the tent flaps into the kootch show. Three underage boys at the end of the line nervously attempted to look older as they approached Junior Stucken. "How old are you, boys?" he barked.

"Eighteen," they said in unison, their voices comically high.

"Enjoy the show, men," Junior said, collecting their tickets. "Keep your hands out of your pockets."

"I've never been to a carnival before," Gloria suddenly volunteered.

Doc looked at her with raised eyebrows. "Never?"

"I spent an afternoon at Coney Island once," she said. She looked down and then quickly added, "I also visited the boardwalk in Atlantic City," as an afterthought offered for acceptance. "They both seemed more permanent than this."

"That's why they call this a traveling show," Doc said, staring intently at her.

"And no, I won't be able to stay to watch Hans wrestle tomorrow. I'm on my way to Iowa City to buy some medical equipment. The train leaves from Mason City in the morning."

"That, indeed, is unfortunate," Doc said. "I'm sure you would have enjoyed his amazing display of athleticism. But the contest is, perhaps, a little too barbaric for the delicate sensibilities of a lady such as you."

Gloria smiled politely but did not avert her gaze. "I spent four years patching up people in Chicago and a year at Saint Vincent's in Manhattan. I assure you I have seen the worst of man's inhumanity to man." She paused and then said, "Of course, cruelty does not always manifest itself physically. Barbarism can take many forms. The exploitation of those unfortunate souls you call freaks—many would consider that rudely uncivilized."

"Jesus jumped-up Judas Priest," Doc said, grinning. "This one's a keeper, Hans. She's got fire. She knows tit for tat. Wait a second," he said, eyeing her skeptically. "You're not a socialist, are you?"

"No."

"A communist?"

"No."

"A prohibitionist?"

Gloria grinned and shook her head. "I'm a Lutheran."

"Mein Gott, Herr Gottlieb, das ist gut," he said, turning to Hans. "She's beautiful, she's smart, and she can patch you up when that dago bastard Lucello is through with you."

Hans glanced nervously at Gloria, who looked totally surprised and suddenly alarmed. Neither of them spoke for a long, uncomfortable moment.

"Wait, don't tell me," Doc said to Hans. "You haven't told her?"

The seductive clarinet from the scratched record on the Victrola signaled that the kootch show was underway. The crowd within the tent had become silent.

"Told me what, Hans?" said Gloria.

"I...I was saving the big surprise for later."

"It appears I've let the cat out of the bag," Doc said apologetically, putting his fedora back on his head. "I'll take my leave and allow you to salvage what's left of the awkward situation I've placed you in, Hans." He turned to Gloria, tipped his hat, and said, "A true pleasure, Doctor Halvorson. Please be easy on the big lout, for he knows not what he has done." With that he nodded, turned, and walked cockily toward the midway.

"I wanted to tell you," Hans said.

Tell me what, Dad?" Will said, leaning forward to hear his father, who had just awakened again from one of his naps. Will knew it was deep sleep by the twitching under his father's eyelids. Rapid eye movements and slow, deep breathing told him his father was not just dozing. Yet he seemed to be able to achieve deep sleep almost at will, as if he preferred it to the reality of the present.

Hans turned his head toward his son and smiled, then closed his eyes and resumed his journey.

How easy it seemed for him, Will thought, to cast aside the burdens of decision making in favor of the randomness of dreams. Will believed it must be like flipping through the channels on a television, watching whatever relieved the viewer from thinking—a mind-numbing experience that simulated sleep.

"Why on earth are you here, Pop?" He whispered as he looked down on the man who had raised him. "Why Deep Lake?"

He glanced at the clock above the door. It was time for round two with Nurse Pond. He felt as though he had been called to the principal's office for some grade school violation. She intimidated him, yet intrigued him. The dichotomy made him uncomfortable. But he had questions, serious questions about his father's safety in light of whatever had

happened at the center to bring the police. He would demand answers. He would take the offensive. Perhaps she did
not know who she was dealing with.

The more Sam thought about being accused of murder, the angrier he became. "Jerk," he snarled. "Butthook," he added for good measure as he dried his lunch dishes and placed them in the cabinet below the trailer's sink. He glanced at L2, who failed to respond. A dusting of snow brightened the unimproved Forest Service campground on the outskirts of Deep Lake.

Years as press secretary to a governor had turned Sam into a cynic, and it disturbed him. Yet his cynicism provided him a competitive edge that bordered on ruthlessness. He learned to assume that everyone had a selfish angle. His job had been to discover what motivated people, then play to it for the benefit of the governor. Fame and fortune were the usual goals. Selfless saints were rare indeed, especially in politics. Maybe that was why he had enjoyed working alone in cemeteries. Sam believed the sheriff wanted to go out a hero and to expend as little energy as possible in doing so. As the sheriff's chief suspect, Sam believed himself to be a gift from heaven, an outsider who had been hanging around the murder scene. Now the sheriff was grasping for a motive. Granted, opportunity was there, but petty theft with no evidence was a challenge.

"Why me, girl?" he said, looking at the puddle of dog flesh at his feet.

L2's eyebrows flicked in acknowledgment of his question.

"I should hire a legal beagle? You always say that. What's your angle, you stink hound?"

In response to the second question, L2 opened her eyes and glanced quickly upward.

"Actually, that's a pretty good idea, girl." He slid open the cupboard door above the stove and pulled out the box of dog biscuits.

L2 struggled to a sitting position in anticipation of the command.

"Of course, it will have to be pro bono since I'm broke. I'll put the kid lawyer on it. Sit," he said, wincing at the strands of saliva descending from the corners of L2's mouth.

Will Gottlieb looked at his wristwatch, something he did when he was nervous or had lost control of the conversation.

Aimee Pond eyed him suspiciously.

"My brother and I were the original latchkey children," he said, as if admitting some dark family secret. He did not make eye contact with Aimee Pond, just absently stirred his coffee. Due to the turmoil caused by Sophie Mickelson's murder, lunch at the Whispering Pines Care Center would be served late today. Aimee and Will sat across from each other at a table near the edge of the quiet dining room. "My parents worked hard to provide for us. Don't misunderstand; they were both very loving and nurturing, but—" He paused and smiled nervously. "They were never there."

Aimee Pond had heard it all before. Children overcompensating for the guilt they felt for placing their parents in a nursing home, justifying their decisions, rationalizing their infrequent visitations. She said nothing.

"It seems strange that I'm able to recall so few family memories from my childhood, times when we did things together. Sure, we had our holiday weekends—boating on the river, picnics in the park, electric trains and erector sets under the Christmas tree." He paused again. A slight smile formed on one side of his mouth. "But the memories are few and far between," he added. "Dad was always gone. He spent as much time on the other end as he did at home."

Aimee furrowed her brow and tilted her head.

Will continued. "The other end is railroad jargon for the place where train crews rested, lived really, before taking another train home. My father was a fireman and later an engineer on the Chicago and North Western Railway. He held the same route for as long as I can remember. Clinton to Boone, Boone to Clinton, back and forth for nearly thirty-two years. Back then, there was mandatory retirement at sixty-five. Otherwise he would have kept going for God knows how long. He didn't cope well with retirement, a bit of a lost soul. He had no hobbies, no outside interests; all he had ever done was work. That was in the early seventies, and he seemed to slip into a state of depression from which he never recovered. My brother and I were both long gone by then."

"What about your mother?" Aimee asked.

"My mother was totally devoted to him. She owned a pet store and gave it up—I think before she wanted to, so they could travel and spend more time together. They bought a motor home and became snowbirds wintering in Texas. They did the things retired people do, I guess. I sort of lost track of them during that period. I was busy building my career and raising a family. We tried to stay in touch, holiday visits and the like, but there was something different about Dad. He just wasn't the same. Mom died in 1982. About ten years later, Dad fell off a ladder and broke his hip. It was then that we started noticing the dementia. I think he noticed it too.

He eventually packed up the house, winterized it, and moved into an assisted care facility. He was very concerned that he not be a burden to either my brother or me."

Aimee's jaw tightened at hearing the same old song and dance, the stories, the snippets of unrelated trivia, the remembrances of the survivors. They sometimes offered glimpses of who the emaciated hulls had once been. They came and they went, both the residents and their descendants. In one way or another, she thought, everybody gets the opportunity to experience the tragic transition, the timeless regression to a state of helplessness. "What do you want to do, Doctor Gottlieb?" she said with a slight edge to her voice.

Will looked at her, his eyes wide as he tried to comprehend the magnitude of the question. "I'm not sure what I want. First and foremost, I want to ensure my father's safety. I heard there was a murder here." He had approached Robyn, the nurse's aide, just outside his father's room, and she had volunteered the news of Sophie Mickelson's death. Finally, he had found the opportunity to take control of the conversation. With renewed confidence, he straightened in his chair. "That troubles me greatly, Nurse Pond. I need to know that you and Whispering Pines are doing everything possible to protect my father and the other residents. If not, I'll be forced to move him sooner rather than later."

"Do you have power of attorney, Doctor Gottlieb?"

"No."

"Do you have a court-issued competency ruling?"

"No," he said defensively. "Where's all this going, Nurse Pond?" He had lost control again.

"Unless you have the legal right to do so, I'm afraid Hans is still in charge of his destiny. I'm assuming you want to take him back to Iowa. What about his remains should he die while he is here? Does he have a will? Are there directives concerning the disposition of his remains?"

"Yes, he has a will, but I have no idea what it contains or if codicils have been added to keep it up to date. Look, I just got here. I need time to figure this out. I have no idea why he chose this nursing home, why he came to Deep Lake, Minnesota. I'll need to find out who his attorney is in Boone."

"Does he have any medical records, special needs that we are unaware of?" she said, still on the offensive.

"I don't know. My mother took care of all that."

"Your mother has been dead for twenty-five years."

"Look," he said sharply. "I know it looks like I have abandoned him. You don't know the circumstances. There's an accusatory note in your voice that I don't like. The fact is I'm here, I've found him, and I'll get this straightened out. Meanwhile, you have conveniently not mentioned that a violent crime was committed here last night. You've given me no assurance that my father is safe in your care. Rather than provide me with that assurance, your approach appears to be an attempt to intimidate me with your third-degree, rapid-fire questions. It's not working, Nurse Pond. Two can play this game. I can bury you in paperwork with a single call to the state agency that oversees nursing homes. Have you even notified the department of health? Your highest priority is to provide a safe environment for those entrusted to your care. Obviously, that has come into question. So, Nurse Pond, you can stop your diversionary tactic of trying to lay a guilt trip on me. Until I can get the legal issues settled, I would appreciate your cooperation." He stared at her intently, his eyes narrowed.

"Is that a threat, Doctor Gottlieb?"

"Yes. But more importantly, it's a statement to let you know that I care about my father and will do what I deem necessary to protect him."

Aimee felt her bravado falter. She had been threatened before, but there was something about Will Gottlieb that caused her to hesitate. She wanted to match him tit for tat, but strangely could not. Instead she fought the urge to take his hand into hers and tell him she was sorry. She dared not speak, for the lump in her throat would surely unmask her.

Will saw it too. He had gained the upper hand, but now wished he had not. Her pretentious swagger had been replaced by a nervous shyness that disarmed him. He would never forget that look.

CHICAGO, ILLINOIS—1935

Hans looked out over the sea of faces and honed in on one in the first row. He recalled that shy look. It often distracted from her attempt to be businesslike and authoritative. There was not a day he did not think of her and the tremulous awkwardness of their first kiss. He could smell her hair, see the tiny creases at the corners of her eyes when she smiled. He had loved her from the moment he met her; she was the one constant in his life. There was never any question about that. Whenever he closed his eyes, she took his breath away. Her glow could fill a room, even an arena. Hers was the only face he saw as she sat at ringside, smiling confidently at him.

"In this corner, weighing two hundred and twenty pounds, from Clinton, Iowa, the challenger, Trapper the Giant Killer!" the ring announcer yelled into the microphone.

The crowd screamed their enthusiastic support for the little-known masked man. They believed he was one of them, an underdog from the hardworking Midwest, an unknown from humble beginnings who held the promise of greatness.

Hans never spoke when in the ring; he never cried out in mock anguish. There was nothing theatrical in his performance, no taunting of the crowd or enlisting their support. He quietly and efficiently did his job. He allowed his opponents to entertain the audience instead. He refused to meet them before a match, demanding his own dressing room. Lucky "Big Ears" Lucello had done his job by working the matchups and building the program of bouts that would gradually give Trapper the push. He would become the champion of Lucky's new American Wrestling Federation, at least until the fan heat wore off. When fan support started to drop, a new champion would be selected and a program developed for their push to the top. So far, the fan heat had been all Trapper's. They liked his masked anonymity and quiet demeanor. They could be him.

"In this corner, weighing two hundred eighty pounds, from Dunkirk, New York, the Fury from Lake Erie, the Hessian Ruffian, Hess the Bear!"

The Chicago crowd booed their distaste for the New Yorker with a thick German accent.

Hess bent over and patted his butt. "You bohunks, Polacks, und Schweinhunds can kiss mein ass." He raised his arm in triumph and yelled, "Für das Mutterland!"

The crowd came to their feet, screaming unintelligible epithets from contorted faces and with the universal shaking of fists to signify their aggression. The Depression had taken away their dignity and replaced it with anger. They needed a villain and a hero to make sense of a complex world over which they had no control. Hess the Bear represented all that was wrong in their lives. He was the Depression. Adding insult to misery, he represented Germany. They had read the newspapers and seen the newsreels of another war in the making. The families they had left behind in Eastern Europe were living under a threat. Hess the Bear must be stopped.

The Fury from Lake Erie *would* be stopped. He had hooked two of his previous opponents, unleashing an ego that planned to go against today's worked outcome. Lucky "Big Ears" Lucello was about to be double-crossed. In addition to being selected for the push, Hans served as the chief enforcer for wrestlers who hooked their opponents. This match was a shoot, a bout designed to get the rogue wrestler's attention. The Bear knew that Hans was the enforcer; all the wrestlers knew it. The Bear had placed himself in this win-at-all-costs situation. If he could defeat Hans, the fan heat would be his. It would be villainous heat, but heat nonetheless. The pressure on Hans was to ensure that Lucky did not lose control.

Gloria sat next to Lucky Lucello, their heads lowered and turned toward each other as they talked intently amid the crowd's noise. Gloria raised her hand and pointed a finger in Lucky's face as though they were arguing. Hans had believed that placing her next to Lucky was the safest place for her. But now he was concerned that their conversation appeared to be heated. Gloria shook her head and looked away. He marveled at the contrast of the beautiful Scandinavian doctor next to the Italian businessman, as Lucky liked to refer to himself. She had not wanted to come and had offered all the usual excuses. Hans was undefeated in eighteen professional matches and she had never seen him wrestle. Her presence produced lightness in his chest and a weakness in his extremities that he hoped would pass when the opening bell rang. He had felt the same way when she stepped from the train at Union Station, this same sensation of weightlessness as they walked down Maxwell Street toward the hotel. He was unsure why she had accepted his invitation to Chicago; she had not wanted to come, but he took it as a positive sign in their long-distance relationship. She diminished her presence by saying that she had some business to attend to and that, based on what she had read in the papers, he would need a good ringside doctor. Suddenly Gloria looked up at Hans and smiled broadly. He nodded in return, since his mask disallowed the conveyance of a smile.

The referee had called them to the center of the ring and was offering the usual instructions and admonishments. Hans's eyes never left those of Hess the Bear. He ignored the fact that the barrel-chested Bear had sixty pounds and five inches on him, that his entire body was covered in dark hair, and that he smelled of body odor and booze. Hess the Bear returned the stare. Hans had seen that same empty look before—seldom in the carnival combatants, but in some of the professional wrestlers. It was the vacuous expression of stupidity. The Bear was all brawn and no brains, easily taunted to aggression. Hans pursed his lips within the mouth slit of the hood, blew the Bear a kiss, and winked at him as the referee instructed them to shake hands and return to their corners. The Hessian's eyes widened, his mouth opened, and he seemed to swell while frantically searching for a response.

"Wunderlich! Sich placken!" he finally shouted. The referee jumped between them and pointed toward the Bear's corner.

"That man is as strong as an ox," William said as Hans approached his corner and waited for the bell. "You best get his attention before going to the mat with him." Hans had insisted that William be written into the contract as his cornerman. Lucello responded by saying that he could have all the darkies he wanted, but their pay and expenses would come from Hans's salary.

"Any suggestions?" said Hans.

"Knock one of his props out. That ought to slow him up a bit and give him something to think about."

"Maybe if you shot him a couple of times, it would slow him up a bit," Hans said as he glanced ringside to see Gloria. She was smiling.

The bell rang and the auditorium ceased to exist. The only sound was from his lungs filling and flushing. Darkness prevailed on all but the Bear. Hans met him in the center of the ring, where they tied up, a ritual designed to eliminate the pre-contact jitters and determine an opponent's strength. The Bear retained his center of gravity well back from the point of contact, his knees bent for power. He was all business as he dug the side of his skull into Hans's ear. Hans signaled that he wished to break up, with a thumb pushed deeply into the soft area below the Bear's clavicle. As they released their grips on the backs of each other's necks, Hans snatched a fistful of the Bear's dark chest hair, pulled hard, and jumped back. Hess the Bear gasped and yelled in protest. He stepped back and straightened up. Hans had anticipated the Bear's reaction, his goal being the straight-legged stance the Bear had now assumed. Hans delivered a flying double-legged dropkick to the Bear's left knee.

The Bear spun ninety degrees and went down clutching his hyperextended knee, writhing in pain. The referee blew

repeatedly on his whistle, his face contorted as he stabbed a
finger toward Trapper's corner. Hans had violated the Greco-Roman rule of no blows below the waist. He obliged,
backing to his corner while the referee attended to the Bear.
The crowd roared their delight. He glanced toward Gloria,
who smiled broadly, thinking the injury feigned and part of
the show. Lucky Lucello looked at Hans and nodded ever
so slightly. Hess the Bear struggled to his feet and limped
in a circle, attempting to walk off the injury. Hans charged
him, grabbed him by the hair, and bent him forward. He
slid behind the Bear and lifted him from the mat while spinning him in the tilt-a-whirl takedown hold. It happened so
fast that the stunned Bear could do little but prepare for the
shock of the tilt-a-whirl backbreaker as Hans delivered the
thunderous slam of Bear's back to the mat. Hans slid down
and lifted the Bear's head, placed a knee in his back, and im-
mobilized him with a rear chinlock. As he stretched the tendons in the Bear's neck to the point of snapping, the Hessian
Ruffian frantically slapped the mat three times, tapping out
his submission. The referee blew his whistle again, signal-
ing an end to the contest. The crowd appeared stunned; the
match they had paid to see was over in less than two minutes.
People slowly rose from their seats and looked around the
arena, anticipating something more than what they had just
experienced.

••••

"Lemme ask you this," Lucky "Big Ears" Lucello said to Hans in the locker room. "What's the most important part of this game?"

"Fan satisfaction, Mr. Lucello," Hans said without looking up.

"Did the fans get their money's worth tonight?"

Hans did not respond.

"No," Lucky said, answering himself.

"I could tell from the moment we tied up that he wanted to hook us." said Hans. "I responded quickly and decisively. Perhaps he'll think twice about going rogue in the future."

"Lemme ask you this: What's more important, teaching that hairy bastard a lesson or making sure the fans come back to the stadium for the next match?"

"You specifically asked me to be the enforcer to this guy—"

"I could've taken him out back and beat the shit out of him myself. But where's the entertainment in that? I pay you to do both."

"Mr. Lucello—"

"The sportswriters gave up on professional wrestling years ago when they found out the Gotch-Hackenschmidt match was worked. We don't get no publicity from the papers. It's all word of mouth in this game. If the fans get screwed, we get screwed. Capiche?"

"Yes, I understand. But—"

"Ain't no buts, Mr. Gottlieb. Trust me on this. Now," he said, turning and walking toward the door, "you have a beautiful lady friend waiting outside for you. Go and enjoy.

Take her to the Drake. She likes the Drake. We can talk business later." He waved his hand in the air without looking
back as he left the locker room. Hans stared after him, his
brow furrowed in confusion. He had wanted the Drake to
be a surprise.

The Cape Cod Room at the Drake. Hoagy Carmichael is playing with the Dorseys," Hans said in response to her question. He could not help smiling when looking at her. She radiated happiness when she spoke. He wanted this night to be special. He was nervous.

"Who's Hoagy Carmichael?" Robyn Threlkeld, the nurse's aide, smiled back at him.

"You know—'Star Dust' and that new Johnny Mercer tune, 'Lazy Bones.' You like that song. Hoagy Carmichael is the cat's meow."

"I don't think I've ever heard it, Hans. What I asked you was, do you want to go to the sunroom or the dining room for your lunch? We don't have a Cape Cod Room."

He smiled at her nervously. She was so beautiful that he sometimes forgot to breathe. He had waited for this for a long time. He had planned it carefully: dinner, drinks, dancing, and lovemaking. They would finally consummate their relationship. He needed to focus, to clear his mind, just like he did before a match. But something was not right. Something in the background was distracting him, something that threatened to expose him—voices.

CLINTON, IOWA—1926

Voices. He was sure he heard voices. Muffled, unintelligible words, some harsh, some pleading: a puppy being scolded that periodically whimpered its suffering. He had heard it before. It had been his voice, his shame. As much as he wanted it to be, it had not been a dream. It was a recurring nightmare that stopped only when he ceased to be a boy.

Returning to the Y for the book that would be discussed in his English literature class the next day, he cussed his stupidity for leaving it behind. He struggled with most of the novels in the class, but this one, *Vanity Fair: A Novel without a Hero*, was god-awful. William Makepeace Thackeray couldn't say shit if he had a mouthful of it. Hans was angry that he had to read it, angry that he had to come back after hours to retrieve it. The Y frightened him at night.

The locker room was dark and the familiar smells of sweat and mildew, that only two hours earlier had not bothered him, now caused his stomach to knot. Again the muted cries from the darkness drifted among the vapors of pain and humiliation. Fear slowly gave way to anger. He stood in the dank blackness under the rusted metal stairway that led from light and normalcy to the bowels of depravity. Soon the door to Coach Carter's office opened and light shot in sharp angles into the locker room. A boy, perhaps eight or ten years old, hurried up the metal stairs, his shoes scraping each tread in a fast staccato on his way to a life of anger and guilt.

Without a sound, Hans appeared in the doorway of Coach Carter's office. "I could kill you, you know," he said. "Someone would find you in the morning with your cock stuffed in your mouth."

"You could, but you won't," Red Carter said, showing no surprise at Hans's presence. "That's the one thing you lack, the one thing that will keep you from greatness, the one thing I haven't been able to teach you. You lack the killer instinct. You can't deliver the coup de grâce and put your opponent away. There's a soft streak that runs right to your core, Hans."

"What you call soft the rest of the world calls normal, you sick bastard."

"The rest of the world won't be wrestling at the Olympic Games. You're off to the university next fall on a full scholarship, thanks to me. You've been state champion four years running. You've become a man, a respected man, thanks to me. You'd still be a scrawny weakling sniffling in the shadows if it weren't for me."

"I'd be able to sleep at night…if it weren't for you. I'd be able to look at myself in a mirror without crying and maybe I'd be able to get through a day without thinking about what you did to me, if it weren't for you. I owe you, Coach. And someday I'll repay you. I'll repay you in full." Tears of rage appeared in his eyes. He had wanted to have this conversation for a very long time. He had rehearsed it. But now there were only tears and the acrimony of words that rose to the surface. Carter was right—he lacked the killer instinct. His own father had seen it, had predicted his weakness and used it as effectively as his belt, lashing Hans at every opportunity. Not once had his father mentioned his son's accomplishments. It was Hans's weakness that allowed what Carter had done to him. His father was right. Carter was right. The coach had seen it early on and had taken advantage of it. What had happened to him was his own fault.

"What are you going to do, Hans? Who are you going to tell? Don't bite the hand that has fed you. You can't crap on me without getting the stink on you. Remember that, Hans."

Remember that, Hans? I told you that today was meatloaf, green beans, and Jell-O. Your favorite," Taneesha said. She wheeled the tray table across his bed and placed the lunch tray on top. "Robyn told me you didn't want to have lunch in the dining room or sunroom today, so here it is. Yum, yum. Open wide," she said as she brought a forkful of meatloaf to his lips, which refused to open. "Listen to me, Hans," she whispered. "They got a strict policy here that when you can't feed yourself, they ship you off to hospice at the hospital. You know what hospice is, don't you, Hans? That's where they let the wolves eat you."

Hans turned his head and looked out the window. It was starting to snow again. Large wet flakes drifted lazily to the ground.

"Ain't no wolves out there, Hans. They's all at the hospital waiting for those who can't feed themselves."

Aimee Pond stood in the doorway to Hans's room, listening, watching, and remembering. She imagined her father aged like Hans, though he had been younger. She had hardly known him. Charles Pond, an Ojibwe Indian, had disappeared when she was a little girl. Everybody assumed he had drowned, but his body was never recovered. They found his overturned canoe, empty bottles of booze floating between the gunnels. Aimee had only two memories of him. One was of him beating her mother; the other was of him beating her. There would be no opportunity to watch the slow progression of death consume him or to see the sallow shell of skin pulled over a life that was once real. Growing up without him had denied her the chance to learn who he was. Though her father was officially considered only missing, for all practical purposes Aimee became orphaned eleven years later in 1965, when she was barely fifteen. She was taken in by her father's older sister, a woman with strong traditional values. They lived on the Winnibigoshish Indian Reservation, forty miles and a hundred years north of Deep Lake. It was considered impolite to speak of the dead, so she learned nothing about her father. White like her mother, she floated in and out of both worlds, accepted by neither. Junior college in Bemidji, followed by a degree in nursing from Saint Cloud University, separated her even further from the reservation. A master's degree in nursing from the University of Southern California allowed her much higher pay and certainly more prestigious options in making a living. She had paid her dues. From emergency rooms in Los Angeles and Minneapolis to working as a physician's assistant in geriatrics, she was used to death. But she had never experienced her own parents' journey into old age.

"Taneesha, I'll tend to Hans if you wouldn't mind helping Robyn with Mrs. Wilson's bath," Aimee said, approaching Hans's bed.

"Uh-oh, Hans, you's in big trouble now," Taneesha said with a serious look on her face. "You don't eat for Nurse Pond, the wolves is next."

"Shut the door, please," Aimee called over her shoulder as Taneesha left the room. She stared down at Hans for a long moment, then moved the tray table to the side and gently sat on the edge of his bed.

"Two months ago, when you checked in here, you were ambulatory and fairly cognitive. We talked briefly. You responded appropriately to all the questions. Our patient representative, Elaine, helped you with all the paperwork, still you got through it. I noted that you were hard of hearing, but not deaf. Both vision and hearing loss are chronic problems among people your age. You don't show signs of the major geriatric impairments. You get around without falling and you don't soil yourself. You're as strong as an ox in spite of significant muscle loss, which will only continue to accelerate. I'm still unsure of your intellectual capacity or whether your memory is corrupted. Dementia is a slow, degenerative, physiological process, Hans. No doubt you have one of the many forms, but I'm almost certain it's not Alzheimer's. At your age, dementia is the norm rather than the exception. The experts all say that dementia, whatever the type, involves memory loss. But I'm not convinced of that. I think the memories are accessible, but there is some dysfunction in sorting and recalling them. Normally, the hippocampus is quite good at sorting between present reality and stored memories. But at your age, I think that region of your brain is struggling and you're aware of it.

"My best guess is that you're suffering from depression, which is one of the many symptoms of dementia. You've given up; you want to die. And you think that acting like you're terminal will make you terminal. Well, it doesn't work that way, Hans. It could take a month, maybe forty-five days for you to starve yourself to death. That probably won't happen. Your son will intervene and we'll hydrate and force-feed you. Most likely, if you lie here long enough, you'll get enough fluid in your lungs that you'll drown. You're ninety-nine years old, Hans, and you will die soon enough—without trying to speed up the process. How? Well, let me give you my best guess. I don't think it will be by stroke or heart attack. You've got the heart and blood pressure of a man half your age. You'll probably break your hip, shatter your pelvis, get some pneumonic infection, and drown anyway." She paused as if waiting for his response. "'What's the difference?' you ask. The difference, Hans, is that you can choose to resist. You can do what you've been doing all your life, fighting to stay alive. You'll lose, of course; we all do. But in the end you will know that you did everything you could, that you didn't give up."

His watery eyes, the color washed to a uniform gray, stared past her. White-beard stubble glistened over his pallid cheeks and chin. His cracked lips parted as if to speak, but instead he inhaled deeply through his nose and exhaled through his mouth. He did not look at her.

Aimee smiled. "I'm guessing your past is a lot more interesting than your present. I'm sure we can learn from the past. But your memories seem more of a refuge for you. They give you someplace to go when things become unpleasant. I think Old Man Death knows that. He counts on it. When you can no longer swim to the surface and gasp one more breath of the present, he'll take you. So, Hans, be careful how deep you dive and how long you stay down. You think your memories will save you, but I truly believe that when you cease to exist, they will too. You don't get to take them with you."

She saw his eyes dart quickly to hers. She had his attention. But she could not tell if there was understanding. "Memory is an electrochemical process that's totally dependent on oxygen, Hans. When you stop breathing, your memories will wither and disappear, forever. Enjoy your trips to wherever it is you go, but you're not going there when you die." She smiled slightly and placed her hand on his. "We'll send your body over to the city morgue in the basement of the hospital in Walker until we can figure out what to do with it. I guess what I'm trying to tell you, Hans, is to cut the crap. You know exactly why you came here. Do the right thing. Make your peace, as they say. Make amends to those you owe, offer your apologies, right your wrongs, and if you want to give those memories some immortality, share them. Give them to someone who will keep them, care for them, and pass them on. I can help you do that, Hans."

He looked out the window again. It was snowing harder. Darkness settled over him.

Y ou're all the lawyer I can afford, Sid," Sam said into the tiny flip phone. He leaned forward over the trailer's dinette table and pushed his hair back with his right hand. "Look, if I think he's actually going to press charges, I'll turn you loose to find the best attorney money can buy. In the meantime, I could use your help in checking out the backgrounds of a few folks....Uh-huh, uh-huh. When is it due?...For crying out loud, Sidney. How many times have I told you not to put off your assignments until the last minute?...She's fine. She spent the morning in the slammer too." Sam glanced at L2, who was stretched on her side across the floor in front of the tiny furnace. "It appears she was severely traumatized. I might sue the bastards.... You'll need your degree first. Then you can represent me. When you get your paper done, I want you to get me everything you can find on Sophie Mickelson. I can't believe this was a random act of violence. Also check out Whispering Pines from top to bottom. See if there's any history here. Take a look at staff too. Leave no stone—...Listen to me, Sid. This sheriff isn't going to do a thing. He's convinced he has his man. It's up to me to prove my innocence. I need to send him off on some other rabbit's trail. Work your magic, kiddo....No, don't tell Pat a thing. If he finds out I've been hanging around a nursing home, he'll blow a fuse....Okay,

okay, I'll be careful. Get that paper done first and don't stay up all night....Love you too. Goodnight."

The wind had started sometime after 9:00 p.m. The weathered clapboard house shivered under the strong gusts that pushed the snow in ghostly patterns between the trees and bushes surrounding it. The soft blue light from the computer screen spilled through the windows of the parlor Aimee Pond had converted into a study, and out into the storm. She sipped tea from a mug that proclaimed "Wyeth Pharmaceuticals" on one side and "Premarin" on the other.

Aimee was scanning the administrator's personnel records for irregularities. Some ambulance-chasing lawyer—if not corporate itself—was bound to claim the center failed to protect its frail, vulnerable residents. There would be allegations of negligent employee supervision, inadequate personnel, or poor staff training. The state regulators would claim the center violated facility licensure rules and regulations regarding quality of life, adequate care, nursing services, and whatever else they could invent to cover their butts. She knew how government worked. Eventually someone would be held responsible. A head needed to roll. She would make sure it was the administrator's—not hers.

Satisfied with her case against Miss MBA, Aimee googled carnival wrestlers, since Hans claimed to be the world's greatest. The search produced a confusing array of websites that all led to professional wrestling. The Midwest, especially Iowa, had produced many of the best-known wrestlers of the first part of the twentieth century. The names Toots Mondt, Martin "Farmer" Burns, Frank Gotch, Ed "Strangler" Lewis, Jim Morgan, and Lou Thesz all occurred repeatedly in articles about the early years of professional wrestling. A little before midnight she gave up her search of dead ends, determining that she needed more information. If his son knew nothing of his father's wrestling past, Hans had obviously kept it a secret from the world in general.

Will Gottlieb's seemingly indifferent attitude was intriguing. He was handsome and successful, and a little too smart for her comfort zone. He was also a pompous jerk who selfishly regarded his father as an annoyance. Sam, on the other hand, viewed the elderly with more compassion than good sense. He said they were more than Social Security numbers or pictures in a yearbook. They were living, breathing beings with a past and with dreams, realized or unrealized. He wanted to know who they were, what had shaped their lives. What were their regrets, and what were their contributions? You spend eighty-some years on the planet, there should be something to show for it, he had told her.

Unable to sleep, Aimee lay in bed listening to the storm's assault, the house groaning in protest. She turned her head toward the window; wind-driven snow smashed against the glass. She knew her concern was not about anybody else. It was about her. She had worked hard her entire life and had little to show for it. No silver spoons, no sugar daddy; she felt cheated. She was in a dead-end job in a dead-end career. Who would remember her, and for what? What was her mark on society? What was her legacy? She had no children, no family to recall her. She forced her eyes shut, scowling under the pressure, and clenched her teeth at the realization that her life had been wasted. A spinster with no close friends, she was a fifty-seven-year-old postmenopausal woman who lived alone with a cat named Emma. The wind heaved against the windowpanes. Aimee sighed.

CHICAGO, ILLINOIS—1935

I'm a doctor; you're a wrestler. I have a home and a practice. You wander around the country like a nomad," Gloria said, her eyes narrowing. "I heal people; you hurt people. Tell me again how this is supposed to work?"

"Attention, passengers with tickets to Minneapolis, Train 2-4-9, Land of Lakes, is now boarding at Gate C. Land of Lakes, Gate C. All aboard," the announcer said, his voice echoing in the cavernous lobby of Union Station.

"All I'm asking is that you give it a chance," Hans said softly, staring down at the marble floor. His hand rubbed along the shiny, rounded edge of the massive oak bench near the center of the station. "These are uncertain times. I don't know what tomorrow will bring. It may not be the noblest profession, but I'm employed. And I'm good at it. It's a young man's game. I'm smart enough to know that it won't last. All I'm asking is that you be patient until we can sort it out."

"Oh, I think I have been very patient, Hans. We've been seeing each other for almost two years. I've traveled hither and yon to be with you. I even came back to Chicago for you, something I swore I would never do. I'm five years older than you and I'm not getting any younger." She took his hand in hers. "I'm more worried about your patience. Your self-control is…is…," she paused as she searched for the word, "noteworthy." She lowered her voice to a whisper.

"It's clear you want to consummate our relationship. And last night…last night…"

"Let's not talk about last night," he said, unable to make eye contact with her, his face turning red.

"Last call for passengers with tickets to Minneapolis. Train 2-4-9, Land of Lakes, is boarding at Gate C. All aboard, please."

"I've got to go. I'll miss my train. Good luck in Cincinnati, Hans."

"Gloria—"

"I wish for you all the best. Really, I do. It's what you want. If only the circumstances were different, perhaps—" Her eyes filled with tears.

"Circumstances? What circumstances? Say what's on your mind, Gloria. Don't you mean if I were someone other than a wrestler, someone more befitting your social status?"

"No, you know that's not true. After two years, how can you even suggest that?" The tears flowed freely down her cheeks. "Can't you see that I love you, Hans? I love you more than you will ever know. I've loved you from the moment you first limped into my clinic. I want to spend every minute of my life with you. I want to wake in the morning and see your face next to mine." She looked down. "But I love what I do too. I've devoted a large portion of my life to it. And just like you, Hans, I'm good at it. Don't make me choose. If you do, I'll choose you and then I'll resent you."

"I won't ask you to choose, but isn't that what you are asking of me?"

"No," she said, shaking her head, then fixing her eyes on his. "Don't you understand? It's the leaving that is tearing me apart. We're two people from different worlds and different times passing each other with outstretched arms, our fingertips touching, but unable to grasp and hold on. You're a powerful drug, Hans, and I'm addicted. When I'm with you, I'm euphoric. When you're withheld from me, I go into withdrawal. I'm a doctor. I know how to deal with addiction. Withdrawal will be painful, but the craving will eventually subside." She could no longer look at him; her lower lip trembled. "Physician, heal thyself," she whispered as she turned and walked away.

"Gloria," he called out after her.

DEEP LAKE, MINNESOTA—2007
DAY 3, 7:05 A.M.

"Glaw-aw-aw-ree-yah, Glaw-ree-yah," Taneesha sang and swiveled her huge hips as she opened the curtains in Hans's room to greet the bright new day. Sun reflected from the carpet of white draped over the landscape. "You remember that one, Hans? Probably not, it was after your time. Mid-sixties, I think, before my time. You know my name ain't Gloria. You know you hurt my feelings when you keep calling me by the wrong name."

Hans appeared both surprised and confused by her presence.

Taneesha stood in front of the window and shook her head. "Well, I'll be. Would you look at that, Hans? There's wolf tracks right below your window. They was here last night, waitin' for you, waitin' to carry you home, sweet chaaa-ree-yuh-uht!" she sang.

Hans looked beyond her; tears welled in his eyes. Billows of gray smoke gave way to charcoal plumes where the land met the sky.

Chicago, Illinois—1935

The black smoke hung in a layer above the receding train. The two giant cylinders thumped with an odd synchrony as the locomotive labored against the snake of cars that followed. He could not tell if it was the platform that trembled or his knees. The acrid smell of burning coal stung his nostrils. Tears of loss stung his eyes. She was gone. The woman whose image burned within his brain, who occupied his thoughts nearly every waking moment was gone. He could not swallow the guilt that swelled in his throat. It was his fault. He had tried to prepare himself for the eventual intimacy that he knew would happen. But in the darkness, her naked body pressed against his only brought fear and the need to escape. In the wrestling ring, he told himself it was competition that drove him to explosively avoid the smothering contact of another human being. But he knew it was fear.

Deep within, perhaps between his shoulder blades or maybe at the base of his skull, he felt the torment begin to roll and swirl. He wished it would escape him with a hiss and roar, the blackness roiling upward in a flourish of released emotion. If only he could forget. If only he had resisted more, screamed louder, told someone. His jaw muscles rippled and his eyes narrowed at the vision of Coach Carter entering the shower room.

Paul Bunyan was in Bemidji with Babe the Blue Ox, his amusement center was in Brainerd, and his name or image was on everything in between. Will Gottlieb looked at the remains of the Paul Bunyan Breakfast Special, syrup glistening on white porcelain. He had made an important decision in the night and was not bothered by the overdone commercialism of Mr. Bunyan. He sipped his coffee and stared out at the black-and-white landscape. A wall of black pine trees, their boughs heavy with snow, provided an impenetrable barrier on the other side of the highway from the Paul Bunyan Diner. A giant northern pike leaped above the billboard at the edge of the parking lot; a red-and-white lure protruded from its mouth. Funny, he thought, that one of the most important decisions of his life was made at 2:00 a.m. from the confines of a Motel 6 room in Deep Lake, Minnesota.

Will hoped the roads to Minneapolis were not icy. He was eager to get back to Fort Collins and meet with his department head. He would resign at the end of the academic year. Having turned sixty-two in May, he was already eligible for Social Security. His accumulated sick leave would pay for his health insurance for the next three years, then Medicare. There was relief in his decision. He was tired, tired of academic bureaucracy, tired of esoteric research, and tired of the students—those starry-eyed veterinarian wannabes who were more interested in shortcuts than what was on the next exam. The demographics of the profession had changed dramatically over the decades. The students were 80 percent female—almost exclusively from urban environments, who were motivated only by their love for animals. They had all read James Herriot in their preteen years and now set out to flood the male-dominated profession with people who would work for less. He was cynical, and that alone was reason to step down. He knew the female vets were more nurturing, caring, and compassionate than the large-animal men who had graduated with him. But companion animal medicine had taken on techniques and pseudoscience disciplines that made him cringe. *Yes, it's time,* he thought, gazing out the window and into his future.

At the next booth, the only other customer, Sam Dawson, stared out the same window toward his Willys and Airstream parked beneath the giant pike.

"You from Laramie?" Will asked suddenly.

Startled, Sam looked toward the well-dressed man sitting in the booth directly behind him. "Excuse me?"

"Laramie," Will said, nodding toward Sam's rig. "I saw the five on your Wyoming tags."

"I live about midway between Cheyenne and Laramie."

"Around Vedauwoo?"

"Just a few miles northeast. You know the area?"

"A little. I'm from Colorado. Fort Collins, just to the south of you. I'm what you folks refer to as a 'greenie,'" Will said, smiling.

"I used to be a greenie," Sam said, referencing the somewhat derogatory term people in Wyoming use in describing people from Colorado. "I got those green license plates off my vehicles as soon as I could. The locals just might accept me in another six generations."

"What part of Colorado are you from?"

"Above Golden, in Jefferson County."

"I know the area," Will said. "White Ranch, Golden Gate Canyon State Park—a beautiful part of the Front Range. Nice views of Denver."

Sam cocked an eyebrow suspiciously. "Yes, I looked down on that fetid, festering miasma of putrid decadence called Denver, the cancer on the plains."

Will tilted his head slightly, squinted, but maintained his smile. "Amen, brother. Smog and people, but I like your description better. What brings you to the Land of Ten Thousand Lakes?"

"Work," Sam said, not wanting to elaborate. "And you?"

Will hesitated. "I'm not sure," he said, scratching the back of his head. "Family, I guess. My dad moved here recently. I came to visit."

The waitress with the red nose brought Sam the remainder of his breakfast in a Styrofoam container. "Will there be anything else?" she asked.

"Just the check, please."

Rhonda pulled the light green check from her pocket and slid it under the edge of his saucer. "Thank you. Come again," she said with perfunctory courtesy and a slight monotone.

Both men stared after her as she walked away.

"Well," Sam said, in an attempt to bring closure to the conversation, "I better feed my dog before she fills the seat with drool."

"It's predigestive," Will said abruptly.

"What?"

"Sure, it's Pavlovian, an unconditioned response to a conditioned stimulus, but it's also predigestive. Her saliva contains an enzyme, salivary amylase, that breaks down—" His voice halted. "Sorry. Old habits die hard," he said with a note of apology. "I'm a professor of veterinary medicine at CSU. I've been there too long. Can't stop professing. I'm retiring soon. I hope someday to carry on a conversation without lecturing."

Sam smiled. "It will probably take a while before you can just say spit without worrying about cause and effect. Sam Dawson," he said, nodding. The seating arrangement prevented him from offering his hand.

"Will Gottlieb. It's nice to meet you, Sam."

Sam looked at him for a long moment. "Any relation to Hans?"

"He's my dad. How do you know him?"

"Whispering Pines, the care facility. I don't really know him, but I look in on him once in a while. Nice guy."

Will Gottlieb seemed to consider Sam's explanation. "That was sure terrible about that poor woman at the home."

"You wouldn't expect something like that to happen in a place like Deep Lake," Sam said before turning to look out the window again.

"How long have you been in Wyoming, Sam?"

"Going on six years now." Had it been that long? Saying it out loud felt like cold water thrown in his face. Originally, his goal had been to establish residency so Sidney could get in-state tuition at UW. "My daughter graduated last year from the university in Laramie."

"A Wyoming cowgirl, huh? What'd she major in?"

"Cowboys, I think. Let's see, there was Cody, Ty, Colt, and Travis. She started in communications, something to do with speech and hearing, but ended up with a degree in criminal justice. Now she's in law school."

"I sense you're not thrilled with her career choice," Will said.

Sam pushed his saucer off the slightly sodden, light green check. "Sidney's a good kid. She'll succeed in whatever she chooses to do."

"They say the average college grad today will have seven or eight career changes during their working lifetime." Will smiled. "You can't pick their boyfriends or their careers. You just have to trust they'll make the right decisions that are best for them."

Sam did not look up. He turned the check over without focusing on the neatly scrawled tab. He knew Sidney had looked for a career in which she could function as a deaf person, a deaf person who would eventually go blind. In the interim, she might make a great attorney. Sam wanted to change the subject. The greenie was talking again, but Sam was not listening. "Excuse me?"

"Snow, they say it's supposed to snow again today," Will said.

"It's that time of year." Sam plucked a five and three ones from his wallet and placed them on top of the check. He gathered L2's breakfast and slid from the booth. The Naugahyde upholstery protested with the sound of simulated flatulence. "Nice talking to you," he said, looking down at the nattily dressed professor.

"You too."

The bells above the diner's door tinkled and a gust of cold air rudely rushed in, roiling over the floor. Aimee Pond brushed flecks of snow from her coat sleeves.

"Nurse Pond," Will Gottlieb called from the center of the diner. Both Aimee and Sam turned to look at him.

She smiled politely at Sam and then looked down as they both stepped in one direction and then the other in an attempt to get around each other. It was perfectly choreographed. Sam chuckled. "How about I stand still and you scoot around me—friend?" he added with emphasis.

Aimee blushed. "I haven't danced like that since the Stones sang *Satisfaction*."

Sam wanted to say that was before his time, but decided against it and simply smiled instead. There was brief eye contact. She demurred and gracefully sidestepped around him. It was his turn to blush. Sam paused momentarily and then nervously started for the door.

"Sam," Aimee called after him.

He turned to face her. Her eyes were puffy, from crying or lack of sleep—he couldn't tell which.

"Sophie Mickelson's funeral is tomorrow, if you're not busy."

"I only met the lady once."

"I know, but I'm looking for warm bodies. She had no one. And the residents are squeamish about funerals. You might be able to get some transition-type shots. You know, the shots between 'the essence of a person,' as you put it, and the carved granite you've been shooting."

Sam stared at her for a long moment. She sounded sincere. "I'll check my calendar." He smiled, nodded, and pushed open the door. The bells above tinkled again and the sting of a Minnesota winter filled his nostrils. L2 stared at him from the passenger seat and drooled in anticipation of what Sam carried in his hand.

"Here you go, Aimee," Rhonda said as she brought the coffee-to-go to the cash register.

Will Gottlieb stared at Aimee. She was an attractive woman, he thought, seasoned, but still very attractive. He had become jaded about the physical appearance of women, being constantly surrounded by nubile coeds. It was the faces of older women that he found alluring.

"Nurse Pond," he called again softly from his booth.

Aimee turned and smiled politely; her eyes felt heavy from lack of sleep.

"Care to join me?"

She hesitated.

"It would save me a trip to Whispering Pines," he said.

"Doctor Gottlieb," she said cautiously as she approached his booth.

"Please sit down. Do you want anything to eat?"

"No, just coffee," she said, sliding into the booth without removing her coat. "Why would you come to the nursing home only to see me?" she said.

Will Gottlieb stared at her curiously. "Oh, what I meant to say was that it would save me a trip to your office after saying goodbye to my father."

"You're leaving?"

"Yes, I'm flying back to Colorado late this afternoon." He looked at his watch. "Actually, I may not have time to stop by to see Dad. I'm not sure he even knows who I am most of the time anyway. When he does recognize me, he sees a ten-year-old boy."

Aimee did not avert her gaze. She felt the slow burn of anger igniting her ears. "That's a good place to start. Tell me about your father a half-century ago." She glared at him. "What were his likes and dislikes? What were his dreams, his ambitions? Are there any major accomplishments that you can remember? You spent, I guess, eighteen years living with the man. Who was he?"

Leaning back from the table, Will crumpled his napkin and tossed it into the clutter of dishes and silverware. "Why is it that you and I can't have a civil conversation? Is it me? Is it you? Why the verbal assault? What have I done to offend you?"

"Don't take offense, Doctor Gottlieb. I'm just curious. I'm interested in knowing if you really know who your father is. Or are you going to let him pass from this earth without finding out?"

"Again, is it just me or do you give the third degree to the families of all your residents?" he shot back.

She pried the lid off the edge of her cup and sipped her coffee as she contemplated his question. "You are the families of all my residents." Her face softened as she met his stare. "I guess I'm using you as the scapegoat for the frustrations I've accumulated over the years, watching family after family visit their loved ones without truly knowing them. Their relationships were superficial, kind and respectful, but superficial. They treated dementia like it was a communicable disease. They observed it from afar, never wanting to touch it or immerse themselves into the perceived reality of their loved one's world. Don't you see that memories—those jumbled, mismatched snippets of a person's life—are who they were or who they wanted to be? You lived with the man for eighteen years. What about the other eighty-one years of his life? I see it all the time, the perfunctory phone calls on holidays or weekends where everyone talks about the weather or what they are going to eat for Sunday dinner." She twisted the Styrofoam cup in a circle. "I see the cards on Mother's Day and Father's Day, poor substitutes for the letters the son or daughter was too lazy to write." She paused and gently wiped the lipstick stain on her cup with her thumb. "We politely avoid finding out anything about their lives before we knew them and, in some cases, even after we entered their lives. We move away, make our own lives and families, introduce them to their in-laws and grandchildren, and refer to them by a title that indicates their degree of relatedness. But we never truly ask them who they are."

They both sat quietly, looking down. Will cleared his throat before he spoke. "My dad worked very hard all his life. It seemed he had little time for anything but work. He didn't keep regular hours, always on call. He liked popcorn and beer, the Friday night fights, and Loretta Young. He didn't like anything in a cream sauce, organized religion, or Ed Sullivan. He wore bibbed overalls, engineer boots, and a starched hat. He could never find shirts that fit his huge neck. The most profound advice he gave me during my formative years was to keep my trap shut and straighten up and fly right. I heard that a lot. When I cried, he always threatened to give me something to cry about." He paused, his eyes searching. "I guess that's it. That's what I remember."

Aimee's eyes narrowed; her lips tightened.

"I know what you're thinking. But I'm telling you again, the man was never there. I can count on one hand the number of basketball games and track meets he attended. I have no memory of him ever helping me with schoolwork. In college, he never asked me what I was studying, what my major was, or what my career aspirations were." He paused again and looked out the window. "My father was a ghost. He moved through my life like a shadow across a doorway."

"And your cold indifference is payback for your fatherless childhood?" Aimee asked.

Will caught Rhonda's attention and held up his coffee cup, which she filled and then moved on without speaking. He sipped the coffee carefully, obviously contemplating either her question or his response.

"That was not a fair question," Aimee said. "I apologize."

"No, no, it was a fair question, an insightful question. Retribution, you ask? I think not, at least from the standpoint of my childhood. But you raise an interesting possibility as it relates to my adult life." He sipped his coffee again. "I turned out like him in many ways. I worked hard all my life. I was never there for my family. I gave them what he gave me: a financially secure childhood. My children are as indifferent to me as I am to him. It's not that I don't love them or they me. It's an intangible aloofness, a defensive barrier we throw up between us to shield the fact that we know very little about each other. My ex resented the lost opportunities of their childhood. She had this mythical image of a family as portrayed by Ozzie and Harriet Nelson or Ward and June Cleaver. What did those guys do for a living?" he asked suddenly. "Anyway, life is about setting priorities. Mine were perhaps selfish, career-oriented priorities. I can't tell you what my dad's were. But back to your original question: Is it payback? No, the answer is no. I don't believe that relationships have scorecards. As Charles Manson said, 'I am what you made me.' I am my father's son. I don't think it is any more complex than that. I treat him as I was taught—a sort of respectful, perhaps cold indifference."

"My original question, Doctor Gottlieb, asked if you knew who your father really was. I think you've given me some very insightful reasons for not knowing the answer. Maybe a better way to ask the question is: Do you want to know who your father is?"

Will looked intently into Aimee's eyes. "Of course, but let me qualify that by saying that finding out that information is a luxury. Most of us can't afford it until we reach a certain point in our lives. My answer would have been different ten years ago, maybe even yesterday. Priorities change. We didn't know who are parents were when we were young because we didn't want to know. We simply didn't think it was important. When we reach that age where we begin to realize our own mortality, we start thinking about tying up those loose ends, finding answers to questions that really don't matter."

Aimee raised her eyebrows.

"What I mean," he continued, "is that they don't matter from the standpoint of finding a cure for cancer, ending poverty, or finding enough to eat for dinner. I think most people are too preoccupied with life—the immediate questions of making a living, of surviving—to worry about lineage or personality traits of their immediate family. Finding the answers doesn't put food on the table or grant world peace. It's a luxury reserved for the affluent to satisfy their curiosity. Frankly, Nurse Pond, I'm more concerned about the safety of my father at your facility than I am about family history. His well-being certainly trumps my need to find out who he really was or aspired to be. As far as I'm concerned, he was the guy I knew for a short period of my life and nothing more. I resent your insinuations regarding my relationship with my father and find it presumptuous that you would even discuss these issues with me. Your time would certainly be better spent doing what you're paid to do: providing care and a safe environment for your clients."

She looked at her watch and then carefully pressed the lid back on her Styrofoam cup. "I'm late. Could I have your card so that I can contact you in case something happens to your father?" she said.

"That's it? No more incrimination? Not even a cigarette or a blindfold before I'm executed?"

Aimee leaned forward and said softly, "You're a heartless, pompous prick, Doctor Gottlieb. It's a shame your mother didn't drown you at birth. I'll not trouble you further." She slid from the booth and calmly exited the diner without looking back.

DEEP LAKE, MINNESOTA—2007
DAY 4, 11:01 A.M.

S ophie Mickelson was all alone in death. Her grave appeared cold and isolated from the others. There were no Madonna statues in Spruce Haven. They were all across the road at Saint Mary's. Sam shook his head and puffed audibly through his nose at the dichotomy of the two mutually exclusive groups of Christians. They were as segregated in death as they had been integrated in life. It was as if everyone had shown up at the train station and the conductor announced the sheep would be on the right and the goats on the left.

Sam had not attended the services at the Trinity Lutheran Church because he had no funeral clothes, not even a white shirt. No tie, nothing dark or solemn, and nothing the Missouri Synod would consider acceptable. Instead he waited at the gravesite, bundled against the cold and popcorn-snow that clattered like static against the hood of his parka. In spite of his winter clothes, he felt naked being in a cemetery without his camera dangling from his neck. He had spent the previous day and most of the morning shooting dull, lifeless winter shots of tombstones to satisfy Pat. He wanted to go home and wondered if the sheriff's order not to leave the county had any legal teeth. He would ask Sidney.

The blanket of green, artificial turf that covered the dark mound of freshly dug earth was turning white by the time the hearse arrived. Funeral home workers, who could easily pass for barflies, were silent as they quickly prepared the site and placed Sophie's casket on the aluminum scaffold above her grave. Six pots of yellow chrysanthemums wrapped in green foil sat on three sides of the casket, symbolically masking the stench of death. Draperies were arranged and guy ropes tightened on the small canopy that did little to protect the site from the blowing sleet. The workers and hearse disappeared with the same silent efficiency as when they had arrived. Sam wished he had not drunk a second cup of coffee before leaving his trailer.

The funeral procession consisted of three cars: one white, one metallic blue, and one black-and-white SUV with the word "Sheriff" boldly printed across the rear quarter panel. The Lutheran minister hurriedly got out of the white car, his Bible clutched to his chest. The sheriff leaned against his cruiser and attempted to retrieve a cigarette from his empty shirt pocket. Aimee Pond, dressed in black, emerged from the blue vehicle and walked solemnly toward the grave; her high heels accentuated her slender features. She wore her pearl-gray hair down. It spilled over her shoulders and flipped up at the ends. She had on makeup.

Neither greeted the other verbally, in observance of the unwritten rule of silence at a funeral. Aimee blinked and offered a slight smile. Sam nodded. They stood shoulder-to-shoulder with their hands clasped in front of them.

Undaunted by the lack of attendance, the young minister made no attempt to abbreviate the graveside service, his voice rising as he looked to the imaginary mourners. Sam shifted his weight, trying to ease the pressure on his bladder. He tipped his head sideways as he stared at Sophie's headstone. Was he the only one to see the contradiction?

Three people stood next to a mound of earth draped in green on a winter's day. The sheriff watched from the road as Sophie Mickelson's body was committed to the ground. In the distance, vapor rose from Hans's mouth as he clutched the iron fence that bordered the cemetery.

••••

There was no funeral reception for Sophie Mickelson, where the sins of the deceased are symbolically devoured in order to clear a pathway to heaven. Instead, Sam and Aimee sat across from each other at the Paul Bunyan Diner on the outskirts of Deep Lake. Neither of them spoke for an uncomfortable length of time.

"I'm glad you came," Aimee finally said, not looking at Sam. She picked at the uneaten slice of coconut cream pie in front of her.

Sam sipped his coffee and said nothing. He offered a slight smile in place of words that would not come. He stared into his coffee and then cleared his throat.

Aimee looked at him, anticipating a response, something difficult or profound after the throat-cleansing prelude.

"Sometimes when I read the obituaries in the paper, I try to imagine what the deceased looked like when they were young, when they had their whole life in front of them and viewed the world as their oyster. I wonder about their dreams and if they ever realized their ambitions, if they were loved, if they are missed. Then I imagine them on their deathbed and puzzle over whether they suffered in their final days or hours. Silly, isn't it?" Sam raised his head to look at her.

"Not at all. I think we all do that to some extent. It's sort of a reality check. We see ourselves as youthful with a life ahead filled with promise. We're probably much less concerned about their achievements than we are with our own. And as to your last point, I think we're all scared of dying. We want to know if it hurts."

"So, it's all about me rather than the deceased?"

"Yep."

Sam looked out the window at the jumping pike. The sheriff pulled into the gravel lot and parked behind Sam's Willys.

"What about your dreams?" Aimee said, leaning forward. "Did they come true?"

Sam looked at her for a long moment. "Only the nightmares."

Aimee smiled. "I don't know what happened to you in Colorado, but I hope someday you can move beyond it."

The bells above the door tinkled, announcing the sheriff's arrival. Sam couldn't help smile as he pictured Matt Dillon pushing open the swinging doors of the Long Branch Saloon.

"Aimee," the sheriff greeted as he approached their booth and touched the brim of his ball cap, an embroidered star centered above the word "Sheriff."

"Joe," Aimee responded, looking up and smiling.

The sheriff reached for his left breast pocket as usual, but this time pulled out a folded, pink paper and handed it to Sam. "This is from Animal Control."

"What is it?" Sam said, unfolding the paper.

"What's it look like, Ace? It's a ticket." The sheriff smiled broadly.

"A ticket! A ticket for what?"

"The folks at animal control said your hound doesn't have a rabies tag. Fifty bucks."

"She had one. She lost it."

"Fifty bucks."

"She's current on all her vaccinations."

"I don't care. She needs a tag. Fifty bucks."

"I can have my vet send a certificate of vaccination."

"Needs a tag. Fifty bucks. If she's picked up again, it'll be a hundred. As ugly as she is, it ought to be a thousand."

Aimee tucked her chin and suppressed a giggle.

Sam looked at the sheriff; his eyes narrowed. "If ugly was a crime, Sheriff, you'd be serving life."

"You got quite a mouth on you, Dawson. You'll be singing a different tune if I haul your ass in again."

Before Sam could respond, Aimee slid toward the window and said, "Sit down, Joe. I'll buy you a cup of coffee."

Sam looked at her with disbelief.

"Thank you, Aimee. I don't mind if I do," the sheriff said, easing in next to her. "Kind of reminds me of old times on the rez, Pond Scum."

"Ancient history, Joe."

Sam shot a glance at the shiny brass name tag above the pocket with the imaginary cigarettes. It read "Whitehorn."

Seeing Sam's confusion, Aimee said, "Joe's wife, Half Sky, was my best friend in high school. She died two years ago from breast cancer," she added as an afterthought. "We go way back." She looked at the sheriff and patted his arm.

"You're just full of surprises," Sam said over the top of his coffee cup.

Skinny Rhonda, her nose more inflamed than usual but missing the tiny diamond stud, brought a cup and saucer. She silently poured the sheriff's coffee and then returned to cleaning the revolving pie cabinet on the counter. Frothy meringue stuck to the glass shelves.

Joe Whitehorn stared at Sam. No one spoke.

"Look, you really don't think I had anything to do with this, do you?" Sam finally said.

"With what?" the sheriff said, finding the handle on his cup.

"You know, with Sophie's murder and rape."

"Who said anything about rape?"

"You did. You implied it when you were interrogating me," Sam glanced nervously at Aimee, who in turn looked at the sheriff, her brow furrowed.

"The medical examiner did a full kit on her, then an autopsy. She wasn't raped." He paused and cleared his throat. "She was suffocated. Doc thinks it might have been a pillow."

Aimee shook her head and covered her face with her hands. "Poor Sophie."

The sheriff brought his cup to his lips with both hands, the liquid sloshing over the brim from his heavy breathing. "What about you, Dawson? Got a pillow in that heap?" he nodded toward Sam's Willys in the parking lot.

"Get a warrant. After, of course, you show probable cause."

"Boys," Aimee interrupted. "Quit measuring your dicks and try to be civil to one another."

Stunned, both Sam and the sheriff looked at her. Sam raised his eyebrows, his eyes wide with disbelief. The sheriff smiled, looked at Sam, and said, "I'd win that contest."

"Only by forfeit. I'd be a no-show," Sam said, meeting the sheriff's stare.

"Quit, both of you," Aimee interjected. "This isn't productive. Nor is it high school. Joe, what do I need to do to make sure this doesn't happen again? I've moved one of the security guards to the night shift and the other to the swing shift, and they're both threatening to quit. We're unprotected during the day. Corporate says no to additional personnel, surveillance cameras, or guns for the guards," she said, counting each denial on raised fingers. "Can you assign some kind of round-the-clock protection?"

"I can lend you my K-9 unit," Sam said with a smile. "She's working undercover now. That's why she doesn't wear a tag."

"Fifty bucks," the sheriff barked.

"Seriously, nothing gets by L2."

"Especially a meal," the sheriff added.

"That's her body shape. She's comfortable in her own skin."

Aimee shook her head. "Enough! I'm serious. There's a killer running around out there and they might come back."

"Chances are they never left," Sam said, sipping his coffee.

No one spoke as the sheriff and Aimee studied Sam.

"Ninety-two percent of nursing homes employ people who have been convicted of crimes. Five percent of all nursing home workers have at least one criminal conviction." Sam had their attention. "Half of all the nursing homes out there employ five or more people with at least one criminal conviction." He took another sip of coffee. "What I'm saying is that rather than rounding up innocent strangers and their dogs, maybe you should look a little closer to home." He stared intently at Sheriff Whitehorn.

"Well, it looks like we got us a Junior G-Man on the trail of crime right here in Timberlane County," the sheriff said from the side of his mouth.

"These are FBI statistics that anybody with half a brain could look up." Sam did not avert his gaze.

"Jesus, Sam," Aimee blurted. "Are you telling me that one of our staff did this?"

"Think beyond primary staff. What about nurse's aides, housekeeping, food service, or laundry? Did anyone do background checks on these people before they were hired?" Turning back to the sheriff, Sam said, "Or now, after a crime has been committed?"

"What else you got, Dawson? Or do I need a decoder ring like yours?"

"Close to twenty percent of these convictions occurred after these people started work in a nursing home."

"So, eighty percent happened before they started working there," said the sheriff.

"The point is, sheriff, nursing homes seem to be a magnet for low-paid, unskilled workers with a criminal record. And rather than skulking around in cemeteries, handing out dog tickets, or sucking coffee in a diner, your time would be better spent investigating the staff at Whispering Pines."

"I resent the implication, Sam," Aimee interrupted. "When were you going to share these amazing statistics with me? I suppose you consider me a suspect too?"

"Sorry, but Barney Fife here keeps barking up my tree. He's either stupid or lazy. I suspect both. Following me around is a waste of everyone's time."

"How about I lock your ass up? Then I won't have to follow you."

"Stop it! Both of you," Aimee said, her lips pursed.

"He's got a real hard-on for me or law enforcement in general. Or maybe it's for you, Pond Scum," the sheriff said, turning to face Aimee.

"Joe, if you're trying to provoke Sam into hitting you, he'll have to get in line because I'm about to slap you."

Ignoring her, the sheriff turned back toward Sam. "This some sort of hobby of yours, Miss Marple? What else you got?"

Sam smiled. "So, you can read. I had you figured for more of a Mickey Spillane–Mike Hammer type of guy rather than an Agatha Christie fan."

"I don't read fiction. It's not factual. I've got cable. There's a PBS series called *Marple*."

Sam cocked his head and squinted his eyes at Joe White-horn's illogical reasoning, but decided to let it go. "Well, as you probably know, Sheriff, most crimes against old folks are perpetrated by people the victim knows—friends or relatives."

"We're not talking petty financial stuff here, Dawson. We're talking serious violence."

"Yeah, and three quarters of violent crimes are committed by a family member, a third of that by a child or grandchild. Women are especially vulnerable. More than half of those who were sexually mistreated said it was by a relative. Maybe you should look at the residents and their families."

"Where do you come up with this crap, Dawson?"

Sam had not thought to write down the sources that Sidney had quoted to him earlier that morning. The kid could pull information off the internet faster than Sam could take notes. She was an electronic whiz kid with a passion for obscure statistics. Her academic background in criminal justice allowed her to find things in places most people would never think to look. "Anybody with a computer or a library card can validate these facts. Again, I'm only trying to point you in a more logical direction and hopefully get you out of my face."

"It sounds to me like you're telling me how to do my job and directing heat away from yourself. Don't leave this county, Dawson."

"Sam," Aimee said, her voice cold. "The fact that you didn't share this information with me earlier is offensive. Joe, come by the home and look through our personnel files if you want. Now let me out of here. I have work to do."

"What about L2?" Sam added to lighten the mood.

"Fifty bucks," Aimee and the sheriff said in unison. Together they stepped out into the cold and snow.

CINCINNATI, OHIO—1935

Cincinnati was cold, colder than Hans had envisioned. Despite the overnight snowfall, "dreary" was the word that best described the gray city and stark countryside. His feet were cold and the air smelled of wet concrete and steel. Looming above Crosley Field, the arena was separated from the ballpark by a huge parking lot. Maintenance men arrived early. Dump trucks with snowplows traversed the pavement in a hectic attempt to clear the snow. It was Saturday and the main event was scheduled to begin at 7:00 p.m. The *Lux Radio Theatre* would not be heard on the NBC airways that evening. Instead, wrestling's World Heavyweight Championship would be broadcast from Ohio.

The Depression had taken its toll on professional wrestling. To increase the gate, promoters added novelty acts for the "B" show. Tonight midgets would warm up the crowd and a stocky Russian woman would wrestle a trained bear. Hans sighed and looked off into the gray morning breaking above the arena roof. He was dreading the breakfast meeting that Lucky Lucello had summoned him to attend. The program had been skillfully developed for nearly two years, the feud built to a fevered pitch. The "A" show was for all the marbles. He was to be the American Wrestling Federation's champion, the likable underdog, the hero the fans would cheer for. It was all settled. So why did Lucky want to see him? He had a sick feeling in his stomach.

The heel was the Mighty Angus MacGregor, the current world champion. Angus knew how to get fan heat. Periodically, he would break from his armed escort on the way to the ring and pummel a shill or two planted in the audience. A near riot ensued in New York when the booing shill Angus attacked was an attractive young woman who gushed fake blood from her mouth as she clutched her torn blouse. At the Kiel Auditorium in Saint Louis he greeted the crowd from the center of the ring by lifting his kilt, bending over, and exposing his hairy butt to his detractors. They hated him almost as much as they hated Wall Street bankers.

••••

"Whaddya know for sure?" Lucky "Big Ears" Lucello said from the corner booth of the hotel restaurant as Hans slid into the seat across from him. "You want something to eat?"

Hans shook his head no. His stomach churned at the sight of Lucky's breakfast, which lay motionless in a pool of yellow ooze. Something was up.

"Lemme ask you this," Lucky said, holding up a copy of *The Ring* magazine. "You seen the latest dirt sheets by Tex Austin?"

Again, Hans shook his head.

"You should keep up on this crap, Hans," Lucky said, pulling the corner of his napkin from his shirt collar. "Lemme read something to you: 'The ritualized spectacle slated for Cincinnati has all the appeal of two dogs mounting each other in the park. The underdog, the hooded Trapper, will attempt to leave his mark higher on the tree than the veteran bully from across the pond, the Mighty Angus MacGregor, known in Europe as the Glasgow Killer. There seems little doubt as to the outcome, given the long buildup and extensive promotion applied to the media-shy Trapper. Righteousness shall prevail in this classic tale of good versus evil—a fairy tale come true for the small-town Midwesterner who has captured the hearts of the downtrodden from across much of the country. Like any fairy tale, we know the ending. But that should not keep gullible young ears from hearing the bedtime story again. Save yourself the price of admission and listen to it on NBC. Better yet, read the story in the next Current Wrestling Gossip column here in *The Ring*.'" Lucky tossed the magazine onto the seat next to him. "I have half a notion to send this guy a nursery rhyme of my own, one that ends with the reporter trying to type with broken fingers."

Hans sat quietly, waiting. The smell of bacon caused his stomach to roll.

"Lemme ask you this: You think we can run this game as a charity benefit? Gate is what pays the bills. We've been building the program for two years. It's not just about the house. If the fans don't show, I got no bargaining power in dealing with that mick bastard, O'Toole. He's got a stranglehold on the New York market. I've been able to consolidate promotion for Philly, Boston, Baltimore, even DC and Hartford. But New York is holding out, waiting to see what kind of gate we bring here in Cincinnati. Then along comes this

Tex Austin guy and tells the marks to stay home because the match is worked."

"Do you believe the fans don't know that?" Hans asked, his eyebrows raised.

"Lemme ask you this: You think they give a shit? It's the show they come for. They want their Prince Charming crowned as king. That Tex guy is right; it's a fairy tale for grownups. They can sleep better at night thinkin' it could happen to them too. But if they think they can save a buck to buy shoes for their snot-nosed kids by listening to the story on the radio, we're screwed. As of last night only half the seats have been sold." Lucky slurped his coffee, his stubby pinkie finger with its large diamond ring stuck out pretentiously. "We're gonna give Mother Goose a screw job. If the marks can't figure the ending of their beddy-bye story, then maybe they'll start showing up to see if they can yell loud enough to change the outcome."

"You're changing the script?" Hans asked, his voice flat, trying to suppress his anger as he felt his dream slipping away.

"We'll do a turn after a bunch of false comebacks. We'll give 'em hope, lots of hope, and then we'll crap in their hats. The dumb bastards won't know whether to spit or go blind." Lucky smiled and snorted from his greasy nose. "The Big Bad Wolf will be fat and sassy while poor Little Red Riding Hood is lying in a heap with her guts torn out. That'll piss 'em off. We'll build the feud and book the challenge for the Garden in May. New York will be a sellout. O'Toole won't have any choice but to join the association. The territory will be ours."

"I'm Little Red Riding Hood?"

"Lemme ask you this: Are you deaf? What the hell have I been saying to you?"

"Two years we've been building the program," Hans said, staring intently at Lucello. "I've hooked for you how many times? You've been able to consolidate more than a dozen territories because I enforced for you. I've stuck to the game plan and now in the eleventh hour you're pulling the rug out from under me and changing the finish?" Hans felt sick to his stomach.

Lucky leaned forward, his dark round face a mere foot from Hans's. "This ain't about you, Hans, you stupid cabbage-eatin' Kraut. This is business. You do what I tell you and you'll be the champ in six months. Screw with me and— let's just say you'll wish you hadn't. Capiche?" His gold incisor flashed menacingly.

Aimee Pond was late. She was never late. Her eyes were puffy with dark circles below. She was not wearing makeup and had not showered.

"Hans is gone again," Taneesha said, placing her hands on her hips and dispensing with her normal singsong morning greeting. "You want that I should I get security?"

"We have no security during the day. I'll handle it. I'm sure he's at the greenbelt."

"Should I get a syringe?" Taneesha offered.

"Not yet. I'll take a wheelchair and see if I can talk him into it."

"Take a blanket. It's cold out there. That old fool is going to freeze himself to death one of these days."

••••

Aimee said nothing as she brushed away the snow and sat down on the park bench next to Hans. He wore his heavy winter coat and a stocking cap pulled over his ears. Five-buckle galoshes hung open on his feet. He looked at her, then removed his glove and took her hand gently in his. He squeezed it as if he were greeting a loved one. He sighed.

She sat quietly, gazing into the white blankness across the greenbelt. She was tired. Her eyes burned from a night of staring at a computer screen. When she finally went to bed at 3:00 a.m., she had not slept. Aimee turned from Hans, took a deep breath, and exhaled through her nose; the steam rose from her face. Without looking at him, she asked loudly, "What happened in Cincinnati, Hans?"

Deep Lake, Minnesota—1935

The whole thing turned into a shoot. That's what happened," Hans said. "It means it went legit. It was my fault. I let my pride get in the way and my temper took over. I started to sandbag him early in the second round. Angus got hot and thought he'd get even with me for the Amsterdam match in '28. Look, Gloria, that's not why I called....His neck's broken. That's his condition. He'll probably never wrestle again....No paralysis; the doctors don't think there will be any permanent damage. They've got him stretched out and trussed up in a bunch of braces. He'll be flat on his back for the next five weeks or so. But that's not why I called."

He turned uncomfortably and looked down at the floor.

"No, Doc's in Texas. I'm laying low until I can figure out what to do." Hans heard someone pick up the phone. "Uh-huh, I know it's a twelve-party line....Yes, I'm the world champion, but Angus was supposed to win. It's a long story. The point is that Lucky is out a lot of dough and thinks that I went rogue on him....You don't understand. There is no explanation. When Lucky doesn't get his way, there's no talking to him. He views me as a traitor, someone who can't be trusted."

He took a deep breath and paused before he spoke. "He's got to send a message, a strong message, to the association that he's in charge," he said. "Right, I'm usually the hooker. That used to be my job. The problem is how do you hook the hooker? This lesson won't be taught in the ring. He'll send some of his boys to—that's not why I called.... No, believe me. It won't do any good to call him. Thanks, but why would he listen to you? Once Lucky makes up his mind....Gloria, I need to talk with you about Chicago."

He heard someone pick up the phone again.

"I agree. We need to talk in person. Can I see you? Can we meet somewhere?...Please," he said softly, turning to cover the phone with his body. "I won't trouble you again. But it's important that we clear the air, that we make a decision we both understand and agree with. Please, Gloria."

Again there was a long, uncomfortable silence except for the crackling and hissing of the line between them. "I'm at Fuller's Grocery Store."

Sophie Mickelson looked up from the magazine she was reading behind the counter.

"I got in this morning....I'd like to think that presumptuous is a word that doesn't apply to us....I know it's Tuesday morning and you have appointments."

He looked at the advertising clock behind the counter. The yellow glass door with red script proclaimed that Clabber Girl was the healthy baking powder. It was ten minutes to seven. Hans held his breath, waiting for a reply.

"Thank you. I'll meet you at the clinic in ten minutes."

••••

He arrived first. His ears ached with cold and he could feel numbness creeping into the toes of his right foot. He grabbed the scoop shovel leaning against the porch and began clearing snow from the walkway to the street. The noise of metal on concrete made his presence conspicuous. He looked nervously up and down the street. A matted shepherd mix—gray in the muzzle with hazy unseeing eyes, tested the air from the middle of the street. Gloria made her way from the west, gingerly walking in a tire rut as she approached the clinic. Her long wool coat and headscarf could not mask her beauty. His heart began to pound and his chest felt hollow.

"Hans," she said as if greeting a casual acquaintance, stepping around him on the narrow path. "Please come in; it's freezing out here."

He nodded without speaking and followed her inside. The heat from the Warm Morning oil stove in the parlor made his ears burn. A faint yellow glow flickered through the isinglass window of the brown porcelain grill.

Without speaking, Gloria removed her coat, hung it on the hall tree, and disappeared through a door at the end of the hall. He heard her descend a wooden stairway, open the furnace door, prod the clinkers, and shake the grates. There were the unmistakable sounds of a shovel scooping coal and dampers being adjusted. When she reappeared in the hallway, she approached him confidently, her almond eyes fixed on his. She cupped his face in her hands and gently brought him to her lips. The kiss, at first, was tender as she stroked the side of his face and the back of his neck. Her body pressed against his as she opened and closed her mouth, her tongue teasing and probing.

His rehearsed pronouncements of love and regret dissolved. There was so much he had wanted to say, but now his arguments seemed unimportant. Neither of them spoke as they embraced, both burrowing into the warmth of the other. She pushed free, took his hand, and led him into the same room where he had stayed after his surgery, where he had been totally captivated by her beauty. She undressed with no hint of shyness. Her eyes sparkled and she smiled confidently as she stood next to the bed. He had never seen a more beautiful woman in his life.

"What was it about Chicago that you wanted to talk with me about?" she asked with a coy smile on her face.

There was so much he wanted to tell her. He could not speak. Instead he pulled her to him and rolled her onto the bed. In the distance he heard Coach Carter's whistle blow, his muffled voice ordering him to the showers. He ignored the past as he found her lips.

Deep Lake, Minnesota—1935

euben "Red" Carter was missing. The *Clinton Herald* rarely printed pictures, but according to Hans's mother, Red's doughboy portrait was above the fold. Decorated war hero, gifted athlete, respected member of the community, and inspirational mentor of young Christian men were some of the many platitudes. Statements from his landlady, the president of the board of directors of the YMCA, the mayor, the chief of police, and others attested to Red Carter's indisputably good character and the many contributions he had made to the community. Monty Harris, who had been collecting trash behind the YMCA, reported seeing a black DeSoto sedan like the one Carter owned parked in the alley on Tuesday morning, the day of Red's disappearance. Anyone with information was asked to come forward.

"I'm here, Mom.... You know he's never been right since the war. He's probably off on a bender. He'll turn up.... Florida, Mom. I'm in Florida," he said. He stole a quick look at Gloria, who stood next to the bed clutching the footboard. "Yes, it's warm here, a beautiful day. I was thinking of going for a swim in the ocean later."

He parted the curtains and gazed out at the wall of snow-covered spruce that defined the boundaries of Deep Lake. He disliked lying to his mother but thought it best. Lucky's attorney, Cortland Davis, had called Gloria twenty minutes earlier with a phony story about wanting to mail a check to him and needing his address. Lucky was on the hunt.

"Do you need anything, Mom?...I will, Mom, as soon as possible, but I've got some business to attend to out of the country. When I get back, I'll visit. I promise....Europe," he said quickly. "I'm going to Scotland....Yes, I have some things I need to take care of for Angus." He had no intention of going to Scotland, but if she were contacted by Lucky's people, she would pass on the information honestly. "I've got to go, Mom. The Cuban lady who sells me fresh grapefruit is coming up the walk. Tell Dad hello for me. I love you."

Gloria stared at him curiously as he hung up the phone. "Where will you really go?" she asked, her almond eyes shining.

"California," he said softly.

"You and most of Oklahoma. You're going to pick fruit?"

"My roommate when I was in Amsterdam, Johnny, was a fish, a swimmer. Now he's a big shot in Hollywood. He put me up in '32 when the games were in Los Angeles. He knows a promoter who's trying to get the West Coast organized."

Her brow wrinkled and her head tilted slightly. "You were in the 1932 Olympics too?"

"Uh-huh. Doc had a conniption fit, threatened to fire me. He wouldn't give me time off to prepare. I went to both the tryouts and the games without training."

"And?" she said, raising her eyebrows.

"I took gold again in the freestyle class."

Gloria looked at him with disbelief. "You're a two-time Olympic champion and you wrestle in carnivals and phony exhibitions?"

"Two gold medals and a nickel will get me a cup of coffee." He shook his head. "Nobody cares. We can't all be movie stars like Johnny. You may not know it up here in the middle of nowhere but there is a depression going on." He ran his fingers gently over the doily covering the telephone stand. Embarrassed, he could not meet her gaze. "It's the one thing I do well. What am I supposed to do? Join the CCCs or the WPA?"

"I don't know, Hans. It just seems like—"

"Thanks for letting me use the telephone," he said, changing the subject. "Mom worries when she doesn't hear from me." He sat in the hardback chair next to the telephone stand and stared at the floor. "That was my first time," he said softly, an admission that he could share only with her. "I'll be twenty-seven in a couple of months and never—I hope I—"

Gloria stepped in front of him and held his head to her stomach. She was still naked. "Yes," was all she said as she combed her fingers through his hair.

"Yes," Aimee Pond said as she pushed his hair back and gently laid his head on the pillow. "You did very well, Hans," referring to his walk back to Whispering Pines from the park bench down the street. "But we're both a little older than twenty-seven." She sat on the edge of the bed and looked into his eyes. "Can you tell me where you were when you were twenty-seven or -eight, Hans?"

"Deep Lake," he whispered immediately.

"No, you're in Deep Lake now. What about when you were a young man, say twenty-eight, where were you then?"

"Deep Lake," he said again.

Aimee smiled and stared down at him. She knew not to argue with her patients. In his mind, he had given the correct response. To argue the point would only yield frustration and lead to anxiety. She smiled and said, "What about after Cincinnati? Trapper seemed to drop off the face of the earth. Where did Trapper go?"

Hans seemed surprised, perhaps confused by the question. His eyes searched hers, moving rapidly across her face.

"Trapper," she repeated. "Yes, I know who you were. But I can't find any mention of you after that January 1935 wrestling match in Cincinnati. You held the World Heavyweight Championship title for nearly eighteen months. You were unchallenged as champion because nobody could find you. You disappeared. Where did you go?"

"Deep Lake," he whispered again.

"After Deep Lake, where did you go?"

Hans turned his head and stared out the window.

"Do you know why you are here?" Aimee asked.

BEMIDJI, MINNESOTA—2007
DAY 5, 1:45 P.M.

S am had skipped lunch when he discovered Sophie Mickelson had died in 1973. His stomach growled loud enough for the reference librarian to take notice. Grand Rapids was closer, but Bemidji had a larger public library that served a five-county area. He smiled weakly at the portly woman behind the desk.

Sidney had told him the night before that she had hit a dead end when researching Sophie, but gave him some ideas to follow up on while she studied for her constitutional law exam. He had found several women named Sophie Mickelson in Minnesota, but only one who was still living after the 1940 census was taken—and she had been fifty-two at the time. He went as far as he could on all the ancestry websites without paying. There was no record of the woman who was brutally murdered in Deep Lake. Timberlane County did have a public viewing station for vital statistics including county birth records from 1898 to present.

The last Minnesota Sophie Mickelson on file had been born ten years before they started keeping records and died in Minneapolis eighty-four years later. He checked all the databases that Sidney had listed. Sophie did not drive, did not own property, and had no medical history or Medicare records. She never paid a utility or phone bill, or taxes. Social Security's Death Master File had no listing for her. Deep Lake's Sophie Mickelson did not exist.

••••

Sam breathed his frustration as he drove the Willys in the direction of Deep Lake. He looked angrily at L2, who sat up front, staring out the windshield. The remainder of Sam's fish sandwich lay uneaten on the seat between them. "It's walleye, you stink hound. Everybody up here eats them." She had devoured nearly all his fries, but refused to even look at the fish sandwich.

Instead of finding out answers, he had generated more questions. Just when he thought he could not be more frustrated, he looked in the rearview mirror. The sheriff's vehicle followed him at a less than respectful distance.

Deep Lake, Minnesota—1935

"Why are you here?" Hans demanded. His fists opened and closed rhythmically on imaginary rubber balls.

Reuben "Red" Carter looked bad and smelled worse. "Aren't you going to invite your old friend and mentor in for a cup of coffee and fond reminiscences?"

Hans quickly positioned himself on the center of the stoop, blocking the front door of the Halvorson farmhouse. He nervously looked over his shoulder to make sure that Gloria or her mother was not listening. "What the hell are you doing here?"

"Can't a guy look up his old protégé?"

"How did you find me?"

"It wasn't so hard. A couple of long-distance calls, a telegram or two, and a few questions here and there. Some of your carny friends were most helpful. If I can find you, so can that nice Italian man, Mr. Lucello. He offered me a pretty good wad of dough if I were to let him know your whereabouts." Coach Carter smiled and slowly looked around, his teeth rotten and filled with food. "I gotta say though, this is the sticks."

"What do you want?"

"You were always one to get straight to the point, huh, Hans? Money, my boy, it's as simple as that."

"You came all the way to Deep Lake, Minnesota, to borrow money from me?"

"'Borrow' is perhaps the wrong word. I have no intention of ever paying you back. I just need a few bucks to help me get back on my feet, or foot as it were. Of course you'll have to match, or better, Mr. Lucello's offer."

"What makes you think I would ever give you one red cent?"

"I know all about you and your doctor friend. So does Mr. Lucello. He gave me this address. Quite a little love nest you've got here in the north woods. Have you told her about us, Hans? Have you told your mother about us? Have you told anybody about your depravity? You're the world wrestling champion, Mr. Trapper. Don't you think your fans would like to know the sordid details of your youthful indiscretions? Surely your doctor friend understands the meaning of the word sodomy."

With blurring speed, Hans grabbed the coach's coat and lifted him off the ground while twisting and pushing him against the side of the house. "You sick bastard. I should have—"

The metallic click of the switchblade stopped him mid-sentence. The knife's point was poking him sharply under the jaw, below his left ear.

"You should've what, Hans? Treated me better? A wealthy world champion like you should treat the man who trained him better. Now put me down or I'll slice you from ear to ear."

Hans eased him down. The stench of booze and urine from Carter's soiled clothes invaded his nostrils.

Carter swayed uneasily as he shifted his weight from his prosthetic leg to his good leg. "That's better, Hans." He folded the knife's blade back into the handle and placed it in his coat pocket, but didn't remove his hand. "Let's not get carried away. No need to get rough. I don't want much. You know I'm not a greedy man."

"How much?" Hans's neck muscles bulged from the pressure of his set jaw.

"That's better. Well, let's see, I'll need some gasoline to continue my journey. They say California has a pleasant climate."

Hans looked over his shoulder toward the street and saw the black 1929 DeSoto Roadster parked at the end of the drive, a black box on wheels that, like the coach, was in need of a bath. "How much?" he asked again.

"A few thousand should do it. Shall we say five?"

"I don't have that kind of money, you crazy—"

"You can get it. I see how you've been keeping that kike mother and Kraut father of yours in style. You've got it. I know you've got it. Get it from your girlfriend. I don't give a damn how you get it or where you get it from. Just get it and get it now or I'll blow the whistle on you."

"All right, all right. I'll scrape together what I can. Give me some time. I'll meet you at the railroad station tonight, say eight o'clock."

"No funny business."

"None, but this is it, Red. I want you to disappear. I don't ever want to see you or hear from you again. Are we clear on that?"

Reuben "Red" Carter sucked his front teeth with his tongue. "You'll get no static from me. Tonight, eight o'clock."

Gloria glanced at the mantle clock in the living room. The afternoon sun cast straight-line shadows—like scalpel cuts—across the wall where she stood listening.

It was eight o'clock on Saturday morning. Sam slipped the old Elgin pocket watch back into his chinos, which he had tucked into the tops of his insulated pack boots. His gloved hand was cupped over the shade of his Nikkor 14–24mm zoom to protect it from the heavy frost that clung to every surface. Sam's fingers tingled from the cold. He was glad he had thrown his flash unit into the well-worn canvas gear bag slung over his shoulder. The frozen forest floor was dark. L2 seemed a little intimidated by the dense boreal forest. She tagged along behind him rather than attempting to lead, as if to say, "Are you sure we're not lost?"

Aimee turned back and smiled at Sam. "I used to come here when I was little. It was my secret place. I pretended no one on earth but me knew about it. It was sacred."

"Out west we can usually see the sun and landmarks, but this is something else. I feel like I should be dropping breadcrumbs or marking waypoints on a GPS or something."

"Deep Lake, the lake, is just over there, maybe two hundred yards," she said, pointing to her left without looking back. "Deep Lake the town is that way," she thrust her thumb suddenly to the right as if she were hitchhiking. "I never told my mother or any of my friends about this place. I believed it was magical and that if anyone but me found out about it, the magic would disappear." She stopped and turned to face him. "As far as I know, you're the only other living person on the planet to know about it." She looked up at Sam, her eyebrows raised and a tight smile on her lips. Sam was not only lost, he was clueless as to where Aimee was taking him. She had simply shown up at the Forest Service campground and told him she had a surprise for him. "Bring your camera. Miss Stinky can ride in the back." Until he could gather more information, he decided not to tell Aimee that Sophie Mickelson had used an alias.

The drive had lasted less than five minutes before she suddenly stopped on the shoulder of the gravel road, bailed from the car, and stomped into the black timber. She wore a heavy flannel shirt under a down vest, comfortable but formfitting jeans tucked into insulated muck boots, and a wool ball cap. Her gray ponytail was pulled through the back of the hat and snugged with a red ponytail holder. Sam was again struck by her cuteness. "So," he said, meeting her stare and realizing the significance of her disclosure, "why are you sharing your secret with me?"

"I've looked at your photos and thumbed through your books. You can't take pictures like that without caring about the subject matter." She paused. Her smile disappeared and her eyes moved incrementally across his. "Your photos belie your stoic exterior, Sam. I think you'll appreciate this place more than anyone else I know. Simply put, I trust you, Sam Dawson." She smiled, winked, and turned back to the overgrown logging trail they had been following. "Come on, it's just ahead."

Sam followed the swishing ponytail, whose movement seemed synchronized with the denim-clad swaying buttocks in front of him.

The presence of a clearing was signaled by the contrasting shafts of gray light that stabbed into the forest floor from above. Angled beams shot earthward from holes in the forest canopy and presented a checkerboard of shadows, light and dark, on the unexpected glade. The presence of geometric structures in somewhat imperfect rows elicited silence. No one spoke, no one moved. Even L2 stood motionless, ears forward, her tail raised as she tested the air.

Tiny gabled houses, their roofs covered with moss, dotted the clearing. "Doghouses" was Sam's first focused thought as he attempted to provide meaning to the surreal image. No, he reasoned, too low for doghouses. The sidewalls were only six to eight inches high and the peaks of the gabled ends were perhaps fifteen to eighteen inches high. Each tiny house, about two feet wide by four feet long, had a small hole cut in one gable. Sam glanced upward to check the angle of the sun filtering through the trees above. He turned his camera on and made sure he had removed the lens cover. The light was hypnotic, dreamlike with shafts angled steeply through the dark canopy. Each beam, sparkling with crystalline particles suspended in the dense early winter air, illuminated a tiny, dilapidated house. His questions could wait. He feared the Disney fairy tale in front of him would disappear if he did not act quickly. There was no time for tripods, flash units, or light meters. He had to act now. Removing his gloves, Sam deftly adjusted the f-stop on his lens and turned the focus ring one direction, then the other as he moved along the edge of the clearing. He would drop to one knee, or both, sometimes stretching prone on the cold forest floor. The click of the shutter and the whine of the motor drive were fakes, built-in auditory cues to let him know that the digital computer shaped like a camera was doing its job. Neither he nor Aimee spoke. L2 sniffed the ground along the walls of the little houses, running excitedly from one to another.

The walls and gabled ends were constructed from wooden boards. Likewise, the steeply pitched roofs were short, horizontal planks of roughly hewn lumber. They were covered with thin, vertical, homemade wooden shingles that had long ago rotted in a mosaic of mossy patterns.

Finally Sam allowed his camera to hang against its tether around his neck as he straightened and turned his head toward Aimee. "What are they?" he whispered.

Aimee smiled and whispered back. "The fact that you are whispering tells me you know what they are. Your reverence is for the dead. The Ojibwe refer to them as *jiibegamig*. They're spirit houses. This is a clan cemetery."

"A family cemetery?"

"Sort of," Aimee smiled and took a deep breath. "It's a long and very confusing story. The *Reader's Digest* version is that the Anishinaabe people, who most people in this country refer to as Chippewa, live in groups referred to as bands. Chippewa is an anglicized name that some refuse to use, including the local tribal members. Here we identify more with Canadian communities and refer to our people as Ojibwe.

The folks in this area are part of the Minnesota Chippewa Tribe, which has six bands, including the Leech Lake Band of Ojibwe. This band," she said, waving her arm in an arc "is the Lake Winnibigoshish Band of Chippewa. We have a patrilineal system based on our father's clan that is so complex that even I have trouble keeping everybody straight. Anthropologists refer to it as a 'bifurcate merging kinship system.' The bottom line is that the Anishinaabe people believe in interconnectedness, a sort of balance between those alive, those dead, and those of the future."

Sam tipped his head and looked at her as if she had just stepped off a spacecraft from Venus.

"I know, I know. It's all really confusing to those who didn't grow up immersed in the culture. Add to that a form of self-regulating government and it really gets dicey. Think of the bands as something like local governments made up of clan representatives. These clans, *odoodeman,* consist of several singular clans known as *doodem,* which sounds like totem, doesn't it? Well, like a totem, the doodem are usually named for some critter. Some of the larger doodem are further subdivided into the body parts of the animal they represent, each with specific responsibilities among their clan. There is a bit of a biological component too, in that you have to marry someone from a different clan. That, of course, limits the possibility of passing on genetic defects or genetically related diseases as a result of inbreeding." She paused, looked down, and then suddenly looked up directly into Sam's eyes. "When we greet other Ojibwe people, we do so with a question: *Aaniin gidoodem?* Which means 'What's your doodem?' That way we know who we're talking to and how to act based on whether they're family, friends, or enemies. Most people today just greet one another with a familiar *Aaniin.*"

"Is this your clan?"

"I have no idea. I found these spirit houses while picking blueberries when I was eleven or twelve. I never told anyone about them."

Sam stared at her but said nothing.

"You're wondering why," she said. "A couple of reasons, I guess. First, it was my private, special place. It was where a pubescent girl could come and share her darkest secrets. Somehow they helped me talk through the problems that plague most adolescents. The Ojibwe are very spiritual and communicate with ancestral spirits, usually in the form of a ceremony. I didn't know any of this at the time—I hadn't gone off to live with my father's people yet. But I connected with them anyway. I found it to be quite therapeutic." She smiled. There was a faraway look in her eyes as she stared off into the forest. "Second," she said a little too loudly as she turned back to face Sam, "in exchange for their silence regarding my most personal issues, I agreed to keep their location secret in order to prevent looting by *Zhaagnaash,* white people."

"Grave robbing?"

"Tourists mostly. They come up here on fishing vacations from the big cities. There's nothing more destructive than unsupervised teenage boys in the forest with their scout

hatchets. These spirit houses are irresistible to them. First
they loot, then they desecrate."

"What's to loot?"

"Nothing really. The older graves may contain some
personal items useful to the deceased in the afterlife. These
artifacts had little intrinsic value. They became souvenirs
stashed in some kid's cigar box. Mostly the offerings were
food and tobacco. The food was left to help nourish the deceased's soul on its four-day journey to the afterlife. Tobacco
was offered as a bribe to the spirits in order that they watch
over the deceased on their journey."

"Four days?"

Aimee smiled. "That's how long it takes for the spirit to
travel to *Gaagige Minawaanigoziwining*, the land of everlasting
happiness. It's to the west. Hence the small opening cut on
the west end of the house," she said, pointing to the gabled
end of the closest spirit house. "That's for the spirit to exit
through. Sometimes personal items are placed outside the
house on the west side so the spirit can take them on the first
day of their journey."

"Why the little house?"

"I don't know." Aimee said as she looked around at the
dilapidated, rotting structures. "It's a practice that occupied
only a brief period in Ojibwe history. But it's fairly pervasive
across a huge area of the country. I think originally they buried their dead in shallow graves and mounded up the soil. At
some point they began placing spirit houses over the graves,
possibly as a way to honor the dead. I guess it would be no
different than setting a tombstone, an upended bathtub with

a Madonna statue in it, or a simple wooden cross on top. Kind of a tribute, I guess. But they're all the same. Nobody tries to build a larger or more ornate one. No little lambs or winged angels on top. No replicas of the Washington Monument. They're just simple, little, rectangular houses to mark the spot or maybe to provide shelter for the spirit of the deceased. I really don't know. I do know that in later times they used to leave the body outside their house for four days. They were afraid the spirit would be reluctant to leave home if they kept the corpse in the house. In the old days, when they still lived in wigwams, the body would lie inside during the spirit's journey to the afterlife. Afterward they would cut a hole in the wigwam and remove the body through it rather than using the door, for fear the spirit would return through the door. Maybe the practice of constructing spirit houses was an attempt to protect the dead from scavengers and the elements. I really don't know," she repeated.

Sam fastened his flash unit to the top of the camera. "Do they still use spirit houses when burying a tribal member?"

"I think it's becoming much less common. Post-European contact resulted in disease, alcoholism, and Christianity. Nearly all of the Ojibwe people have been converted over the last couple hundred years. Much of their culture has been assimilated into the mostly northern European culture that settled this part of the country. The dead get buried in regular cemeteries like everybody else. Don't get me wrong, they maintain their traditions, especially as they relate to death. There's traditional music, dancing, eating, drinking, and ceremonial smoking. The family of the deceased grieves for a year following the death of a loved one. You can still find recently constructed spirit houses in Christian cemeteries. Old beliefs die hard."

Sam deftly adjusted the manual settings on both the camera and flash while he crawled on hands and knees around a spirit house. L2 sat, as if commanded, next to a house on the edge of the clearing. "How old do you think these are?"

"Hard to say, but I remember them being in better shape when I was a young girl. I'm thinking turn of the century, maybe teens. Possibly later, but I doubt it."

"What about that old road we followed in here?"

"Like the spirit houses, it was in better shape nearly fifty years ago. I'm pretty sure it's an old logging road from the late eighteen hundreds. They used draft horses to skid the logs out of the forest. Later, hunters probably used it. There's even an old abandoned car just up ahead. I remember it as a rusted hulk shot full of holes. I fantasized that it belonged to a bootlegger who got caught in an ambush by revenuers."

Sam glanced upward. The morning sun was yielding to thick, gray clouds. He had lost his light. "Would you mind if I came back here sometime when the light is better and took some more shots?"

"Do you always work alone?" Aimee smiled, her eyes sparkling.

Sam thought for a moment. "I do. I guess I never thought about it. It's kind of morbid work in a way. Not many people are up for the task. The last person who helped me—" He paused. "Let's just say I fell for her in a big way and she broke my heart."

"I'm sorry to hear that, Sam."

"Don't be. We're still friends. It was sort of an age difference thing." As soon as he said it, he wished he hadn't. He desperately wanted to take it back. Instead he looked down and adjusted the camera's f-stop and hoped she would let it pass.

"Yes, that can be a real deal breaker." She paused but did not look away. She absently pushed several strands of hair under her ball cap just behind her ear. "How much?"

"Excuse me?"

"How many years? I assume you were the older one. That seems to be the way it always works."

Sam looked at her and smiled. "You're not going to let it go, are you?"

"Nope."

"Ten. Actually nine years and seven months. She was twenty-seven and I was thirty-seven, divorced with a teenage daughter. You can't really blame her."

"How long ago was that?"

"Eight years ago."

"You're forty-five?"

"Yeah, well, very soon. Is that what this is all about? You wanted to know how old I am?" Sam stared at her, his brow furrowed. "For what purpose?"

"I was fifteen when my mother died and I was essentially orphaned," she said, looking directly into Sam's eyes. "That's when I went to live with my father's people on the reservation. I guess you could say I grew up pretty fast. I had to." She looked down, then back up at him. "That was in 1965. ...You were—what? Two or three years old?"

Sam didn't reply. A light breeze entered the clearing from the north and brushed gently against Sam's cheek. He looked away nervously. L2 still sat attentively next to the little house she had claimed as her own.

"The purpose, you ask?" she said softly. "At my age, there's no time for games. Get to the point, process the information, make a decision, and move on. Know what I mean?"

"No."

"Liar."

Sam smiled and took a deep breath. "What do you want from me, Nurse Pond?"

"Honesty, Sam. That's what I want. No games. You need to process the fact that I'm fifty-seven, make a decision, and move on. In the meantime, stop looking at my butt."

MISSION, TEXAS—1935

During the day the north country moved slowly past the window. But at night, only his reflection appeared in the framed glass of the rail coach. When he closed his eyes, she came to him. Over and over again he relived the scene. She stood naked in front of him. Then he felt the warmth of her body, smelled her delicate scent, tasted her lips, and caressed her softness. There was no sleep. At Shelby he stood on the platform and watched the train slowly disappear into the cold Montana night. He had no intention of going to California.

Wyoming, Colorado, across the northeastern tip of New Mexico, and into the Texas Panhandle gave him time to think, to justify the lies. At Smithville he wired William, who met him the next morning at the Harlingen station.

"You're a sight for sore eyes," he said, brushing William's extended hand aside and engulfing him in a bear hug.

"You too, Trap. I've been worried sick for you."

"Any sign of Lucky's boys? Anybody sniffing around?"

"Not a peep," William said as he grabbed Hans's suitcase.

Hans took William's arm and pulled the suitcase from his hand. "You're my cutman, not my porter," he said, smiling.

Neither man spoke as William drove northwest toward McAllen. The fertile floodplain of the Rio Grande was seg-

mented into a checkerboard of irrigated fields, straight green
lines of year-round agriculture that stood in sharp contrast
to the frozen rocky soil and forests of northern Minnesota.
Just outside of Mission, nestled against a large irrigation ca-
nal, was the winter camp of O'Brien's Wonders of the World
Travelling Show. Rows of grapefruit trees surrounded the
camp and provided a pastoral view from afar. Doc had purchased the land, a former migrant labor camp, from a local
bank that had foreclosed on the property at the start of the
Depression. He paid a Mexican family to maintain the buildings and irrigate the grapefruit trees. A large outdoor summer kitchen with adobe ovens connected to a sheltered plaza of serape-covered picnic tables that served as the dining
hall. Barefoot Mexican children with sticks chased chickens
through the plaza. Penelope the Pinhead followed gleefully
behind. He wore his trademark dress and work boots with a
pink bow in his topknot. The other freaks, with the exception of Edna the Bearded Lady, Larry the Human Tattoo,
and Sheila the Fat Lady, blended in with the other carnival
workers. Even Harriet the Hermaphrodite appeared nondescript in her Mexican skirt and blouse.

"Jesus jumped-up Judas Priest," Doc smiled as he pulled
the cigar butt from his mouth. "Look what the cat dragged
in, you big charley horse."

"It's good to see you too, Doc," Hans said as he yanked
his suitcase from the bed of the truck.

"I knew you'd come crawlin' back." He stuffed the cigar
in his mouth again. "I told you that dago bastard Lucello
was no good, didn't I? No, you wouldn't listen to me. You

had to run off and hitch your wagon to that big-eared wop. I want you to look me in the eye, you cauliflowered piece of elephant crap, and tell me I told you so." Doc folded his arms across his chest and squinted up at Hans.

"Doc, you told me so. I should have listened to you," Hans said with a hint of a smile.

"You're goddamned right you should have. Now look at the kettle of fish you got." He searched Hans's eyes. "I know the man," he said softly. "If he's got nothing else, he's got a code, a code he lives by. And that code has kept him alive all these years. He has neither friend nor foe that he hasn't re-paid in full. It's that simple. He decides both the reward and the punishment. When it's over, it's over. He moves on. But until it's over, you'll need to watch your backside."

"And which one are you, Doc, Lucky's friend or foe?"

Doc considered the question for a long moment before raising his head and smiling. "I'm in Lucky's gray area. I keep him guessing, and that's right where I want that dago."

Hans sensed, as he had before, a history between Doc and Lucky. These two unlikely acquaintances knew each oth-er. Like two street dogs circling one another, they observed each other's territory.

"He knows you'll come here," Doc said with certainty. "He also knows we showmen protect our own. There isn't a roughy, an agent, or a talker in this carnival that would rat you out. You did right coming here. There's no safer place in the country for the time being."

Hans considered Doc's statement for a moment. He thought it strange how such a ragtag band of societal misfits could provide him sanctuary. He nodded his agreement to Doc.

"William," Doc suddenly barked. "Take our armpit-sniffing friend to the bachelor officer's quarters and get him settled. Please," he added politely. "*Table d'hôte*—dinner, as you call it, is at seven. Tomorrow you'll report to Gummy for maintenance duty. You can use those muscles to pull bearings on the Ferris wheel and Tilt-O-Whirl." Doc turned and walked away. Without stopping he called over his shoulder, "By the way, keep a lookout for Blackie. Reba is beside herself."

"She better hope I don't find his black snake ass first," William said, his eyes wide with mock fear. "I'll turn him into licorice drops."

Hans put his arm around William as they headed for the dormitory-looking building beyond the plaza. "You're not afraid of snakes, are you, William?"

"Not them that slithers, Trap. It's the ones with legs that will hurt you."

••••

She came to him in the night as she had each time he closed his eyes. She stood so near he could feel her warmth, smell her nakedness. His heart raced with anticipation, his breathing was labored. He could not swallow.

"Trapper," she whispered seductively, her breath warm against his eyelid and cheek as she leaned over him.

He smiled as he allowed himself to slip further into that foggy area between consciousness and sleep.

"Trapper," she whispered again. The heat of her hand caressed his shoulder.

His smile gave way and he felt his brow furrow with confusion. She had never called him Trapper, always Hans. He could smell the gin on her breath. He opened his eyes.

"Have you seen Blackie?" Reba asked softly, her face only inches from his as she leaned over his bunk. She was naked.

"What the hell are you doing in my room?" he asked weakly as he struggled to sit up.

I work here. Don't you remember me, Hans? I'm Robyn, the nurse's aide. I come here mostly on weekends to help with meals and baths and stuff. Mostly stuff," she said as she worked the remote control to place his bed in a sitting position. "Smelly stuff," she added, talking to herself. "I hope I didn't frighten you, but it's time to wake up and have your bath. They'll be serving breakfast soon."

He watched her as she hurried around the room, opening curtains, filling the water pitcher, and hanging up his clothes.

"Have you been to the bathroom this morning, Hans?" She pulled back his covers. "Do you need some help? Can you go by yourself?" She swung his legs from the bed while reaching behind him and pulling him upward. "Are you okay? Can you walk? From what I hear, you can walk better than anybody here. When you've gone to the toilet, we'll see about your bath. Come on, Hans, up you go," she said, pulling him to his feet. "I'm going down the hall to fetch you some fresh towels and linens."

"Robyn, Mrs. Ostler soiled her bed," the shift supervisor said as she passed Robyn in the hall. "They're cleaning her up now. Would you please get her sheets changed before they bring her back to her room?"

"Sure," Robyn said as she did an about-face and headed for Mrs. Ostler's room. She had wanted to study nursing next year at the university but was now beginning to question her career choice. She found herself smelling her hands, sometimes hours after work.

••••

"Hans, are you in there?" Robyn tapped on the bathroom door again. "Hans?"

H ans?" Aimee Pond stood in the open doorway of her small clapboard house, her arms clasped around her shoulders in an attempt to fend off the morning cold. She was in her bathrobe. "It's Sunday morning. What are you doing here?"

His breath escaped in slow surges of cloudy vapors barely rising in the subzero temperature. He stood on the shoveled walkway at the foot of the steps. They stared at each other.

The phone began to ring from somewhere behind her. "Don't move," she said sternly while pointing a finger at him. She turned and started back into the house, stopped, then quickly walked back to Hans. "Come in, Hans, while I get that. It's freezing out here. I've just made coffee." The phone continued to ring. She slipped her arm through his and escorted him into the hallway.

"No, no he's fine," she said, speaking into the cordless phone. "I'll warm him up and drive him back in a little while. Tell Robyn it's not her fault. Call off the dogs. All right, see you shortly." She pushed a button and then slipped the phone into the pocket of her robe. "I'm glad you came by, Hans," she said as she positioned herself in front of him. "I want to talk with you."

She took his coat in the hallway and then led him into the kitchen. Sam Dawson stood with his back to the sink, sipping coffee from a mug cupped in his hands.

Sam had shown up at Aimee's the night before and told her he had more questions about spirit houses and Ojibwe burial customs. He had been unsure of his motivation and had allowed his curiosity to override his better judgment. His hesitancy was obvious. As a result, Aimee kept Sam at arm's length. They spent most of the night working on the computer, researching Hans Gottlieb, and talking with Sam's daughter, Sidney, who followed Sam's advice and said nothing about their investigations into Sophie Mickelson's background. Sam had retired to his travel trailer, which Aimee had allowed him to park in her driveway so he could attend to L2.

"Morning, Hans," Sam said, a curious smile on his face. "Funny, we were just talking about you."

Sam liked Hans. The old man asked for nothing. Unlike so many of the people in their nineties that Sam had met, Hans never complained or fished for sympathy for his aches and pains, loved ones lost, or his plight in life. He seemed to fade in and out of conscious reality, catching himself, and abruptly becoming silent as he searched his listener's face for understanding. Sam was unsure of what Hans could hear, so he kept verbal conversation to a minimum and used pantomime to convey simple thoughts. Mostly he just listened. He smiled and nodded, conveyed surprise, displeasure, and agreement when he listened to the always disparate and sometimes incoherent statements that occasionally flowed from Hans's lips.

Hans's son, Will, on the other hand, yelled at a decibel level that caused Sam to grimace in pain. He was patronizing and condescending, always quick to correct rather than attempt to understand. Sam was unsure how he felt about Will. He neither liked nor disliked the man and he believed the feeling was mutual. It was obvious, however, that Will was attracted to Aimee and he seemed unconcerned, or perhaps did not notice, that Sam was too.

"Coffee, Hans?" Sam asked in a normal voice, pointing at his mug. The old man gazed back at him through cloudy eyes and then began searching the kitchen floor, looking to each of the corners.

"She's in the trailer," Sam gestured with his thumb over his shoulder toward the kitchen window where the Airstream totally blocked the view. "Aimee, Nurse Pond, has a cat that's not very fond of large, smelly dogs."

Aimee helped Hans out of his overshoes while Sam poured him a cup of coffee. She busied herself at the counter without speaking, slicing banana nut bread and arranging it neatly on a small plate. "It's not much," she said, sweeping her arm outward, "but it's home. It suits an old maid like me fine." She looked around the kitchen and suddenly felt self-conscious of the eclectic collection of meaningful junk that made her comfortable when alone but embarrassed when with company. The entire house was like that, she thought, a neatly arranged hodgepodge of mismatched furniture and decorations that were important to her and no one else. She thought it strange that she felt no embarrassment about her home in front of Sam. She slid the plate of banana bread toward Hans. "I don't have many gentleman callers." She glanced nervously at Sam. "Actually, before you guys showed up, I didn't have any gentleman callers at all. It's a shame we don't have Fuller Brush men anymore. I bought a Eureka vacuum cleaner a few years ago because the guy promised to come back periodically with bags and attachments. I have a lifetime supply of Eureka stuff." She pushed the plate even closer to him. "Try the coffee, Hans. It's a gourmet blend, not like the institutional coffee we serve at the home."

Hans looked down at the mug in front of him, but made no attempt to pick it up.

"So, what brings you out on a cold morning like this?" she asked, squinting over the coffee mug she held to her face. "Did you come to hear more about our research into the life and times of Hans Gottlieb? You know, it's funny. I know more about you, a complete stranger, than I do about my own family. Not because I didn't want to know about them, it was just that I never took the time to find out." She looked at Sam. They'd had a similar conversation the previous evening. "I don't remember my father. He disappeared in 1954. I hadn't even started school yet. My mother died when I was fifteen. When you're that age, you don't ask those types of questions. You don't care. Now I care and there's no one to ask. My mother's people have been gone for decades. My father's people had a life expectancy of less than thirty years and politely avoided the half-breed kid who came to live with them. You didn't know that, did you, Hans? I favor my mother, but I'm part Ojibwe. Everybody in Deep Lake knows it. Why'd I come back here, you ask? I don't know. Roots, I guess. It's where I came from. You've got to stop asking so many questions, Hans," she smiled. "You didn't come here to talk about me. Your coffee is getting cold."

Hans glanced down again at the mug in front of him.

"Hans, do you remember a guy by the name of Ralph McCready?" Sam asked suddenly.

Hans looked at Sam blankly.

"Ralph wrestled for Oklahoma State—it was A&M in 1928," he corrected. I don't know how you could remember someone you were only on the mat with for nineteen seconds. It was the very first NCAA Wrestling Tournament. You didn't have to travel far; it was in Ames. I went through the brackets for each weight class and never found a faster fall than two-and-a-half minutes. You won the NCAA heavyweight title in '28. You took gold in the '28 Olympics in Amsterdam and again in 1932 in Los Angeles. I saw a picture of you in the *Los Angeles Times.* You were posing with Johnny Weissmuller and Maureen O'Sullivan. In 1934 you took on the World Heavyweight Champion in boxing, Max Baer, in a publicity stunt in Saint Louis. What were you thinking, Hans? The guy had killed two men in the ring. It should have been like taking a knife to a gunfight, but you managed to humiliate him, pinning him in the first round. A year later in '35 you won wrestling's World Heavyweight Championship in Cincinnati." Sam took a sip from his mug, but he never took his eyes off Hans.

Aimee lowered her head and leaned across the table. "And then you disappeared," she said softly. "I think you resurfaced a couple years later as the Masked Marvel."

His eyes shot back to hers.

"It was mostly exhibitions in the Southwest and even Mexico. But I'm pretty sure it was you." Aimee glanced at Hans's untouched coffee. "The heyday of modern professional wrestling was just beginning and you dropped off the face of the earth. Was it because of what happened to that guy in Cincinnati, the Mighty Angus MacGregor?"

With both hands Hans slowly brought the coffee mug to his lips. His knarred and misshaped fingers trembled. He said nothing but continued to look at her.

"I know it was the Depression," Sam said. "But there must have been opportunities for you. You were a great athlete. Was it because you saw the direction professional wrestling was going? Gorgeous George, Wild Billy Wicks, 'Classy' Freddie Blassie, and that Monroe fella, Sputnic Monroe, were all just kids. They were ten or fifteen years away from transforming the sport into what it is today. Did you see that coming and decide to get out rather than become a spectacle?"

Hans's head rolled slightly backward and his eyes seemed to focus on something distant.

"But you were already a spectacle," Aimee said, answering Sam's question. "You wore a mask, for crying out loud. When you weren't beating up drunken amateurs along the carnival circuit, you were wrestling fixed matches in exhibition halls and bars." She paused and delicately wiped her fin-

ger around the rim of her coffee mug. "You were the missing link in the evolution of professional wrestling, Hans. A
legitimate athlete turned showman....Try the banana bread."

He looked at the plate in front of him.

It was Sam's turn. "You were still a young man, early
thirties, when you went to work for the railroad in 1941.
That was the same year you filed for a marriage license in
Muscatine, Iowa. Did you decide to settle down?" Sam
stepped forward and took a slice of banana bread from the
plate in front of Hans. "War was on the horizon," he said
loudly, unsure of what Hans could hear. "The economy was
starting to pick up, especially for railroads. Did you see the
war coming? Were you looking for an occupational deferment? Is that why you quit wrestling and went to work on
the railroad?"

The telephone rang again. Aimee pulled it from her robe
pocket and looked at it as if she had never seen one before.
She scowled and said, "Excuse me."

Aimee took the phone into the hallway. "Yes, he's still
here. We'll be along shortly. No, I'm fine." There was a long
pause. "Give her twenty milligrams of Omeprazole a half
hour before lunch and keep her bed elevated. After lunch
give her a hundred fifty milligrams of Ranitidine. I'll do the
scribe when I come in with Hans."

Hans shuffled through the doorway behind her, turned
left, and proceeded down the hall to the bathroom. Sam
watched as Hans stopped briefly to look at the small drawing of a nude woman that hung crookedly in the hallway, the
same drawing Sam stared at each time he went by.

"No, no, tell her she's not having a heart attack. It's just indigestion, for crying out loud. Don't call Doc Payson unless you want to do all the paperwork. I'll have a look at her when I get there. All right, see you in a little while." She hung up the phone. "Just once I'd like to have an entire weekend off," she said, smiling at Sam. "The administrator told me she would not approve any overtime. I'm tired of donating nights and weekends to Whispering Pines. I know how lucrative the business is. The corporate officers in Los Angeles are raking in the profits at the expense of the people who keep the doors open." They heard the toilet flush.

Hans came shuffling back up the hallway. Aimee stared at him curiously. "Have a seat, Hans. We need to get your galoshes on and get you back to the home. Mrs. Gruen thinks she's having a heart attack. We'll continue our walk down memory lane later. I want to know why you never told your children about your wrestling past. Did your wife know? Why the big secret? I don't know what you're hiding, but I aim to find out. You're almost a hundred years old, Hans. Nobody cares anymore."

Timberlane County, Minnesota—2007
Day 7, 2:20 p.m.

Nobody cares anymore. Is that what you think?" Will Gottlieb said into his cell phone. "That's simply not true, Nurse Pond. Look, you and I somehow got off on the wrong foot when we first met. Do you think it would be possible for us to start over and perhaps communicate civilly with one another?...Good, that's a start. Yes, I'm sure you're quite busy. I'm glad I caught you at your office. I wasn't sure you'd be there on a Sunday afternoon....I think having this conversation later is a wonderful idea. Shall we say seven, over dinner? I'm about fifty miles north of Brainerd on my way to Deep Lake. I flew into Saint Paul this afternoon and rented a car....Why so surprised?...No, don't transfer me to the front desk to schedule an appointment. I don't know what my schedule is tomorrow....I'm sorry? You're breaking up, Nurse Pond," he lied. "I'll meet you at the Iron Range Inn just down the road from the Motel 6 at seven. I look forward to—" He pushed the end button and hung up. He smiled.

••••

The Iron Range Inn had been built during the Deep Lake expansion. The city council had listened to a fast-talking developer from the Twin Cities who convinced them if they built it, they would come. The term "they" was never defined and everyone seemed to have their own vision, all of which involved free-spending tourists. An eighteen-hole golf course, an indoor water park, two hundred rooms, a convention center, and a supposed five-star restaurant with a rustic mining motif comprised the most underutilized, ill-conceived development in Minnesota history. It was for sale.

Aimee arrived at seven. She had struggled with what to wear, angry that she had agreed to meet with someone after hours. In the end she decided it was a business meeting and chose a navy blue suit. Heels and a single strand of pearls gave her the professional look she desired. She wore her shoulder-length gray hair down. Will Gottlieb had impressed her as being an uncaring, self-centered jerk. She had treated him rudely both times they had spoken and deservedly so. He was handsome, smart, and successful, but there was something about this guy that just rubbed her the wrong way—aside from his threats of contacting the Minnesota Board of Examiners. She had not had dinner with a man in a real restaurant in more than three years and resented that it would be with someone she disliked.

"Nurse Pond," Will said as he approached her in the lobby. "It's great to see you again."

"Doctor Gottlieb," she said, extending her hand. He too wore a navy wool blazer. Tan slacks and a light blue dress shirt, open at the neck, gave him a professional yet relaxed appearance.

"I made a reservation, but it looks as though we didn't need one," he said, guiding her by the elbow toward the Tipple restaurant at one side of the lobby.

When the waitress came to take their drink order they both declined, asking for hot tea instead. Aimee decided it was irrelevant for her to tell him she was a teetotaler.

"If you don't mind me saying, Nurse Pond, you look really nice this evening."

Aimee cocked her head slightly and her eyes narrowed. "I do mind you saying that, Doctor Gottlieb. This is a business meeting and your comment is inappropriate. And by the way, that little trick with your cell phone was equally sophomoric. What exactly is it that you want to discuss that couldn't wait until tomorrow?"

Will shook his head and smiled. "Wow! Is it me or is it you?" He leaned forward and said, "Why is it that you and I can't be in the same room for more than five minutes without totally pissing each other off?"

The waitress brought their tea and asked if they were ready to order.

"Could you give us a few more minutes, please?" Will asked.

"You look really nice this evening, Aimee," the waitress said.

"Thanks, Linda. How are Larry and the kids?"

"They're fine. I'll give you some more time. I'd tell you about the specials, but they're not. I'll be back."

"You see, she agrees with me," Will said as he picked up his menu.

"Answer my question, Doctor Gottlieb. Why are we having this meeting?"

"Did you have trouble choosing what to wear this evening?"

"Excuse me?" she said, her anger growing.

"How many outfits did you try on before deciding on business attire? Your feet must be killing you in those pointy-toed high heels. You wore your hair down rather than up. Your nails are freshly painted and match your lipstick perfectly. Your mascara, eye shadow, and makeup are flawless. It must have taken you close to an hour to prepare yourself for this business meeting."

"Your point is?"

"My point is that I recognized your efforts and paid you a compliment. Accept it and move on, for Christ's sake. What's good here?" he said, holding up the menu.

"Nothing," she said, staring at him intently. "Nothing's good here. That's why the place is empty." Aimee looked at her watch. "The diner is open until ten, and thank you for the compliment," she said without smiling.

"You're welcome," Will said, placing a five dollar bill on the table for Linda.

••••

They sat in the corner booth of the empty diner. Green plastic baskets lined with grease-stained paper held the remains of their pork tenderloin sandwiches and French fries. The conversation had been polite, mostly about Aimee's frustration with the lack of security at Whispering Pines and not knowing if any progress was being made in the investigation of Sophie Mickelson's murder. Both had removed their jackets, and Will had rolled up the sleeves of his shirt to avoid the puddles of ketchup that decorated his basket. He had tactfully avoided discussing his concern for the safety of his father, based on Aimee's hit-and-run responses from previous conversations.

"Anyway, May 12 is commencement and my last time to wear the silly robe and funny hat," Will said. "I'm on a nine-month contract, so I'll be paid through the summer, but my obligations to the university are over when the last student crosses the stage. I've got a couple of grad students who'll drag it out until December, but for the most part I'll be free at last, free at last," he smiled broadly. "Every day will be Saturday," he added with his eyebrows raised and eyes large with anticipation.

"The fact that I'm envious tells me that I'm getting close to making the same decision," Aimee said. "But I'm nowhere near as old as you are," she said, smiling. "It will be years before I can draw Social Security."

"Your time will come, Nurse Pond."

"Aimee. You can call me Aimee," she smiled.

"And you can call me Doctor Gottlieb, lest you forget your station in life."

They both laughed.

"Aimee, I've thought a lot about the things you said during my last visit."

"About you being a heartless, pompous prick and all," she said, leaning forward, a toothy grin on her face.

"I especially liked the part where you thought it was a shame my mother didn't drown me at birth. That was good," he said, shaking his head. "Yes, I've thought about those things and more. Some of your admonitions turned out to be revelations that have been haunting me ever since you slapped me across the face with them. You're right. I don't have a clue as to who my father is and I wish to correct that."

Aimee had not said a word about Sam's and her research on his father's past. "Sometimes we need to be careful what we wish for, Doctor Gottlieb."

"It takes a lot to surprise me at my age. And please call me Will," he said. "My biggest regret is that I waited too long to take an interest in him as a person, not just as my father. I'm not sure how cognizant he is. It's like I'm running a race against his dementia—"

"I'm not sure of his condition," Aimee interrupted. "It's not Alzheimer's. He shows some signs of age-related dementia, but it could be depression or a combination of both. I don't think he's disoriented, even though he showed up at my place today."

Will raised his eyebrows in concern.

"He's sneaky about it. He watches and waits, calculates his escapes. That's behavior you don't see in someone with moderate or severe dementia. He handles daily tasks like getting dressed, eating, and going to the bathroom just fine. His behavior isn't really disruptive and when he has demonstrated aggressive behavior, it was simply an instinctive response, not hostile. He never seems agitated or irritable. He seems confused at times, but it's as though he's awakening from a dream." She looked directly at Will. "It's as though he prefers the past and he goes there almost at will in a sort of self-induced trance or sleep. I'm really thinking it's more depression than anything else. People who are depressed often seek relief through sleep and can do so almost on cue."

"But why is he depressed?" Will asked. "He never showed signs of depression when I was growing up. Is it purely clinical, based on neurochemical imbalances?"

"Perhaps, but I think it's something else." Aimee slipped the straw from her cherry Coke into her mouth and drank. "I think he's a man with a mission. There's some underlying purpose for his being here."

"That makes two of us," he said, looking directly into her eyes.

Aimee did not respond immediately. She studied his face for a moment and then leaned forward over the table. "Will, I'm a fifty-seven-year-old spinster. There's a reason for that."

He straightened in astonishment.

"No, I'm not a lesbian," she smiled. "Let's be honest here. I'm well beyond middle age, unless I'm planning to live to be a hundred and fourteen. I've lived alone for so long that everything has to be my way. In case you haven't noticed, I'm short-tempered with an acerbic tongue and I don't look that good naked anymore. I take care of old people all day long. I'm not looking to take care of another one when I come home in the evening. I'd be lying if I said I wasn't flattered. But frankly, I'm not interested in a personal relationship with you. Where the hell were you thirty years ago when I needed the company of something other than a cat?"

Will smiled nervously and looked down at the table. "When I said I, too, was a man on a mission, I meant that my underlying purpose was to bring Dad home to Iowa and spend time with him, learn who he really is."

Aimee looked toward the door of the diner. "This is awkward," she said finally. "I thought you—"

"I'm kidding you, Aimee," he said, cutting her off. "The only thing awkward is my feeble attempt at humor and how to balance the competing emotions about what my real mission is. I don't like admitting that my father might be the excuse I needed to see you again. He's very important to me. But I'd be lying if I said I wasn't attracted to you. The problem is I can't figure out why I'm attracted to you. And yes, you're ill-tempered and rude and I'm pretty sure I don't want to see you naked. But I like being around you. I'm comfortable around you, and I can't say that about many people. Maybe we could just take it one day at a time and see what happens."

Aimee looked at the 7Up clock on the wall. It was 9:50. The boombox on the shelf between the kitchen and the lunch counter sounded a bouncy salsa tune. The waitress was filling saltshakers and the Mexican cook looked out from the tiny kitchen.

Aimee met Will's eyes. "I'm glad you're comfortable around me, Doctor Gottlieb. Sort of like a dog that you're pretty sure won't bite."

"That's not an analogy I would use."

"Look, I've got work tomorrow. Normally I would thank you for a lovely evening, but I'm not sure it was. What I am sure of, however, is that this conversation is over."

TIMBERLANE COUNTY, MINNESOTA—2007
DAY 8, 8:37 A.M.

S am focused his camera on the bullet-riddled frame that once encircled the radiator. Bulbous headlights stared vacuously into the forest's darkness, empty sockets rimmed with chrome. The faceted lamps had been shot out decades earlier. Bullet holes were small reminders of their fate. The honeycombed radiator had offered little resistance to the tiny missiles that had punctured it. Rusted fenders gracefully arced upward from the forest floor, still attempting to protect the rotted rubber surrounding the wood-spoked wheels. The running boards had sunk beneath the forest's litter. A spruce tree, crooked and leaning, had grown between the front bumper and right wheel well. Louvers, like gill slits, ran vertically on each side of the car's tapered snout, a hood unraised in decades. A small gold emblem just below the radiator cap had been the target. The word proclaiming the model of the car had not survived the hail of gunfire or the years. All that was recognizable was the image of two spread-winged birds, falcons perhaps, at opposite corners of the emblem. The camera's fake shutter opened and closed. It was a comforting sound to his sleep-deprived brain. The sheriff's accusations crawled beneath his skin like a parasitic worm. He needed this distraction.

Sam had followed the overgrown logging road past the spirit houses, searching for the vehicle shot full of holes that

Aimee had mentioned. Old abandoned cars, like old abandoned people, had character. Their rusted exteriors belied their once opulent interiors where, long ago, real people had enjoyed the adventures unique to automobiles. Whether it was sexual discovery in the oversized luxury of the backseat, or simply flinging empty beer bottles out the window on the way to the town dump to shoot rats, it was a place where memories were made. Sam smiled as he remembered his first car, a 1971 Toyota Land Cruiser, powder blue with a white top. He had driven it all through high school and college, traversing every trail leading to a trout stream along the front range of Colorado. There was no backseat to speak of, just two little jump seats, but he and Marcie had made do. He had never told Sidney of her Land Cruiser conception, but was tempted to whenever she poked fun at his '53 Willys Station Wagon, which had a remarkable resemblance to the Toyota.

••••

The sun's angle was just right when he backtracked to the clearing. The spirit houses seemed more three-dimensional than when he had passed through earlier on his way to the abandoned car. Tiny ice crystals were suspended in the shafts of sunlight that angled down through the trees overhead. The light sparkled like delicate fireworks above the moss-covered structures. Sam worked quickly to take advantage of Mother Nature's display. He envisioned a separate section of the Minnesota book devoted to these unique graves. He thought he had seen every type of tombstone invented and carved, but these were truly different. Simple yet original, they represented a culture he had not thought to include in his odyssey of discovery. The Minnesota book would be different. He was thinking "jacket photo" as he framed his last shot.

The crystalline fireworks had suddenly given way to a bland evenness of light that seemed to take away the mystery. The sky had turned dark gray to the northwest. Change was in the air. The north woods would soon yield to snow and penetrating frost, short days, and long cold nights. He wished he could capture the silence on film. Sam took a deep breath and blinked his acknowledgment that there was no film. How could he capture sunlight on the side of a house or the silence of a cold forest when he didn't understand how his camera worked? Pixels were the fairy dust of his profession. Sidney and the next generation seemed to accept technology without question, but he struggled. His resistance was now a source of embarrassment to him. Extinction was his destiny.

Sam smiled at the juxtaposition of his camera, cell phone, and computer with the two L-shaped brazing rods that dangled from his belt. "And now for the real magic show," he said aloud as he pulled the brass welding rods from his belt with the flourish of a medieval knight.

A rancher, Vern, with an MS degree in physics and a keen interest in the immigrant trails that traversed Wyoming, had introduced Sam to the concept of grave dowsing. Unmarked graves littered the westward path of eastern expansionism and Vern had found many of them. Sam had been skeptical but could not deny the results. He could find no scientific basis for witching or divining, and all credible investigations had shown that dowsing was no better than random selection in locating graves. He didn't understand it and couldn't explain it, but neither could he understand or explain ground-penetrating radar, resistivity, conductivity, or magnetometry—all conventional techniques for locating lost graves. He couldn't tell you how his camera worked, but the pictures it produced left little doubt as to its effectiveness. He understood soil coring, rod probing, and formal excavation, but they were invasive and there was no magic involved. The excitement he felt when his rods gently crossed was akin to discovering buried treasure. He had to admit that finding graves in a cemetery was likely. The killjoy scientists who explained it away as chance or unconscious hand or body movements in response to ground surface depressions were the same people who debunked the existence of Santa Claus and the Easter Bunny. Some beliefs are better left alone, he determined.

When Aimee had brought him to her secret place two mornings before, Sam had noticed almost immediately that two of the spirit houses were slightly askew and the uneven forest floor appeared to have surface depressions. With a hip pocket full of engineering flags and a grid pattern in mind, Sam began walking while holding the dowsing rods in front of him. The morning chill had yielded to the warm flush of anticipation.

MISSION, TEXAS—1936

The heavy bass cords of the accordion, a shrill trumpet, and the slap of guitar strings sounded the repetitive melody of Mexican music drifting from Rosalita's on the outskirts of Mission. The Texas clip joint was south of the city limits and owned by the Hidalgo County sheriff's brother. There were no laws. The unwritten rules were enforced by the bouncer. Hans had worked the smoke-filled bar and brothel the two previous seasons when the carnival was in winter camp. The pachuco who normally bounced the joint took a much needed vacation to visit one of his wives in Reynosa. The clientele, mostly Mexican cowboys with a few seasoned enlisted men on leave from Fort Hood, were as hard-boiled as the whores. Guns were rare, but knife fights broke out frequently. Hans never attempted to argue with or physically overpower a man with a knife. Instead, he used a baseball bat. For close-up work, he sometimes relied on the claw hammer that always hung from the hammer loop on his dungarees.

Drunken men bent over dead-hoofer whores on the dance floor and shuffled around, oblivious to the monotonous rhythm of the music, while the women made their financial pitch for sex. Hans hung in the shadows, watching, waiting. His job was to protect the property, the employees, and the patrons, in that order, but not to be so obvious that it stifled the free-spending and often raucous atmosphere.

"Trap," William called from the Rosalita's doorway.

"No shines!" Jesus Hernandez, the bartender, shouted from behind the bar, pointing at William. It was the same warning he issued each time William came to the cantina looking for Hans.

William was careful not to step inside the doorway. He knew the rules. Instead he leaned around the door frame, scanning the smoky room for Hans.

"What's up, William?" Hans said, stepping from the shadows.

"Sorry to bother you at work, Trap, but there's something hinky going on. You know Lefty Coleman, the ride jock for the wheel?"

Hans nodded his acknowledgment of the man who operated the Ferris wheel.

"Lefty's got a friend who's a cinder dick for the railroad," William said. "He came into camp tonight and told Lefty that a couple of goons, togged to the bricks, got off the train in McAllen this afternoon. One of 'em was carrying a case that the dick said looked like it might have a Chicago typewriter in it. He said they looked like button men to him."

"You think they're Lucky's boys?"

"You know well as me that he's put the curse on you. It was just a matter of time before they found you."

"Does Doc know?" Hans said, looking over William's shoulder to the gravel parking lot.

"Everybody knows. Doc's on it like a chicken on a June bug. Those punks won't be able to pass gas without us knowing about it. He sent me. Says I'm not to let you out of my sight. What time you get off?"

"Two o'clock," Hans said.

Two o'clock? No, Dad, it's nine o'clock," Will said as he stood next to his father's bed. "It's nine o'clock in the morning."

Hans looked at him suspiciously. "Why aren't you in school?" he said.

"It's Saturday, Pop. There's no school," Will said, smiling, knowing it was Monday. "As a matter of fact, from now on every day is Saturday. Come on. Get up. Get dressed. I'm taking you out for breakfast. We'll get some real food, something with grease on it."

Will helped his father dress. He studied his dad's feet. Knarred by age and arthritis, the big toes turned inward, overlapped by their next of kin. The nails were a yellowish brown with numerous parallel ridges running their length. Veins were as prominent as tendons. Hans's ankles rattled loosely, the bones vibrating in Will's hands as he pulled up the sweat socks that his father apparently preferred due to the absence of elastic.

••••

Aimee Pond waited for them at the diner. She smiled and fiddled with her coffee cup as Will guided his father to the table.

"Good morning, Nurse Pond," Will said.

"Good morning, Doctor Gottlieb," she said, attempting to sound professional. "Good morning, Hans," she said cheerfully. Her hair was pulled loosely into a ponytail. She wore dark slacks with a knit pullover.

Aimee and Will silently studied the breakfast menu. Hans stared at Aimee. Will ordered a green chili breakfast burrito for his father. Aimee raised her eyebrows but said nothing.

"I've retired, Pop," Will said suddenly. "I've come to take you home—if you like," he added a few seconds later. He remembered the conversation he had with Aimee on his first visit. Unless he had power of attorney or legal guardianship, he could not compel his father to go anywhere.

The food came and Aimee and Will pushed it around their plates without talking. Hans stared at the untouched burrito.

"Is everything okay here?" the waitress said as she poured more coffee into Will's and Aimee's cups.

"Rhonda," Aimee said with an overly pleasant lilt in her voice, "could you please take his burrito, put it in a blender, and puree it? Add enough water so I can get it through the stomach tube I'm going to insert in him after breakfast."

"Sure thing, Aimee. You want me to throw in his coffee?" Rhonda said, totally deadpan. "He ain't touched that either."

"No, the caffeine will keep him awake. I'd just as soon he stays asleep. He's a lot less trouble then."

"Very funny," Will said. "You two are quite the comedy team."

"Excuse me, but green chili? You had that coming," Aimee said.

Rhonda retrieved Hans's plate and hustled behind the counter to the far end of the diner. A minute later she leaned over their table and placed a piece of fresh apple pie in front of Hans, then walked away without saying a word. Hans immediately picked up his fork and began to eat.

"Why not?" Aimee said. "Pie won't kill him."

His unsteady hands worked the fork methodically until only a brownish stain remained on the plate.

"So, what do you think, Pop? Do you want to go home?" Will asked.

Aimee leaned back and looked seriously at Will. "Did you know he liked pie?"

"Can't say as I did," Will said, meeting her gaze. He saw where this was going and attempted to head it off. "But everybody likes pie."

"What else does he like?" Aimee shot back.

"He likes radish sandwiches." Will twisted in his seat. "Hot dinner rolls, buttered, with sliced radishes. Don't do this, Aimee. I'm trying. Stop beating me over the head with it, for Christ's sake."

"I'm sorry," Aimee said, shaking her head. "But I find it absolutely incredible that you don't know what your father did between 1922 when he started high school and 1941 when he went to work for the railroad. Did you ever stop to think about those missing nineteen years?"

"Hell, I don't know what he did from 1945 when I was born to 1963 when I graduated from high school and left home," he said, his anger rising. "There's eighteen years for you to think about," he offered. "As I told you before, he was never there. I'm trying to fill in the blanks now, if you'd just give me a chance."

"Well, let me help you, Doctor. This man with apple pie filling on his shirt was the star player on the state high school championship football team; set a state record in the hundred-yard dash that held for forty-six years; was state high school wrestling champion four years in a row in five different weight classes; went to Iowa State on a wrestling scholarship; was the NCAA champion in 1928; was a two-time Olympian, winning gold medals in Amsterdam in '28 and Los Angeles in 1932; hung around with movie stars; was world heavyweight wrestling champion in 1935; and was billed as the world's greatest carnival wrestler for the rest of the 1930s. He was known as Trapper in his carnival days and as the Masked Marvel when he went professional." She stopped, but did not take her eyes from his. "Those were his athletic accomplishments that anybody with a computer can find out."

Will looked at her blankly. "Are you sure?" he said weakly. "Yes."

"I don't understand. Why would he keep that sort of thing secret? Why would you keep this secret, Pop?"

Aimee did not respond.

"Pop," Will said too loudly, reaching for his father's arm. "Is any of this true?"

Hans looked at his son benignly; a half-smile formed on his lips. He said nothing.

"I haven't a clue as to who he really was," Aimee interrupted. "Besides radish sandwiches and apple pie, what else did he like? What were his dislikes? Who were his friends? Did he like Truman? Did he have a dog?" She turned her gaze to Hans, who watched her intently. "You're not going to tell us, are you? You've purposely kept your past from your family. Why, Hans? What are you hiding?"

"Liebchen," Hans half-whispered.

Both Aimee and Will looked at him, stunned.

"What did you say?" Aimee said.

Hans inhaled slowly and looked out the window, his eyes glassed over with tears.

"His dog," Will said, his voice cracking. "I remember when I was a kid and was begging for a dog, he told me that he had a dog named Liebchen, a dachshund, I believe. I remember it because it was years later when I was in grad school and was taking German, I came across the word. It means lover or sweetheart." He looked at Aimee. "What's going on here?" He shook his head. "Jesus, Aimee, what the hell's going on here? I'm sixty-two years old, I've announced my retirement, and you tell me my father is somebody I don't know?"

"Yes, that's what I'm trying to tell you. That's what I've been saying all along. I see it every day. Our loved ones are people. They had long, rich lives filled with accomplishments and failures, loves and hates, good times and bad times. At best, we only see glimpses of who they really were, snippets represented by an old photograph or a newspaper clipping in a scrapbook. Parents protect their children from what they consider harmful. They concentrate on shaping their children's lives based on the present. They often view their own past as something they want their children to avoid. I see it more in Depression-era people. They don't look back, only forward." She looked at Hans, then back at Will. "I'm sorry for making all this sound like it was your fault, that somehow you didn't care enough to find out. I'm no different. I know virtually nothing of my parents' past and it haunts me. The fact that I've spent more time researching your father's life than my own parents is just as troubling."

"An Olympian?" Will asked, looking into his father's face. "You went to college? Did Mom know any of this?"

Hans turned his gaze to Aimee's, slowly reached over the table, and placed his hand on hers.

"What about Mom, Pop? She knew, didn't she? Why the secret? All those years growing up—you were an automaton, a guy in bibbed overalls who went back and forth, back and forth. Why? Jesus, Pop! You were going to take this to the grave? And what the hell are you doing here? Why come to the north woods of Minnesota? What are you running from?"

"Or," Aimee interrupted softly, "running toward."

"Is that it, Pop? You came here to do something, to get your affairs in order? Did you come here to die? Why here? Why Deep Lake?"

Hans sipped his coffee and looked down at the table.

"How about you tell me, or we go back to Whispering Pines, pack your bag, and head for Iowa this afternoon? You can die there just as easily. We'll put you in the ground right next to Mom. What do you want on your stone? One word comes to mind: Deception. There's your legacy, Pop. I'll put a vase full of plastic flowers on top, fake flowers, just like your fake life."

Hans released Aimee's hand and slowly pushed up the left sleeve of his shirt. The purple flower with green leaves on the inside of his forearm was still there, faded and blurred around the edges, but still there.

S torm clouds rolled in from the northwest, churning masses of moisture-laden air that descended down the back of Sam's neck, sending a chill deep into his core. His mood had turned dark as the sky as he moved deeper into the thick forest surrounding the Ojibwe burial ground. He wished he had brought a compass. It was beginning to snow much harder and the temperature had dropped ten degrees since L2 had disappeared. Moss on the stumps of long-fallen trees indicated he was moving in a southward direction.

"L2!" he yelled, his hands cupped around his mouth. His voice was quickly absorbed by the softness of the dark forest.

"Damn dog," he said between clenched teeth. He had owned two bloodhounds in his life and both of them demonstrated blind allegiance to their noses. There was no turning them off a scent once they began tracking. Elle used to give voice that clued Sam as to her general direction. But L2 was a silent tracker. He had watched her run into trees as she trotted along, head down with her brow wrinkles flowing over her eyes. A powerful scent had turned her, yanking her by an invisible rope as they made their way along the old logging trail that led back from the spirit houses.

A twig snapped ahead and to his left. Sam stopped and listened, his heart pulsing inside his head. The wet flakes of snow tickled his ears. He hunched up his shoulders to keep the cold from the back of his neck. A flash of movement behind the bristle of trees startled him. "L2?" he questioned weakly. "C'mon girl, let's go."

Her tracks appeared much larger in the fresh dusting of snow. Sam followed them. Again there was movement ahead, but this time to his right. The track he was following suddenly merged with another set and then another and another, all headed in the same direction. Confused, Sam stopped and turned left, then right as he stared at the jumble of tracks. It took a moment for the reality of the situation to seize him, but when it did, it was with the force of a lightning bolt. He could feel the hair on the back of his neck begin to rise. He stopped breathing and listened.

"L2!" he yelled with all the force within him as he began to run in the same direction as the tracks. Sam knew that documented attacks on humans were rare, but wolves were deadly when it came to domestic dogs. He had a vision of the snarling beasts huddled over their kill with bloody muzzles and flattened ears as they pulled steaming viscera from L2's lifeless body.

Ahead the forest's darkness seemed to give way to light where the tracks converged on a trail that led to a clearing. Sam stopped, his chest heaving as he looked toward the mound of fur and blood at the edge of the forest. Bright red against virgin white, the scene looked like a Jackson Pollock canvas stretched over the ground. His arms felt heavy with fear as the flush of grief swept upward over his neck and face, culminating in the burn of tears below his eyes. He stumbled toward the lifeless, blood-soaked body, the butchery animated by the falling snow.

The doe's lifeless, steel-blue eye looked back at Sam with expressive gentleness. But his relief was only temporary. The crunch of a pinecone from the darkness of the forest spun him around with the forceful reminder that danger was imminent. Sam backed slowly away from the kill toward the clearing that he now recognized as a lake. Deep Lake, he guessed. The heavy snowfall limited visibility to less than fifty yards. He stepped toward the dried sedges and small white spruce that extended toward open water. L2 sat obediently in the thick, snow-covered vegetation as if she had been waiting for Sam to return.

"You're in big trouble, you sow," Sam said as he bent over the dog and immediately inspected her for injuries. Blood on her lips and muzzle indicated she had investigated, and perhaps sampled, the venison before being displaced by the wolves who had been driven from their lunch by Sam's noisy arrival. Movement from several points along the tree line indicated the wolves' reluctance to expose themselves as they approached, then avoided the openness of the lake's edge. "This is a fine mess you've gotten us into," Sam whispered as he led L2 by the collar deeper into the tangle of sedges. There appeared to be a path of trampled vegetation that led toward the lake and Sam quickly followed it. Suddenly feeling nauseous, he fought the urge to stop and vomit.

A large, almost black wolf boldly walked into the clearing, its head down as it sniffed the ground that Sam had walked on. Then another lighter-colored animal stepped forward, followed by another and another—the wolves hesitantly gathering their courage to approach the edge of the field of sedges. Sam counted seven of the animals as they darted nervously back and forth along an invisible line that paralleled the lake's shoreline behind him.

L2 planted her feet widely and refused to be dragged any farther toward the water's edge. Sam bent over her and was about to snarl a threat when he nearly toppled forward, dizzy and disoriented. Water filled the depressions under L2's feet. He looked down at his own feet, which were now submerged almost to his ankles. Raising his head, Sam saw the surface rolling between the wolves and him. Like waves on open water, the ground heaved and dipped in an undulating pattern around him. He had motion sickness, the same malaise he suffered from the spin-and-puke rides he used to take Sidney on at Lakeside Amusement Park in Denver. He and L2 were on a floating bog. A mat of sedges and sphagnum moss were all that separated them from the tannic-colored depths of icy water below. "Easy, girl," he said as panic threatened to overtake him. He had no way of knowing the depth of the lake below. It was more of a fear of the unknown that made him shudder. The thought of falling through the tangle of moss and surfacing against the black tentacles of a thick, floating mat of impenetrable vegetation was nightmarish, to say the least.

The wolves appeared to line up in a coordinated effort to make their final assault. Sam had no weapons other than a penknife. His camera was slung around his neck, and the brass dowsing rods hung from his belt. He pulled out the rods and swung them violently over his head in a circular motion. The whirring noise caused seven sets of ears to point forward, then backward as fear threatened their resolve. Still they maintained their spacing along the invisible line. "It's the bog, girl," Sam almost smiled. "They're afraid to walk on the bog." He looked down at his feet. The water was now over his ankles. "Me too," he added as he tried to step toward firmer ground. A dark hole appeared next to him. He could see the edges of the sphagnum mat. It was maybe eighteen inches thick floating above the inky unknown. L2 snuffled loudly as she leaned hesitantly over the watery abyss.

The dark wolf, large and scarred, broke ranks and trotted away toward the tree line. The other wolves quickly followed suit. They melded into the forest verdure with the ease of fog lifting off water.

Sam stood motionless, watching. He waited. His feet were numb and his fingers tingled with cold as he went to separate the dowsing rods before slipping them through his belt. The rods unexpectedly pulled toward each other, crossing forcefully. Sam yanked them apart and held them outward over the dark hole in the bog. Again they crossed, almost harshly. His breathing was shallow and he was unable to move at the realization that someone was below him.

Mission, Texas—1936

He traced the edges of the tattoo with his finger as the phone rang on the other end of the line.

"Gloria, it's Hans....I'm fine. I know you've been worried. I just got off work and I really needed to hear your voice. Sorry it's so late....I'm with Doc." He looked around the tidy room that served as Doc's office at the compound. "I changed my mind about California. I needed some time to think, someplace safe....Yes, I needed the extra cash too."

Not expecting the next question, he hesitated.

"I'm in charge of customer relations for an exclusive club, a swanky place....Uh-huh. Customer relations sounds better than bouncer. It's just temporary. It'll buy me some time to think while I figure out what my next move is.... About you, about us, about where we go from here. I miss you." He stared at the red clay tiles on the floor. "I miss you too, and yes, I know it's three in the morning.

"Look, Gloria, things are heating up a little down here and it might be best if I hit the road for a while. I was wondering if you'd like to meet me somewhere?" He realized he had said the wrong thing and attempted to cover it. "No, no, it's getting too hot down here. It was over ninety again today. I can't take that kind of heat....No, it's not Lucky....No, nothing has happened. Nothing is going to happen. But it would be best if I didn't stay in one place too long, especially someplace where they know to look for me.

"Are you still there?"…"I know you have responsibilities.…Your practice needs you. So does your mother.…I understand," he said, the disappointment evident in his voice. "It was just a thought.

"Gloria? Are you still there?…Boone," he said quickly. "When I was at Ames, my coach let me use a little cottage on the outskirts of Boone. He'd inherited it from some aunt. It was beautiful, sits on a creek surrounded by hardwoods, a place I could get my mind straight before a big match. I could call him.…You bet. The Chicago and North Western goes right through town. Let me put it together," he said excitedly. "When I get there, I'll call you. That'll give me time to get the place cleaned up and buy some groceries. I've got a little dough. I'll see about getting a boiler, maybe a Ford. There are plenty of high-gear roads in the area. We can see the sights. Don't say no. I'll pick you up at the station."

I 'll pick you up at the station?" Taneesha said, her voice going falsetto. "Who you gonna meet at the station? 'Meet me at four thirty and don't be late—,'" she sang under her breath. "The Monkees, I think. I'll have to look that one up. You been listening to the oldies station again, Hans?"

"Gloria," he responded clearly.

"Here we go again," she said, rolling her eyes. "I did look that one up. It was a group called Them. A big hit in 1964. Written by Van Morrison, I believe. 'Glaw-ree-yah,'" she sang.

Hans looked at her, his brow wrinkled in confusion.

"Can you drag your boney butt out of the sack? Your son is here again. He and Nurse Pond are the talk of the home, you know. He's a handsome man, your son. I think he's been making eyes at Nurse Pond. It's not like she's a dog in heat or nothin'. But you can tell he's been sniffin' around. Maybe they'll hook up and adopt you. Maybe they'll take two or three of the other orphans too. Make my life a lot easier."

Hans followed her with his eyes but made no attempt to get up.

"You know what they do to old men that won't get up, don't you? They carry them out back into the woods and let the wolves have 'em. Then in a couple of days we go out and gather up all the bones, put 'em in a cardboard box, and send them to the 3M Company in Saint Paul. They make glue out of them bones. The kind of glue they put on the flaps of envelopes. Think about that, Hans, next time you're lapping the back of an envelope. Yum, yum, tastes like old Mrs. Ostler with a hint of poop."

Hans turned his head to look out the window. The boughs of the whispering pines sagged beneath the rounded pillows of snow that clung to each branch.

"Ain't no wolves out there, Hans. I'm just funnin' ya. But there is snakes in your bed. I slip 'em under the covers of those that won't get up in the mornin'."

"Blackie," he said clearly.

"Excuse me?" Taneesha said, turning to face him, her hands on her hips. "What did you just call me?"

Hans stared back at her.

"I don't mind you callin' me William once in a while, but I'll whoop your skinny ass if you start making racial slurs."

He tilted his head and frowned at her.

"Knock, knock," Will said as he opened the door and poked his head into the room.

"You're just in time, Doctor Gottlieb. I was about to twist this old man's head off and spit in his neck for being ugly to me."

"I'm sorry, Taneesha, but you'll have to get in line for that. There are several people ahead of you who want a piece of that old man's hide."

Hans looked at Will, an expression of both surprise and confusion on his face.

"It's Saturday, Pop. There is no school," Will said, heading off the expected question. "Rise and shine, Champ, we've got a busy day ahead. First, I need to establish power of attorney. A local attorney that Aimee, Nurse Pond…," he said, glancing at Taneesha, "knows here in Deep Lake will draw up the papers. Second, we have an appointment with a county judge in Walker this afternoon who will issue a competency ruling declaring you a stubborn old goat and thereby giving me total control over your fraudulent life."

Hans stared at him blankly. There was nothing behind the dullness of his gray eyes that could be mistaken for comprehension.

"Up and at 'em, Pop. We're out of here. You're headed for the state hospital in Independence back in Iowa. They know how to handle troublemakers like you."

"They got wolves in Iowa?" Taneesha asked.

Will looked at her curiously. "No," he said skeptically.

"How 'bout snakes?"

"Yes," Will said, cocking his head.

"Now you're talkin'. I'll fetch his suitcase," Taneesha said, smiling as she opened the closet door.

Will gathered his father's clothes from the closet and laid them on the foot of the bed. "While you're getting dressed, I'll fetch us some breakfast from the cafeteria. We can eat in the room. You might stand a little closer to your razor this morning. Or were you planning to wear a mask to the courthouse?"

Hans reached with both hands to his face and gently ran his fingertips along his cheeks from the tips of his ear lobes to his chin.

Natchitoches, Louisiana—1937

The smooth coolness of the calfskin mask reassured him. The reinforced stitching around the cutouts for his mouth and eyes provided an ominous depth to the shiny black hood stretched tightly over his head and face. William claimed it made him look like a vaudeville actor portraying a Negro by accentuating his lips and the whiteness of his eyes, a stereotype that William thought degrading. But Hans believed it provided a Halloween-like creepiness while giving him the anonymity that he needed. The nameless man behind the mask could inflict pain without remorse and incite the crowd without shame. He checked the tightness of the drawstring at the back of his neck and traced his fingers along the laces that ran from his crown to the base of his skull. He was ready.

"Ladies and gentlemen," the announcer proclaimed slowly from the center of the ring. He gave the usual ballyhoo that echoed from the cavernous depths of the small-town armory.

Hans had lost track of the towns, sometimes the states. The night before it was Nacogdoches, Texas, and tonight it was Natchitoches, Louisiana. It smelled the same—sweat and dust. It sounded the same, the agitated anticipatory rumble of men looking for a fight, the squeal of the public address system, and the bark of kids hawking peanuts and popcorn. The clems thought it might be rigged, but they didn't care.

It was the Depression and life was rigged. There was no control. They were just along for the ride. Someone in Washington would determine where they were going. It was the same for the combatants, performers who trudged from one town to the next hoping to heal the cuts that would open night after night, spilling the blood that energized the crowd. Promoters determined where they were going and the outcome. They did their work from an office using a telephone. Newspaper ads, handbills, rent agreements, concessions, day laborers, police, medical, and all the other preparations were made over the line, sometimes over the wire, from afar. The whole kit and caboodle was greased.

"And in this corner, our challenger from a tiny island between Oakland and San Francisco in the Golden State, weighing two hundred thirty pounds, the Masked Marvel, masked because he skipped out on his rent and the landlord keeps putting his picture in the post office."

There was no response from the crowd. They didn't care if he was from the moon. They wanted entertainment. Hans ran his hand over his paunch. He had added ten pounds in the last three months. He ate incessantly to overcome the boredom of long days on the road. That, added to winter-camp Mexican food and inactivity, had made him a little cushy around the edges. He inhaled and sucked in his stomach. "Tomorrow," he whispered to himself.

"And in this corner!" the announcer yelled with a sweep of his arm, "the current heavyweight champion of the world, from Wall Street, New York, the man with more property than God, the banker with rancor, the mortgage monster, the property pirate, the Fore-close-zer!"

The crowd came to their feet and booed as Bill Ganzel strutted around the ring in his three-piece suit, tipping his creased fedora and waving a briefcase. Saturday-night white shirts flashed brightly from beneath bibbed overalls and work jackets at the edge of the ring spotlights. Squinting his eyes, Hans blurred the angry crowd to a foggy black-and-white shoreline with waves crashing over rocks. He saw himself as a rabbit on a canvas-colored, sandy beach, dark cliffs looming above him, the tide eagerly consuming the earth beneath him.

Joe Turner, the referee, called them to the center of the ring and pretended to give them the usual instructions and warnings. With a finger stuck alternately in each of their faces, Joe spelled out the rules for the evening poker game and whose responsibility it was to bring beer and snacks.

"Why are one-eyed jacks always wild?" Bill snarled as he reached beyond Joe and grabbed Hans by the neck of his cape.

Joe pushed Bill back and pointed, directing him toward his corner.

"Because if they weren't wild, you dumb jackass, you'd never have more than a pair of deuces," Hans shot back. Hans smiled to himself beneath his dark hood. He liked Bill Ganzel. After three months on the road, they viewed each other as veteran dance partners. There was no need to choreograph their routines, no need to practice. Subtle signals telegraphed each wrestler's next move, and responses were automatic. A camel clutch, chicken wing, crucifix armbar, wheelbarrow, or pumphandle were easily recognized and performed theatrically. After nine rounds of gut-wrenching punishment, the Masked Marvel would make an amazing comeback in the tenth with the Forecloser screaming for mercy as the referee tapped him out amid the bloodthirsty screams of the avenging audience. Again, justice would prevail and the crowd would receive vicarious pleasure, however brief, from the symbolic beating of the Wall Street mortgage banker. The Masked Marvel had, once again, stood up to the mighty Goliath and made the world right.

After the match William placed Hans's cape over his shoulders and wrapped a towel around his neck. "Don't look now, Trap, but there's a couple of goons hanging out next to the locker-room door."

"How do you know?"

"'Cause the way they's dressed."

Hans stole a look in their direction. Two no-necks stood on either side of the doorway to the Armory locker room. They were dressed to the nines with their hats pulled down to their eyebrows.

"I told you not to look," William scolded.

"Lucky's boys," Hans whispered. "Probably dispatched out of Kansas City."

"Ain't they ever gonna give up?"

"They've got a code," Hans said, remembering what Doc had told him about Lucky and his philosophy of always paying back in full, either friend or foe. "When will this end?"

"I got an idea, Trap," William said, looking into Hans's eyes. "You mingle with the crowd till I come back for ya."

Before Hans could question him, William had slipped off into the throng of people milling around the ring and was making his way toward the main exit. Hans ducked between the ropes and stepped down to the arena floor.

"That was some beatin' you gave that ole boy," a man with a long white beard said, staring up at Hans's masked face. "'Course he deserved it and then some," he added. "When you get done with them bankers, I'd like to see you take on Bruno Hauptmann and then maybe that Hitler fella from Germany. Now that'd be somethin' to see."

Hans never spoke to the fans. Instead, he looked intently at the man, then nodded. He reluctantly accepted his role of doling out vigilante justice to all the evildoers of the world. In an instant he saw the future of professional wrestling and it paralyzed him with sadness. He was, in part, responsible for the demise of athletic exhibition and the birth of wrestling's theatrical sideshow. How could he argue that, he thought, as he stood there dressed in a cape and hood.

"All right, Mr. Marvel," William said as he slipped his arm through Hans's, "we need to get to the locker room right away."

"But—"

"No buts, Trap. It's greased. Just come with me," William said, steering Hans through the crowd toward the locker room and the two thugs posted on either side.

Hans could feel the goons staring holes through his mask as he passed within inches of them.

William pushed the locker room door open and said loudly: "You get showered while I pack up things and bring the car 'round back."

Someone stepped from behind the door, startling Hans, who immediately assumed a defensive posture.

"Easy, Trap," William whispered. "It's Pete Harrison."

Pete Harrison was one of three advance men who would arrive a day ahead of the wrestlers to do setup. Ten years younger than Hans, Pete was a well-proportioned, redheaded Nebraska farm boy who was not afraid of hard work. Pete was wearing Hans's back-up outfit, complete with cape and mask.

"Out the back, Trap," William whispered. "Quick," he said, pointing to the back door that opened to the alley. "There's a car waiting for you. We'll catch up with you in Texarkana."

"But—"

"Get," William said. His eyes were wide and his jaw set. He pointed toward the back door.

"My clothes...where's my grip?"

"Here's your suitcase," William said, handing Hans the scuffed leather bag.

"Thanks, William," he said, pausing to look him in the eyes.

Y ou're welcome," Taneesha said as she placed the
suitcase on the foot of his bed. "And how many
times I gotta tell you my name's not William?"

Hans looked down at his misshapen feet hanging over
the edge of the bed. The yellowed nails needed trimming.

"Now get out of that bed and get dressed. Your son
will be back shortly with some breakfast. And then I'll be rid
of you, you old goat. You've been more trouble than you're
worth. They'll know what to do with you in Iowa."

Hans lifted his head and turned toward Taneesha.

"That's right," she said. "Don't look so surprised. Didn't
you hear your son say they was takin' you back to Iowa?
Soon as they get that judge in Walker to say you are incompetent. That won't take long. You're as crazy as a loon. Now
get washed up and dressed. Don't forget to shave too," she
added as she headed for the door. She turned and looked
at him affectionately. "You'll fit right in there. You know
what Iowa stands for, don't ya, Hans? Idiots Out Wandering
Around. I-O-W-A. Get it? Iowa," she repeated.

BOONE COUNTY, IOWA—1936

Iowa," she said again. "Who would have guessed it was so beautiful?" The early spring breeze teased the hair around her face. Gloria turned to the north, then to the south, looking up and down the length of the Des Moines River from the hill high above it. The skeletons of dark hardwoods covered the rough sea of light green hills on either side. Occasionally a white steeple pierced the dark tangle. Beyond the wooded river corridor, a patchwork of green and black squares formed the breadbasket of the heartland.

"I used to come up here before a big match in order to put things in the right perspective," Hans said. "Looking at this made everything else seem small and unimportant."

"Does it still work for you?" she asked, pulling a strand of hair from the corner of her mouth, her eyes searching his.

"Being here with you makes everything go away," he said, taking a step closer to her. "I wish we could stay here for the rest of our lives, that this moment would last forever."

"For a guy who beats up people for a living, you can also be the most romantic person I've ever met." She smiled and reached out to him. They kissed tenderly and then embraced, her feet dangling off the ground as he pulled her into his massive chest.

"What's for dinner?" he said, smiling inches from her face.

"Is that why you brought me to Iowa? Come to Boone and cook for you?"

"Among other things," he said, opening the door to the well-used '34 Ford Coupe he had managed to rent from the Ford dealer in Boone. "I'll cook tonight. We can take turns. I bought plenty of groceries and a couple blocks of ice. There's no electricity to the cottage. The joint is snazzy in a rustic sort of way. You'll love it."

Gloria gave him a sideways look dripping with doubt as she slid into the car.

••••

The sun was setting as they pulled into the clearing between the cottage and Sauk Creek. Gloria leaned forward, her mouth partially open.

The cottage was made of quarried limestone blocks, most of which were now covered in ivy. Rough-hewn timbers defined the windows and doorway. The cedar shingles were covered with moss and years of dead leaves. A giant weeping willow tree with a hint of green from new buds towered over the structure as in a fairy tale. Cottonwood, oak, juniper, and box elder trees surrounded the property, isolating it from the pastoral countryside that rose gently from the creek on either side. A small, dilapidated barn with an attached chicken coop sat across the lot, surrounded by new growth from the encroaching woods.

"It's beautiful, Hans. It's right out of a storybook. It looks like a Hopper painting you would see in a museum."

"It needs work," Hans said as he opened her car door. He retrieved her suitcase from the trunk and led the way down the flagstone path to the cottage doorway. "The privy is out back. There's a cistern that collects water from a spring and a pitcher pump in the kitchen. It's not exactly the Waldorf, but—"

"It's fine, Hans. You've been to Deep Lake. The twentieth century hasn't reached that far north either."

He opened the door and stood to one side for Gloria to enter.

"Only one bedroom," he added nervously.

Gloria smiled as she took in the warmth of the shadowy interior. An Imperial Crown cookstove and porcelain sink defined the kitchen. A large double-burner Round Oak sat against the rock wall of the small living room. A pine trestle table with press back oak chairs separated the kitchen from the living room. A bentwood rocker, morris chair, and overstuffed couch crowded the tiny parlor.

"It's gorgeous," Gloria proclaimed, turning to Hans, her eyes flashing. "I'm glad I came. I think I could stay here forever."

••••

"Then let's," Hans said suddenly, lifting his head from the pillow and turning to Gloria, who was cradled in the crook of his arm.

"Let's what?" she said, furrowing her brow and tucking her chin.

"Let's stay here forever."

Gloria raised herself on her elbow and rolled toward him, her breasts gently brushing against his chest. She stared into his eyes and then said, "You're serious, aren't you?"

"We could start a new life together. You could open a practice in Boone. I could get a job, a real job, maybe teaching school and coaching or, if worse came to worst, the railroad. My father probably has connections on this division. He could get me on."

"Hold on, what are you saying? Is this some roundabout way of proposing to me?"

"I guess so. I mean yes, yes. I'm asking you to marry me. You keep asking me how this is supposed to work and I'm telling you this is how it could work. I'll give up wrestling. Trapper and the Masked Marvel will disappear from the face of the earth. I'll go legit, settle down in one place, here in Boone. I'll give up anything and everything for you, Gloria. I love you. I want to be with you for the rest of my life."

Gloria sat up, her slender, naked back to Hans. She said nothing, then without turning, "What about Lucky?"

Now he sat up, bristling. "We can't let that greasy little dago run our lives."

She turned toward him and half-smiled. "But he's already running our lives. Don't you see? You're running all over the country like a fugitive. You've had to leave the circus…I'm sorry, the carnival. Today, you tell me you're the Shadow or Captain Courageous or something—"

"Masked Marvel," he interrupted.

"The point is, you've changed your identity, changed your job, and make me sneak around like a common criminal. Besides that mess, what about my practice in Deep Lake and all the people who depend on me? What about my mother? Who will care for her?"

"I'll fix up the chicken coop," he said with a smile.

Gloria sat up and pulled the sheet around her. "Hans, I'm older than you. I've got my own history. The country is still in an economic depression with no end in sight. Things are heating up in Europe. At some point we'll be dragged into another war."

"My God, Gloria, listen to yourself," he interrupted. "What if your mother had told your father that they couldn't get married because somebody's cow was going to kick over a lantern and burn Chicago to the ground?" Or that San Francisco was going to be flattened in an earthquake? There will always be hardship. Life goes on. If two people love each other, they find a way. They endure."

Gloria looked away and whispered, "Sometimes I wish Chicago would burn to the ground." She stood and carefully slipped on her robe, her head bowed as she studied the knot she tied with the sash. She stepped into her slippers and quietly left the room.

He heard her shake the grates of the cookstove and open the firebox door to place kindling on the coals. The screech and clang of the pitcher pump only partially masked her sobs as she filled the teakettle. Outside a raven cawed repeatedly, harsh and grating.

Sidney's hearing aid squealed its miniature version of auditory feedback into the phone's receiver. "Are you on the right program?" Sam asked. "I thought the snaggletooth feature allowed you to hear the phone through both ears....Sorry, I meant Bluetooth." Her hearing aids were top of the line with more features than a new car. He half-joked with her that she could have a new car or hear. It was up to her. She always picked the new car option. She disliked the inconvenience of having to wear them and was self-conscious enough that she no longer wore her hair up or back. She wore another device around her neck, but under her clothes, that allowed her to discreetly change program functions and volume. Sam had fought bitterly with his health insurance company in an attempt to have them cover the cost, even a part of the cost of the hearing aids. He had argued that Usher syndrome was a genetic disorder, which, in Sidney's case, caused gradual deafness and visual impairment. At twenty-four she could no longer drive at night and was showing signs of losing her peripheral vision. Hearing aids and glasses were not covered. Case closed. Self-employed, his monthly insurance premiums were staggering and kept him awake at night. He needed to get back to work. He needed to go home.

"You know I don't like you skipping class....Well, if you put it that way, I guess it's okay. But, this sheriff has nothing. Legally, he can't even make me stay here....Yeah, I know. How come I have to prove my innocence anyway? I thought it was the other way around....Uh-huh, uh-huh, yes, dear. I'll give him the plate number. He won't do anything with it. He's convinced I'm trying to lead him on a wild-goose chase....Work your magic, Sid, but nothing illegal. Okay? ... Yeah, there is one more thing. See what you can dig up about the artist Edward Hopper. Specifically, find out everything you can about an etching or a pen and ink of a nude sitting in an armchair looking out her apartment window....That's right, except for a pair of shoes....I don't know, probably nothing. Just let me know what you find....No, that's it. Wait, I forgot. Remember that woman you met on campus who heads up the American Indian Studies program?....Yeah, she's the one. When you get a chance see what she has on Ojibwe or Chippewa burial customs, especially the use of spirit houses....Uh-huh, just like it sounds—spirit houses.... All right, kiddo. Call when you have something. Love you."

Sam chose not to tell Sidney about his and L2's run-in with the Deep Lake wolf pack. He did not need another lecture on responsible pet ownership. He looked at L2, who was sprawled across the floor beneath the Airstream's oven. He dialed information.

"Um, let's try Duluth....Yes, could I please have the number for a synagogue, any synagogue? Thank you."

The black, almost iridescent wings of the raven stretched above the lake at the timber's edge. Only the bird's head moved as it floated effortlessly along the snowy shoreline. Its sharp call pierced the morning calm. Hans's breath left him in vaporous surges as his eyes followed the arc of the bird's path over the lake skimmed with ice. White smoke rose above the black spruce from the chimney of the farmhouse beyond the trees.

••••

"Taneesha, you stay here in case he comes back. Have security continue to check the greenbelt periodically. Both the sheriff and the marshal are out looking for him now. Come on, Will, we'll go to my house. He went there once; he may do it again," Aimee said in her take-charge tone that staff knew not to argue with.

"He couldn't have gotten very far," Will said. "I was only gone for a few minutes. When I came back with his breakfast I thought he was in the bathroom."

"Do you see now how calculating he is?" Aimee said with an accusatory note to her voice. "There's cognition at work. That old man, in spite of his refusal to communicate, has perception, memory, and decision-making processes going on. He knows what's happening around him. He has an agenda." She looked sharply at Will.

"Don't ask me what it is," he said. "I just got here. I don't have a clue as to who this guy is. I just thought he was my father."

••••

"Mommy, there's a man outside," the little girl said as she rushed into the kitchen, her blonde ponytail bobbing behind her.

"The school bus will be here any minute. Have you brushed your teeth? Where's your backpack?" her mother said as she quickly scanned the kitchen.

"But Mommy, there's a man outside."

"Honey, we don't have time for games this morning." The day before it was a rhinoceros and last week her daughter had insisted there was a gnome living under the house. Last summer, a giant shark patrolled the lake, just beyond the trees. Her imagination had blossomed when she started first grade the previous fall.

The skeletal remains of potted geraniums sat on either side of the front door. A snow shovel was leaning against the door frame. He heard voices from inside the house.

"I hear the bus coming. Get your coat and boots on. Where is your backpack?"

"But Mommy—"

"Now, young lady, no games!" she said, walking briskly toward the front door in her pink chenille bathrobe and gray slipper socks. She was a trim woman with long dark hair and kind eyes.

Her daughter rounded the corner of the living room, the backpack slung over her shoulder, her yellow overshoes flopping noisily against the hardwood floor.

"Here's your lunch," the mother said as she opened the door. "No trading for junk food. And straight to the bus stop after—" She stopped mid-sentence as she stared at the aged figure of Hans Gottlieb standing on the threshold.

"I told you there was a man outside," the little girl said matter-of-factly.

DEEP LAKE, MINNESOTA—1956

It had been more than seven years since she had seen him on that crisp fall morning of 1949. She smelled the sulfurous coal smoke that drifted down from the chimney above, engulfing the tiny front porch. A scoop shovel was leaning against the door frame. Their eyes searched each other's, minute horizontal movements darting frantically in an attempt to read the mood, to predict intentions. She pushed her silver-streaked hair back from her face. She was as beautiful as when he had first seen her at the clinic so many years ago. She was fifty-three years old, but she looked the same to him as she had twenty years ago when he asked her to marry him. Hans carried a few more pounds and his hair had receded at the temples, but he still filled the door frame with his presence.

The school bus roared to a stop at the end of the shoveled path. In the front yard, a large circle had been trampled in the snow where children had played fox and geese, the pie cut in near-perfect slices.

Gloria was the first to avert her gaze. She handed the little girl her lunchbox; a smiling Gene Autry with his six-shooter drawn was painted on the lid. She kissed her on top of the head and pointed toward the school bus.

The little girl looked at her mother, then at Hans and then back to her mother.

Gloria smiled and nodded approvingly and gently nudged her daughter out the door. They both watched her as she made her way toward the waiting bus.

"She favors you," Hans said.

Excuse me?" she said, her eyes creasing as she studied the old man's face.

"She favors you," Hans repeated, this time more unsure of himself.

"Yes," she answered, her voice faltering. "She's a chip off the old block."

Hans's lips trembled and he averted his eyes downward.

"Do I know you?" the woman asked.

Hans turned slowly and watched as the little girl boarded the school bus.

"Are you by yourself?" Her eyes scanned the shivering man in front of her. He was wearing pajamas tucked into his open overshoes. His coat was buttoned crookedly and his ungloved hands were blue with cold.

Hans turned to face her and she saw the confusion in his eyes. "Would you like to come in and have a cup of coffee and warm up?"

Hans hesitated.

"Come in," she said as she backed away from the door and gestured for him to enter.

Hans stepped across the threshold and kept going. He shuffled across the living room, turned left at the second door, and entered the kitchen. He surveyed the room, his lips moving as if he were about to speak. The built-in dishwasher, microwave oven, stainless steel refrigerator, and birch cabinets were foreign. Only the sink was in the right place, but it was no longer porcelain with a red pitcher pump. Instead it was stainless steel, divided, and had a tall arching faucet that loomed over it. The room was warm and smelled of cinnamon.

"Please sit down," the woman said, pulling a chair out from the table. She poured him a mug of coffee and placed it in front of him. "Do you take anything in it?"

Hans sat but did not respond.

"I'll get my husband for you," she lied. "Make yourself at home," she said as she disappeared into the living room. Her husband had left for work at 6:00 a.m., as he did every morning.

Hans searched the room as if looking for something, anything familiar. He could hear the woman's voice in the next room but none of it made sense. He looked at the jumble of photographs held by an assortment of decorative magnets on the refrigerator door. Almost all of them were of the little girl.

"Hans, are you hungry?" the woman said calmly as she entered the kitchen. A man that age deserved to be called by his last name with mister placed in front of it, but she couldn't remember the name the sheriff's dispatcher had told her. It was German-sounding.

"She favors you," Hans said again softly.

"Most people think so."

"She's six, isn't she?" he said as he raised the shaking mug of coffee to his lips.

She pushed her dark hair away from her face and studied him, her brow furrowed. She had not forgotten his direct path to the kitchen. "Have you been here before, Hans?"

"What's her name?"

"I made cinnamon rolls for breakfast. Would you like one?" she said.

Outside, the sound of tires skidding on gravel gave her reassurance. Car doors slammed and voices rang out.

"She's six, isn't she?" he said, tears welling up in his eyes.

Deep Lake, Minnesota—1956

She nodded, not taking her eyes from his. Her daughter would be seven next June.

Hans said nothing for several uncomfortable seconds. "She favors you," he repeated.

Gloria looked down.

"I heard sometime back that you were married," he said.

She exhaled loudly.

"An Indian from Federal Dam told me that your husband might have died a couple of years ago."

Gloria nodded, her eyes glassy.

Now Hans looked down. He had also heard that her husband was a mean drunk who used to beat her. He looked out the corner of his eye at the scoop shovel. He repressed the urge to grab it and start clearing her sidewalk.

"You suppose a guy could get a cup of coffee and a chance to thaw out his toes?" He shifted his weight from one foot to the other.

Gloria stared at him for a long moment. She clutched her arms against the cold and then looked past him.

"I'm alone," he said. "My wife took the boys to Chicago. Will has discovered dinosaurs and wouldn't stop badgering us until someone took him to the Chicago museum of natural history. Carl went too. He's got a real mouth on him lately. He's hard to be around." He looked at the shovel again. "They're growing like weeds," he added softly. When he looked up she was staring at him again. "It's been seven years, Gloria." He paused and nervously cleared his throat. "Just a cup of coffee and I'll be on my way."

Gloria looked into his eyes and forced a smile. She stepped aside.

••••

The silence was palpable. Storm clouds, almost blue, had moved in by late morning. It was snowing. She stared at the wall, not seeing anything. From behind her he stared at the roundness of her bare shoulder. His left arm cradled her stomach, his massive hand flat against her abdomen below her navel.

"Did you ever wish you could just start over?" he said softly. The shadow of a bird angled across the bedroom wall. "I do," he said, answering himself. "Every day, ten times a day."

Gloria rolled over to face him. She pulled the bedsheet and quilt up to cover herself.

"Gloria, there hasn't been a day gone by in more than twenty years that I haven't thought of you and how much I love you. I'll always love you." He paused. "Do I wish things had turned out differently? I stopped wishing for things I couldn't have long ago. We are who we are. We made our decisions. Right or wrong, we live with them. There's no use in looking back. We can't change a thing." He gently pushed her hair back from the side of her face. "But there isn't a minute of the day that passes without me wishing I could take back what happened to you. Not a moment that I don't feel your pain. Not a second that I don't feel the guilt." His eyes became glassy as he cupped her face in his hand. "And now this," he said, tears spilling down his cheeks.

She placed her index finger gently across his lips to stop what she knew was next.

"She has my eyes," he whispered.

This just gets better all the time," Sheriff Whitehorn said, leaning back in his chair and stroking his left front shirt pocket with a shaking hand. "You're my prime suspect in a homicide and you waltz in here with a crazy story like that? What do you take me for, Dawson—an idiot, a dumb Indian, a hick sheriff in a hick town? I know a diversion when I see one and that's all this is, a poor attempt to draw my attention away from you."

Sam leaned forward and cocked his head slightly. He slowly scratched an imaginary itch under his left eye with his index finger, never taking his eyes off Joe Whitehorn. "You do what you want with it, sheriff. I didn't come here just to make you mad. I've come here as a concerned citizen."

"Citizen? You're not my citizen. You're a Zhaagnaash from Wyoming. You don't belong here, Dawson. You're trouble with a capital T."

"I may be a white guy from Wyoming, but I know a bit about finding dead bodies."

"Look, Dawson, if I had my way, you'd be in my jail awaiting arraignment. I did some checking up on you and it led me to Pueblo County in Colorado. I met Tony Garcia several years ago at the National Sheriffs' Association annual conference. I trust him. He said you could find a cemetery on the dark side of the moon. He also said you're unconventional in your methods and push the envelope when it comes to abiding the law. Long story short, Dawson, he vouched for you and that's the main reason I haven't gotten a warrant."

Sam smiled. "That, and the fact that you have no physical evidence linking me to Sophie Mickleson's murder. But it's nice to know you actually got off your fat butt and did something."

Joe Whitehorn again reached for his breast pocket as he inhaled deeply and leaned back dangerously in his chair. Sam noted the dark perspiration stains that now appeared under the sheriff's arms.

"Ever hear of textile interweaving, Dawson?"

Sam stared blankly at him.

"I got a call from the lab rats in Saint Paul. We pulled fibers from your dinette cushions that match the throw on Sophie Mickelson's bed. As soon as I get the final lab report, I'll have what I need to convince the judge to issue a warrant."

"Good luck with that, Sheriff. Both you and your deputies were all over the crime scene and then tore through my trailer like Tasmanian devils. I suspect those fibers came in with you, Andy, or your deputy, Barney. My attorneys will turn you and Mayberry into the laughingstock of the state."

"We'll see, Dawson. I'll take my chances with hard evidence any day over the psycho-babble you're talking about." He smiled. "Let me see if I have this straight. You want me to call the state archaeologist, the Bureau of Criminal Apprehension, and God knows who else, and start digging around in an old Ojibwe burial ground because you divined the presence of human remains using a couple of bent wires." He shook his head from side to side. "It's a cemetery, for crying out loud. Bodies are supposed to be buried there."

"You might want to give the Indian Affairs Council over in Bemidji a call too," Sam said, remembering his phone conversation with their representative that morning. "You don't want to infringe on their sovereignty or spiritual values, do you?"

"Don't tell me how to do my job, Dawson."

"Then don't tell me how to do mine, Sheriff. Just like you, I think I'm pretty good at what I do. And I'm here to tell you that there's a little something rotten in Denmark when it comes to that burial ground."

"That ought to convince the state archaeologist to get involved," Whitehorn laughed.

"A place to start would be to request the unplatted burial sites the archaeologist has mapped out. I would've done it already, but it's password protected. Aimee said she never told anyone else about the site. But if it has been surveyed, we need to know when, and how many graves were recorded."

The sheriff leaned forward and placed his forearms on his desk. "Just because you think you have more bodies than spirit houses, doesn't necessarily mean there's been a crime committed, other than somebody made off with a few spirit houses. I've seen them for sale in antique stores and at flea markets."

"But that doesn't explain the variable intensity of the dowsing rods over some houses and not others."

"Are you listening to yourself, Dawson? You're talking major quackery here. I don't know what you're selling, but I'm not buying this ESP, clairvoyance crap. It's pseudoscience. And then there's your wild-ass story about wolves and the bog on the north end of Deep Lake. I've lived in these parts my entire life and I've seen wolves maybe three times." He shook his head. "Can you tell me why a sane person would wander out onto a floating bog? Do you have any idea how dangerous that was, especially in winter?"

Sam stood and began to button his coat. "It won't be long the ground will be frozen like concrete. State agencies couldn't respond quickly if their hair was on fire. You'll need to get on this fast."

"You just can't help yourself, can you?"

Sam reached into his pocket and retrieved a crumpled scrap of paper. He placed it on the sheriff's desk and oriented it so the sheriff could read it. "That's the plate number from an old car I found less than a quarter mile from the burial ground. It's probably unrelated, but you won't know unless you run it through your system."

The sheriff looked at the carefully printed letters and numbers. "Get out of my office."

Sam placed his University of Wyoming Cowboys ball cap on his head, snugged it down, and carefully shaped the bill. "One last thing, sheriff," Sam said. "You've failed to secure the crime scene at Whispering Pines. It's not going to look good for you or the prosecutor if this should ever go to trial." He paused and attempted a smile. "Have a good day, Sheriff," he said, then turned and walked out.

The cold morning air stuck to the inside of his nostrils and constricted his throat as he looked up and down the nearly deserted streets of Walker. The tendons behind his right knee quivered but he was able to smile to himself. He had Joe Whitehorn's attention.

J esus jumped-up Judas Priest, you're back. You always
come back. Did you ever stop to consider that this is
where you belong? You're a freak of nature, a human
charley horse," Doc said, cigar juice staining the white-beard
stubble below the corner of his mouth. "What happened?
Don't tell me—you dropped the soap and your agent slipped
you the wet willy. No? How about, Doctor Lutefisk handed you your hat? As she should have after meeting me," he
added. "Your ebony-colored friend, William, said you'd gone
to Iowa to build a nest. Your grizzled presence tells me that
didn't work out."

"How about I squeeze your neck till your head pops?"
Hans said.

Madame Marguerite quietly appeared from behind Doc
in the wagon doorway. She offered a half-smile to Hans then
placed her hand on Doc's shoulder.

"You can bunk with William. We'll jump to Saint Joseph
on Friday. I'll send the advance man word that you'll take
on all comers. He can start building the pitch. If that namby-pamby, socialist cripple in Washington doesn't do something pretty damn quick, there won't be any clems for you to
thump. They'll all be in Europe fightin' your Nazi relatives."

Hans furrowed his brow.

"He's married to his horse-faced cousin, for Christ's
sake," Doc added for justification.

"It's good to see you too," Hans said as Doc turned and started up the steps of his wagon.

Doc stopped and turned back toward Hans. He pulled the cigar butt from his mouth. "You're more damn trouble than you're worth, Trap. If I had any sense, I'd turn you away. As soon as you step in that ring, no matter what masked creature you call yourself, Lucky's boys will be on you like stink on a turd. You're trouble, I tell ya." He paused, stuffed the cigar back in his mouth, and squinted at Hans. "But now you're my trouble, and woe be to the man that tries to bring harm to you." He smiled. "It's good to see you too, Hans." With that, Doc disappeared into the wagon.

••••

The G-top was the social core of the odd conglomerate comprising the carnival. Townies were not allowed. It was where the carnies gathered after the show closed for the evening. There was food, booze, gambling, and even women, who sifted in from the darkness like stray dogs. Everything was for sale, but no money changed hands. Instead, tabs were run and deducted from the workers' pay. Like a company store in a mining town, all proceeds went to the show. Carnies often ended up owing more than they made and were forced to work off their debt, thus assuring an adequate workforce. The tent smelled of grease, body odor, and cigarettes. Carnies, Hans thought, were like orphans who were occasionally adopted out but would find their way back to the orphanage when things didn't work out. No one was surprised to see him—they were glad, but not surprised. Penelope was particularly affectionate. His sleeveless dress and pink topknot bow were soiled and he smelled of urine.

"Mind if I sit with you?" Reba the Snake Girl said, suddenly appearing in front of Hans, a plate of food in her hands.

Looking up, he hardly recognized her. Her hair was combed and pulled back into a ponytail. She wore a white blouse tucked into a pleated skirt. Dangling earrings, a matching necklace, and tasteful makeup gave her a sorority girl appearance. William had told him of Reba's transformation to which Hans had responded, "What's her angle?" No one knew. She had quit drinking and whoring, and taken up backstage costume design for the tawdry outfits of the kootch show. She was now Madame Marguerite's apprentice for the All Girl Review.

"Not at all," Hans said, half-rising from his folding chair.

"I heard you were back. What's it been—six months?" she said.

"About," he said, eyeing her suspiciously. "But enough about me, what's going on with you?"

"I heard your lady friend, the doctor, gave you the brush."

"You still throwing rubber snakes at the lot lice?"

"For now, I guess. Doc said I'd have to get rid of my babies if I didn't do the snake girl routine." She looked at him and smiled. "Are you going to play grab ass with boys again?"

His ears began to burn. Reba may have changed her appearance, but she still knew how to pick up a scab and look under it. He thought about trading insults with her. After all, if anyone knew about playing grab ass with boys, it was Reba. He smiled and shook his head. "You look very nice, Reba." He stood and walked away.

••••

Both he and Doc had been uneasy about Illinois. Galesburg was less than two hundred miles southwest of Chicago. Doc had agreed to play the fairgrounds during the town's anniversary. The mayor was presenting the key to the city to some poet who had been born there, whom no one except Doc had heard of. "You illiterate bastards!" Doc had shouted at a group of roughies who had asked who the hell Carl Sandburg was.

There had been no advance buildup and Doc decided it would be best if Myron took on all comers while Hans was the shill. With the usual ethnic slurs and feigned drunken taunts, Hans, playing the part of a local hayseed, would narrowly defeat Myron, the strongman, and then challenge the audience with mock bravado. The townies would line up, money in hand, for a chance at the hundred-dollar purse. It was almost 10:00 p.m. and the crowd was starting to thin when Doc appeared just inside the sweltering tent. He talked with William, who nodded and looked nervously at Hans, who was trying to ignore the charges of the local fat man, a four-hundred-pounder in bibbed overalls. William twirled his finger discreetly, the sign to wrap it up, the show was over.

"Time to say goodnight, Clem," Hans said as he grabbed the charging man by his bib straps, fell backward, and jammed both feet into the man's plush underbelly. Kicking upward as he rolled, Hans flipped the rotund man over the ring ropes and into the front row of panicked spectators.

"Two goons, one at each exit—could be droppers," William said as he walked past Hans. "Free beer at the Ferris wheel!" William yelled. "Free beer at the Ferris wheel!" he repeated as the crowd suddenly moved with purpose toward the exits.

Operators, talkers, agents, roughies, and ride jocks materialized from the dust of the midway, each carrying their version of a war club: monkey wrenches, baseball bats, wheel spokes, and mauls. Reba, dressed as the snake girl, carried a boa constrictor over her neck and shoulders. They silently converged on the two entrances to the tent, the button men backing helplessly into the tent ahead of them, their eyes wide with fear.

"D-eeyuhz-on't k-eeyuhz-ill th-eeyuhz—em!" Doc shouted from the rear of the throng. "B-eeyuhz-ut br-eeyuhz-eak s-eeyuhz-ome b-eeyuhz-ones." The showmen understood not to kill the men, but to break some bones. Doc was sending a message to Lucky.

William took Hans by the arm and led him from the tent. "Free beer at the simp heister," he said.

I don't understand," Aimee Pond said, sitting on the edge of Hans's bed. "What's a simp heister?"

Hans stared past her as if waking from a dream.

"There's free beer at the simp heister?" Will asked from behind her.

Aimee attempted to hush him with a raised finger.

"It's all gibberish, disparate thoughts that bubble to the surface without continuity. Give it up, Aimee. It's random flotsam and jetsam," Will said, fidgeting with frustration.

"Hans, why did you go to that house this morning?" Aimee asked.

Hans turned toward the window.

"Do you know the people who live there? How did you know to go to that house? Is there something important about that house?"

Hans continued to stare out the window.

"Hans," Aimee said sharply. "Why were you there?"

Will stepped forward and leaned over Aimee's shoulder. "Perhaps after he's rested he'll respond. I'll call Walker and cancel with the judge; we can't make it anyway."

"Hans, answer me. Why that house?" she said with anger in her voice.

"Let's get a cup of coffee," Will said.

"I don't want any stinking coffee. I want to know why the hell, out of all the houses in Deep Lake, he chose that one to show up at. You heard the woman. He knew right where the kitchen was. He'd been there before. Don't you see, Will? He has a purpose here. He came here for a reason."

"He has dementia," Will snapped back. "You're reading way too much into this. Clever Hans, the math horse, couldn't count, but thousands of people all over the world were convinced he possessed cognitive and analytical abilities. What they didn't know was that the animal was responding to very subtle cues that his trainer was unconsciously giving."

Aimee looked at him as though he were from outer space.

"My point is," Will continued, "we don't know what stimuli elicit his responses or what associations there might be. Most likely he's generalizing. Something about that house triggered a memory from his past. It wasn't necessarily that house. It could have been a house from anywhere."

Aimee ignored him. "Hans, listen to me. Did you know someone who lived in that house a long time ago?"

"Aimee, give it a rest," Will protested as he turned toward the door, making eye contact with a wide-eyed Taneesha, who looked in from the hallway.

"Hans," Aimee pleaded, "who lived in that house?"

Hans turned and searched her eyes; his were glassy with tears. His bottom lip quivered, but no words came. He looked down and with trembling fingers pulled up the sleeve on his left arm.

Aimee stared at the nondescript blotch of purple and green on Hans's forearm. She shook her head slightly. "I don't understand. A tattoo? Of what?"

"A morning glory," Will and Taneesha said in unison from behind her.

Winter resisted the dawning of a new day. The sharp edges of cold dulled slightly with the rising sun, but Minnesota was sliding farther from the yellow warmth with each passing day. The tiny furnace in the trailer kept the upper half of the ancient Airstream warm while the floor was uncomfortably cold. At first Sam had resisted L2's attempts to sleep on the bed, but her shivering was pitiful and he succumbed to her advances. Now she acted as if she owned the converted dinette. She spread her ninety-two pounds of hound-smelling wrinkles across the foot of the bed so that Sam could not straighten out his legs. "Jeez O'Pete, you stink hound." He pushed against her with his feet. It was an expression Annie used when surprised or angered. He missed her. He wanted to call her. It was a little disconcerting that Sidney and Annie talked on the phone every week. They had become best friends and seemed to have much more in common than either of them had with him. The ten years between Annie and him were somehow more of a barrier than the twelve years that separated her from his daughter.

The thirteen years between Aimee Pond and him was a chasm in time that seemed impossible to bridge. He wanted to like her. He had been drawn to her, a certain sexual attraction, but it was different in a way that he couldn't explain. It wasn't an eye-popping physical magnetism that would cause the wolf to whistle in a Looney Tune. She wasn't a starlet or a fashion model, but seemed more comfortable in her skin than any woman he had ever known. She had told him to make a decision and move forward. But he had hesitated, and now was thankful for it. "Get over, you cur bitch," he said as he kicked at L2 from under the covers. He needed coffee, he needed to urinate, but not in that order.

"Sam!" Will Gottlieb yelled and then rapped his knuckles on the trailer door. "Aimee's making omelets. Coffee's on. Drag your carcass out of the sack and come over."

"Thanks, Will. I'll be over in a few minutes, as soon as I regain circulation in my feet."

"That cold, huh?"

"No, bloodhound."

"Get a woman, Sam."

"Easier said than done, my friend."

"Tell me about it. I could make you cry with my tales of woe. Get dressed and come over."

Sam heard the back door to Aimee's house slam. He was beginning to change his opinion of Will Gottlieb. It was apparent that Will liked Aimee. But like Sam, he too appeared to be held at arm's length. Sam thought Will treated his father like a distant relative and seemed less interested in Hans than he was in Aimee. He understood that family relationships were complicated and he tried not to judge Will harshly. He liked Will Gottlieb but could not help resenting him at the same time. It appeared that Aimee was simply enjoying the attentions of both men.

Sam yawned. He and Sidney had talked on the phone until after midnight. The kid was a genius. She had done what Sam had asked of her and more. She had discovered things that caused doubt to creep into everything he once believed.

••••

"Where's Miss Stinky?" Aimee said, turning from the stove to greet Sam.

"She's still in the sack, too cold to get up." Sam poured himself a cup of coffee. "She ordered extra cheese on her omelet and that you hold the onions."

Aimee smiled. "That dog is spoiled."

"You think?" Sam said.

"Eggs are okay, being the obligate omnivore that she is. But go easy on the cheese. Dogs are lactose intolerant, and onions are toxic," Will said without looking up from the morning paper.

Both Sam and Aimee stared at him. "You get free veterinary advice if you let him sleep on your couch," Aimee said.

Sam easily recognized her attempt to explain Will's presence and remove any speculation of a romantic relationship between them.

"Sam," Aimee said a little too loudly as she turned back to the stove. "Do you have any food allergies? If so, I'd like to put a large dose of them in your omelet." Not waiting for him to respond, she continued. "You betrayed my trust, Sam."

"Excuse me?"

"You told Joe Whitehorn about my secret place. That's bad enough, but you tried to convince him to go dig it up."

"News travels fast in the north country."

"This is a small town in a sparsely populated county, Sam. When were you going to tell me? And why do you continue to aggravate Joe? The guy is sick, really sick, and you keep poking at him like a kid with a stick. Put two slices of bread in the toaster." She pointed at the counter with her spatula. "And you might try standing a little closer to your razor in the morning."

Sam stroked the stubble on his face, then dutifully loaded and cocked the toaster.

Will sipped his coffee while looking at Sam above the rim of his cup. His eyes were squinted as he suppressed a smile. He said nothing.

"Guilty, your honor," Sam said, turning back toward Aimee. "I should have talked with you before going to the sheriff. I apologize. But there's something strange about that place." He decided not to say anything about the bog unless she mentioned it.

"It's a cemetery, for Pete's sake," Aimee shot back. "It deserves your respect," she said more softly as she folded an omelet.

"Believe me, I know about cemeteries. But this one—"

"What do you gain by digging it up, Sam? What is it with you white tourists that you feel compelled to dig up Indian graves?"

"I never said to dig it up. There is specialized equipment that can be used to map out the graves."

"They're pretty obvious. They have jiibegamig on top of them." She placed one hand on her hip and raised the spatula with the other.

Will carefully folded the paper and leaned back in his chair. He was enjoying this.

"Not all of them."

"What?"

"Not all of the graves have spirit houses over them. There's at least two that don't, possibly more. A couple of the houses have been moved too. Burial grounds are very symmetrical. It's human nature. We space everything evenly. We line up the markers and everything faces the same direction. Think of Arlington or other national cemeteries. The uniformity is striking. The Chippewa were no different."

"Kids, hunters, loggers—somebody moved them, probably looking for artifacts." Aimee lifted a perfectly formed omelet from the pan and placed it in front of Will. "There's salsa in the fridge."

"But there are bodies buried beneath each of the houses, and some graves aren't marked with a spirit house." Sam said.

Aimee thought for a moment. "People steal them. Tourists will buy anything. You're missing a few houses. What's the big deal? There's no mystery here."

"What about the symmetry?"

"Rocks, tree roots, or something made it hard to place the graves in a perfect row. You're really grasping, Sam. I'm sorry I took you there. Sit down. Your breakfast is almost ready. Butter that toast, please." She nodded toward the toaster.

"I'm not buying the tourist desecration argument. It was your secret place because of its isolation. It's pretty unlikely that tourists would find it. Hunters are too focused and stealthy. They're not going to be dragging spirit houses through the woods. And that forest hasn't been logged since the late eighteen hundreds. Those graves were dug long after that skid road was built. But here's the clincher. The hole in the gable end always faces west. You said it allowed the deceased's spirit to exit and begin their four-day journey to the west. Two of the houses have their openings facing almost due east. I doubt if the Chippewa carpenters, gravediggers, or whoever oversees the burial process would have overlooked such a glaring error."

Aimee hesitated. She seemed to consider Sam's argument for a moment and then dismissed it. "Back to Joe; he's got another year left on his term. He has an incurable, terminal disease and a murder investigation on his plate. Can't you understand that slightly out-of-kilter spirit houses are a low priority with him?"

"Oh, believe me, I understand. I'm his chief suspect and he's determined to leave office a hero by pinning this on me. That isn't going to happen. Sickness or not, I'll be his worst nightmare if he continues down that road."

Will sat back in his chair and dabbed the corners of his mouth with his napkin. Sam's threat had gotten his attention. He waited.

"I'll bite," Aimee finally said. "What're you going to do, Sam, take a bad picture of him?" She handed Sam a plate with a near-perfect omelet in the center.

"Before I was a photographer I was a damn good press secretary for a governor who couldn't keep his feet out of his mouth. My job was to put a spin on political issues to ensure the proper outcome. My unofficial title was 'The Spin Doctor.'"

"Eat that before it gets cold." Aimee nodded toward Sam's plate. "I'm sure Joe Whitehorn will rue the day he ever crossed swords with a wordsmith."

Sam sat down across from Will, who stared at him eagerly.

"I had a journalism professor in college," Sam said as he cut into his omelet, "who was fond of saying that a good writer can make their readers cry. And that a very good writer can make their readers laugh. But an exceptional writer can make their readers take action." He took a bite of the fluffy egg-and-cheese mixture and said, "Mmm, now that's an omelet." Then he looked up to see both Aimee and Will waiting for the punch line and put down his fork. "The governor of Minnesota will have to call out the National Guard in order to quell the civil unrest and restore order to Timberlane County when I'm done spinning my story of what has and hasn't happened here. Joe Whitehorn will take up smoking again in his final days."

The carnival sweltered in the heat of late August. The river towns had been the worst; humidity amplified the high temperatures. Night brought little relief and hordes of mosquitoes. The canvas shelters of the midway games and concessions held the daytime heat well into the night. The smell of humankind mixed with dust clung to the inside of nostrils and created dark threads of grime at the creases of elbows, wrists, and necks. Maquoketa was higher ground, but was no relief from heat or insects. They would move to the northwest: Anamosa, Independence, Waverly, Mason City, then across southwestern Minnesota and into the Dakotas before turning south and slowly making their way toward winter camp, the Midwestern circle complete.

The mighty Trapper, descended from Greek gods, the world's greatest wrestler, ran the new Tilt-O-Whirl. Wrestling exhibitions had been suspended indefinitely as carnies waited anxiously and watched suspiciously for Lucky's response to Doc's message.

"Why don't you call her up, Trap?" William said, crawling out from under the ride's motor and gearbox.

Hans was leaning on the long clutch handle that engaged the drive that spun the tilting floor. By moving the handle at the right moment, he could add spin to a particular car. The centrifugal force would cause the townies to scream with a mixture of fear and delight. "Say what?" he said, looking at William, who was covered in oil and held a grease gun.

"I said the U-joints have got enough play that if you're not careful, you'll send hot little bearings out into the crowd. And why don't you call her?"

"Who?"

"You poop through feathers? Who do you think? The lady doctor, that's who. You been standing around pining like a lovesick hound for weeks. Your sufferin's about to drive us all batty."

"Mind your own beeswax," Hans said, turning away from him.

"It is my business when you start tearing up machinery 'cause you're mad. Call her up. Tell her you is sorry for whatever you done," William said.

"I didn't do anything."

"It don't matter. Just tell her you're sorry."

"Are you the voice of experience?" Hans asked. "In all these years, I've never seen you with a woman. Maybe you don't like women," he said suspiciously.

"I like women," William said defensively. "I like all women, but I'm particularly partial to Negro women, mostly 'cause I don't want to be hanged by an angry mob of white men. Besides, how many Negro women have you seen in these lily-white, cornpone Midwestern towns? And don't change the subject. We was talking about you, not me. Why don't you go into town and call her on the telephone?"

"It's complicated," Hans said.

"Too complicated for a darky like me?"

Hans rolled his eyes. "It's complicated because there isn't a solution. We're from two different worlds. She's not leaving hers and I can't get out of mine. I offered her a solution with plenty of compromise on my part, but she didn't take it and offered nothing in return. She's a doctor and I'm a ride jock. It's as simple as that."

"I thought you said it was complicated."

"The problem is simple. It's the solution that's complicated. If times were different, we might have a chance."

William looked at him skeptically. "And what would you be doing if times was different?"

Hans stared back at him blankly. It was a question he had asked himself many times.

"Seems to me, you might be making excuses because you're scared you might lose."

"What the hell are you talking about?" Hans said, slapping a mosquito on his neck and avoiding eye contact. He knew exactly what William was saying.

"You do what you're good at. You always win. None of the clems in these hick towns can beat you at wrestling. That's one of the reasons you hide out in this two-bit carnival; you know you're gonna win. That's a good feeling. It's easy to blame the times for your lot in life. Fact is, it's a scary world out there 'cause you don't know if you're gonna win or not. This carnival is like a mother's lap for all the misfits who can't make it on the outside."

"Are you calling me a misfit?"

"You're as queer as a three-dollar bill, Trap. You're a cauliflowered charley horse, as Doc would say. This carnival is to you what Notre Dame was to the hunchback—sanctuary."

Hans pulled in his chin as his mouth dropped open. "Jesus, William, I didn't know you were a literary scholar too."

"You don't need a bunch of schoolin' to see what's as plain as day. You're not hidin' from Lucky. He knows where to find you. You're hiding from what you don't know."

Hans's face began to flush red. He had long ago realized what William was saying was true. But he was embarrassed by the truth, by being found out. "So let me see if I've got this straight.…The solution to my problem is to shed my peasant clothes, ignore my deformities, and tell Esmeralda that I'm ready to settle down and open a bell foundry in Paris?"

"That's right. Roll the dice. Show her your willin' to—"

"Trap, Trap!" Junior Stucken yelled as he made his way through the crowd toward the Tilt-O-Whirl. "Doc said to fetch you right now. He's down at the annex to the ten-in-one."

"Hey Rube?" Hans asked.

"No, he just said to come get ya. It must be important, 'cause I was just about to give the blowoff for Harriet when Doc comes up and says he's taking over and for me to fetch ya."

Hans looked at William, who raised his eyebrows and shrugged his shoulders. "Can you spell me? I'll be back shortly."

••••

After the ten-in-one display of human oddities ended, Doc paced slowly across the show's platform. He had already dismissed the women and children toward the midway, where the freaks hawked miniature Bibles and pitch cards with their photos and outlandish biographies. He rubbed the stubble on his chin and looked down the midway to where the women and children were gathered. He lowered his voice. "Now, gentlemen, allow me to draw your attention to a special attraction that you won't see advertised anywhere. This is the good stuff, the real thing, the reason you're here. I can't tell you everything out here because of the more delicate sensibilities of our female patrons, but...," he looked up and down the midway again and lowered his voice even further, "you will see it all. I'm not talking about a nice set of knockers here. I'm talking about the whole thing, every bit of it; you'll see it all. It's going to cost you a little extra. You saw a good show already, worth every cent. Am I right? For two bits, another twenty-five cents, you will witness one of the rarest oddities of humankind, a biological mistake, a medical marvel, an anatomical mystery that has baffled the scientific world. See it, believe it. But first, let me tell you a little story.

"Sometime back, she came to me on a cold and rainy night, her tears masked by the rain that fell in those remote Appalachian hills. A fugitive from parents that had kept her chained in the bowels of a coal mine for most of her life. In her arms, wrapped in rags, was a newborn whose face shone as though illuminated from an unseen celestial body. Behind that curtain, gentlemen, you will see the woman that teenage mother has become, and what's more, you'll meet the father too, for they are one in the same. That's right, you heard me correctly. Man and woman, father and mother in one person, in one body. Chained in a cave like a dog, this beautiful young girl turned into a woman with all the desires of a woman and the parts of a man to fulfill those desires."

Hans could hear the crowd of Saturday-night cake eaters breathing in unison. Doc had them hooked and was now reeling them in.

"It's going to cost you another two bits to see her genitals. Here's how it's going to work, men. She's sitting in a chair on a platform right behind that curtain," Doc said, waving his hand behind him. "For twenty-five cents, one quarter of a dollar, you'll file back behind that curtain. She will lift up her dress, spread her legs, and you'll find yourself at eye level with her external genitalia. See them. Examine them. But please, no touching. You'll not forget what you're about to see. There is no finer specimen of a hermaphrodite in all the world, gentlemen. And what happened to the baby, you ask? She's now a gorgeous young woman, an exact duplicate of the young woman who came to me on that rainy night in the hills of Kentucky. Step right up. The show will begin as soon as you assemble behind that curtain."

The ragtag crowd of men and boys, their mouths agape, moved as a millipede, only their legs shuffling forward as they approached the mystical slit in the curtain.

"Junior said you wanted to see me," Hans said as the last man disappeared into the darkness of the ten-in-one tent.

"Jesus jumped-up Judas Priest, now I'm an overpaid mick delivery boy," Doc said, pulling a crumpled paper from his pocket and handing it to Hans. "It's from Doctor Halvorson's mother. It sounds serious."

Hans read then reread the two-sentence telegram: "Gloria hurt (stop) Come quickly (stop)."

He was unaware of the noise and confusion of the midway as he made his way toward the end of the lot. His mind raced and there was a sickening hollowness in his chest. Burning droplets of fear filled his eyes.

Hans lay on his back. Tears ran slowly down his face, darting left and right as they followed the crevices of time. Tears of sadness, tears of anger—he could not differentiate. Seventy-one years had not dulled the pain of guilt.

"I'd cry too," Taneesha said with her hands on her hips. "You're in big trouble now, Hans. I ain't never seen Nurse Pond so upset. You're gone. You're history, old man. I'm not going to miss your raggedy ass either. You've been nothin' but trouble since the day you set foot in Deep Lake."

Hans suddenly cocked his head and looked at Taneesha as if unsure of what she had said. He waited for clarification.

Taneesha studied him curiously, then repeated "Deep Lake" loudly.

Hans struggled to sit up. He stared out the window, his head still cocked with alertness. He listened, he waited. Had he heard the conductor correctly?

D eep Lake," the conductor repeated as he passed down the aisle.

Hans looked out the window and wiped the sleep from his eyes. The dark forest was interrupted occasionally by cleared fields with piles of stones at the center. He remembered little of the trip from Dubuque to Saint Paul, even less from Saint Paul to Deep Lake. He had tried to call her from Maquoketa, but there was no answer. The crumpled telegram in his pocket said little, but it had been enough. Four words that raised the hair on his arms: "Gloria hurt. Come quickly."

••••

Fear gnawed at his empty stomach as he approached the clinic. The window shades were pulled and uniformly yellowed. Light shone through the curtained window of the door. He saw a shadow pass along the hallway. The doctor was injured. *Who doctors the doctor?* he wondered. He did not knock.

"Oh my God," Mrs. Halvorson said as Hans stepped into the kitchen. "You came." She started to cry and struggled to her feet from the small table; tea sloshed over the rim of her teacup.

An older man in a dark suit and a crooked bow tie stood up slowly, studying Hans from behind wire-rimmed glasses.

"You came. Thank goodness you came," Mrs. Halvorson said as she embraced Hans. She introduced Doctor Peterson from Grand Rapids.

"I'm pleased to make your acquaintance, Mr. Gottlieb," Peterson said. "I wish it were under different circumstances."

"How's Gloria? What happened? Where is she?" Hans said, uninterested in cordialities.

"She's resting," Peterson said.

"Can I see her?" Hans asked, taking a step backward.

"First, let's have a little chat, Mr. Gottlieb," Peterson said, motioning for Hans to take a seat at the table.

"I don't want to talk. I want to see Gloria," Hans said.

"Sit down, Hans," Mrs. Halvorson said, attempting a smile in spite of the tears in her eyes. "It's important that you hear this."

••••

The room smelled of alcohol. Gloria lay sleeping on her back. A clean, white sheet was folded neatly and tucked tightly over her arms below her chin. He might not have recognized her if he hadn't known it was her. Her dark hair spilled across the pillow on either side of the purple-black swollen mass that was her face; cadaverous eyes were recessed and blackened. Her lower lip was split deeply where it had been caught between her teeth and the pliers.

He began to cry. He could not help himself. His large chest heaved up and down as he attempted to control his anguish. He covered his eyes with his hands to hide his shame. He had done this to her.

Gloria opened her eyes when he took her hand in his. She closed them again and breathed deeply, unable to overcome the morphine-induced sleep that allowed her to escape the pain.

He blew his nose and swallowed the painful lump in his throat. How could he have allowed this to happen? Why hadn't he thought to protect her? He would kill those who had done this to her, he told himself. He would start with Lucky Lucello. It would be painful, and he would be glad to do it. He would hold that fat, greasy bastard down and yank his tongue out with pliers and slice it off with a razor. Lucky would feel Gloria's pain before he died.

••••

She could smile with her eyes like no one he had ever met. The morning sun brought her eyes to life. They were her essence, windows to her soul that would speak the words she could no longer say.

"Good morning," he said, attempting a smile.

DEEP LAKE, MINNESOTA—2007
DAY 10, 9:00 A.M.

Good morning," she responded back to Hans, surprised by the clarity of his words. Aimee Pond leaned over his bed and studied his worn-out face, his remote eyes, once green. She wondered what he saw and how his brain processed the cloudy images.

He squeezed her hand gently and she returned the greeting.

"Do you feel like talking this morning?" Aimee asked.

Hans continued to stare at her. He turned his head slightly as though trying to look around the opacity of his lenses. He did not respond.

Down the hall someone dropped a tray of breakfast dishes. The unmistakable sound of breaking glass and clattering silverware caused him to look beyond her, not toward the doorway and the source of the sound, but over her shoulder toward the rubble of the Ristorante La Roma.

William stood guard just inside the doorway of the restaurant, his bloody hammer hung at his side. Nearly a dozen carnies kept lookout from strategic locations up and down the block. Every able-bodied man in the carnival had answered Doc's "Hey Rube" call. His selection had been strategic. A lifetime of moving a carnival across the country had honed his organizational skills. He commanded logistical support with the ease of a field general. Lucky had gone too far. War had been declared.

Doc remained with the show, herding the caravan into western Minnesota and then North Dakota before descending toward winter camp. He had turned over the Chicago field operations to William, who some thought was a curious choice. But Doc was a student of human behavior. He discerned that a Negro from the South must possess refined survival skills. William could sense danger instinctively and knew how to avoid it. He was quick on his feet and loyal to a fault. Doc respected him much more than he let on.

Lucky's routine was easily established by the advance man. He always took his Friday night dinners at the Ristorante La Roma on the lower South Side. A driver and two goons were his usual entourage. The driver would wait in the car, and the bodyguards would sip coffee while seated at a separate table from Lucky's.

"Gimme the veal parmigiana," Lucky said as the waiter approached his table and stood over his right shoulder. "And don't be so goddamn stingy with the mozzarella."

The waiter did not respond.

"You deaf or something'?" Lucky said, twisting his fat body in the chair to confront the waiter.

As still as a statue, Hans loomed over him. His eyes burned with hate.

"Well, if it ain't my old cabbage-eatin' Kraut friend from days gone by," Lucky said, smiling.

Neither Lucky nor Hans blinked at the sound of breaking dishes and furniture being overturned behind them, as both bodyguards were subdued and patrons were hurried into the kitchen.

"Why?" Hans said, slightly above a whisper.

"Why?" Lucky repeated. "You askin' me why? Lemme tell you this, you dumb carny hick, it ain't none of your damn business. You don't know the half of it. But you think I should turn my head that you gave me the screw job? You cost me a lot of dough."

Hans could see the nickel and ivory handle of Lucky's automatic under his left armpit, his fat breast protruding next to it.

"You think I could do business in this town or any other if I let punks like you off the hook?" Lucky asked.

"Your fight was with me, not Gloria. She did nothing to you."

"Like I say, you don't know the half of it. That dame was a mouthy bitch. I bet she's not so mouthy now," Lucky said. He grinned broadly and his gold tooth suddenly appeared between his lips.

The unmistakable four clicks of a Colt revolver being cocked caused Lucky's smile to dissipate. The old .44 looked huge even in Hans's large hand as he brought the gun up and leveled it at Lucky. His other hand extracted the automatic from under Lucky's coat. "This is for Gloria," he said, and he squeezed the trigger. The hammer fell with a loud metallic click on an empty cylinder. Lucky blinked painfully. "I want you to live every day with the knowledge that I can show up when you least expect it. Who knows, the next time the hammer falls it might be on a loaded cylinder. In the meantime, you've called me a cabbage-eating Kraut—or anything else for that matter—for the last time.

Several carnies hurried through the front door. Dark and stealthy, they swarmed over Lucky silently. Dishes crashed to the floor. The glint of a straight razor and the clatter of a pair of pliers replaced the fang and claw of the pack. Hans looked out the window to the empty street. The muffled screams that filled the restaurant reminded him of the rabbits' terrified calls when his father would come for them. He had become his father.

Hans stepped outside, closing the front door behind him. The moonless Chicago night was sticky; the air smelled of oregano and blood. He thought he might be sick.

"It had to be done, Trap," William said. "There was no call for what he did to Miss Gloria. He needed to feel what she did. Don't you ever forget that." William placed his arm around Hans's broad shoulders. "Let's go home, Trap."

"Home?" Hans asked, surprised by the realization that a traveling carnival made up of freaks and societal misfits was in fact his home. "Home," he repeated softly as he stared blankly ahead.

H ome, is that where you want to go, Pop?" Will
said, stepping into the room.

Aimee pulled a stethoscope from her coat
pocket. She deftly listened to Hans's chest, then rolled him
on his side and listened again. She pulled the earpieces from
her ears and handed the stethoscope to Will.

Will repeated Aimee's examination. "There's a lot of fluid in there," he said softly. "He's in congestive heart failure."
He pulled back the sheet at the bottom of the bed and noted
the significant swelling around Hans's ankles.

"He's not going anywhere," Aimee said, "unless it's to
the hospital or hospice. What do you want to do, Will?"

"What do I want? I want to have a meaningful conversation with him. I want to find out who he is. I want to know
why he's here. That's what I want. In the interim, I'd suggest
a potent diuretic like furosemide."

"Lasix? What dosage?" Aimee asked.

"I'd start with forty milligrams and see how he re-
sponds."

"I'll call in the prescription."

"Get a vial of Sodium Pentothal too. I want truthful
answers to my questions."

The look Aimee gave him told him that he should have
asked those questions years ago.

"I know, I know," he said, grimacing. "I can't undo the past. But am I asking for too much now?"

"Will, we need to talk," Aimee said softly. "But not here."

••••

The administrator's window was covered with ice, layers of moist air frozen in place like thick coats of mother-of-pearl on the inside of an oyster's shell. "Would you like some tea?" Aimee asked.

"No thanks. It stains my teeth," Will said. "Plus I have an overactive bladder. Diuretics tear me up."

"You wet the couch and you'll buy me a new one."

Will scowled at her. "What did you want to talk about?"

Aimee believed that Will Gottlieb irritated her more than anyone she had ever known. "Cookie?"

"Sorry, I don't eat sweets."

"You're an easy keeper."

"Wheat gluten is killing our society."

"As a species, how did we ever make it this far?" she whispered.

"Excuse me?"

"Your father is dying," Aimee suddenly blurted out. "You heard what I heard, Will. You don't have to be a cardiologist to see that your father is dying. I have no idea what that man hears and understands, but it's rude to talk about his dying in front of him. Your bedside manner tells me you've been around horses and dogs more than people."

"Where are you going with this, Aimee?"

"Your dad is a mystery to me, an enigma. But with each day I'm more convinced that he's here for a reason. I don't believe in fate or karma or the random behaviors of dementia. There are a lot of unanswered questions concerning Hans Gottlieb. It's not my place to interrogate him. If you want to find out why he came to Deep Lake, you better find out soon. You need to put aside your self-absorbed interests and start asking questions that don't necessarily relate to you."

"Is that why you brought me in here? You want to lecture me again on family relationships? I have a better idea. Let's talk about your family. I thought we were trying to get to know one another better. You seem to know everything about my family. Well, let's hear about yours for a change."

"Bite me, Will. You don't need to know about my family."

"Touché."

Aimee contemplated his challenge, then leaned back in her chair and said nothing.

"I'm waiting," Will smiled.

Aimee leaned forward and placed her elbows on the desk. "Fair enough," she said without smiling. "My mother died in 1965—uterine cancer," she added matter-of-factly. "She was sixty-two years old and I was fifteen." She paused but continued to stare at Will. "I was fifteen. I was embarrassed to have a mother that old." She shook her head and smiled. "She was your age. I'm pretty sure she was embarrassed by me too. Looking back, I'd have to say the relationship was a bit cold and indifferent. I'm not sure she ever really liked me."

Will looked at her and was uncertain how to respond. "What about your father?" he said, changing the subject.

"He disappeared when I was four. I only have a couple of memories of him, or maybe none at all. I'm not sure. The memories seem to be related to photographs that my mother had and a dislocated shoulder I suffered. Rumor had it that he had been some sort of bootlegger during prohibition." Aimee continued to stare at him.

Will studied her face but said nothing.

"Everyone always referred to him as Charles, Charles Pond—never Charlie or Chuck, and he was a half-breed Chippewa," she said as if admitting a dark secret. "When my mother died, I went to live with my father's sister on the Winnibigoshish Indian Reservation. She claimed to be Ojibwe. It was all very confusing to a fifteen-year-old," she said, shaking her head. "I was a quarter-breed who didn't fit in at first. I had no history with those people. Family was everything to them. I was an orphan who dreamed of going to medical school while the other girls my age dreamed of having babies and getting high. They called me Pond Scum. That was my nickname all through high school. They thought I was a stuck-up, rich, white kid. My meager inheritance was in a trust that I couldn't access until I was twenty-one. My aunt received a monthly allowance that she and her boyfriend drank up by the end of the first week. We lived mostly on poached deer and fish." She paused again.

Will looked down.

"Don't get me wrong, I wouldn't trade my life on the rez for anything. My aunt was the sweetest, most loving, nurturing woman in the world. It was just different, that's all. There was a sense of community there. Everyone loved everyone, warts and all. But deep down, there was something that nagged at me, something that haunted me. It was just a feeling, but there was something missing, out of place. I've never been able to explain it. I still can't." She turned and looked toward the iced-over window. "The Spanish poet Machado once said that we should look in the mirror for the other one, the one who accompanies us." She turned back to Will. "All my life I've had this feeling that someone was standing behind me looking over my shoulder, staring into the mirror. Don't know who. Don't know why. It was just a presence, sort of like a void that needed to be filled, an itch that needed to be scratched."

Will waited.

"Pond Scum," she said sharply. "My nickname eventually became a term of endearment, an expression of their love for me. Nicknames are like that. They become an affectionate symbol of you. Don't you see, Will?"

Startled, Will looked at her. "No."

"Hans's tattoo, my mother's nickname—Morning Glory."

am's parents were dead. It was hard for him to imagine them as young and fun-loving, especially his father. The years following the disappearance of Sam's sister had been dark. Then his father died, but not before he ceased to live. Sam learned later that it was his father who had taught his mother to roller-skate, more specifically, roller dance. Waltzes were their specialty, played on an organ, a rotating ball of colored lights shooting straight beams around the rink. Pompoms on the toes of their white skates, they glided in each other's arms in the animated light, smiling, laughing. Sam had seen the medals they had won. They were young and healthy with the bulk of their lives ahead of them. Their children were yet to be born but they knew they would be exceptional. They were defiant of all future harm. How could they foresee their loss?

Digging and sifting through the debris of other people's lives made Sam melancholy at best, angry at worst. He had not taken the time to know his parents and he resented having to discover who other people's parents were. He still had boxes of pictures and keepsakes from his mother's basement, unlabeled evidence of lives he knew nothing about. Always smiling, always posed with the subject of the photo in the background, they were a photographic version of Kilroy Was Here. Someday, he would organize their lives. The photos of canyons, dams, waterfalls, and cement dinosaurs with the smiling couple in the foreground would tell their story. It would give no clue of what was to come.

••••

The calls to government offices were easy. Cities offered up professional licenses and permits. Counties kept marriage licenses and property tax records. The state had vehicle registrations and birth and death records. The feds had everything else. Once Sam obtained the person of interest's Social Security number, which was plastered on everything, he could write their biography.

Lawyers, however, were not so easy. They were universally evasive and noncommittal. They easily poked holes in his fabricated stories through which he sought information. Questions about the probate of wills often yielded a dial tone. Real estate agents were most helpful. If he pretended to have commercial property for sale, agents would eagerly provide him with deeds of trust, amounts of debt, legal descriptions and values, lien holders, and previous owners of property. Feigning an interest in making a major donation in the name of an alumnus, universities would give him anything he wanted.

Sam glanced at the alarm clock. Funny or sad—he was unsure which, he was able to condense a person's life onto a single page of a legal ruled pad of paper in less than an hour. It was sad, he concluded.

"Stow your tennis ball, girl. We're moving to the KOA. I need a shower and I'm down to my last pair of clean socks." Sam pulled back the curtains and secured them with Velcro ties. The sheriff's deputy had parked behind the trailer. His emergency lights were flashing.

Ogallala, Nebraska—1941

There's no glory in tucking tail and pretending you're an isolationist," Doc growled. "Jesus jumped-up Judas Priest. Roosevelt is an idiot. You mark my words," he said, pointing a bony finger at Hans. "This will make the Great War look like child's play. While that pacifist, socialist nancy in the White House watches London burn and our own freighters sink off our eastern coast, Benito, Joe, and Adolf are dividing up most of Europe and laughing at us. Then the dumb bastard cuts off oil and steel to the Japs because they started kickin' China's ass." Doc pulled the cigar stub from his mouth and squinted at Hans. "That little embargo will come back to haunt us. We'll rue the day we didn't let the Japs take care of those Communist bastards. When Chiang Kai-shek jumped into the sack with Mao Tse-tung and Chou En-lai, we should have rallied for the Nips." Doc shook his head. "It's 1941, for Christ's sake," he said, waving his arms. "We're going on a dozen years of economic drought, and Comrade Roosevelt in eight years has delivered what? Working Piss Ants—those shovel-leaning sons-of-bitches of the WPA have built parks nobody uses, buildings that sit empty in the middle of nowhere, and roads that lead to 'em. 'We Piddle Around' is their motto."

Hans stifled a yawn. He knew better than to interrupt Doc when he was on a rant.

"There's only one way to pull this country out of the sinkhole we're in." Doc paused as though he heard an imaginary drumroll. "War," he proclaimed. "Screw all the noble intentions of making wrong, right. War will put this country back to work. Not only will we recover, we'll prosper."

Hans looked at him, one eyebrow raised, questioning Doc's sanity.

"Sure, there's risk," Doc shot back, answering the unspoken question. "We have to win it. None of this embargo crap. We have to kill the bastards. 'At what cost?' you ask. At all costs," he said slowly, his voice lowered. "But there will be opportunity too." A smile formed at the corners of his mouth.

"Here we go," Hans said, his head rolling back. "Doc O'Brien's money-back guarantee on how to profit in times of misfortune."

"You're absolutely right, you oversized charley horse. That's what this great nation is founded upon: finding opportunity and sticking it to the chumps. Capitalism, my cauliflowered friend, is what we're all about. Money is the grease that lubricates the gears that turn the wheels that grind the grist of a competitive economic machine—the machine that pays your salary, Lumpy. Oh, they'll come all right. The tired, the poor, the huddled masses will all come." Doc's eyes were glassy as he gazed into the future. "The war-weary widows and orphans will come, unsure of why; they'll line up to escape their sorrowful little lives. They'll hand over their money and say, 'Thank you, Doctor O'Brien, for bringing me joy.' Oh, they'll fork it over, Hans," he said, smiling.

"I'm sure you're right, Doc. But my mind is made up. I'm quitting. Railroad pay is good and the hours are decent. It's not what I want to do, but it will do for now. Who knows? Maybe in a couple of years I'll land that teaching and coaching job I've dreamed about. But for now, it'll pay the bills and I won't have to beat anybody up. I'm catching the eastbound from North Platte in the morning."

"You'll be back," Doc said. "You always come back. Like a bad penny, you'll turn up when I least expect it." Doc stared at him as if debating whether to argue his decision. Finally he said, "And when you do, there will always be a place for you. Good luck, Hans." He turned and walked into the midway.

Hans watched him disappear into the Nebraska night, a little man with a slight limp who held himself tall. The carnival lights reflected off the leaves of the giant cottonwood trees that stood between the fairgrounds and the river. They fluttered with a late summer breeze, creating a kaleidoscope of muted colors. He caught a glimpse of Doc, who had stopped midway through the carnival lot and had turned back to look at him. Doc touched the brim of his hat and nodded, then was gone. It would be the last time he ever saw him.

••••

The railroad consumed him. It was no different from the fiery maw of the locomotives into which he funneled coal. It took all he could give and wanted more. In his off-time, he slept. William's telegram found him in Boone. It was October. The show's last billing was in Big Spring before heading south to winter camp. Doc was dead, a stroke.

Less than two months later, Doc's prophecy about Japan was realized. A galvanized nation was at war. Hans would be thirty-four years old in March, too old to go, too young to stay. An occupational deferment settled the argument. The country needed him to help ferry the munitions of war across Iowa.

S am had been summoned. The sheriff's deputy had offered nothing other than where Joe Whitehorn wanted to meet him. The morning air was cold and heavy. Thick gray clouds descended on the tops of spruce trees and down the back of his neck, producing a shiver and triggering disparate memories. This was the time of day for reflection, for remembrance. Snippets of trivia from the past would suddenly appear in his mind's eye without warning or context. Sam remembered the warm convection of stored heat from deep within the smooth stones of the fireplace's hearth. On cold winter mornings he would often lie on the uneven river rocks, absorbing the energy from the previous night's fire as he watched his father get ready for work—silent tasks deftly conducted in the same sequence each day. The warmth reassured him at a time when his life seemed so ephemeral. His sister was presumed dead and his father had withered inside. Sam remembered the stones' warmth, his father's frightening silence, the wait.

Joe Whitehorn appeared small as he emerged from the forest's edge and stood staring at Sam from across the meadow. His breath rose in vaporous puffs, like the smoke that had surrounded him for decades. From a distance, the dark fur earflaps of his bomber hat looked like Mouseketeer ears. His brown nylon coat, with the embroidered gold star and faux fur collar, made him look healthy despite the pallid, de-generated body it covered. He turned his head sharply down and to the left, speaking into the epaulet microphone on his shoulder. In the distance Sam heard the distinctive rise and fall of a siren, the sound rebounding from the thin coat of ice that had formed overnight on the edges of Deep Lake.

Making his way toward Sam, Sheriff Whitehorn gasped for air in open-mouthed inhalations, as if attempting to yawn. Behind him a swarm of deputies and investigators from the Bureau of Criminal Apprehension moved in and out of the tree-lined edge of the clearing.

"Well?" Sam said, his irritation and impatience obvious.

The sheriff pulled off his hat and wiped the perspira-tion from his hairline. He placed it back on his head before looking at Sam. "Tell me about the bog."

"What do you mean? I already told you about the bog. What about the graves? Why don't you return my phone calls?"

"What led you to walk out on that bog?"

"Seven pissed-off wolves. I had no other place to go. There was somewhat of a trail that headed out there. I fol-lowed it."

"What day was that?"

"A couple of days ago. You know what day it was. I came to see you at your office the very next day."

The sheriff reached inside his coat searching for the cigarettes that were no longer there.

"Why don't you try lollipops, Kojak?"

The sheriff glared at Sam for a long moment. "Why would you pull out your magic rods and douse for bodies in the middle of a bog?"

"It was an accident. I was using the rods to scare away the wolves. What does it matter? Did you find anything?"

"I'll ask the questions, Dawson."

Sam looked down at L2. She was beginning to drool. "Where are you going with this Joe Friday routine?"

"Did you think that ground penetrating radar would work on a bog?" the sheriff asked.

Sam thought for a moment. "I never thought about it. Does it?"

"Nope, I had to bring in the sonar fish finder that I use for ice fishing."

"And?"

"Don't leave town, Dawson." The sheriff turned and started to walk away. Stopping, he turned back toward Sam. "And I won't tell you again. Get a tag on that dog."

Geneneral Eisenhower's wife was from Boone. That, and the fact that they had a roundhouse capable of turning the giant Big Boy and Challenger locomotives around, seemed to be their claim to fame. The Fairmont Hotel, where the road crews stayed while awaiting orders for their return trips, had a television in the lounge. No one that Hans knew owned a TV or even wanted one, but the rails gathered twice a week in the smoke-filled lounge to stare at the tiny, colorless screen. Baseball games, Chesterfield cigarettes, and Pabst Blue Ribbon beer kept the men occupied on the other end. Jackie Robinson had been the target of their frustration for the last couple of years, as if they needed another reason to hate the Dodgers. It was Tuesday night and the ceiling fans did nothing to stem the August heat. Milton Berle and Judy Canova had the sweaty men roaring with laughter. It was 1949 and the country could laugh again.

Hans felt stagnant, adrift. His conversations with Gloria, of course always one-sided, had become infrequent and then had stopped altogether. He had learned to frame his questions so that a simple "uh-huh" or "huh-uh" could be used to respond. A long "mmmm" signaled either a maybe or a didn't know. She was silent when he had asked again for her forgiveness.

The Axis had been routed out of North Africa and the Allies were about to clean up Sicily and Italy, when her mother died in 1943. His condolences were minimally accepted. The war years seemed to pull them further apart as the railroad continued to devour both his time and energy. By the time the country was able to concentrate on northern Europe, their relationship had become like one between distant relatives, cordial but lacking emotion.

"Hans," the nervous desk clerk said discreetly, leaning over Hans's shoulder. "There's a Negro here to see you."

Hans looked at him as if he had not heard him.

"He's in the lobby. You know the hotel's policy, Hans. I can't let him in here. Would you take him out the back—"

"I'll handle it," Hans said.

William stood proudly at the end of the reservation desk. "Trap," he said, smiling broadly, and held out his hand.

Hans dismissed the gesture and threw his arms around him. "William, it's great to see you. What a surprise. What are you doing in Boone, Iowa?"

"The show's set up just outside of town. Since we was in a couple hundred miles of Clinton, I thought I would give you a call. Your boy Carl answered the phone and said you was in Boone. Too good to be true, I thought, so I called the railroad and found out where you was staying. Gosh, it's good to see you, Trap. How's the family? Carl was just born when we talked last."

"Carl's seven now and I've added another to the brood. William turned four in May."

"William?"

"That's right. He's the namesake of a friend of mine from the old days," Hans said, grinning.

William scratched behind his ear and smiled. "Now don't that beat all," he said, shaking his head.

"I'd buy you a beer, but they don't allow the likes of you in a fine establishment like this. I know a little place down the street where we can get a milkshake, if you like, and we can catch up."

••••

Madame Marguerite had died in June of 1945 just after V-E Day, but before Hiroshima and Nagasaki. She willed her entire estate, the carnival, to William.

"The writin's on the wall, Trap. Get big or fold up your tent. The little shows are droppin' like flies." William took a long draw on the straw standing in the center of his chocolate shake. "The money is in long-term contracts with state fairs, livestock shows, rodeos, and the like. Ten-in-ones are on their way out. Single-Os are the name of the game. They want rides for the huge crop of young'ns that's been hittin' the ground since the end of the war. They don't want freaks or kootch shows. Pickled punks are okay, but you gotta have more center joints and cook shacks for the clems. Too many flat stores or bunko and you won't be asked back. And you've seen what's happened to wrestling. It's all about the show."

Hans nodded his head. Gorgeous George with his outrageous costumes, hair, and behavior was taking the country by storm. Killer Kowalski, Verne Gagne, the French Angel, the Sheik, and others filled the auditorium seats with well-rehearsed theatrical productions.

"I think we got a chance of gettin' Cheyenne Frontier Days next year and I've been talking to the state fair folks in Minnesota, which brings me to one of the reasons I wanted to look you up."

Hans raised his eyebrows.

"You ain't never gonna guess who I ran into when we played Grand Rapids last month."

He could feel his heart race and he was afraid to swallow the obvious lump in his throat. "I give up." Hans stirred his milkshake slowly and deliberately, avoiding eye contact with William.

"We was set up at the fairgrounds west of town, a real pretty spot with a little lake, and all the buildings were white-washed. Big ole pine trees all around."

"Who?" Hans interrupted, looking him straight in the eye.

"Miss Gloria—I mean Doctor Halvorson. That's who. She came walking right up to me, tall and straight, that long brown hair of hers shining like a halo, a big smile on her face. She was a real sight for these sore old eyes. I wanted to give her a big hug but had a vision of myself hanging from the archway into the fairgrounds. I ain't forgettin' those lynchings of black circus workers in Duluth. My, my, she's a handsome woman, pretty as a picture."

Hans gave him a hard look.

"Of course, I forgot she couldn't talk and I started blab-bing questions at her. But she just smiled and pulled out a pencil and paper. You're both damn lucky to know a Negro who can read."

Hans rolled his eyes. "Will you get to the point before I put one on you?"

"The point is, she asked about you and I could tell she was nervous about it. You know how white folks turn red in the face and get blotches on their necks when they is upset? Anyway, a long story short, I told her I would be down here in a month and I would try to look you up." William leaned forward and reached into his hip pocket. He pulled out a slightly soiled and dog-eared envelope that had been folded in half. He straightened it awkwardly and handed it to Hans. "She wanted me to give you this."

Hans hesitated, then gently took the envelope. He turned it over and back again. It was blank.

"I'm pretty sure she could afford the four cents to mail it, but I guess she didn't know your address or was scared your missus might open it. Speakin' of who—"

"I'll open it later." Hans cut him off. He folded the envelope on its original crease and placed it in his shirt pocket. "I don't get to see you every day, so let's make the most of it. I'm firing the packer back to Clinton in a few hours, California produce on ice headed for Chicago. It's a hotshot with priority. It only takes four hours to get home. How about I take you to dinner and—"

"Thanks, Trap, but I better get back to the show." William nudged his empty glass to the center of the table and scooted back his chair. "We're only here for two nights. We open in Storm Lake on Saturday. I got a crew working for me now that would steal the pennies off a dead man's eyes. It's hard to find good help these days with more jobs than people to fill 'em. 'Bout all I can get is ex-cons and white trash. It's not like the good ole days when there was honor among us thieves."

"Yeah," Hans smiled, "we were an honorable lot."

••••

The truck with William behind the wheel shrank in the distance, turned, and then it was gone, erased from the future. But the past remained. Hans stood on the curb for nearly a minute staring after it, remembering.

••••

Hans's knees felt weak as he climbed the stairs to the hotel's second floor. The envelope protruded from his breast pocket, its presence both ominous and jubilant. It had been six years since he had called, when her mother died. Had she forgiven him? He turned the envelope over and over in his hands as he sat on the edge of the bed. Finally, he took a deep breath and carefully tore it open.

My Dearest Hans,

I have debated for a very long time whether to write this letter. I believe there comes a time in everyone's life when they can see the whole of their existence—the beginning, the middle, and the end—when we realize our mortality. Preparations must be made. Truths must be spoken, especially those that haunt the soul.

Your last words to me asked if I would ever forgive you. It took me years to conclude there was nothing you had done for which you needed my forgiveness. Indeed, it is I who needs your forgiveness.

You loved me and a very bad man took advantage of that. You could not have predicted what happened to me. There is no forgiveness needed.

You loved me and asked me to marry you. I dismissed your proposal and you moved on with your life. You married and found happiness. There is no forgiveness needed. It is I who should have predicted my fate. You do not know the whole story, my love. I have made serious mistakes in my life for which I have profound regrets. But these errors in judgment pale in comparison to the blunder committed when I rejected your love.

The truth is, Hans, I love you. I have always loved you. I would do anything and sacrifice everything to protect you. There is scarcely a moment of the day that passes without me thinking of you, of regretting the path taken. I doubted my love for you and made the wrong decision. I never stop imagining what our lives could have been and the happiness I would have received by spending my life with you. I know that I hurt you. My body aches with sorrow each time I think of what I have done to you and to us. I beg your forgiveness. But forgiveness does not change the past. Some believe absolution clears the conscience. I am not sure that is possible. But I feel compelled to tell you that I love you and that I am sorry I pushed you away. My hope is that someday you can find it in your heart to forgive me.

Hans, I wish for you the happiness that you so richly deserve. A response to this letter is unnecessary. My intention is not to cause you anguish. Rather, it is to free you from the guilt you have assumed is only yours. I wish I could prescribe a medicine or perform a surgery that would restore our lives. I can only hope that forgiveness will aid the healing process.

Be well, my dearest. Remember us as we were, Hans. Never forget the time we shared together. I am hopeful it will comfort us both to know that our love is secure for the rest of our lives. And if there is life after this mortal existence, perhaps we will meet again. Until then, I remain

Affectionately yours,

Gloria

Darkness crept into the room unnoticed. He stared at nothing. He startled when the telephone rang at 10:00 p.m. He was ordered for midnight. Ordered to accept what was real: a wife, two kids, a house, and a job that stole his life. He resented that he resented. He thought he had been moderately happy. But her letter was a sucker punch that left him dizzy with swirling images of a life that could have been. He had questions—questions that, if left unanswered, would consume him. Anger crept slowly to the surface. She had cleared her conscience, but what about him? Didn't he deserve equal opportunity to clear the air? A letter would be too open-ended and a telephone call totally one-sided. "Deep Lake," he said, his voice scratchy. He would go to Minnesota and settle this once and for all. "Deep Lake," he repeated with conviction.

Deep Lake, Minnesota—2007
Day 10, 3:42 p.m.

That's right, Hans. You're in Deep Lake. Where did you think you were?" Robyn said, her huge blue eyes reflected his withered image back to him. "When I got here after school, Taneesha said you weren't feeling so well. Is there anything I can get for you?"

Hans's eyes followed her lips.

Robyn Threlkeld pushed her long, blonde hair from her face. She tucked it behind her pink ear and straightened the name tag pinned above her right breast. "I've been in Deep Lake my whole life," she said unexpectedly with a sigh. "Except for band trips to football games, I've never left this place." She stared at him and smiled. "I bet you've been lots of places, haven't you, Hans?"

She sat on the edge of his bed. Cartoon characters in bright colors were scattered across her scrubs. Hans continued to stare at her face.

"My folks are divorced. My dad works in the mine over at Hibbing. I don't see him very often. Sometimes in the summer he takes me walleye fishing." She smiled with a faraway look in her eyes as she stared out the window. "He's about as talkative as you are." She smiled again. "My mom works for the school district. She really has a hard time making ends meet with me and my little brother. I guess you could say we're poor," she looked down, embarrassed by her disclosure. "And now—" She sighed and looked away. "She doesn't like my boyfriend, Mike. His name is Michael Wies, but everyone calls him Weasel or Weas for short. Mom says he won't ever amount to anything. He's older, dropped out of high school a few years back. He works at the pulp mill over in Grand Rapids. Mom says he has no future. He's really a great guy and I love him. The problem is, you see, he's twenty-one and I just turned seventeen." She looked down.

Hans stared at her.

Robyn's eyes filled with tears. "My mom said she would have him arrested if he ever, you know, went too far with me." She took a deep breath. "Well, guess what? I've missed my period and I'm pretty sure I'm pregnant. And I haven't heard from him or seen my keycard in more than a week." She paused and took his hand in hers. "You're the only other person on the planet who knows, Hans. I haven't even told my best friend, Kim. But I know you can keep a secret. And I'd appreciate any advice you might have," she said, wiping the tears from her eyes and looking at him. "What am I supposed to do?" The tears came again. "Maybe if I just left Deep Lake." She thought about that for a few seconds and then said, "But how far would I get on a bicycle? Besides, this is my home. It's where I grew up." Robyn looked away, embarrassed. "And I love him." She stood and smiled at him, then bent down and placed her cheek against his. "Thanks for listening, Hans. I feel better already," she whispered.

His lips parted but no sound came. He felt her warmth and smelled her freshness, a mixture of shampoo and soap. Her words were soft but most were unheard. They were inti-

mate to his ear and stirred passion in his heart as he remembered.

Robyn dabbed at the tears in her eyes. "Would you like
something to eat?"

Deep Lake, Minnesota—1949

He thought about her question for a long moment and then laid the tablet with her scrawl on the bed beside him. He couldn't remember when he had eaten last. Pushing himself up on an elbow, he looked at the Baby Ben on the dresser. It was Saturday, and the rest of the world did not exist. He wished he could stop Ben's ticking and freeze the moment in time. There would be no future, no past, only the present. He savored the feel of cool sheets on his bare legs and the warmth of her skin pressed against his side in the tangle of dangerous flesh. Above the dresser was the unlikely etching of a naked woman sitting in an armchair looking out the window of her home, as if waiting for someone to arrive. Her elbows on her knees and her hands clasped together, she appeared relaxed. She was wearing shoes. Her long hair covered her face and her body was turned slightly away from the viewer, hiding any graphic details of the female form. Her white flesh amid the darkness of the room drew the viewer to her nakedness and created a sensual, almost erotic scene—a scene isolated above Gloria's dresser within a house devoid of similar art. Long ago he had asked her about it. She said she had gotten it in Manhattan when she was a resident. He had never asked her why.

Closing his eyes, he inhaled deeply through his nose and drank in her scent. Reality seemed to fade into a hazy, gray ring on the periphery of his imagination. He allowed the present to consume him. The past did not exist. There was no future. A rhythmic throbbing in his ears was synchronized with the beat of his heart, his deceitful heart. His eyes opened suddenly as guilt and fear oozed upward from his stomach into his throat. He was afraid to move, as if movement would give away his location and allow both the past and future to overtake him.

Gloria tapped his nose gently with the tablet, flashing the question at him again.

"I could eat," he said, his voice cracking.

••••

She sipped her coffee and stared at him as he pushed his uneaten food around his plate. She cleared her throat.

Hans looked up, almost surprised by her presence.

Gloria raised her eyebrows.

"She thinks I'm in Galena for training," he said, looking down again. "There's no end to the training lately. They're buying almost all diesel-electric locomotives this year. Steam is on its way out, lots of retirements too. Everything is changing. The unions even negotiated a forty-hour work week this year. There'll be more time for watching that little box of tubes with moving pictures that everyone gawks at every night." He sipped his coffee and said nothing for a long while. "This whole red thing is getting out of hand. We've got Red China and Russia both blowing smoke, Congress looking for traitors under every rock, and Truman giving our money to any country that might be threatened by the commies. In a little over two months it'll be 1950. Who would have thought we would make it this far?" He shook his head. "Isn't it funny where you end up? When you're young you think you have all these choices and you can pick and choose and even back up if things don't work out. The truth is if you make a mistake, you're stuck. There's no going back."

Gloria attempted a half-smile before setting her coffee cup down.

"Regrets," he said, looking away. "Life's full of them." He sipped his coffee again. "Don't get me wrong, I love my family. But once you start down that path...life sort of pulls you along and there are no more choices. A house, a mortgage, a car—all the things a modern family requires. You do what you have to do in order to survive. There's no going back."

Gloria reached across the table and took his hand with both of hers. She smiled a tight-lipped smile, her eyes moist with tears. They stared silently at each other, remembering, imagining. They were saying goodbye.

Outside, the black spruce were motionless, their tops illuminated by the rising August sun, the earth rotating toward a new day.

Timberlane County, Minnesota—2007
Day 10, 4:01 p.m.

Sam breathed heavily. He moved his jaw sideways in an attempt to massage the ache in his right ear, a cramp from gritting his teeth. The metal button on his Wranglers clanked annoyingly against the wall of the dryer with each revolution. He sighed. After stepping down as press secretary—a highly respected member of the governor's office, he could have started his own public relations firm. Big money clients were lined up and waiting. Instead he pursued his dream of becoming a photographer, and now he sat watching his laundry go 'round in a musty KOA in the north woods of Minnesota. His tiny Airstream shone like a diamond in the otherwise empty, spacious campground. The front of the weathered, red A-frame proclaimed "Kampground Of America" in large black letters. He had pulled up stakes from Aimee's driveway earlier in the day. She made it plain she was angry with him for telling the sheriff about her secret cemetery. And as far as he knew, he was still the prime suspect for a murder that occurred on her watch. It would be better all around if he distanced himself right now.

He hadn't expected Sidney's call earlier in the afternoon, but should have. Sam's publisher had cancelled his contract. Pat had been looking for an excuse, and a call from the sheriff of Timberlane County, Minnesota, stating that Sam was a suspect in a murder investigation was all he needed to part company and demand his advance back. Sidney was in the process of lining up some pro bono legal help and was confident they could at least keep what he had already spent. But all that news paled in comparison to the real shocker when Sidney let the other shoe fall. Annie had broken up with Mark, quit her job, and was moving to Cheyenne to assume the position of publisher/managing editor/president and CEO of a newly formed independent book publishing company with a single client—Sam.

"Let me see if I have this straight," Sam said into the phone after a long, long pause. "I've been fired, I'm broke, my former girlfriend—my cousin—is my new boss, and my daughter, former daughter I should add, negotiated all this without my input or permission. Is that the gist?…Uh-huh, no I didn't forget the part about being a suspect in a murder investigation.…You've got my back? That's comforting."

His daughter had his back, an interesting and somewhat depressing revelation, he thought, as he watched his clothes tumble noisily in the dryer. He had come full circle, from parent/guardian/teacher/caregiver to dependent welfare recipient. Sidney had explained that both she and Annie believed in Sam's artistic capabilities and how he had paid his dues, and he now deserved the opportunity to pursue photographic projects without being a slave to the almighty dollar. He smiled at her naïveté. Neither she nor Annie had a clue about the costs associated with the publishing business. From production to marketing, it operated on thin profit margins and false promises, especially for coffee table books like his. But the glaring question was what did Annie's sudden presence mean in terms of their relationship? He sighed again. Too young for Aimee and too old for Annie, he thought. He was frustrated in every sense of the word. "What's wrong with me, girl?" L2 flicked her eyebrows back in a halfhearted attempt at recognition. The rest of her face spilled onto the floor like a melted taffy apple.

As concerned as he was about his future, it could not overshadow the results of Sidney's investigations of old cars, old artists, and old Indian graves.

"Sheriff wants to see you again!" the deputy yelled over the noise of the dryer.

Both Sam and L2 jumped, startled by the sudden intrusion of the corpulent officer dressed like a mannequin from an army surplus store. "Not again?" Sam whined.

"Yes again. Let's go."

"Where? I hope it's not another trip to the lake."

"Nope. He's on his way back to Walker."

"Does he have a warrant?"

"No." The deputy smiled. "He said he'd buy you dinner."

H ans, we're running out of time," Aimee Pond
whispered as she leaned over him, her face only
inches from his. "You need to tell me about Gloria, Gloria Halvorson."

His eyes suddenly met hers. The cloudiness seemed to
disappear as he stared intently at her.

"She was my mother and I believe you knew her." Aimee smiled at him, the type of smile one gives when admitting something without speaking. "She was born in that
house you visited yesterday." She paused as she searched his
face for any response. "The house I live in now used to be
her medical clinic. It's pretty obvious you knew your way
around there too. You've been in both of them before. How
did you know her, Hans? I'm guessing, but the morning glory on your arm tells me it was more than a casual relationship. When did you know her? Was it before the car accident
when she lost her tongue? Talk to me, Hans. Do you remember why you are here?" Aimee's eyes narrowed with intensity.

Hans took her hand in his and sighed deeply but made
no attempt to talk.

Aimee clutched his hand and sat down on the edge of
the bed. "I was only fifteen when she died and I'm forgetting
her," she admitted. "I've tried to hold on to the few memories I have of her. But now those seem so distant. They show

up now and then. It's like finding a piece of a jigsaw puzzle under the couch. You have no idea where it fits, but without it the puzzle can't be completed." She squeezed his hand and smiled at him. "And now, looking closely at the corner of the lid to the puzzle box, I see a man in the distance. He's on the edge of the picture but he's looking in." She paused, "That man is you, Hans. You're much younger, but it's you. You're a part of the puzzle. Maybe a big part, maybe a little part. I don't know.

"What's so frustrating is that you and I seem to be competing for her memory. I'm thinking that maybe you knew her longer than I did. I'll bet your memories make more sense than mine. Mine are bits and pieces scattered randomly through time. The context is often lost. I remember arguments. They usually involved things I wanted that she denied. You know, she wouldn't let me date? Do you think that explains why I've never married? That somehow I'm afraid of angering my dead mother, of doing something she disapproved of when I was fifteen? That I've inherited her cautiousness with men? Maybe it's the religious doctrine the Lutherans beat me over the head with. Their entire faith is based on guilt, you know. The saintly spirit of my long-dead mother watches over me. She sees everything I do and is making a list to confront me with someday." She smiled. "But enough about me." She turned back toward Hans. His eyes were closed.

"Gloria," he whispered. His mouth opened slightly. He slept.

Deep Lake, Minnesota—2007
Day 11, 6:27 a.m.

Darkness gave way reluctantly. The uncertain light of dawn spread across the landscape, red at first, then orange. Aimee sensed that he was watching her and she was afraid to move. Conversation would be awkward again. After all, they barely knew each other.

"You awake?" Will said, his head poking around the doorjamb of her bedroom.

"I am now. What time is it?"

"Almost six thirty. I'd start the coffee, but I don't know where you keep it."

"Door of the refrigerator. Aren't you afraid it will stain your teeth and make you pee?"

"That's tea. Besides it's for you, not me."

Her bladder ached, but relief would necessitate confronting Will Gottlieb, who stood in the hallway just outside her bedroom door. She had allowed him to sleep on the couch in the living room again. It had been after midnight and snowing hard when he finally stopped talking about himself. He seemed totally unconcerned that his father may have known her mother. Aimee glanced at the closet door where her robe was hung.

As if sensing the awkwardness of the moment, Will suddenly entered the room and retrieved her robe. He was already dressed. "Here you go," he said, smiling. "I'm calling

dibs on the john first. I have a prostate the size of a canta-
loupe and, frankly, I can't hold it any longer." With that, he
turned and dashed out of the bedroom and down the hall
toward the bathroom.

••••

At breakfast they made small talk, meaningless com-
ments about strawberry preserves, the body's response to
the gluten in the wheat bread that filled Aimee's mouth, how
most coffees tasted the same in spite of what it said on the
bag, and the fact that he was lactose intolerant.

"Aimee," Will said, looking over his glass of apple juice,
"why is it that you never married?"

She held her hand over her mouth while she quickly
chewed a mouthful of poisonous toast. Swallowing, she
looked at him with narrowing eyes. "Normally, I would take
offense at the boldness of such a personal question and answer with an equally offensive question such as: Why is it
that you never considered reconstructive surgery? Or, why is
it that you lack the basic social graces that would inhibit you
from unabashedly asking a question of that nature? However, since I've allowed you to sleep in my house and eat my
food like the stray dog you are, I'll respond in terms you'll
understand." She smiled and raised her middle finger.

Will laughed and shook his head. "Touché! That's what
I like about you, Aimee Pond: hostile irreverence instead of
the expected. How refreshing. Unfortunately, it appears the
men in your life, if there were any, were never able to take

you anywhere without a muzzle and a leash. I suppose that's the price they had to pay for being attracted to a sociopath."

"Speaking of a price to pay, now that you're going to be living on a fixed income, it will be tough to come up with the fifty-bucks-a-pop you're used to paying for a woman's company." She smiled and batted her eyelashes at him.

Will smiled back and said, "I guess I got my answer. But at the risk of offending you, if that were even possible, why Deep Lake, Minnesota? Why did you stay here?

Aimee said nothing for a long moment as she stared into her coffee cup. "It's funny where you end up. It's even funnier where you don't end up," she said as if talking to herself. "I stopped asking myself that question years ago." She looked across the table at Will. "The simple answer is—I used to like it here. I used to like what I do, in spite of an incompetent administration, and I used to be content. I think I used to be afraid to be anywhere else."

Will looked at her doubtfully. "That's a lot of 'used to' statements. What's different now?"

Aimee sipped her coffee and smiled. "I guess I'm starting to realize my mortality and I'm frustrated. I'm hopelessly middle class and I want to see how the other half lives. I've been in Deep Lake most of my life and I don't know why. I don't want to end up like the people I care for. I hear it at Whispering Pines all the time. People telling me they were born here and they want to die here. It seems to give them comfort when facing the uncertainty of death, the familiar overriding the unfamiliar." She paused and turned to look out the kitchen window. "Many believe their loved ones wait for them at the place where they shared their lives. Again, that anticipated reunion gives them comfort. They've made that choice, regardless of where life has taken them since the one they loved passed on." She paused and then smiled. "I've seen people choose to be buried next to a spouse who died decades before them, even though they had remarried and raised a family with someone else. It's who they choose to spend eternity with. I think that's why your father came here to Deep Lake," she said, suddenly changing the subject.

"He has a lot bought and paid for next to my mother back in Iowa," Will said, a note of defensiveness in his voice. "He was born in Clinton. He raised his family in the area. He may have traveled the world in his younger years but that was his home. Besides, there's no one here—"

"Where will you be buried?" Aimee interrupted.

"I'll be cremated."

"And what about your ashes? What are your instructions?"

"I own some property in the mountains west of Fort Collins, a beautiful meadow surrounded by aspen, a small stream, a log cabin. It's where our pet cemetery is," he added, looking down.

"But your home is in Iowa," Aimee protested.

"I left home when I was eighteen."

"So let me get this straight. Your family, who loved you and raised you, is interred in Iowa and you want your remains sprinkled over the graves of dead animals in Colorado. That's who you want to spend eternity with?"

"It's a personal choice, not a social statement. It doesn't mean that I don't love my parents. I dug each of those pets' graves. I built that cabin. I laid in that meadow and contemplated the universe. It was my sanctuary. It's where I took refuge."

Aimee smiled. "Do you remember your first kiss?"

"Of course," he said, furrowing his brow.

"When was it? Where was it? Describe your surroundings. Give me the details."

"I don't see what this has to do with—"

"Humor me."

"It was around 1960, I think, probably late July or early August, one of those sultry Illinois summer nights where you could wring water out of the air. Mosquitoes the size of hummingbirds gave me something to do with my awkward hands. She lived just up the block, and her mother had issued the second call for her to come in for the night. I was fifteen and she was twelve going on twenty-seven. We were sitting in my brother's '34 Ford Coupe parked behind our garage. It smelled of oil and dust. We both loved dogs but had run out of dog things to talk about. She wanted me to kiss her, but I was too shy. I remember my heart was pounding so hard I could barely catch my breath. It was her mother's third-and-final warning, accompanied by a slammed screen door, which prompted her to latch on to me with a lip-lock that lasted all of two seconds before she bolted out of the car and ran for home. I was dizzy for two weeks."

"Were you in love?"

"I must have been. I carved our initials into every picnic table, teeter-totter, and outhouse door in the city park. I would have painted them on the water tower, except I froze halfway up."

"How long were you sweethearts?"

"That was it. We never kissed again, or talked to one another for that matter. It was our secret. She was an eighth grader, for crying out loud, and I was in high school. The guys would have laughed me out of town. Funny, I ran into her years later, after college. She had morphed into this beautiful woman who still made my heart pound with desire. I could tell she felt the same way, but it was too late. I was a newly minted assistant professor and was already married to my career. I think about her every now and then and wonder what might have been."

Aimee was beaming. "The fact that you remember a kiss that took place nearly half a century ago with such clarity proves my point."

"What point was that?"

"When you meet someone and they ask where you're from, what do you say?"

"I tell them I was born in Iowa, raised in Illinois, but I've lived in Colorado for the last—"

"My point is," Aimee cut him off again, "that home is where the heart is. That's where you came of age. That's where your emotional attachments are. Why else would you tell someone where you spent a mere eighteen years of your life? Illinois is your home."

"She still lives in Illinois, by the way."

"You've never forgotten her. You've even kept track of her."

"It doesn't mean I want to be buried next to her."

"Of course not. You've moved on with your life, developed other emotional attachments. Or maybe...," she hesitated.

"What?" he asked a little too loudly.

"Oh, sometimes people who want to be interred with their animals are folks who haven't developed strong emotional relationships with people."

"Or maybe they're veterinarians," he said, straightening in his chair.

"Sorry, I didn't mean that as an indictment. It's just a general observation."

Neither of them spoke for several seconds. Aimee sipped her coffee and then cleared her throat. "Your dad has nearly forty years on you. Who's to say what your wishes will be forty years from now? Maybe you'll show up in Illinois."

"He has dementia," Will said flatly.

"So will you at that age," she smiled. "I had a nutty roommate in college who was fond of saying that her madness caused her to see things more clearly. I've often wondered if dementia allows the truth to rise up from the depths of repression to show us who we really are, warts and all. Typically people say and do things that seem totally out of character. They cuss like sailors, seem preoccupied with sex, and are often aggressive—all the things they actively inhibited throughout their lives. It's that lack of social inhibition that causes them to be institutionalized."

STEVEN W. HORN

"Interesting theory, Doctor Pond. You just described the average domestic dog. Don't you hate it when they hump the sofa pillows in front of company? Look, I'm not buying your idea that he came here to die. I don't think he has a clue as to why or how he ended up in Deep Lake. Dementia is a complex physiological phenomenon. It's neuroelectrical and neurochemical in nature. You're trying to describe it in behavioral terms, which, frankly, adds little to the ultimate explanation of the disease. Again, I've lost the point of this most interesting but irrelevant conversation."

"He has a purpose, Will. Don't you see it? He came here to die. Morning Glory, my mother's nickname, was an expression of love. He had it tattooed on his arm, for crying out loud."

"I think you're reading way too much into—"

"Why didn't I think of this before?" Aimee said, suddenly jumping up from the table. "Mom's files are in the basement. She was meticulous about record keeping."

"Did you just change the subject again?"

Aimee was halfway down the hall. "Come on. You can make yourself useful by holding the flashlight."

••••

The basement was dank and smelled of coal. A single light bulb at the bottom of the stairs seemed overwhelmed by the cold darkness. A dozen or more cardboard boxes were piled upon each other along the wall behind the open staircase.

"Here," Aimee said, pointing to one end of the pile. "These are the patient files."

Cobwebs and dust covered the boxes, but they were clearly labeled alphabetically. Aimee read off the groupings. "Here we go, A through H," she said as she pulled the box to the floor and removed the lid. "Give me some light," she commanded, her fingers walking across the file tabs. "Christensen, Dierksen, Everettson, Erikson, Ferguson, Gilbertson—" She stopped and looked up at Will. The next file was labeled "Gottlieb, Hans R." She pulled the thick folder from the box as if it were fragile and laid it on top of the others. Neither of them spoke. The flashlight's beam bounced in Will's unsteady hand. He inhaled deeply.

Will exhaled loudly through his nose as though he had achieved resolution or proclaimed finality.

Aimee looked up from the kitchen table; her eyes were red and puffy. She held a tissue in her hand. She waited and then realized his gesture was one of frustration rather than conclusion. She desperately needed someone to collate the information, summarize it, and put a period at the end. She stared at the kitchen door as if expecting the jury to file in and deliver the verdict. But she knew what their judgment would be. The sentence was what she was unsure of. She would plead for mercy.

Will cleared his throat. "I sure as hell didn't need that. Any of it," he added a moment later, as though he were trying to rid his mouth of a bad taste.

Aimee shook her head and looked away. She flicked the back of her hand toward an official-looking piece of paper. "You know, there were probably a half-dozen times in my life when I needed *that*," she said softly, "and nobody could find it. No record at all."

The birth certificate lay atop a pile of medical forms, newspaper clippings, and letters. The yellowed newsprint with bold headlines that declared "The Trapper Heavyweight Champion of the World" was as insignificant as the medical records that described his gunshot wound and the stack of love letters from Hans postmarked from Boone, Iowa. But it all paled in contrast to the Minnesota State Department of Health, Division of Vital Statistics, Certificate of Birth that boldly proclaimed the birth of Aimee Frances Halvorson. She was born June 9, 1950, in Timberlane County, Town of Deep Lake; at home at 11:30 a.m. Gloria R. Halvorson was both the MD and the mother. Sophie Mickelson served as midwife. Father of the Child was Hans Rudolf Gottlieb, age 42, a white man born in Clinton, Iowa. His usual occupation was listed as "Fireman, C.N.W.R.R." There was no mention of Charles Pond, no Social Security numbers, addresses, or embossed seal of the State Department of Health. The mother was unmarried.

"What did I do to deserve this? I got an education, worked hard all my life, dedicated myself to helping others, and this is how I'm repaid—I'm given a brother?" She shook her head in disbelief. "I want to cry, but I'm too stunned. I never saw this one coming."

"Half brother," Will said weakly.

"What?"

"If any of this is true, I'm your half brother. It would be the same degree of relatedness as if we were first cousins. We share a quarter of our genotype."

"Shut up, Will. Just shut up." Her eyes filled with tears. "You're my brother, for crying out loud. I don't need a lecture on genetics."

"You're not the only victim here, Aimee. I've had a lifetime of being my father's son. You were only fifteen when your mother died. I understand your image of her has been shattered. Perhaps the pedestal you'd placed her on was unrealistically high. But we're talking about my dad too."

"You were eighteen when you left home, Will. You never went back. It's not as though you and he were joined at the hip. You said it yourself—he was never there. I'm just saying that maybe I was as close to my mother in memory as you were to your father in reality."

Will attempted a smile. "Let's not concern ourselves with who's been hurt the most. There's no winner in that contest. It might be best if we try to focus on where we go from here."

"What are you talking about?"

"I'm talking about the immediate concern of what we do with this information. Who do we tell? What are the implications? Is there some resolution we should work toward? I mean, now what? I'm really confused right now, but—"

"You're confused? Christ, Will, I don't know whether to welcome you to the family or swab your cheek for DNA." The tears came again. "Sophie Mickelson knew who I was and never said a word." She wiped her eyes with each hand. "And what is all this stuff? What does it mean?" She swirled her hand through the pile of papers on the table. She picked out a pair of ticket stubs to the Skylight Room in Boone, Iowa. "Who the hell is Artie Shaw?" she asked. "What about this?" She lifted a yellowed newspaper clipping with the headline "Mob Boss Lucello Missing." "Or this?" she asked, holding up a handbill for O'Brien's Wonders of the World Travelling Show that proclaimed "Freaks, Oddities,

Wrestling, Burlesque, and Death Defying Rides." A picture of a scantily clad woman with a snake around her neck was labeled "Reba The Snake Girl."

"Wait a second. Let me see that," Will said, taking the handbill from Aimee. He studied it for a few seconds before he shook his head no. He sat back in his chair, his mouth open, his face ashen. "I can't believe this. Tell me this isn't happening."

"What?" Aimee asked. "What is it, Will?"

"That's my mother," he said, pointing at the picture. "The snake girl is my mother. Her name was Rebecca and she insisted on being called by her full, given name. Sometimes when Dad was angry with her, he would call her Reba in order to goad her."

"Are you sure?"

"You don't think I recognize my own mother?" he said with obvious irritation. "Mary, Mother of Christ, my mother was a circus freak." He stood and ran his fingers through his hair. He began to pace back and forth the length of the tiny kitchen. "She had no history," he said suddenly. "She said her family had died when she was young and she was raised by some Irish doctor who moved around a lot." He stopped and turned toward Aimee. "When's this going to end? How many more secrets are there?"

"I don't know, Will."

"The big family secret," Will said, stopping and looking directly at Aimee, "that nobody talked about was the fact that she was a closet alcoholic. It was worse when Dad was on the other end—Boone or Des Moines. We never saw her drink and she never got hammered, but she sometimes slurred her words and seemed to forget things. Don't get me wrong. She was a wonderful, loving mother who doted on my brother and me. But she always seemed a little down. In the end, she died of cirrhosis of the liver. I saw the pathology report."

"So," Aimee said a little too loudly. "Let me summarize: My father—our father," she corrected, "was a carnival wrestler, your mother was an alcoholic snake charmer, and my mother was the other woman, who was married to an Indian. Whew, I'm glad that's settled. Would you like a cup of tea?" She paused and then added weakly, "To hell with your teeth."

He saw the tears welling up in her eyes again. He hesitated, then stepped toward her and held out his arms.

She stared up at him; the tears spilled down her cheeks. She rose slowly and allowed him to embrace her.

"None of this changes who we are," he paused and then added, "Sis."

Aimee smiled and sniffed. "I always wanted a big brother."

They held each other briefly and then pushed apart, not making eye contact.

"This is awkward, isn't it?" Will said finally.

"Yes," Aimee said, looking out the kitchen window. The large dial thermometer with a picture of a loon on it showed a temperature of eight.

The pinkish dawn had yielded to dark gray clouds that cast an even dullness over Deep Lake. It was snowing lightly. The phone rang.

Robyn met them at the front door to Whispering Pines. She was crying. Taneesha stood at the nursing station, her hands on her hips in a defensive "I told you so" posture.

"Nurse Pond, I was only gone for a few minutes. I went to get his breakfast before I left for school and when I came back—"

"Quit your blubbering, Robyn," Aimee said. "Did he say anything? Did he get dressed? Tell me what happened."

"You want that I should call the sheriff?" Taneesha said matter-of-factly, but loud enough for all the residents in the dining room to hear.

"Not yet. Let's look in all the usual places first. Robyn, how long has he been gone?"

"I don't know, maybe an hour or so. I searched the entire home before I told anyone."

"Taneesha, check his closet to see what he's wearing. The temperature is dropping and it's snowing harder."

"Where does he usually go?" Will asked.

"Just down the road," Aimee said. "There's a little park, sort of a greenbelt with a bike path. There's a park bench he seems to like. But he could be anywhere. He's shown up at both my mother's house—where the Jorgensons live now, and her clinic—my house."

"His coat and overshoes are still in the closet," Taneesha said, out of breath, her eyes wide. "He's got on that old suit he was wearin' when he showed up here. But look here what I found on his tray table." She waved the piece of paper in the air as if it were a ransom note.

Aimee took it from her and held it at arm's length, not bothering to find her glasses. Will looked over her shoulder. He recognized his father's sharp script that Will always thought looked like he was trying to cut something out of the paper rather than apply ink. It was a $10,000 check made out to Robyn Threlkeld.

"Who's Robyn Threlkeld?" Will asked.

Both Aimee and Taneesha turned toward Robyn, who stood shyly at the nursing station. No one spoke.

Will rubbed the back of his neck. "I don't get it," he said.

Aimee slipped the check into her coat pocket. "We'll discuss this later. Right now we need to concentrate on finding Hans. Taneesha, drive over to the Jorgensons' and see if he shows up there again. Will, he might be headed to my house. Search all the roads between here and there. I'll check the greenbelt. Let's go, people. It's cold out there and there's a storm coming."

••••

Each time Aimee inhaled, the cold air cut at her nose and throat like broken glass. She sat on Hans's favorite park bench; she peeled back the cuff of her glove and looked at her watch. She felt strangely relieved; she had purpose. It was snowing much harder than when she had left Whispering Pines, a fine below-zero snow. A cold wind was driving the tiny flakes in waves, opaque curtains of white—parting, closing, billowing. The tops of her ears ached and she felt a burning numbness in her toes. Her face stung from the assault of wind-driven ice crystals. She stared at the tracks Hans had left in the snow. The lethal wind was erasing them before her eyes.

The swirling curtain of flakes parted momentarily. Across the greenbelt, on the other side of the bike path, a dark row of trees and a wrought iron fence emerged against the white background. It was the back side of Spruce Haven Cemetery, where her mother and the rest of the Halvorson family were buried. As the sole descendant, Aimee decorated each of the graves every Memorial Day, graves of people she never or barely knew, including her mother. Charles Pond was still missing. Her mother had taken his abuse, but never the name of her husband. Even if his body had been found, there were no Indians allowed in Spruce Haven.

She looked at her watch again. It was time. She struggled to her feet. With head down against the driving storm, she made her way across the greenbelt. The ground was rough with pinecones and sticks below the fluff of fresh snow. She easily squeezed through the gap in the fence she had used as a child, the same opening Hans had pulled himself through as evidenced by his tracks. The cold metallic odor of wrought iron stuck to the inside of her nostrils. Her fingers stung and her toes ached with numbness as she moved among the graves toward the older section of the cemetery. Here the tombstones were crooked, tilted from the huge spruce roots pushing up from below. She slipped and then awkwardly recovered as she made her way around a clump of trees—dark sentinels guarding the remains of her family.

Hans's body lay facedown beneath the gray monolith of granite that proclaimed "Halvorson, Gloria 1903–1965." The mighty Trapper, the world's greatest carnival wrestler, descended from Greek gods, appeared small, subdued by the white vastness of the storm. His left forearm was extended toward the headstone, the sleeve pushed upward, exposing the dark blotch that had once been a delicate, funnel-shaped flower. The same flower was chiseled into the stone that loomed above him, its granite bloom forever open, even in darkness.

TIMBERLANE COUNTY, MINNESOTA—2007
DAY 15, 8:12 P.M.

The snow came straight down. Large, silent flakes, the kind a child could catch on her tongue. A snowplow emerged from the east, yellow lights rotating above the bed filled with sand. Whiskers of fire flashed from the edges of the noisy blade as the truck chased the highway west. Silence followed.

The diner was illuminated softly, a silvery torpedo glowing warmly with manmade light easily held back by glass and nature. Its isolation shone through like a beacon in a sea of dark timber and waves of windswept snow. Rhonda, the anemic, red-nosed waitress, poured coffee into four coffee cups spaced evenly on the table. The four dark figures, squeezed into the booth with heads lowered, appeared lonely in spite of the gathering.

Sam was tired. He had slept little in the four days since Hans's death. The marathon telephone conversations with Sidney and others had taken their toll. He cleared his throat and was first to speak. "The Greek poet Euripides said something to the effect that when good men die, their goodness stays with us; it lives on. As for the bad, it also dies and is buried with them. Of course there's the opposite view. Shakespeare said the evil men do lives after them and the good is buried with their bones."

Aimee and Will raised their heads from across the table and stared at him blankly. Aimee attempted a smile before asking, "And our dad? Was Hans a good guy or a bad guy? I've got to tell you, Sam, this whole thing seems pretty bad to me."

Sam pulled his cup and saucer toward him. "I'd like to think that a man is as good as what he leaves behind." He sipped his coffee, avoiding any eye contact. "There was certainly a time when I believed, as did Euripides, that bad things were buried with the evildoer, that bad wasn't inherited."

"Good or bad, Sam?" Aimee interrupted. "Help me out here."

"I guess it depends on your perspective. Mine is certainly different from yours, and yours is probably different from Will's. I think we can all agree that Hans was a very interesting guy with a past that he kept well hidden. I think it's hard to categorize most people as being either good or bad. None of us is perfect. And who decides? From what Will has told me, Hans seemed like a pretty average guy who never drew attention to himself, and that was purposeful."

"Of course it was purposeful," Aimee shot back. "He was hiding his secret life of being a gifted athlete, a philandering adulterer, and a killer."

"Hold on, Aimee," Will said, the red-and-black Naugahyde protesting as he leaned back in the booth. "There's no reason to suspect Dad had anything to do with those bodies out in the forest."

Aimee looked at Joe Whitehorn.

Joe fumbled with his shirt pocket. "There were at least four bodies in the forest and one at Whispering Pines that need resolution. Forensics are still coming in. Everything's pretty old. The only thing recent was Mike Wies's body. He was a punk and small-time thief. The ME said somebody broke the Weasel's right arm and nose a couple of hours before he was stuffed into the bog at the north end of Deep Lake. He still had Robyn Threlkeld's keycard in his pocket with the jewelry he stole."

"Is she part of this? What about the check Hans wrote her?" Aimee asked.

"We don't think so. She's just an innocent kid who got taken advantage of by Mike Wies. The guy was a real bottom-feeder," Joe added. "I say give the kid her check. But that's up to Will."

Will nodded his head in agreement. "But what about the other three bodies, the ones under the doghouses?"

"Spirit houses—," Joe said with an edge to his voice.

Sam interrupted. "Joe was able to run the 1935 plate number from the 1929 DeSoto Roadster that Aimee had told me about. The Iowa Department of Transportation, working through their state archives, came up with a registration to one Reuben Carter. My daughter worked her computer magic and sent Joe this." Sam retrieved from his coat pocket the folded copy of a newspaper article from 1935 that proclaimed Carter missing. "The guy was from Hans's hometown and was some sort of local sports and war hero who had lost a leg in France."

"One of the bodies we dug up from under a spirit house was a male Caucasian with a prosthetic leg," Joe said, looking at Sam. "We may never know for sure who he was. There just aren't any records. We've got a guy at the FBI Laboratory Division at Quantico who's trying to match the hardware that was on the prosthetic leg to known manufacturers during World War I. The ME thinks the cause of death had something to do with the broken-off scalpel blade he found lodged between neck vertebrae below the victim's jaw."

"What about the head in the bucket?" Aimee asked, her nose wrinkled and eyes squinted in disgust. "Any idea about who that was?"

"We're waiting on dental records. We're hopeful we'll get a match, since the guy had a gold central incisor." Joe looked at Sam again. "The ME thinks that both Gold Tooth and Peg Leg were buried back in the '30s. If we had the money, we could turn the forensic anthropologists loose on them. Those people can tell you everything from their dietary habits to what kinds of trees were planted in their front yards."

Aimee looked at Sam for a long moment and then turned again toward Joe. "I heard one of the bodies was more recent, maybe from the 1950s?"

Again Joe reached for his breast pocket. "Based on the radioisotopes in his bones, the victim died sometime after the early fifties."

"I thought carbon-14 dating yielded ranges that were much too broad for something that recent," Will said.

The sheriff looked at Sam.

Sam smiled. "That's right, Will. What they find in all of us alive since the atomic age is the presence of certain elements like carbon-14, strontium, cesium, and tritium. Those nuclear tests in the Nevada desert in the 1950s and '60s left us all with radioactive souvenirs in our bones."

"All we know so far," Joe said, "is that the ME thinks he may have been Native American or perhaps of mixed racial heritage. There were Mongoloid features characteristic of American Indians, but the skeletal features that distinguish race were a little inconclusive." The sheriff paused. "I know what you're thinking, Aimee, but we need a lot more information before anyone can say it's the body of Charles Pond. The crime lab was able to extract DNA from a tooth. I'll head up to the rez next week and see if I can get a sample from your aunt's side of the family."

"I can save you the trip, Joe," Sam said, reaching across the table and sliding Aimee's coffee cup toward Joe Whitehorn. "Swab that. I'm pretty sure you'll get some very specific variable number tandem repeats. The VNTR pattern analysis will show a high probability of match with the DNA fingerprint from that corpse."

"What are you saying, Sam?" Aimee said, leaning back and fixing her eyes on him.

"Bear with me, Aimee. I'm going to tell you a little story, and hopefully I'll be able to answer some of your questions." He stared back at her. Sam inhaled deeply as if he were about to dive into deep water. "Peh-Nun," he said, not taking his eyes from hers.

"Excuse me?"

"It's Hebrew for 'here lies.' It was carved in Sophie Mickelson's tombstone just above her name. I found a rabbi in Duluth to translate it for me. She had ordered the marker from a monument company in Duluth nearly two decades ago and left final instructions for cemetery lettering with the local funeral home. Sophie was a member of Trinity Lutheran Church, same as your mother, so I found that very strange."

"So?"

"There's no Jewish section in Spruce Haven. No Jewish graves anywhere. There's no synagogue within a hundred miles. With a Scandinavian name like Mickelson, it got me wondering why Sophie would have had her tombstone inscribed with a Hebrew expression. So I put Sidney on it, made a few phone calls, and connected a few dots." Sam looked around the table. "I've got to tell you, there are a lot of dots in a person's life. It's hard to connect them all. At best we might be able to get an outline, but the details are often lost to history." He paused then looked directly at Aimee. "The name Sophie Mickelson was an alias. Her real name was Nicollet Blumenfeld." He waited for her reaction.

Aimee shrugged her shoulders and shook her head. "I'm not familiar with that name."

"Surely growing up in Minnesota you've heard of her brother, Isadore Blumenfeld?"

"Can't say as I have. Who is he?"

"Isadore Blumenfeld, aka Kid Cann, was a notorious mobster in the Twin Cities during Prohibition. He bootlegged huge amounts of booze into Minnesota from Canada. It was rumored he even had a pipeline that brought industrial grade alcohol from Canada to distilleries hidden all through the north woods. He was involved in the protection rackets and prostitution, and linked to a number of high-profile murders.

"Kid Cann's little sister Nicky saw the direction Kid and her other brothers were going. She left the Jewish neighborhood of north Minneapolis sometime in the late '20s. She came to Deep Lake to escape the family business and changed her name to Sophie Mickelson. She ended up working at Fuller's Grocery Store and became the best friend of the local physician, Doctor Gloria Halvorson. Surely you knew that, Aimee?"

"I guess that explains why Sophie was listed as midwife on my birth certificate and why she used to babysit me when I was little. My memories of her during those years are pretty vague. I have my doubts that she was actually that close to my mother."

Sam pulled a folded piece of notebook paper from his jacket pocket. It was yellowed with age and brittle. He unfolded it carefully. "Joe found this in your mother's hymnal, the one she got from her parents. They inscribed it to her on Palm Sunday 1914, when she was confirmed. Joe collected it from Sophie's room at Whispering Pines after her murder. Let me read it to you.

Deep Lake,
June 4, 1935

Dearest Gloria,
Remembrance loves to linger near
The ties of one I hold most dear
Remembrance oft brings back to view,
The happy hours I've spent with you.

Your best friend forever,
Sophie Mickelson

"They were best friends," Sam said, smiling. He slowly folded the paper and placed it back in his pocket.

"But I still don't see where you're going with all this," Aimee said.

"Me neither, Sam," Will said. "Is there a point coming?"

"Again, bear with me. Lives are complex and when you're trying to reconstruct them three-quarters of a century later, it gets real tricky. It's not easy to compress decades into a few sentences. I won't even begin to try to explain the connection between Hans and Gloria. The letters and clippings you and Will found in Gloria's files attest to the long and complex relationship the two of them had. Suffice it to say that they were lovers for a very long time. It would be an injustice to attempt to tell their story here. But the backstory on some of these other people is important. Trust me.... Where was I?"

"You were playing Ralph Edwards on *This Is Your Life* with Sophie Mickelson," Will said, somewhat sarcastically.

"Before my time," Sam said, returning the sarcasm. "I'll come back to Sophie in a minute. First, I'd like to give you a little background on Doctor Halvorson."

Will shook his head and smiled. But Aimee seemed to bristle at the presumptiveness of someone who never knew her mother, talking about her.

"I know, Aimee. I apologize. It's a personality flaw that I have to live with. I'm like a badger. Once I start digging, I can't stop until I get my gopher, which is a clumsy segue into your mother's college years."

"I'm all ears," she said, tucking her chin.

"Your mom graduated high school in 1920. She left Deep Lake for Minneapolis where she attended the University of Minnesota for two years. I assume they were called Gophers back then. Anyway, she was accepted into the College of Medicine of the University of Illinois in 1922 where she spent the next four years. Even by the standards of the day, med school was expensive. There were only a handful of women and they were shamefully discriminated against, but your mother made it. Not only did she graduate with distinction, she seems to have prospered financially. In 1923 she acquired an apartment building on Taylor Street in Little Italy on the Near West Side of Chicago, right smack-dab in the middle of University Village. She rented apartments to medical students and, while I can't confirm it, provided medical care to Lucky "Big Ears" Lucello and his mob. She showed up on the FBI's radar in 1924 in their investigations of money laundering by Lucello. It gets real sketchy here, but it appears that Lucky bought several buildings in Gloria's name between 1923 and 1927. Lucky's attorney, Cortland Davis, represented Gloria in all the transactions. No one seems to know how or why this relationship developed, but the speculation is that Lucky was smitten with her."

"You're making this up!" Aimee almost yelled, unable to contain herself any longer. "You're telling me that my mother owned properties in Chicago and consorted with gangsters?"

"Yes."

"Well, I'm telling you that you're mistaken. This is—"

"Hold on, Pond Scum," Joe said, raising his hand. "Let the man finish. You'll have your turn."

Aimee shot a defiant look at Joe but bit her tongue.

"Thank you," Sam said. He took a sip of his coffee. "In those days a physician wasn't required to do an internship or residency. They simply took a test and hung out their shingle. Doctor Halvorson, for unknown reasons, applied for and was accepted into a residency program at Saint Vincent Hospital in Lower Manhattan in 1926. At the end of her first year, the internship year, she was expelled from the program by the Sisters of Charity. Saint Vincent's records show the reason for expulsion was moral turpitude."

"This is crap, Sam. You expect me to sit here and listen to you slander my mother? Why would you even take the time to investigate her?"

"Why, Aimee? Because you lied to me the first day we met. When you, Hans, and I were sitting in my trailer I asked if you had heard of the painter Edward Hopper. You said no."

"Who the hell is Edward Hopper?"

"He's the artist who did that little seven-by-eight-inch etching that's hanging in your hallway."

"I'm supposed to know that?"

"It's an original printmaker etching done in 1926. Hopper used the original copperplate and acid method. He only did about seventy etchings in his lifetime, all with a very limited number of copies produced. This one, however, is unique. Only one print was ever made from the copper stencil. It's titled *Eleven A.M.* The original oil-on-canvas version was done later in 1926 and was apparently based on the etching. It's hanging in the Hirshhorn Museum in Washington, DC. Hopper, as best as I can tell, rarely based his oil or watercolor paintings on his etchings, which, of course, were an entirely separate art form. That, in part, is what makes this one so special. Also, Hopper had just married Josephine Nivison in 1924. Jo Hopper was his primary model, posing for virtually all of his later nudes, except for this one. Hopper's studio was in Washington Square in Greenwich Village. You'll never guess who lived in the apartment below. That's right—your mother, a scant twenty-four years before you were conceived."

"I've looked at that drawing," Will said. "You can't see the model's face, or much else for that matter."

"Well, Jo Hopper knew who it was, and she and Hopper had a very public knock-down, drag-out fight about it when he unveiled the painting in 1926. At the time I don't think she or anyone else knew about the etching. But when the Sisters of Charity finally caught wind of the scandal, they promptly kicked Gloria out of Saint Vincent's residency program."

Aimee raised both hands palms-up and shrugged her shoulders. "Your point, Sherlock?"

"My point, Aimee, is that for whatever reason, your mother ended up with the etching. Sidney called several art buyers and auction houses in New York, including Christie's, in order to get a value. If authenticated, it will sell for approximately forty-five million dollars, give or take ten million."

Silence descended over the booth like a cold fog. "You're rich, Sis," Will finally said, smiling broadly. "As your closest living heir, let me be the first to congratulate you."

Aimee looked stunned, her mouth partially open. "I had no idea," she managed to whisper.

"Yes you did," Sam smiled. "But let's come back to that in a minute. First, let me tell Will about his good fortune."

"Pray tell, Sam," Will said, expectantly.

Sam inhaled deeply again. "According to the Minnesota and Iowa Departments of Revenue and the IRS, when Gloria Halvorson died in 1965, she left Aimee the family homestead and the medical clinic plus a small trust for her education. She willed her valuable Chicago real estate holdings to Hans Gottlieb. But there was no comparison in terms of how her assets were divided. We'll never know what her true motivation was. Perhaps it was love, perhaps guilt—who knows?"

"I don't understand," Will said. "You're telling me that Pop was some sort of zillionaire the whole time I'm growing up middle-class and struggling to pay back student loans?"

"Not the whole time. You had graduated from high school two years before Hans acquired the properties. He put everything in an irrevocable trust and hired a legal firm in Boone to manage the trust for him. He liquidated all the physical assets in 1980 and set up a charitable trust for the interest on the corpus. That corpus was over a hundred million dollars."

"A hundred million dollars! A charitable trust for what?" Will complained.

"Oh, there were more than two dozen charities and educational institutions. His anonymous gifts to Iowa State University alone funded everything from their athletic center to their wrestling scholarship program. He even bought an acreage north of Boone and turned it into a rehab center for sexually abused children."

It was Will's turn to look shocked. "I spent most of my adult life writing research proposals and grubbing for money to keep my lab funded, and all the while my dad is giving money away by the truckload. I don't get it."

"We may never get it, Will," Sam said. "My guess is that your dad discovered where that money came from and didn't want to gain from it personally. So he put it to good use for the benefit of others. We can't second-guess history. We can judge it, we can even distort it, but we can't crawl inside the heads of dead people and see what they saw. We can only make decisions about the future. Sometimes those decisions can become so clouded by hate, by love, by greed, and all the other frailties of human emotion that we forget about the past. We all remember the old admonition that says if you can't remember the past you're condemned to repeat it."

"Spare me the philosophy lesson, Sam. Am I, I mean, are we...," Will corrected himself, quickly looking at Aimee, "rich?"

Sam smiled broadly. "I have no idea what's in Hans's will. You'll have to wait for the reading. The chairman of the board of trustees that oversees his trust did confide in me that provisions were made for his heirs long ago. And that brings up an interesting point. Let me go back to my story about Sophie Mickelson and I'll see if I can tie up some of the loose ends."

Aimee rolled her eyes.

"I think you'll like this part, Aimee. Wait for it, okay?" Sam turned to watch a car pull into the diner's parking lot. The falling snow was illuminated brightly in the funnels of light from its headlights. "Nicky Blumenfeld, aka Sophie Mickelson, was always her brother's sister, even though she had moved away and changed her name. Kid Cann, if nothing else, was loyal to his family. He would do anything for his sister. I should mention here that Kid Cann's empire was somewhat limited by the rural nature of Minnesota. He needed to exploit a larger population base and he set his sights on Chicago.

"Of course, I have no way of knowing how it occurred, but Kid Cann and Lucky 'Big Ears' Lucello became business partners. It makes me wonder if Gloria might have facilitated that arrangement since she surely knew her best friend's brother was Kid Cann. Or maybe it was the other way around. If Lucky already knew Kid in the late '20s, he could have introduced Gloria to Kid's sister. That would explain why Nicky chose Deep Lake as a haven, to be near her friend. Anyway, Kid provided the booze and Lucky provided the distribution. Life was good until they started infringing on the territory of other well-known mobsters in Chicago. When the gang wars broke out, Lucky decided to get out of the liquor business and diversify his operations by organizing professional wrestling, but not before putting the screws to Kid Cann.

"Bad blood developed between the two crime bosses. They were both smart enough to see the writing on the wall that Prohibition was coming to an end. Kid expanded his extortion and prostitution businesses. Lucky concentrated on wrestling. Then he found himself cash poor—especially after a botched attempt to fix the world heavyweight wrestling championship in Cincinnati, and attempted to sell off his real estate holdings in Little Italy. The problem was that, for money-laundering purposes, the properties were in your mom's name," Sam said, nodding toward Aimee. "Like you, Aimee, your mother was a very strong woman, determined to protect herself and the one thing she loved above all else, Hans Gottlieb.

"Lucky probably felt double-crossed by his star wrestler, Trapper, in that he lost a colossal amount of money on that Cincinnati match. Most likely he ordered a hit on Hans. But that wasn't going to make him financially solvent. He needed that real estate. I think, and I'm just guessing here, your mother attempted to broker a deal with Lucky: real estate for Hans's life. I don't know the outcome of that negotiation, but Lucky wasn't one to trifle with. If I were a betting man, I'd say Lucky tortured and mutilated her to get her to sign over the Chicago properties. My first clue, Aimee, was when I saw you sign to the cook the first time we came to this diner. I figured you might have grown up with someone who was deaf. I was wrong. She was mute."

The bells over the door tinkled softly when a slender, dark-haired woman entered the diner. She brushed the snow from her shoulders and gently stamped her feet before looking up and smiling at the four sets of eyes fixed on her. She was beautiful. Her long, wool coat and Russian-style hat gave her a tall and mysterious air. She took a seat at the counter, her back to the group. She ordered hot chocolate and talked softly with Rhonda the red-nosed waitress.

"Let's see…where was I?" Sam said, turning back to Aimee.

"You were fabricating some nonsense about how my mother had lost her tongue."

"Right. Thanks. Let me close the loop on Lucky 'Big Ears' Lucello," Sam said, placing both hands palms-down on the table. "You might imagine the anger felt by the two people who loved Gloria Halvorson the most. Both Hans and Sophie, I'm sure, were devastated by the brutality of cutting Gloria's tongue out. I think Hans would have beaten Lucky to death—dealt with it head-on. Sophie, on the other hand, would have called her brother. We're still waiting for dental records, but it looks like the head in the paint bucket belonged to Lucky. The gold central incisor is a dead give-away—pardon my pun. The ME said the head was missing a tongue. Kid Cann probably sent the head up to Sophie or Gloria with the best intentions. In any case, it ended up under a spirit house north of the lake."

"Again, Sam, I don't see the relevance of any of this," Aimee complained. "Why are we here this evening?"

"The first question you asked me tonight was whether Hans was a good guy or a bad guy. I struggled with that same question for the last several days." Sam stared at the table for a long moment before speaking. "Hans was a good guy, at least from the standpoint of his involvement with those bodies. Here's what I think happened to each of them: Reuben Carter and Hans surely knew each other, but to what extent we'll probably never know. If Peg Leg out in the woods is, in fact, Reuben Carter, I suspicion he was killed by some-one who knew precisely where the carotid artery was located and had access to a scalpel."

"Now wait just a damn minute. You are not going to pin this on my mother." Aimee's lips were drawn tight and she glared angrily at Sam.

"I don't think anybody can pin this on your mother. Too many years have passed. I'm simply speculating. You can't deny that your mother was in love with Hans. You found the letters he wrote her. And she left him a fortune. It's pos-sible that she defended and protected him from whoever she perceived as a potential threat. And, Aimee, I believe she was equally protective of you. If you won't voluntarily give Joe a

DNA sample, he'll pull one off your coffee cup, which takes us back to the beginning of this convoluted story. I believe the mixed ancestry corpse is Charles Pond, your father."

"Hans is my father. I have the birth certificate."

"You forged that birth certificate. You should have taken the time to check with the Minnesota Department of Health. Their Office of Vital Records has your original birth certificate that lists Charles Pond as your father. You forged the one you planted in your mother's files. The folks in the forensics lab at the Bureau of Criminal Apprehension will analyze the paper and ink and prove it's a forgery."

"Does this mean you're not my sister?" Will asked. "I don't understand. Will somebody tell me what's going on here?"

Aimee ignored Will, putting her whole focus on Sam.

Sam continued. "Charles Pond was a violent drunk who was abusive to both you and your mother. The FBI had a file on him. Apparently, he was the local bootlegger for Kid Cann and was linked to homicides here and in Canada."

"This just keeps getting better and better," Aimee said, shaking her head slowly. "Why are you doing this to me?"

Sam smiled. "This is all Joe's fault. He was intent on charging me with Sophie's murder. I was only trying to defend myself." He paused before continuing. "We don't know, but it seems reasonable to assume that Gloria was introduced to Charles Pond at some point through Sophie Mickelson. Never forget that she was Gloria's best friend and confidante. Sophie knew about Gloria's wealth and who your father really was."

"Who cares who my father really is?" Aimee shouted.

"You care," Sam snapped back. "You cared enough to forge a birth certificate and to lure Hans to Deep Lake, with the hope of convincing him that you were his daughter and that he needed to include you in his will. But you had no way of knowing how rapid and progressive his dementia was."

"I don't know what you're talking about. This is preposterous. It has nothing to do with me," Aimee said. She looked around the table, but no one offered her support. "You all think I'm some sort of monster, spawned by a family of killers."

"Killers who beget killers is an interesting possibility. Both your parents were killers," Sam said, raising his eyebrows. "But as a defense it will never hold up in court. Truth be told, I think we're all grasping for an explanation to help us deal with the fact that you're a heartless murderer—"

"Okay," Aimee cut Sam off. "Who is it you think I've killed? What's the motive here? Shouldn't there be a motive?"

Joe Whitehorn cleared his throat and spoke without making eye contact with Aimee. His right hand reached for his left breast pocket as he spoke. "Anyone who watches television cop shows knows there has to be both motive and opportunity. The motive is simple: money. It's always money. It's the greed I don't understand. You might have been able to get away with stealing the etching from Sophie Mickelson. But you couldn't wait for her to die naturally. She knew Hans was not your father. Plus you needed to get all this done before the administrator got back, while you were still in charge."

"You think I killed Sophie Mickelson? I never stole that etching. It belonged to my mother. I remember it in our house from when I was a little girl."

"I'm sure you do, but at some point before your mother died, she gave it to her friend Sophie. I don't think you had any idea of its worth until Sam brought the artist's name to your attention. Your phone records show you called art dealers in New York the very day Sam mentioned Edward Hopper to you."

"My phone records?" Aimee shouted; her face turned red. "I hope to hell you got a court order, Joe."

"You know me, Aimee. Of course I did," Joe said matter-of-factly. "Sidney used the same phone numbers to come up with a value. As for ownership, most of your staff at Whispering Pines will attest to seeing the etching on the wall in Sophie's room. Even better…" The sheriff reached into the inside pocket of his coat and retrieved a photograph. "Here's a picture that Sam took the morning before Sophie was murdered." He tossed it on the table. "There's Sophie sitting in her room, and there's that etching hanging on the wall behind her." Joe fumbled with his shirt pocket again. "We have motive. We have opportunity."

"You have nothing, Joe," Aimee said. "It's just circumstantial and coincidental. My mother never gave that drawing to Sophie. I loaned it to her when she moved into Whispering Pines because she liked it and it reminded her of my mother. After Sophie was killed, I took the etching home where it belonged."

"That's not true." Joe pulled another photo from his pocket and tossed it on the table. "The evidence boys, who arrived shortly after my deputies, snapped this shot of Sophie's room. The etching is no longer on the wall. Tell me, how could you have retrieved it after her death if you didn't arrive on the scene until a little after six o'clock in the morning? This alone was enough to convince the judge to issue an order for your phone records."

"I took it the night before, Joe, at the end of my shift. I'm just a little confused about times. We can play this stupid game all day. The bottom line is that the etching is mine. It was always mine. Are we done here?"

"Sadly, no," Joe said. "I don't think the etching was your motivation to kill Sophie Mickelson. Stealing her artwork was a crime of opportunity. You had to get rid of Sophie because she knew Hans was not your father. And you got greedy. You still wanted a piece of Hans's fortune."

"Why am I the suspect? I thought Mike Wies was the killer."

"He should have been," Sam interjected. "You botched that opportunity. You weren't thinking clearly when the Weasel stumbled into Sophie's room with a broken nose and arm, the result of trying to steal from Hans in the next room. My guess is that he walked in on you while you were still holding the pillow over Sophie's face. Who knows what he saw? Given the extent of his facial fractures, his eyes would have been watering and swelling shut. You should have killed him on the spot and framed him for Sophie's murder."

"Instead," Joe took over, "you loaded the punk up with pentobarbital and led him out back, shoved him into your car, and drove him to Deep Lake. Then you overdosed him and stuffed his skinny ass through a hole in the floating bog on the north end of the lake, where he drowned. The chemists at the crime lab told me they can trace the Nembutal in his system to a specific batch produced by the manufacturer. Since it's a controlled substance, we'll be able to track it right to your supply room at Whispering Pines. We're running a tox panel on the night nurse's coffee cup now to see what you used to drug her. Our evidence crew is very thorough."

"He was a druggie, Joe. No doubt he got into the medicine supply cabinet when he broke in. He probably drugged Kate. No telling what a high junkie was doing walking across that bog at night."

"Let's get back to motive," Sam said, changing the subject. "I don't know when you discovered your mother's will, or how long it took you to track down Hans, or what you said to convince him to come to Deep Lake. But your mother's files right downstairs in your basement the whole time. Joe has a record of your calls last summer to the legal firm that manages Hans's trust, and your own phone records that show nearly a dozen calls to the Majestic Oaks Assisted Living Center in Clinton, Iowa."

"I interviewed the staff at Majestic Oaks," the sheriff offered. "They attempted to send Hans's medical records to you, but the address you gave them doesn't exist. Obviously you didn't care about his medical conditions. You only wanted to get him here so you could convince him to include you in his will." Joe leaned back in the booth and exhaled loudly. "When you discovered that Hans would never be able to pass the test of being of sound mind and body, you abandoned your efforts to have him provide a codicil to his will."

It was Sam's turn. "You knew you would have to challenge the will by claiming you were Hans's long-lost daughter. You needed the acceptance of his only living heir. It was someone from Whispering Pines that contacted Will Gottlieb to tell him where his father was on your instructions. You lured Will here just like you did Hans. You cultivated the relationship, planted the birth certificate, and gave an Academy Award performance to win over Will as your long-lost brother."

"Is this true, Aimee?" Will said, leaning forward to look into her face.

"None of it," Aimee shot back.

"The sad thing," Sam continued, "was that Hans was in congestive heart failure and was probably not long for this world anyway. You went so far as to convince Will that Hans needed Lasix to pull off some of the fluid surrounding his heart. You knew the interaction between Haldol and Lasix would cause serious heart rhythm problems that would most likely kill him."

Joe leaned forward. "The ME found enough haloperidol and furosemide in Hans's system to stop the heart of a Clydesdale."

"You killed my father?" Will asked loudly, anger in his voice as he started to rise from the booth.

Joe reached across the table and put his hand on Will's shoulder.

"No, Will," Aimee said. "You listened to his lungs. You saw the swelling in his extremities. He was critical so I increased the dosage of Lasix a little."

"My God, Aimee, what have you done? Why on earth would you give him Haldol?" Will demanded, his voice shaking with emotion.

"He wouldn't let me give him the Lasix. He became abusive. I was only trying to calm him down a little."

Will's knuckles turned white as he clutched the edge of the table. He looked like a man about to burst into flames. "Do you have any idea what you have done?" he snarled through clenched teeth. "I thought you understood medicine. The electrolyte imbalance alone demanded monitoring. But to combine it with an antipsychotic—the extrapyramidal effects on a man that age would cause unbearable muscle pain before it killed him." Tears of anger welled up in his eyes. "I hope there is a special place in hell with your name on it, you psycho bitch."

"I'll be dead before you get to that special place, Aimee," Joe said just above a whisper. He stared at her, his eyes glassy. He looked tired. "You were my friend, Pond Scum. *Gimikwenden ina?*"

"Of course I remember, Joe."

"*Ningashkendam,*" he said, looking away.

"I'm sad too," Aimee said, her eyes suddenly filling with tears.

Sam pulled a manila file folder from the corner of the booth and slid it slowly across the table toward Will. "I thought you might want this."

Without picking it up, Will opened the file. Tears suddenly spilled from his eyes. It was an eight-by-ten-inch, black-and-white photograph of Hans. He was standing next to the window in his room, sunlight softly illuminating one side of his creased face. He was looking toward the whispering pines, but not seeing them. His eyes searched beyond them. He was peering into the past.

"He was a good man," Sam said. The finality of his statement was undeniable, his voice emphatic.

A curtain of snow drifted from the roof of the diner. It descended briefly in wispy gauze that momentarily obscured the four dark figures behind the yellow window. The giant pike still leaped above the billboard, defiant of both snow and time, as if it knew that below the surface all was calm and time was endless.

EPILOGUE

Small Minnesota towns appeared without warning through the divided windshield of the Willys. Some had main streets that radiated despair, scarred with abandoned reminders of better times. Others simply waited—municipal versions of subway panhandlers, always hopeful that someone would stop and drop money in their hat. The decaying buildings disappeared just as quickly in the rearview mirror, their only reminder a faded Storz Beer sign on the side of somebody's dream. It was four hundred sixty-one miles to Wall Drug.

They had barely spoken since leaving Deep Lake early that morning. Annie George wore the same wool coat and Russian faux fur hat she had the night before. The Willys's heater struggled to keep them warm as they pushed through the arctic blast that had descended over much of the state. They were both tired. It had been well after midnight before Sam finished recounting to her the details of the investigation that he, Sidney, and Sheriff Whitehorn had conducted during the previous five days following Hans Gottlieb's death.

At Detroit Lakes, Sam suddenly veered the Willys, pulling the tiny Airstream south toward Fergus Falls.

"Jeez O'Pete, Sam, I wish you'd tell me when you're about to roll this thing over." She braced herself with one gloved hand on the passenger door and the other on the

dash. Even L2 raised her head from the backseat in response
to the sudden change in course. "I thought we were going to
Fargo?" Annie said.

"This rig wasn't designed for interstate travel," Sam
said, referring to I-94 that, beginning at Fargo, stretched in a
pencil-straight line across the lower half of North Dakota.
"Interstates were still Eisenhower's dream when this thing
rolled off the assembly line in 1953. I guess I don't like being passed by semis all day. The slightly slower pace of the
blue highways and back roads is more relaxing. I think this
country is best seen at speeds of less than sixty."

"Are we there yet?" she mumbled.

"Look, this was something you and Sidney cooked up.
I thought it was a bad idea from the start. I'm not sure what
you were hoping to accomplish by flying to Minneapolis and
renting a car to join me in Deep Lake for a two-day drive
back to Cheyenne. You could have flown to Denver faster
and cheaper."

"I need to look for a place to live, and rent some office
space in Cheyenne or Laramie. I also thought it might be an
opportunity for us to catch up. On the publishing business,
I mean," she quickly added.

Sam laughed. "First, you'll be lucky to afford an apartment, let alone office space. Second, how do you catch up on
a business you know nothing about?"

Annie stared at him for a long moment. "You better be
nice to your new publisher. I'll cut your royalties."

"You can't pay any royalties. You can't pay my advance
from which to deduct my royalties. You can't pay for printing

or distribution or shelf space or editing or cover or interior design or any of the other costs associated with the publishing business." Sam shook his head and then shifted the Muncie overdrive into high. "What were you thinking?"

"Banks. That's what banks are for, Sam."

"They generally require that you pay them back."

"I've done my homework. There are some low-interest start-up loans, various tax incentives, and grants available. I'm hoping for a meeting with the Wyoming Business Council later this week."

"I'm sure they're willing to roll out the red carpet for a business without a plan, a business with no employees or start-up capital."

"I thought you'd be glad to see me," she said, looking out the side window. "We're going to be business partners, you know."

Sam did not respond. He pushed aside his key ring to check the bank of gauges below the dash. He wanted to remind her that it was she who had broken up with him, that he hadn't gotten any younger or less related to her, that she was responsible for the stink hound in the backseat, and that she had broken his heart. "I am glad to see you, Annie. I'm just a little concerned about the future right now. I think you and Sidney are a bit naive about what it takes to run a publishing business, especially the costs."

"Not to worry, Sam. Sidney says that as soon as she finishes her law degree and gets her license, she's filing a Sherman Antitrust Act suit against the dot-coms. We'll be rich."

"I rest my case."

Neither of them spoke. After Pelican Rapids the lake country gave way to cultivated agriculture. First, they saw hay production with evenly spaced round bales dotting the flat fields, then the remains of corn and soybean rotations, and finally wheat stubble as they pushed closer to the Dakotas.

"Sam, last night at the diner I overheard you say something that got my attention."

"What was that?"

"It was when you were talking about killers begetting killers, implying there might be some genetic cause."

"I remember."

Annie looked at him. "I read this really interesting article recently. Nothing has been published yet; it's all pretty preliminary. But there has been this ongoing study in Sweden where they sequenced the genomes of a huge number of violent prisoners in a score of Finnish prisons. Apparently they found a genetic predisposition to committing acts of extreme violence."

"So what are you saying? That Aimee is a chip off the old block?"

"I think it's more related to impulsive violence or aggression rather than planned or calculated crime. Aimee took planning to a whole new level. I don't know what her excuse is." Annie looked out the side window again. "You know, what kept me awake most of last night was the possibility that she might get away with it." She paused. "She killed three people that we know of, and there's no hard evidence. She's got an excuse for everything. The thought of her going scot-free sends a chill up my spine."

Sam smiled. "I wouldn't underestimate Joe Whitehorn. He's a lot sharper than I initially gave him credit for. I'd be willing to bet that he has some evidence he's holding back. He'll quietly go about his business of building a case against her and then get his warrant. Also I don't think Will Gottlieb will let it rest. I asked him to call me if there are any developments."

The highway sign read "Fergus Falls 9 Miles." Sam said, "I've got to gas up when we get to town. Are you hungry?"

"I skipped the complimentary breakfast at Motel 6," Annie said. "I could use a bite to eat."

Sam's cell phone rang. He thought it odd since he knew Sidney had classes. He fished the flip phone from his coat pocket and opened it.

"Hello?...Oh, hi, Will. How you holdin' up?" As Sam listened he froze, staring straight ahead, the phone held tightly to his right ear. "I see," he said finally, his voice barely audible above the engine's noise.

Annie could hear Will Gottlieb's voice but could not make out what he was saying.

"What do you think? You buying it?...Me neither.... Uh-huh....Uh-huh....All right. Thanks, Will. Keep me posted....I will. You too....Bye."

Sam pushed the end button, folded the phone, and carefully slipped it back into his coat pocket. He took a deep breath and continued to stare at the road ahead. The brown-and-white countryside faded away on both sides of the asphalt artery that sustained the unsophisticated honesty of rural places. Barbed-wire fences chased along the thoroughfare, their strands rimed with puffy crystals of frozen air. In the distance he saw a man walking along the edge of the road, his shoulders hunched against the cold. As the Willys approached, the man turned to face them and absently reached for his left breast pocket.

"What is it, Sam? You look like you've seen a ghost."

He pursed his lips and his eyes narrowed. "They found Joe Whitehorn dead in his vehicle out at Deep Lake. He took a bullet through the brain."

Annie was silent. She gently placed her hand on his shoulder.

"They're calling it a probable suicide. Did I tell you he had terminal cancer?" He turned to look at her. "He was a good man too."

Annie searched his eyes and nodded her agreement.

A series of small, faded, red rectangular signs with white letters appeared at the edge of the borrow ditch, remnants of an earlier time, each separated by a distance that allowed them to be read one at a time:

She put
    A bullet
        Thru his hat
            But he's had
                Closer shaves than that
                    .....Burma-Shave

Sam smiled tightly. He shook his head and whispered something as he leaned forward to look at the receding signs in the side mirror, his knuckles white against the dark steering wheel.

"What?" Annie said.

Sam cleared his throat and swallowed hard. "Scot-free," he said. "Scot-free."

THE END

ACKNOWLEDGMENTS

Thomas Mann said, "A writer is somebody for whom writing is more difficult than it is for other people." The people who support, encourage and assist in the process of bringing a story to print know how true this is. They often coddle, cajole, provoke and inspire until the words come together and a book is born.

I owe many thanks to Peter Decker, Tonya Talbert, Jane Seiler, Rachel Girt, David Worthman, and V.A. Stephens for suffering through earlier drafts and gently reminding me of what my responsibilities as a writer are. Your suggestions were invaluable.

The conventions of the English language would have been daunting without the editorial skills of Kate Deubert. She is more than amazing.

Graphic designer Tina Worthman truly knows the definition of fickle. Her artistic skills are exceeded only by her creative genius and quiet patience.

Daughters Tiffany, Melissa and Amanda are the reason I tell stories. I value their honest input. They still inspire me.

As always special thanks are given to my biggest fan and most beautiful critic, my wife Margaret. This novel would not exist without her dogged enthusiasm and unfailing support. She makes me write better books.

CPSIA information can be obtained at www.ICGtesting.com
Printed in the USA
LVOW11*0134080715

445208LV00002B/3/P